MW00948718

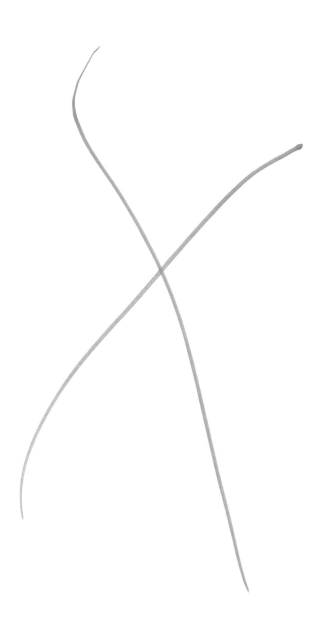

Rough Edges

Books 4-6

A SMALL TOWN FIREFIGHTER SERIES

USA TODAY BESTSELLING AUTHOR

ASHLEY ZAKRZEWSKI

CONTENTS

TREASURE ME

SAVOR ME

RAVISH ME

TREASURE ME

BOOK 4

1

JEREMY

*M*y chair scuffs the floor loudly because of the inability to stay still while Hazel hounds me. I rub the back of my neck, trying to keep myself calm, but my feet have a different idea. I just want to get the hell out of here, but I'm practically cornered with no path of escape. She claims it's not healthy to be at home on a Friday evening, even as a single man. I'm not a pitiful thirty-five-year-old living with his father. There's more to it than that, and she knows it.

Heat runs through my body as it tenses, not wanting to listen to anymore of her crap. Why is my personal life any of her concern? She only arrived an hour ago from Massachusetts for a visit, and already I find myself longing for her departure.

"Surely there's something you would rather be doing tonight," Hazel says, her arms draped over the back of the couch.

Is she trying to provoke me? My arms cross, and my feet begin to tap, waiting for her to be finished. My gaze flips upward as my father comes downstairs.

"What are you two going on about now?"

I open my mouth to criticize, but decide against it. She doesn't make it down often, and my father deserves to enjoy her visit. Maybe she will understand after spending some time with him alone, that I don't have the luxury of going places.

Our father is my life right now. His fight with Alzheimer's doesn't award me with an abundance of free time and as it progresses, our window gets smaller and smaller.

"Just trying to talk Jeremy into getting out and doing something tonight. Damon is throwing a barbecue and invited him. For some reason, he'd rather stay here, cooped up in the house."

Dad passes through the living room and goes into the kitchen.

I clench my jaw, trying to keep my cool, but it's hard when she won't let it go. "My life isn't a burden. You need to get off your high horse. You have no fucking idea what it's been like taking care of dad."

She might lead a lavish life in Massachusetts, and I'm thrilled for her, but that means I'm liable for staying in Grapevine with our dad and taking care of him. Some days are smoother than others, but when Hazel brought in the at-home assistant, it made our lives much simpler to maintain. Living with Alzheimer's is tough, but we keep on trudging.

"You act like I choose to not be here. I'm sorry that my fucking job and life is in Cambridge. If it wasn't for that, we couldn't afford the nurse, or anything else for that matter."

She makes me sound like a spoiled little brat, and that couldn't be farther from the truth. Ever since his diagnosis, it's just been him and I. There's never been time for friends, dates, or even the occasional hang out. If I'm not at work, I'm here in this house with him. My priority is taking care of my father.

"Yes, Hazel, but what the hell does any of that have to do with me going to some stupid party? I'm not in my twenties anymore. In fact, they were never my thing."

Why does she need to intrude on my life? She just keeps pushing and needs to let it go before I blow up. It's not like I've just been sitting around all day. I've been working on a construction site for the last nine hours in the blazing hot sun, and right now all I want to do is take a shower and lay in bed.

"When did you last have a date? Or just went out with friends?" Hazel suggests.

I glance up at the ceiling, struggling to recall. "A long time, okay?"

She chuckles. "Why don't you go to Damon's party? He would love to see you. You guys used to be best buds."

Damon and my relationship has changed tremendously over the last couple of years. Like most people, our paths drifted away from each other. It happens. The party will have most of the guys from the fire department, and since I start there on Monday, he thinks it will be a good way to hang out beforehand.

My phone vibrates in my pocket with his name on it.

Damon: *Just bring your ass here. Drink a couple of beers. All I'm asking for is two hours.*

My excuse is mute now since she has agreed to stay here with dad. *Damnit.* I close my eyes and sigh, knowing I don't have a fucking choice. Might as well bite the bullet and just comply. If this will make everybody happy, then it's done.

Me: *Fine. Two hours is all you're getting. See you soon.*

Dad is sitting in his recliner, watching an action movie, and Hazel is reading a book on her tablet.

"You decide to go?" she inquires, leaning over the rear of the couch. "Get out and have some fun. I've got this handled."

It's not that I don't think she can deal with it, but his time is precious and I don't wish to squander the insufficient time I have left. Pathetic, right? I don't sit around here all day, but I guess that's what she thinks.

"Yeah, yeah. I'm leaving. Damon won't fucking leave me alone about it. See you in a couple hours," I say, clutching the keys off the bench and shutting the door behind me.

Perspiration forms on my upper lip after walking outside, and it emphasizes why I didn't prefer to go. Who the hell wants to stand around outside when it's this fucking hot out? I get into my silver pickup, start the engine, and roll the windows down. It's like a hot box in here, fuck. The sky is clear and blue, but that means the chance to have any shade is gone.

The closer I get to Damon's, the more my anxiety heightens. The sweat from my hands coupled with the over hundred-degree weather is making the steering wheel slippery. I'm not good with meeting a bunch of new people at once. Tonight, I'm stepping outside my comfort zone long enough to meet some of the guys, have a beer, and then I'm going home. Everybody gets what they want, and I can get some much required sleep. The sun has already been on me all day, and the first thing I plan to do is find somewhere to get out of it.

As I turn onto his road, there are at least ten cars lined up in front of his home. How many people are here, anyway? I rock my head and park behind a gold Toyota. What the hell am I getting myself into? I rub my sweaty hands on my pants, and hike up the driveway.

"Glad you could make it," Aiden says.

A nod is my return, and I stroll past them. "Where is everyone?" There doesn't appear to be anyone in the house.

"We are all out in the backyard. Come on, man."

He slides the glass door open and I practically throw up. There must be at least thirty people in his backyard right now, but my eyes settle on a woman in a long lavender sundress with aviators on.

"Everybody, this is Jeremy. He'll be joining us starting next week," Damon reveals, and everybody turns to look at me.

My hand raises, and I force a half smile onto my face for the sake of not offending anyone. I'm not the type of person who likes to be in the spotlight; it gives me anxiety. Damon knows this. Once the eyes come off of me, I follow him, waiting for my chest to untighten.

"Come on, we're barbecuing over here. Need a beer?" Aiden asks.

He drops into the container and hands me one. "Come on, drink one for me. I'm sober."

My sister cleaned his ass up, and I'm glad for it. Aiden, up until recently, was known as the township slut and drunk, until she showed up back into town for Damon's wedding and whacked him off his feet again. It's nice to see him sober and still having a good time. "Alright, this one's for you."

This is the first time I've been to his new house, and it surprises me how extravagant it is. A shiny red swing set and matching slide pushed toward the back of it, and a tree house settled high in the branches of a huge oak tree. Around the back of the house are painted rocks speckling the flowerbeds. What catches my attention the most is the radio set up blaring country music now. Damon has always seemed to me like someone who is frugal with his money.

"Ready to start Monday? It'll be nice having you around. It's a different pace than construction for sure," Damon says.

'Yeah," I respond, but not fully paying attention to what he is saying. The woman is speaking to Tessa, but every so often, her attention shifts to me. Who is she? I can't seem to take my eyes off of her, and her lengthy brown hair and fair skin.

I try to pay attention to Aiden as he speaks about his bookstore, and how well it's been operating, which I couldn't be more thrilled about, but my focus isn't on him. The eye makeup she has on enhances her brown eyes, and it only makes me want to approach her even more.

Self-doubt takes effect, speculating if I should even pursue to present myself. What if we hit it off? It's not like I have time for anybody else in my world right now. My old man would instruct me to go for it.

"Are you even paying attention?" Aiden asks, whacking me on the arm.

I rattle my head. "Who's that girl?"

"Not sure. Never seen her before. Go talk to her, bro. Never hurts to try."

Can I put the time and effort it takes to bloom a new relationship?

"It's been way too long for you. You need some pleasure in your life," Aiden says, patting me on the shoulder and trying to instill confidence.

Fuck it, I'm doing it.

My chest rises and falls as I get closer, and I try not to chicken out. "Hey, Tess. Who's your friend?"

Tessa glances at me, brings her palms up, and answers, "No need for the banter. I'll go hang out with Damon. She's single, by the way."

When she leaves, the woman remains in front of me, offering a flash of a smile that doesn't meet her eyes. I don't wish to be assertive, so I take a sip of my beer, and evaluate her interest. She has been staring me down since I entered, so that means she must be keen, right?

My pulse quickens, not wanting to be rejected. "And you are?" Someone with her elegance should keep her head high, but her eyes keep finding the ground. Who demolished her confidence?

"I'm, uh, Raquel." Her left hand is holding her right elbow.

She is still not making direct eye contact with me, and self-doubt has me considering maybe it was very forward of me to come over here and introduce myself. My hand grazes across the back of my neck. "Not to sound like a total crackpot, but want to go sit down?"

She nods, and I follow her over to a section with a couple of tables and armchairs in the grass, off from most of the guests. The warmth isn't doing us any favors, but at least this spot brings us some much desired shade from the sun with an oak tree protecting us. There is still an hour until the sun sets. I try to get her to open up a bit, show me some of her charm. Her disposition transforms once we are elsewhere from everyone, and she grins. *There it is.*

"You from here? I don't think I've seen you around town before," I ask. The question is theoretical. Grapevine is small enough to where, if I had seen her around before, I would remember.

She raises her hair in a bun while replying. "No, I moved here about eight months ago from Dallas. Needed a bit of a scenery change. My brother lived here, so it seemed like the best place to come."

Not many people come here from the bigger cities, and that's probably because it's a different way of life. Small towns are famous for imposing in other's business, but also for banding collectively as a community when needed. The best example of that is the housing that the Jacksons provide to those that need somewhere safe to stay. They weren't required to do that, but helping others out that need it reminded me why I would never want to live in a big city.

"Big city girl, huh? Too much traffic for me. I like to keep it simple."

She smiles. "Tell me about your simplicity."

I smile, set my beer on the table edge, and lean in. The discussion tracks as I reveal how the folks in Grapevine are a meaningful form of support for what's happening with my dad right now. She needs to know that she has picked a wonderful city to live in.

"It's a refreshing pace here. Between construction and congestion, it takes too long to get anywhere in Dallas."

Our conversation turns, and we end up discussing sunsets. Living in Dallas, it's hard to enjoy it because there are high buildings everywhere, but here there is nothing obstructing the view. You can sit on your porch and enjoy it every night. Raquel would look stunning on a blanket underneath the sky with a backdrop such as that. It might be a plan for a date if she says yes. First, I will need to work up enough courage to ask her. It's been, what, like almost two years since I have asked someone out. What if she says no? Rejection isn't something that I do well with, but who does.

Something about her instills confidence in me, and the way our conversation flows easily without having to force it only makes matters better. Raquel needs someone to give hers back, because she is too beautiful to be staring at the ground. Her head should be held high, and someone needs to tell her how beautiful she is.

"Serious question, ready?"

"Okay? Shoot," I respond.

"If you could choose one superpower, which one would it be?"

Well, that's one hell of a question. Every action has repercussions and those need to be considered delicately. Super strength is great, but that also means you can crush everything. It's not something you can switch on and off. Being invisible sounds nice, but I'm not going for that one. "To heal people. Or, to take away people's pain."

Okay, I know how cliche that resonates, but I would do anything to diminish my dad's condition.

"You are the first person who has presented that as a superpower. Great choice. Mine would be to fly. So, I can just get up and go wherever I want while looking down at the magnificent sights."

Tessa serves her another refreshment, winks at her, and shuffles away.

"So, you're joining the department, huh?" Raquel asks.

"Start on Monday. Was looking for a change."

"Don't let my brother haze you. He can be a real jackass sometimes."

Fuck, of course. Why else would she be here? Not even officially part of the team and already I'm talking to someone's sister.

"Don't worry, he's not here yet."

"Well, if your brother doesn't kill me on Monday, wanna go to dinner sometime?"

She fidgets with her fingers. "I'd love to."

Her smile wavers, but we swap phones. My stomach sinks knowing that her brother might be upset with me once he finds out, but nothing worth it comes easily, right?

"It's been fantastic talking to you. It's time to head home for me, but I'll call you."

She watches me wander away, and I wave once I get to Damon and Liam. "Alright, guys. I'm outta here. We have so much to get done this weekend while Hazel's in town. Thanks for the invite."

As much as I'd love to stay longer and chat with Raquel all night, sleep is calling my name after a long exhausting day outside. I marvel in my confidence tonight. It's been too long since I've asked a woman out and rejection is always a fear of mine. Women prefer bad boys, most of the time, and I don't have time to play cat and mouse games.

Once inside my truck, I head toward the house, thinking about how I would have left earlier if she hadn't been there. Damon is my friend, but things like that just aren't something I'm interested in. I'm skeptical because if Hazel and Damon didn't push me to go, then I wouldn't have met Raquel. Even with everything going on with my father, I still want to make time for her.

I pull in behind Aiden's truck and park, wondering how Hazel's night is going with our father. She doesn't get to come down as often as he would like, but at least she is making the effort. We have no way of knowing if he has years or months left, and like me, she needs to spend as much time with him as she can. Regret is a terrible thing, and I don't wish it upon anyone.

The front door opens, and Hazel steps out. "So, who's the girl? Aiden claimed you were talking to someone."

Does he always tell her everything? What I do is none of her business. Jesus, we're adults. "Yes. Don't make a big deal out of it."

"It's been a while since you've been on a date. Good for you."

I roll my eyes and go up the stairs.

"Make sure you call her," Hazel yells up the stairs.

I'm not the type of guy that asks for your phone number and then never calls. Some guys wait a day or two, but I find myself wanting to talk to her. Will she think it's weird if I message her now?

I shake my head, and put all my worries aside as I click on her name and bring the message screen up.

What the hell do I even say?

2

RAQUEL

The crisp air is rejuvenating resting underneath a beautiful oak tree concealing me from the brutal conditions of the sunlight. Most of the guests have taken off now, and Tessa has taken Jeremy's seat. Aiden and Damon are cleaning the grill, and we are savoring our beers, just enjoying the night. After pondering over today's events, why were Tessa and I the only women? Did she invite me to meet someone? Jeremy is charming, but is it in my best interest to get entangled with someone my brother is working with?

My relationship situation has come up several times in conversation and this might have been her plan of seeking to set me up. I'm not keen on blind dates, because when do those usually work out? Although Jeremy has been a delightful shock. He is the first man to ask me out since being in Grapevine, and he didn't sit around hitting on me the entire time. Maybe that's why I am attracted to him. He seems like a gentleman, and those are troublesome to find these days.

Tessa knows about my situation, and being divorced isn't something that I holler from the rooftops. It's embarrassing to know my marriage failed, but not for the lack of trying. Dean had straying eyes, and that's not something I could solve. I would much rather be divorced, than stuck with a man who is not faithful.

"Did you have any trouble dropping Lily off?" Tessa asks, searching around the backyard.

I have met many of the men from the fire department, but they all seem rather playerish. Men in uniform seem to have an ego problem, and that's not something I'm seeking at all. Confidence is sexy, but I don't need to know how many women you could have other than me. Yes, I had one of them tell me something along these lines, and I ended up laughing in his face. Bryan is someone I try to steer clear of, especially after that conversation, but he is always wanting to strike up a discussion if he sees me. I'm thankful he did not show up tonight.

"His new girlfriend or whatever she is, came outside when I dropped her off. Who does that?"

My phone vibrates and I take it out of my pocket.

Jeremy: *I'm headed to bed after a long day's work, but I wanted to let you know I will call you tomorrow. Have a great time at the party.*

A smile emerges and Tessa notices it. I didn't predict he would contact me so soon. He proves to be a gentleman and I want to find out more about him. Sometimes men are good at putting on an act to get what they want, and I don't have time for players.

"What's that for?"

I lean over, and present the text.

"I'm all for you getting back out there after what you have been through with your divorce. Jeremy's a good guy, and my husband has known him since their junior high days."

This is a good sign. Texting me within an hour of leaving. Maybe Tessa can give me some knowledge about him. Jeremy has already gained points in my book. Yet, I don't know how my brother is going to react if I date one of his coworkers. Should I even care? We are both adults, and it's not like he has dated none of my friends.

"I wonder how sexy he looks in his uniform, though. Did you see his arms?" I ask, giggling.

Things have been turbulent since the divorce, but it's not like my ex-husband isn't already living with some new woman. In fact, she moved in about a week after the divorce was finalized.

"I say go for it, girl. You deserve to be happy. Your brother will get over it."

The glass door opens, and Eli steps into the backyard. I know he is going to come talk to me but, should I mention Jeremy? Will he flip out and cause a scene?

He approaches me and Tessa. "Enjoying yourself, sis?"

I thrust my shoulders, and glimpse over at Tess. "You missed the special guest."

He searches around. "What special guest?"

"The new guy, Jeremy," Tessa responds. "He asked your sister out, you know."

Damnit, Tess.

"Hold on a damn minute. The guy hasn't even started yet and already he's trying to date my sister? What the hell."

Why did she have to bring it up? Let him get some alcohol in his system first.

"I mean, you've been trying to screw Brittaney for ten years. So, why does it matter?"

To be fair, Brittaney has never been interested in my brother at all. And I think she has spelled out that it's never going to happen. She isn't the dating type, and by that I mean she does short-term relationships, but nothing long-term. For the decade I've known her, the longest one she has had is five months. Speaking of her, I haven't heard from her in a while, and that's an indicator she has met someone new. Every time she gets a new boyfriend, she goes MIA. I'm used to it by now, but sometimes it's hard to consider her a friend when she can go months without even speaking to me.

"Listen, I don't care who you date, but it can't be someone I work with, that's weird. The guys talk about our relationships at work, and I don't want to hear anything about you. That's crossing a line."

"Grow the hell up, Eli. That's such a double standard. You can try to screw my best friend, but I can't go out with someone who works with you? Don't be an indignant ass."

Why is he trying to act like my father? He has no say in who I date, but this could cause a problem between Jeremy and my brother at work, and he doesn't need me making things harder for him. Damnit, what do I do?

"My bed is calling my name. See you later, Tess."

I brush past Eli, knocking shoulders, and don't look back. It's one thing for him to be protective of me, but giving me orders of who not to date, that will not happen. He seems to still be upset about Dean, because Eli liked him, but who would want their sister to stay in an unhealthy marriage?

The front door slams behind me before I get to my car and start it up. Things in my life haven't been going great, but I refuse to let anyone stand in my way of being happy. And that might be with Jeremy or someone else.

After trekking the six blocks back to my house, and getting inside, I text him back.

Me: *Party was lame after you left. Wish you could've stayed longer. =)*

I take my shoes off by the door, and grab water from the fridge before ending up in the bedroom. My king sized bed is big enough for three of me, but I always end up smack dab in the middle. It's only like ten o'clock, but I can feel my eyes drooping. So, I go to YouTube and search to see if my favorite author has posted anything new this week.

The notification pops up that he has responded.

Jeremy: *I could've talked to you all night. Parties aren't my thing. Being from Dallas though, you are used to them, aren't you?*

His assumptions are false, because being married, we didn't get invited to things like that. He doesn't know much about me yet, and I hope I don't scare him away. The way I look at it, if being divorced is a problem, then he's not the right guy for me.

Me: *Nope. Something you don't know, I'm divorced. Most people don't invite married couples to parties, I guess.*

I watch my screen to see if the three dots appear.

Jeremy: *What fucking guy would divorce you? Have you seen yourself? I could literally stare into your eyes forever, and still not be sick of it. Okay, that's a little sappy, but oh well.*

I laugh, and lay back in bed. His humor is great, and we vibe on a level that my ex-husband and I never did. When we first got together, he was a very serious person, but after a couple years, he changed. He became very spontaneous and happy go-lucky. It's then that I thought he was cheating on me, but I never could prove it.

Me: *I like sappy. Give me more!*

I switch on the tv and flip through the channels until I land on some rom-com. Some might call me a hopeless romantic, but learning love languages is my favorite thing to do. Each person has one and knowing which one they respond to will help your relationship be more successful.

Jeremy: *Okay, is it weird to say I want to know everything about you? When I saw you tonight, it's like I could see our future. You are probably blocking me now thinking I'm some psychopath, right?*

Quite the opposite. It's refreshing to have a man be upfront about things, instead of acting uninterested to keep up on the leash. Jeremy being truthful and telling me about how he feels is a plus for me. It shows he isn't afraid to tell me things.

Me: *I find it sexy how open you are. Please don't end up being some serial killer or something. I've watched way too many crime shows. LMAO*

My head hits the pillow, and I know it's time for me to shut my eyes, but I'm enjoying talking to him. Plus, he is supposed to be asleep too.

Me: *Aren't you supposed to be passed out? I didn't mean to wake you up.*

The phone sits beside my pillow with my eyes closed, pretending to fall asleep, until it vibrates again.

Jeremy: *Your text woke me up, but I'm not complaining. So, are we still on for dinner tomorrow?*

I do nothing on the days I work because of my schedule, but there's no way I'm turning him down. Guys like Jeremy don't come around very often, and I'm not letting him slip between the cracks.

Me: *Pick me up at 7?*

Any earlier and I wouldn't have time to get home and get ready after work. It's been years since I've been on an actual date. What the hell am I going to wear?

Jeremy: *Perfect. See you tomorrow. Get some rest, beautiful.*

I don't respond, but put my phone back next to my pillow and close my eyes. If Tessa didn't invite me to the party tonight, then Jeremy and I wouldn't have crossed paths. So, I'm thankful she didn't tell me about her plans or the likelihood of me showing up is slim. Damon and Tessa's relationship is what I hope to have one day. Someone who loves me, and doesn't want me to change who I am to please them.

Can Jeremy be the perfect guy for me? Or, will my brother get in our way?

3

JEREMY

When Hazel took off to travel back to Massachusetts with Aiden, things with our father escalated. The couch squeaks at me when I take a seat, waiting for him to come downstairs and have his morning cup of coffee. It's practically seven in the morning and he's typically awake by now. The specialists pointed out that he might be more exasperated than normal as the disease advances. Alzheimer's is a bitch, and I never know what kind of day he is going to have. Sometimes he's himself and others he's not. I'll never reveal it to Hazel, but the horrifying notion of waking up one morning and discovering him passed has influenced my sleep. Most nights, I'm fortuitous to receive four hours, and that's risky when you work with heavy equipment. Yet, no matter what, even with sleeping aids, I'm wide awake after a meager four hours. Death is something that everybody deals with, but not something they come to terms with until an older age. That's when matters become real, but how do you prepare yourself for losing someone? The doctors say he doesn't have too much longer with how fast it's progressing.

From the minute we take our initial breath, our clocks are tallying down to our death. There are many components that go into how short that can be; like health, disease, and unanticipated occurrences like crashes and serial killers, but when a doctor tells you to prepare yourself, what do they mean? Am I expected to somehow come to terms with the fact that my father will no longer be on this Earth? He's the only man that has been there for me a hundred percent since I met him. I refuse to accept that he is going to be gone. Yet, I have always known this day would come.

Hazel is having a hard time with it, too, even if she doesn't tell me about it. Aiden has messaged me a couple times saying he's had to console her, and it's okay to be furious at the world right now. We all look at our parents as bulletproof, and don't realize there will come a time where they won't be around. So, we need to soak up their knowledge and advice while we can. No one knows for certain what happens to us after our hearts stop, but I hope I get to see the ones I love on the other side.

To pass some time, I pull out my phone and bring the thread between Raquel and I. Will it seem desperate for me to text her this morning? With everything going on, will I still be able to go tonight? She might think I'm not interested if I cancel, or maybe she will understand. Taking care of an ill parent isn't something for the faint hearted. Many do not have patience required to take care of someone with this disease. Episodes come and go, but you have to be able to handle it. If the doctors hadn't explained to me the importance of not tearing down their delusion, then I would be clueless.

Me: I'm excited for tonight. Hope you got some sleep and have a good day.

Short and sweet. The point is to let her know I'm thinking about her, even if it's seven in the morning. She seems like the type to be up this early, whether she is working or not.

Raquel: Slept like a baby. Do you know where we will be going? Need to know how to dress.

There are only so many places in Grapevine, and we could venture outside the town, but would rather not. I need to be close just in case Hazel needs my help with our father. She hasn't been around during any of his episodes yet. So, if he does end up having one, she might not be able to handle it like I do.

Me: Need to stay close because of Dad. Are you okay with the diner? Maybe next time we can go someplace more romantic.

A part of me wonders if she thinks I'm a cheap date, and I almost send a text saying never mind, but I don't. A materialistic women is not something I'm searching for, and the right one will understand my reasoning for staying close and be okay with it.

Raquel: The place we eat doesn't matter. See you at 7.

A noise from his door shutting upstairs catches my attention, and I soon hear footsteps coming down the staircase. Let's hope he is in a good mood. He isn't much of a morning person, and then throw an episode into the mix, and that can make matters far worse.

"Morning, pop. Sleep okay?"

He pauses at the bottom of the stairs, and his eyebrows arch. "Who the hell are you, boy?"

My heart drops. This isn't the first episode I've witnessed and it won't be the last. No matter how many times I go through it, it still breaks my heart to see him like this.

He walks right past me to the kitchen and starts loading the coffee maker. "Regina?"

His episodes have often revolved around when his wife was still alive. If there is ever a time for him to be on the precipice of being happy, that's the best place for him to go. She passed years ago, and so I just go along with it. He has been having them more frequently over the last couple of months, but it comes with the territory. The doctors cautioned us this day would come, but it still never truly prepares you for it. All we can do is be someone else until he comes out of it, because telling him who we are will only set him off and confuse him further. If this happens, he could become violent.

"She's not here. We've met before, I'm Jeremy, sir." I extend my hand out to him. "I'm just waiting for her to get back."

His forehead creases as he pours his coffee into his #1 Dad mug, and then takes a sip. He doesn't even read it. "Well, you will be here for a while. When my wife goes to the store, she's there for hours. Have a seat."

I don't mention the fact that I'm his son, and that helps him stay calm and collection. It's my only option. So, I use this opportunity to have a conversation with him. He takes a seat in his recliner and turns the television on.

"Let's see what's fucked up in the world today."

We watch stories about robberies and murders in Dallas, but they don't even make him bat an eye. He must think it's the weekend or he would get ready for work right now. At least his brain gives him that out, because if he went to the school, they would ruin it. He used to be a schoolteacher, but retired a couple years ago. I can't say I blame him, he seems to enjoy his life on the couch binge-watching old movies.

"How long have you and Mrs. Regina been married, sir?"

He sets his cup down on the table and peers over at me. "A long time, son. When you find your soulmate, you don't let them go. Remember that. Obstacles will pop up, but you hurdle over them and keep moving."

I remember when she was still alive, and how perfect they always seemed, but no one is perfect. The catch is finding someone that loves you despite your flaws. As he has already stated, she was always the one that could say she was going for milk and be gone for a couple of hours. Regina would always return with bags of unnecessary groceries.

My phone rings, and I see Hazel's name scrolling across the screen. "Hello?"

Her voice is on the other end. "We are on our way over. Need me to pick up breakfast?"

I glance at him, and get up and go toward the front door so he can't hear me. "Not a good time yet. Right now, he thinks I'm waiting for his wife to get home from the grocery store. Oddly enough, he never asked me my reason for being here. But he doesn't even recognize me."

"Jer, I think it might be time we think about the home option. A nurse is helpful, but he is declining and I don't know if you should have to go through that alone. Nurse or not."

She's right. His deterioration has been hitting fast, and the doctors have said they don't know how much longer because of the advancement of the disease. If we can find someplace that specializes in Alzheimer cases, he might be better off. I can't imagine how painful it will be for him when he wakes up one day and he can't remember anything. The specialists have tried to get me to prepare for that day, but I don't want to. Is it awful of me to think maybe he will somehow be magically cured? That maybe one morning he will wake up and the episodes will just go away? Miracles happen, right?

"I'll be over in an hour whether or not he's back to normal. Find some places for us to look at today while I'm in town. Dad wouldn't want you to suffer, and having to pretend to be someone else other than his son is just that."

I hang up the phone, and collapse back down on the couch, waiting to see if my dad reemerges. He is just resting in his recliner, still sipping on his coffee, now watching an action movie.

"Would you like me to make you something for breakfast?" I ask, only to gauge where his headspace is. The episodes can last minutes or hours.

"I could go for some scrambled eggs right about now. Do we have any salsa in the fridge?" he asks.

He's back. If he was still expecting for my mother, he would have asked why I would offer to make him breakfast? The episode is over, and I can be myself again. As petrifying as that situation was, I wouldn't trade being able to spend time with him for anything.

The most baffling part of this disease is walking on eggshells, never knowing what to expect. Some days he's fine, and other days he has multiple episodes. He's approaching final stages, the doctor's say, but he has had no trouble speaking or getting around. That's what we have to watch out for, because that means it's the beginning of the end.

I venture into the kitchen, snagging a bowl, fork, and the container of eggs out of the fridge and set them on the island.

Scrambled eggs aren't that hard to make, all you do is crack the egg, whisk them, and put them into a skillet and let it cook. It's one of the very few things I know how to make. The nurse prepares him breakfast, but she's off today. Thank god for Hazel and her big time salary because if not for her, I would have to quit my job and take care of him. Not that I wouldn't do it in a heartbeat, after everything he has done for me. The nurse stays with him during the day while I work which is great, but when his episodes become more frequent, he is going to question why someone is in his house. He could get violent toward her, and she doesn't deserve that.

My development job was becoming more demanding and begging me to work greater hours, so I took Damon up on his offer to go work for the Fire Department. In Aiden's absence, they haven't hired a replacement yet, so it works out. At least, there I will have a set schedule whereas the construction company could work me thirty hours a week or sixty with no warning. Right now is not the time for me to spend an insane amount of time at work. It's better spent with him.

I move the eggs around the skillet, waiting for them not to be so runny, and I peek in on dad to make sure he's alright while I wait. I will not mention the episode to him, but we will at some point have to explain why he's going to a facility, and Hazel might be the best person for that. I'm afraid I might be too emotional.

The eggs are ready and I take a spoon and dish them out onto two plates, adding salsa on top for my dad. It's the only way he'll eat them. I've tried it, but thought it was disgusting. Just plain ole eggs for me.

"Here you go."

We sit and eat them while ending the action movie that's already playing on television. I'm not much of an action fan, but when my dad's around it's pretty much all he watches. He's a huge fan of Bruce Willis. When we were younger, he would drag both Hazel and me to the theaters to watch the premiers, and we never complained. It was nice to have someone who wanted to be around us. Being a foster kid, bouncing around from home to home, the parents never bonded with us, and most didn't want to. It was all about the monthly paycheck.

"Hazel will be over in a bit and then we are all going to go out."

"What do you guys have in mind?"

"We will see what Hazel has planned when she gets here," I reply.

I'll miss this. Just hanging out with him, and watching television together. Why did this have to happen to him? How is he going to take it?

4

RAQUEL

*I*n my line of work, it's exceedingly troublesome not to become close to my residents. It's hard to follow when you check in on them every day, and see how fast the disease takes someone. It's a horrible sight, and my only job is to keep them comfortable until it's their time. My friend, Brittaney, asks me why I choose to stay here all the time. It's where I feel I'm doing the most good. Nurses can be bitchy sometimes, and these people deserve someone who will make them laugh and smile. It's not their fault they have Alzheimer's and yes, they might have a sporadic episode and become violent, but it passes. Another patient is being brought in today to take over the deserted room from Richard's passing.

One of my patients, Daniel, has been here for two years, and his doctor told him he had six months. Now, about ninety-percent of the time, he doesn't comprehend what year it is, but he remains tranquil enough to go throughout his daily routine. The disease doesn't advance the same for everyone. He is one of the lucky ones.

"Hey, how are you feeling today?" I ask, laying my hand on his shoulder.

"Still alive, so great."

Things have gotten worse, and he has come to terms with his

passing, and that's one thing that the support group tackles here. Some people aren't able to fathom being gone, and what that will do to their families. A gentleman comes in once a month to talk to the residents and discuss legalities. Most of them don't even have wills when they come in here, and he explains how important one is, and how to take care of things beforehand. It's morbid, but it has to get done.

My grandpa never established a will , and at a young age, I had to watch my dad struggle over after his death. It developed into a troubling time for him, and had to stand by and watch his family home be auctioned.

My parents aren't wealthy by any means, and back then, they were struggling just to keep the lights on. If a will had been drawn up, it would have been left to my father, and we could have been raised there. It defeated him, knowing that someone else was going to be living in the very home he spent his entire childhood.

That's something that lingered with me, and when I turned twenty-one, the first thing I did was go to an attorney to get a will in place. I don't have many assets, but after the divorce, Lily has been established as the beneficiary. Anything I have will be passed down to her without question. She doesn't need to have to go through what my father did.

The eight-hour shift always goes by fast, because I enjoy my job, not the losing people part, but getting to interact with the residents and hear the stories of their lives. Some of them are quite fascinating, and I never turn down the chance to hear a good story.

Many of the residents are still asleep, but it's seven in the morning, and there are lots of things to do today. I'm the onsite attendant, and I have some flu vaccines to administer today, and some basic check-ups to report to their doctors. I keep their charts amended with their weight and their medications. That's my to-do list today.

Brittaney is supposed to meet me for lunch today, since we haven't seen each other since she started seeing this new guy. I love her, but her entire world changes when a man comes into it. It's like she has no time for me anymore. She gets tunnel vision, perhaps, and stops reaching out. Brittaney is always saying I need to get out there, and put up a profile on one of these dating apps, but no thanks. All you get on those are one-night stands or men who aren't looking for something long-term. At thirty-five, I'm not a one-night stand type of girl. I've always dreamed of having the white picket fence, beautiful house, and a family. Although, it doesn't seem to be in the cards for me.

Dean wrecked that for me. My piece of shit ex-husband who declared I wasn't spontaneous enough for him. We were together for almost seven years, and one day, he just up and petitioned for a divorce. I still think he was having an affair, but I could never prove it. What the hell did he expect? How am I supposed to be spontaneous when I have a job that requires me to be here? I can't just up and take a week vacation at the drop of a pin because I want to. His job allowed that, as long as he had the time. Here, I have to give at least a two-week notice before using any vacation time. Dean, such an asshole, and I hope he rots in hell.

My phone beeps, and I pull it out to read the text.

Brittaney: *Still on for lunch?*

Wow, I'm amazed she isn't bailing on me.

Me: *Yup. The diner at 11?*

The only place in town besides fast food that can get us served quickly is the diner. I only get an hour and even though there is no one to get mad if I'm late, I don't exploit the policy. No reason to give them ammunition to use against me if it ever comes down to budget cuts, which happens often in this line of work.

The time until lunch flies by, strolling around and chatting to the girls in the crochet club. They always talk about the good ol' days, decades ago, when things were much simpler. They dismiss technology, and don't believe in cell phones, internet, and all that jazz. I recall a couple of weeks ago, I overheard their discussion about the way girls dress today, and how they shouldn't show so much skin or go out in public in pajamas. When they were younger, if you were in public, you had your makeup done, and your hair perfect. They didn't peruse around town in anything less. To be fair, I'm glad that it's not like that because I don't have enough energy every morning to fix my hair and put on makeup. I just throw it up in a bun and go on my merry way. Boy, how things have changed.

"I'll see you in a bit, ladies. Heading to lunch."

I hang my white coat in the office, and lock the door behind me, before roaming through the main sitting area to the front door. You have to swipe your badge for them to open from the inside, so no one can go drifting around town. So I do that, and make the two block walk to the diner from the facility. It's not too bad outside, in the mid-eighties, and a slight breeze that makes me want to let my hair down, but I don't. I can detect the flowers blossoming in the air, and it helps that it's my favorite season. See, I don't like the cold, but also hate the hot. The perfect temperature for me is seventy-five with a slight breeze and the sun shining.

A squeal comes from down the street and I see Brittaney's hands flapping around. "Girl, it's been too long."

I'm speculating what news she has to tell me. This isn't like her, especially if she is still dating that guy. Usually by now, she has called me crying cause they broke up. So, when she texted me this morning about lunch, it caught me off guard. Yet, I couldn't turn down a chance to catch up with my best friend, no matter what news she has. I love her regardless, even if she ditches me sometimes.

Her arms fasten around me, and I let it happen, but then she pulls away and takes a good look at me. Almost to where it makes me uneasy.

"Let's go inside and eat," she says, tugging my arm.

She chooses the booth farthest from the door, and opens the menu. So I follow her lead, not wishing to pry on this impromptu luncheon. The French dip and Swiss is amazing here, but a bacon cheeseburger sounds to die for right now. So, I decide to go with that, and add guacamole to it.

"So, while we wait for our food, we have so much to catch up on."

I roll my eyes, wondering what the hell she is going to throw at me now. Brittaney doesn't have a good track record with men. She once said she doesn't believe in long-term commitment, because all that amounts to is getting cheated on or hurt in the long run. How would she even know if she has never taken the chance? Yet, I just let her do her thing, and listen about it when the time comes she needs a shoulder to cry on.

Brittaney takes my hand in hers. "I'm getting married."

My eyes land on the enormous diamond ring on her finger. What the hell is she talking about? Since the day I met her she has been anti-commitment and now, she is getting married to a man she hasn't even been with for a year? Brittaney must be out of her fucking mind. "When did you get engaged?"

I haven't even met the guy, and that's ludicrous. You don't get engaged to a guy that your best friend has never even fucking met. I'm becoming a little flustered now, and it seems she is waiting for me to say congratulations, but I can't.

"What are you thinking? You are not a long-term person, remember? I mean, you just said that three months ago. And now you are engaged? Did Chad drug you or something?"

Her neck cocks back. "What the hell are you talking about? We're in love. You should be happy for me."

Maybe I am being too hard on her, and need to cut her some slack. However, I'm still stuck wondering how she could fall in love with this guy in such a short time, enough to get engaged? "When do I get to meet him? I mean, being your maid of honor, I think it should happen soon. We will have so much to plan."

The smile comes back, and she pulls out a binder. "Already started. I'm going to send this with you to look over, and maybe we can have you over for dinner next week."

Have me over? Did she move in with this guy and not even tell me? What the hell has she been doing since we last went out for girl's night? My gut feeling tells me something is wrong, because this is out of character for Brittaney.

The waitress brings our food, and I flip through the folder while plucking at my food. My appetite is gone, and now I'm just worried. She could make the biggest mistake of her life, and she isn't about to listen to me. Why? I'm a thirty-five-year-old divorcee. Maybe this is the guy she's been waiting for all along and she is ready to settle down. It's just a hard pill to swallow for her entire persona to change in such a short amount of time. I never thought this day would come and sitting here looking over her wedding ideas is preposterous. She will change her mind in a couple weeks, and be back to sobbing on my shoulder again.

"Listen, I'm happy that you are excited about this, but aren't you jumping into this too soon?"

She crinkles her nose, and grabs the binder. "I knew you wouldn't be happy for me. That's why I waited to tell you. Why can't you just be happy for me? Fuck."

How can I be happy knowing this isn't who she is. Something has to be causing this, a chemical imbalance in her brain, or hormones. Brittaney is not a settle down type of woman, especially after spending three months with someone. How can she expect to just stand by and not say anything? Isn't that what best friends are for? Pointing out when things aren't right?

"All I'm saying is not to rush into marriage. Have a long engagement. Don't you want to make sure that he isn't some creep? How well do you even know this guy?"

She gets up from the booth, and clutches the binder in her arms. "I told Chad you would be against it. When you are ready to come to terms with this, give me a call. I don't need anyone dampening the most exciting time in my life. Best friend or not."

Brittaney struts down the aisle and out the door, leaving me sitting there like a fool.

5

JEREMY

The atmosphere is stuffy, and it has a lot to do with the impending conversation that is going to take place. Hazel and I would like nothing more to have him at home until he passes, but it's becoming difficult with the frequency of his episodes. A center might be the best option for him to keep him safe. I fear he is beginning the final stages of this disease, and specialists told us that this is the most difficult to handle. The person forgets most of their life, becomes confused, and will need around the clock care. Hazel might make a shit ton of money, but that would cost almost all of her salary and we just can't afford that. The thought of robbing a bank crosses my mind, just to keep him here with me, but it's not feasible. If I end up in prison, what good does that do?

Hazel has been showing him pictures of Jake, and knowing that he might never get to meet his grandson is heartbreaking. This man, more than anything, has been excited to have grandchildren around, and to know that he can't travel to meet Jake kills me. He has gotten to talk to him on the phone, and video chat once, but it's not the same. I hope that we can get Jake out here, at least once, before he goes. It will mean the world to him.

My dad is always inquiring about the bookstore, and her pile of fresh cases. I'm not a jealous person, but sometimes, I feel like Hazel gets more attention because she doesn't live here. My father is proud of me, and I know that, but he harps on Hazel. I get it, she's a high profile lawyer, but still.

Aiden lets us know the bookstore is thriving and is finally in the green, and now he is phasing in book signings for local authors. He seems to think it will bring in a new set of readers which will have a good impact on his business. I never gauged him to be a business man, but he's been doing pretty well for himself out there.

"Will Jake be coming down with you next time?" he asks.

"We are working it out with his parents, dad. Believe me, we are trying."

His doctor doesn't know if he is in the best condition to go such a distance. If he has one of his episodes, being in a different city poses a risk. There will be nothing to ground him, whereas in his home, he knows this place. So, making the trip out there is out of the question.

My eyes scan the feel of the room, which is uneasy, because Hazel and I know what is approaching. The walkthrough is scheduled soon and we haven't even talked to him about it yet. She has decided to bring it up herself, and I'm not ready for this. Even as an adult, I want to shield my father from heartache.

"So, we have an appointment at Grapevine Memory Care. You might go get some jeans on."

He looks at me, and then to Hazel. "What do you mean? I thought we weren't going to do that?" His demeanor changes and his hand shakes. "I don't want to live in one of those places, son."

His eyes penetrate to my very core, and I try to hold it together, because we need to be a united front. We want to clarify that we aren't abandoning him.

Hazel stands up, and pops a squat in front of him. "Do you remember the episode from this morning, dad?"

He shakes his head. "No – I didn't have one."

"But you did. We aren't blaming you for anything. It's not your fault, but you didn't even recognize Jeremy. You thought Mom was still alive."

"No – that's ridiculous. That didn't happen."

He bolts out of the recliner, and shoots past us on the couch to go upstairs. When he gets up to his bedroom, the door slams behind him.

We knew this wouldn't be easy. I want this no more than he does. "Maybe we should reconsider?"

"Jer, I know it's hard, but the doctors think he will do better at one. He needs to be around those that specialize in this disease. We can only do so much. It's not like we won't visit him."

Tears fall from my eyes, and then Hazel joins me. I never thought I'd be in this position; not with him. The man gave us so much, and now his memory of us is going to fade. Soon, he won't remember us, and that's going to be the most heartbreaking part. I want to cherish the moments we have left, and putting him in a home, won't that diminish that? Will he ever forgive us for this?

"We need to get him adjusted before it gets worse. Do you know how bad things could escalate if he wakes up one morning and thinks you're an intruder?" Hazel says. "He could shoot you, for heaven's sakes. The doctors were clear. When his episodes began happening every day, we should look into round the clock care. We need to do what's best for him even if he doesn't see it that way."

She gets up from her knees, and takes a seat on the couch next to Aiden.

"If it's the right thing to do, then why does it feel so awful?"

She takes my hand and walks me upstairs to outside his bedroom. *Knock. Knock. Knock.*

"Dad, let's talk about this, please. We don't want you mad at us. Can you open the door?"

The silence on the other side scares me so I open the door, and find him lying in bed, the blankets over his head like a child.

"I don't want to go. This house is the only thing left of your mother."

Hazel and I glance at each other and we crawl into the bed, slide under the covers, enveloping him a family hug. This transition is going to be rough, but it is the best thing for him right now. He needs someone with knowledge of Alzheimer's and how to handle the episodes.

"Dad, I'll stay in the house, and make sure everything stays in tip top shape. I will never let this house go. It's our family home. I promise you."

We stay hugged against each other for a few minutes, giving him the opportunity to calm down and listen to reason. I understand his frustration and wanting to hold on to the memory of his wife, but right now his health is depleting. It must come first, and she would want that. Leaving everything you know, to an unknown place can be scary, but I will be there for him every step of the way.

Hazel gets off the bed, allowing me the chance to escape, too, and we leave him alone as our feet make the staircase squeak some more on the way down.

"Is he okay?" Aiden asks. "I hate this for your dad."

I nod, and go to the kitchen, preparing myself a small cup of coffee for the day we are about to go through. It's not only going to be exhausting for him, but for us as well. We don't want to do this, but with his episodes getting worse, we have no choice. Waiting around would be dangerous. I know many parents get thrown into nursing homes because their kids don't want to take care of them, and that isn't us at all. If it wasn't for the episodes, he would just continue living with me, and the nurse could assist, but the chance of violent episodes are something to think about in this case. When he has these, it's not our father in there, he doesn't know who we are. This only heightens the chance of him being violent if he finds an unfamiliar person in his home. We can't take that chance, and as much as he is against it, our father wouldn't want to put that risk on us.

"What should we do? We are supposed to be there in thirty-minutes. Should I call and reschedule for later?" I ask.

She shakes her hand, puts down the coffee cup on the island, and heads toward the stairs, but then we hear his door open, and foot-steps coming down the hall.

"Kids, before we go, we need to discuss something. Have a seat."

Hazel and I look at each other and sit down as asked. I'm not sure what he is going to say, and I can't take anymore tears right now.

"I will go, but you should know where my important documents are in case something happens. In the filing cabinet in your mother's old office is my will and life insurance paperwork."

Hazel scoffs. "Don't talk like that. You are going to a facility. It doesn't mean you're dying tomorrow."

My dad knows his episodes are getting worse. Nobody wants to wake up and not be able to take care of themselves.

"At any rate, I'm not getting any younger and with this disease, my time is limited. Please keep the house in the family. Your mother bought this house hoping to hand it down to our kids. Don't let it go."

I put my hand on his shoulder. "I'm not going anywhere."

He stands up from the recliner, and shifts his pants. "Okay, I'm ready. Let's get this over with, shall we."

Why does my heart hurt walking out the door? A piece of me wants to take care of him and not have to do this, but the other side also understands the progression. No matter what I want, we need to do what's best for him. If he were to hurt someone during one of his episodes, he could never live with himself.

We all pile up into my truck, and head to the facility. Dad just stares out the window, and I can't even remember the last time he got out of the house. Poor man. He turns up the radio, and doesn't say a word, just stares out the window and lets the breeze hit his face.

When we come up on the sign for Grapevine Memory Care, he sighs, and sits up straight until we come to a stop in our parking spot. Dad unbuckles and gets out of the car.

Hazel takes his hand in hers, and walks up to the double doors, holding it open for him, and we all step inside to the wide open area. We see residents around, and most look to be much older than dad.

There are four women sitting in chairs by the front door, and they are babbling away while crocheting. They seem to have a good time. It catches dad's eye, and he looks back at me.

"I'm not taking up crocheting."

I laugh in response. "You don't have to."

"Hi, Can I help you?" a woman asks, walking up to us. And that's when I realize it's Raquel.

"Yeah, we have an appointment for my father, Donald," Hazel replies.

She double takes me, and then responds. "Oh, yes. Right this way."

Things just keep getting worse for us. Not only is she related to one of my coworkers, but now she is going to be working where my dad will be living. I know Grapevine is small, but not that damn small. The universe fucking hates me.

I watch her ass sway in the skirt she is wearing, and notice the wondrous curves god gave her. It's been a while, and it's not against the law to stare at a beautiful woman.

"This is the main common area," she says, her hands gesturing toward a vast room with three televisions, plenty of recliners, and some tables and chairs where there are people playing card games and watching the news. "And if you follow me next door... this is the eating area. We serve breakfast from 4:30 to 7:00 in the morning, lunch from eleven to one in the afternoon and then dinner starts at five and ends around seven as well."

My eyes search my dad's to see how he is doing. His hands are by his side in fists. Nobody is excited about living in an assisted living home, so I can't blame him, but he knows it's the best thing for him.

"And where would I sleep?"

She touches his shoulder, "Of course, let's take you to your room."

We all follow her down the hallway, to a room without a name on it yet. The rest have wreaths with their last name. "This will be all yours to decorate how you want."

He walks in, and it's bigger than I expected. It's about the size of the living room at the house and has its own flat screen, a king size bed, dresser, closet, and bathroom.

"What do you think?" Hazel asks.

He doesn't answer, but continues to walk around the room, examining everything. Raquel looks back at me, doe eyes wide, and smiles. She's thinking the same thing I am. Can we pursue this relationship now? I've been looking forward to dinner tonight since she said yes, and now I'm not even sure if it's still going to happen.

"It's difficult to get used to at first. We promise to make you feel at home here. And family can visit anytime they want," Raquel says. "Would you like to walk around and meet some others?"

He nods, and takes off to the common room leaving us behind. I'm not sure what to ask, and so I let Hazel take over from here. She is the one paying for it, and wants her to feel comfortable, too.

"I am the resident nurse here at the facility. If you decide to have him here, I promise to take good care of him. His doctor sent over his file, and I think you're doing this at the right time."

Hazel asks a bunch of questions about how they will handle his episodes, if he may leave the center with a family member, and what the specifics are. She mentions wanting her to meet his grandson if he comes down.

"Family is welcome anytime here. Our residents thrive on interaction. As far as leaving the facility, they can be checked out for a period of up to four hours. However, we suggest you don't do this once they show signs of not recognizing family. This is more for your safety."

Hazel cries again, and then tries to talk us out of doing this. "What if he hates it here? I don't want him to think we don't love him, you know? This has all been so hard, and I can't imagine what he is going through."

I pull her close into my shoulder. "He knows we would do anything for him. This is the right thing, no matter how hard it is."

Raquel glances at me with a smile, and puts in her two cents. "You don't have to decide today, ma'am. We will hold his spot for three days to give you time. I will say this though, after seeing his file, and hearing about the episode this morning, it's going to progress fast and it's best to get him comfortable while he's still himself."

She excuses herself, and we go try to find him. He's sitting in the common room, talking to some gentleman about the war, and smiles when he sees us. This might not be a bad place for him, and it will be nice for him to make some friends.

"You ready to go?" I ask, approaching the table with the men.

"So, when do I move in?" he asks. "This is Paul. He fought in Vietnam."

I wave Hazel over, and repeat the question.

"So, this is where you would like to go?" she asks.

"Paul and I have some common interests, and it seems like an alright place, I guess."

Hazel smiles, and goes to find Raquel to let her know he has decided. I stand behind him and let him finish talking with Paul until she gets back.

"You're all set to move in tomorrow. Looks like we have some packing to do tonight. We better get started," Hazel says.

He waves bye to Paul, and then Raquel lets us out of the double doors. I'm glad he didn't freak out about this, and took it like a champ.

My dad is my hero, and nothing will ever change that.

6

RAQUEL

The initial visit is hard on every family, because no one wants to live in a facility. Many of our residents are dropped off here and family barely comes by. The crucial part of having a loved one live here is for them to have support from their family. Sometimes, it causes depression in our residents when no one visits.

I watch Jeremy walk away to the truck and can't take my eyes off that man's ass, but who knew a man could have such a perfect one? *Snap out of it*!

The nurse before me made the mistake of getting involved with a patient's family member and when they broke up, it caused many problems for the facility. All I know is the man showed up here ranting and raving about how big of a slut she was, and it ended up getting her fired. The company suggested when they hired me not to have any romantic interests in the residents or their family members. And up until now, it's never been an issue.

The ladies by the front door are gabbing about their first boyfriends and having a good time. It's nice to see they made friends after coming here. So many of the elderly get pushed to the side, and depression kicks in. Being lonely is one thing that can make someone's health deplete. I always encourage the family to come back and visit anytime, because that's what's best for the patient.

I do my last round of the day, and my phone vibrates in my pocket.

Jeremy: *So, that was awkward. This probably changes things, but are we still on for dinner tonight?*

Damnit, I'm not even sure how to respond. We made the agreement before I knew I would be his dad's nurse, and seeing him could cost me my job. Yet, I want to say fuck it and just do it, anyway. They say we find love in the weirdest places, and sometimes you have to just embrace it. What if Jeremy and I are meant to be together and my job is the only thing standing in the way? Do I just go for it or walk away? It's a hard decision to make, but one that could have dire consequences.

After rounds are complete, it's the end of my shift, and I take my jacket off, grab my keys, and head out the door. The big piece of the grill missing on my brand new Kia Soul kills me every time I see it. The day after I bought it, with only ten miles on it, someone rammed it in the grocery store parking lot. No note, nothing. Of course, the cameras weren't working so I couldn't get any video, but it's supposed to be fixed next week. The insurance company wrote it off as an uninsured vehicle accident. The car beeps and I open the driver's door, slip in, and turn the key. One of my favorite things about it, when I get in, the GPS asks if I want to go home, and then starts it for me. Not that I need directions, but it's a nice feature.

I pull out onto Lamar Avenue, and come to the first light. There is a man in the truck next to me, waiting for the green light, and just staring straight ahead. It's Jeremy. For a moment, I think about rolling down my window and saying hi, but then I talk myself out of it. I haven't even texted him back, and honestly at this point, don't even know what to say.

At the next light, I turn left into my subdivision, and then into my driveway. Okay, my home is nothing spectacular, but it's just what I need. I have no need for a mansion or six bedrooms. I close the car door behind me, and unlock the front door, and then sit my keys in the bowl right inside.

When I bought this place, I had just been divorced, and needed some place that was my own, and that's when I stumbled across this place. It's got three enormous bedrooms, two full baths, and a nice sized backyard. I have some room on both sides if I wanted to add on to the house, which I might do in the future, because the master bathroom is smaller than what I like. It's only got a shower and not a tub, and after a long day at work, sometimes I want to just relax in a hot bubble bath, but to do that I have to use the guest bathroom.

My phone sits on the counter, and I pull his text up with no response. I do not know what to say. He will understand if I say no, especially after finding out I'm his dad's nurse. Yet, something inside tells me I should just go for it. Grapevine has become my new home and my job means the world to me, and if they decide to retaliate against me, where will I go?

As the bath draws, I grab my robe from my bathroom and put it on the hook on the back of the door. A nice, warm bath might help me decide, and this one could be one that I might regret no matter what. If I walk away, there's a chance he could be the man for me, but if I go, it could end badly and I could lose my job. Why did Grapevine have to be so small? I deserve better than this impossible decision.

The bath is full, so I turn it off and get inside, letting the warm water help with the tense muscles in my back. My neck rests on the lip of the back, and I close my eyes. Moving here to be closer to my brother, and have a change of pace, changed my look on things. The divorce ruined the first half of the year, and then finding out that bimbo moved into his house right after we finalized the papers, only it put the nail in the coffin. I couldn't stay in Dallas, and the only family I have close is Eli. We were close when we were younger, but I moved away for college, and we saw each other a couple times a year around holidays. Maybe this is all a sign telling me not to go out with Jeremy. First, he was my brother's coworker, and now I'm his dad's nurse. The universe must try to show me it's not a good idea.

It's like a lightbulb goes off in my head, and I stand up, wrap a towel around my torso, and grab my phone.

Me: *Listen, I think it's best if we don't. Things are complicated now.*

Before I change my mind, I respond. It's for the best. My job is my livelihood and losing it could cause me not to be able to support my daughter, and that's has to be my primary concern. Lily deserves everything in the world and without a job, I can't do that. Plus, this position is what I want to do, and helping people. Jeremy messages me right back.

Jeremy: *What if we are just friends? You said you were new to town. I can be your tour guide. Unless Tessa is already doing that.*

Fuck. Can I be just friends with him? He poses a good point, and even though Tessa has shown me most of what there is to see, Jeremy might know some different spots. I may regret this.

Me: *Fine, but only friends. I'll meet you at the restaurant. Where?*

I take the towel off and replace it with my red robe. Since it's not a date, I don't have to go crazy when I dress up, which will save me some time. It's already after six. My feet are still wet, so I leave a trail straight to the bedroom. The robe comes off, and I slip on a pair of black lace panties and a matching bra. Yes, I know it's not a date, but they give me confidence. And after the ex-husband scandal, I could use all of it I can get.

I browse through my closet, trying to decide what to wear, because it can't be anything too dressy but nothing too casual either. Of course, I want to look nice, but not take me home and fuck me good. The red dress is too provocative, and the purple one hugs my ass too well. I need something in between. My eyes set on a powder pink short dress I wore to a wedding last year, and it's perfect. The length is just long enough, but it hugs my curves, too. I slip it on over my head and then zip up the side.

I take a second to check my phone to see his response.

Jeremy: *Have you been to the diner?*

I laugh because Brittaney and I were there for lunch. Everyone raves over that place, and I have to agree they have some good food, especially breakfast. Pancakes are good for lunch and dinner, too.

Me: *Yes, and I love it. See you in 20.*

I pull black flats off the top shelf and put them on before going back to the bathroom to at least line my eyes. This not being a date works for me, because I don't have to curl my hair or do a full face of makeup, yet I'm still nervous. Why? Jeremy is fucking attractive, like he should be on a cover of a magazine, and he asked me out. As exhilarating as that is, we are doing the right thing by just being friends. Being divorced is already complicated, no need to add to the pot.

I turn off the lights in the kitchen and living room, grab my keys from the bowl by the door, and head to the restaurant. The pressure is a little less since we aren't going to some fancy restaurant, just the diner. Yet, on my way over, I think about how the date would have gone if we hadn't run into each other today. We could've had a great time and then I would've found out later. It's better it happened this way, because once I had a piece of Jeremy, it would have been harder to say no.

There is one spot left on the street in front of the diner, and I swipe it. There is a parking lot a couple of blocks down, but I don't want to walk there. It's still hot outside, and in Texas, that's pretty much normal in the summer.

"Hey there, gorgeous," Jeremy says, leaning up against his truck with a smile. "I thought you were going to ditch me for a minute."

I close my door and walk over to him. "It's not a date, so why would I do that?"

"Things are complicated. Like you said."

I shake my head, and he opens the door for me and follows me to the back booth. The same server from this afternoon is still here.

"Back again, darling?"

Jeremy looks at me. "Again?"

"She was just here for lunch. Our food is good, but not that good," the waitress laughs. She sets down the menus and walks away.

"Why didn't you tell me? We could've gone somewhere else."

I don't even respond, but pick up the menu and start browsing. I had a burger earlier, so breakfast it is.

"Breakfast platter for me. What about you?" I ask, laying down the menu toward the edge of the table.

"I always get breakfast. Never fails," he responds, putting his menu on top of mine.

He puts his elbow on the table, and his hand on his chin. "So, tell me all about you. What made you decide to move to Grapevine? Why did you want to become a nurse?"

This sounds a lot like date talk, but can be construed as getting to know a friend as well. I take his questions and decide to answer them as honestly as possible. He knows I'm divorced, so that's off the table, but he doesn't know the whole story. When Dean and I met, things didn't start out romantic. When I went to work at Dallas Memorial, he was my attending doctor, and we worked together.

The server interrupts us by bringing us coffee.

After she walks away, I continue. It was within a few weeks, we started sneaking around, and then stupid me fell in love with the guy, and we got married. The biggest mistake of my life. Not only did I fuck and marry one of my bosses, but I couldn't stay at the hospital after that. Seeing his damn face every day, no thanks.

"Holy shit. So, you came to Grapevine to be closer to your brother then?" he asks.

"Yeah, my parents live in Washington, so he is the closest relative to me. Plus, I like Texas."

He seems interested in me, and it's refreshing for a change. Dean had always been very focused on himself in conversation and the bedroom. I wish I had noticed the signs before we got married, but love clouds our judgment sometimes.

"Ain't that the truth? So, what made you want to become a nurse?"

My fingers tap on the table, making me remember my first run in with a hospital. When I was about seven years old, we were in a car accident. We were on our way back from a dance recital of mine, and someone fell asleep at the wheel and hit us. My mother called 911, and they took us to the hospital. My nurse's name was Paula, and she took great care of me. Somehow, she inspired me at such a young age to want to become a nurse. Over my childhood, seeing the brave women on tv and movies helping save lives, it just motivated me to pursue it. I felt like it was my calling. Just like working at memory care. The residents need someone on their side, and I can be that person.

The conversation is flowing great, and we do have a connection, but we aren't here to harp on that. Questions are important to get to know someone, and I still know nothing about Jeremy. *Time to dive in.*

7

JEREMY

You can tell a lot about a person by their motivation behind certain things. Raquel's want to become a nurse because of someone who she saw to be brave and kind means she wants to be like Paula. She wants to make a difference. Motivations like this can have a tremendous impact on who a person becomes, and looking at Raquel, it's proof.

She has this thing she keeps doing where she bites her lower lip when I ask her a question, almost like she's scared whatever she says is going to make me run. Everyone has baggage, especially at our age, so she doesn't need to worry. I've got my own shit to work out, too.

Raquel gets more interesting the more I learn about her, and we might just be friends right now, but I'm hoping eventually we can give this a shot. She might have said this isn't a date, but I like how her outfit of choice shows she wants it to be.

As she is talking to me, my eyes focus on hers, and they gleam a little when she talks about her job. It lets me know my dad will be in expert hands. Things don't always go the best in places like these, so it's nice to know I have someone on the inside monitoring him.

"So, how long have you lived in Grapevine?" she asks, adding some cream and sugar to her coffee.

Sometimes, I hate talking about my childhood because it's depressing, and on dates, it can ruin the mood, but it always comes up. The part that irritates me is sometimes I can see the pity in their eyes, and it's unnecessary. I ended up okay, thanks to Don and Regina.

"Since I was a teenager..." Raquel has been upfront with me, and I can only extend the same truth. "The foster care system is a joke. As a child, I bounced around home after home for years, and never stayed anywhere over six months. Making friends or getting close to people isn't something I could do. This went on for about six years, and then I was placed with Don and Regina. At first, it was hard. After every family has let you down for six years, it's hard to imagine finding one that wants to keep you around."

I search for her reaction, because talking about this is personal, and normally not something I share with someone I just met, but it's not like that with her. Raquel has been easy to talk to, and I don't see any judgment from her.

"Foster care needs to be revamped. I've seen firsthand some people that are verified foster parents, and it's terrifying," Raquel says.

Usually, when I talk about this, the person thinks I'm being over-dramatic, but no one can attest to it unless they have been in the system. Being a foster parent is not the same as being a foster kid. I bet the parents that housed Hazel and myself thought they were doing right by us, but they weren't. Bringing a child into your home for only monetary purposes is downright despicable. They have already lost enough, and being in a home that doesn't want them only makes matter worse in their eyes.

"I can't tell you how many places they sent me to that only used me for the check. They didn't care about me or want to get to know me," I respond, and don't want to get too far deep into this topic.

"So, are you staying in Grapevine long term?" she asks.

Where does she think I'll go? "It's my home and always will be. The small town vibe is perfect and knowing the people in this town means I have thousands of people I can trust. It's like a family community, and we are all here to help each other. Trivial things aren't important to me, so a big city isn't on my radar. Plus, it's a great place to raise a family."

I stop myself after mentioning that. This isn't a fucking date. No need to talk about having a family. Her eyes search mine, and it's obvious my demeanor has changed. Why would I mention starting a family with a girl that I'm not even on an actual date with? Stupid, Jeremy.

The waitress shows up with our food, and I don't know if it's because of my last statement, but it feels like we've been here forever. I thank her and start digging in. Maybe that will help change the subject.

"And becoming a firefighter?" she asks.

Construction has always been my job since I turned eighteen, and it pays very well, but the hours are long and horrible. There is no set schedule with it, and with everything going on with my dad, it isn't fair to waste what precious time I might have left working. So, when Aiden and my sister got back together, a spot opened up.

"So, it just kind of fell into your lap?"

"You could say that."

Damon has been asking me for years to come and join the team, but it's a pay cut. So, I never took it seriously until now. Helping the community will be beneficial and rewarding. The Jackson brothers are always talking about how doing the job changes their perspective on a lot of things, and makes them feel like they are helping the community every day. So, when the spot became open, I applied and got it. Simple as that.

"Do you see yourself staying in Grapevine long term?" I ask.

The friend zone is somewhere I've been pushed into many times, and it's hard to crawl out of there once you are so far in. I like Raquel and if we need to start out friends to give this a chance later, I'll do it. Yet, none of that matters if she doesn't plan on staying here long term. Grapevine is my home, and it is my responsibility to make sure my dad's house is taken care of and doesn't get sold to some random person.

Raquel takes a big bite out of her burger, and her head bobs while chewing it before answering. "I like it here. Working at the memory center is something I didn't know I needed."

So, that's not a direct answer, which throws me off guard. She might just be here to get away for a couple of years, and then plans on moving back to Dallas. Raquel isn't going to break my heart before we even get started, is she?

Here I am, listening to her talk about how much she loves her job, and all I can think about it taking her from behind while wearing nothing but her white coat. I twitch, and try to keep on the back-burner, but it's impossible. My dirty ass mind is full of angst and when I get to have her, she will know why I'm the perfect man for her.

"Hello?"

She's waving her hand in front of my face because I haven't been paying attention to much of anything that she's said in the last few minutes.

"Earth to Jeremy."

Right then, my phone vibrates with a text from Hazel. What the hell does she want?

Hazel: *How's the date going?*

I roll my eyes, but Raquel catches it.

"Everything okay?"

"Just my nosey ass sister. That's all."

Hazel's intentions mean well, but she never knows when to stop. My love life is none of her concern, and the meddling needs to die down. I can handle it on my own.

I place my phone back on the table, after responding fine, and continue to eat my breakfast, which is getting cold at this point. Raquel tells me about some residents at the center, and how she thinks it's going to be a great fit for my dad. I don't know how she does it; dealing with the episodes with multiple people, and still maintaining a smile. I would think it would be sad to watch people slip away from themselves. Maybe she can give me some advice. I'm going to need all the help I can get.

She might have a relative that is going through this, but every day she goes to work and helps others dealing with Alzheimer's. It can't be an easy job, which only makes me like her even more.

"I admire your dedication to your job. Not everyone is cut off for it. You seem to handle it pretty well."

She maneuvers her hair behind her left ear and blushes. "Those people need someone to care for them, and even a brief conversation can make their whole day. Many don't have visitors, and that breaks my heart."

She doesn't have to worry about that with me. My dad will see me every day, and he deserves that. It'll be nice for him to have others to socialize with to, instead of being stuck at home, with just me and his nurse all the time.

Her phone rings, and she answers it.

"What is it?"

All I can hear is a man on the other side of the phone. He doesn't sound pleased.

"I'll pick her up tomorrow at five p.m. like the papers state. Don't pull this shit, Dean. Bye"

It's her ex-husband. He sounds like a complete asshole.

"Sorry about that."

"Don't be. Everything okay?" I ask, wondering who she is picking up.

"He wants to keep our daughter longer, and the arrangement is in place for a reason. He knows that. Yet, he thinks he can always talk me into giving him more time."

She has a daughter? There is something I didn't know.

"How old is she?"

"Eight. Sorry, since this wasn't a date, I didn't mention it."

Is the fact that she has a daughter supposed to scare me away? It just makes me attracted to her even more.

"No need to be sorry. We are just friends, remember?"

She smiles, and we finish up the last couple of bites of our food. The conversation goes silent, but Dean put a damper on our evening, and I'll have to remember to thank him for that later on.

"Need anything else before you go?" the waitress asks.

"Nope, just the check," I reply.

She hands me the check and I hand her two twenties.

I stand up and maneuver out of the booth, and Raquel follows. The bell rings above our heads, letting the diner know someone is leaving. The night went well, and it is nice to get to know her a little better.

Raquel stands by her car, fidgeting with her hands, and I almost think she wants me to kiss her, but don't want to ruin the night. She has made it clear this isn't a date. As much as I would love to bring her close and see just how soft her lips are, it's not happening tonight.

"I had a great time tonight. We'll see each other tomorrow when I drop off my dad and get him settled."

Her eyes meet mine, and she licks her lips, as if begging for a kiss. She might be in denial about wanting to be more than friends and wish she would just take the leap.

"I'll see you tomorrow," Raquel says, getting into her car.

I wonder how long she can resist our chemistry?

8

RAQUEL

I hate Sundays. Or any day that I have to see Dean and his girlfriend. Am I crazy for feeling like it should be illegal for parents to bring random women around their kids? They should at least wait a couple of months... right? Yet, he did even wait a week. This only proves my theory that he was having an affair. It's the only thing that makes sense.

"I wish there was some way around having to see him every weekend. It dampers my whole damn day," I say to Tessa.

After last night, as I thought, my phone started ringing at nine in the morning. Somehow, she found out about the date, and wouldn't let up until I agreed to meet her. She doesn't know about our complicated situation.

"Girl, divorces can be brutal, but don't let him get to you. Believe me, I had plenty of problems with Emily's dad."

The sun is beating down on me and even this little sun dress isn't keeping me cool. Why couldn't we meet up somewhere that has shade? Emily is climbing up the stairs to go down the big red slide again. We should petition the city to plant some trees out here. I don't know how anyone can sit out here for hours while their kids play. At least, there is a slim breeze today.

"So, enough about your ex. I wanna know about Jeremy," Tessa says.

I'm interested to see her reaction when I tell her about what happened yesterday. Either she will think I'm out of my mind or smart. Things can be harder than they seem, and sitting across from him last night in that booth, well, it made me want to rethink my decision. Yet, I know it is the right one for now. Hell, am I even ready to date someone after all the chaos with Dean?

"There's a lot to tell you since the party. We were all set to go on a date last night, but... then he showed up with his dad at the memory center and he's going to be my resident."

She looks at me and then rolls her eyes. "And?"

"How the fuck am I supposed to date a man that is related to one of my patients? Especially, after all that nonsense that happened when I first got hired, remember?"

Tessa shakes her head. "I don't think you ever told me about that. But do dish."

"The old nurse slept around with a patient's son and when she broke it off, he came up to the center and made a scene, calling her a slut and some other things. Once the higher-ups found out, she got fired."

Emily comes running up to us to get a drink of water. "The red slide is fun." She takes a sip and runs back to the playground.

"They need to mind their own business. We are all human and sometimes, love finds itself in odd places. Here's what I think; go with your gut, not the employee handbook."

I wipe the sweat accumulating on my forehead and lean in to her. "But what if it goes sideways? My job means a lot to me, and I just don't know if it's worth it."

"Let's just say I overheard some girls at our wedding talking about him, and they seem to think he is. In many unique positions," Tessa says, winking.

A chuckle escapes my throat, and I look around to make sure no one else heard her. Tessa isn't a prude by any means, and sometimes she can be inappropriate, but I love it. Harper is even worse, but I don't judge. That girl can get down and let's just say she has some kinks that Liam happily obliges.

I pull up Jeremy on my phone and go to type a message, but do not know what to say. Things went well at the diner, and he seems like an amazing guy. Kudos points for wanting a family, too. Men don't bring that up in casual conversation, but he did.

Does his family know about me? I think back to yesterday, and none of them seemed bothered by it, but they could be in the dark about him knowing me prior to their visit. Will his family be okay with this? They say don't let fear guide you, and I'm trying not to, but it's building.

"I'll talk to him about it, and we will see how it goes. It's kind of nice being just friends with no pretext."

Tessa slugs me on the shoulder and then goes in for a hug. "Let's just say, if you decide to go out with him for real, I don't think he will disappoint. He's nothing like Dean."

It's time for me to head to get Lily from Dallas, and I want to do anything but go to his damn house. He gets off on making my life a living hell. After he asked for the divorce, Dean demanded that I pack my things and get out. Who the hell does that to the mother of their children? The person they are supposed to love and cherish for all eternity? Our marriage felt like we were both walking on eggshells when around each other, so it's not like I can say it surprised me.

The next day, I booked a hotel room and packed most of my things. And the worst part of it all, having to go back to work and face him. After a couple of days, I decided for me to get the hell out of dodge, and that's when I reached out to Eli and let him know I'd be moving to Grapevine. It's close enough to where the drive to see her dad isn't too bad, but far enough, I won't ever run into him. I knew I would not stay at the hospital, so I put in my two weeks' notice. My brother mentioned the center, and it didn't take but two days for them to call me in for an interview and hired the same day. My plan to move to Grapevine was a go.

I put the car in reverse and head out of the parking lot and straight for the interstate to swerve through traffic to Dallas. The best thing about the drive is knowing that my Lily is coming back with me. She has loved school since coming here, and I think the main reason is there doesn't seem to be a bullying problem in this town. The kids seem to be friendly, and her previous school that was not the case. So, it's nice to see her opening up to new people and make friends.

I connected the Bluetooth and I turn on my 90s playlist because you can never go wrong with that era. I'm talking about Spice Girls, TLC, and Monica. They helped me through the anger of my divorce, and damn, did they do a stellar job. Lately, I've been into another genre like NSYNC and Backstreet Boys. Their songs hit me differently now that I'm in my thirties.

My fingers are tapping on the steering wheel and I'm blurting out the lyrics to Barbie Girl when the exit approaches, and it's only a few blocks until I'm at Deans. It always takes mental preparation when going to his house, because Lily doesn't deserve to see or hear the hostility between us. She's a child, and I would never put her in a position to choose one of us. He might be an asshole, but he is her father.

I could've asked for the house in the divorce, but with moving out of Dallas, there was no point except to piss him off. When we got married, he let me pick out the house and decorate how I wanted it, and I can already see that bitch has made some changes. Not pretty ones, either.

When I pull up to the curb of the street in front of his house, Lily is already waiting outside, her bag sitting on the steps. Why do they have her outside by herself? I keep forgetting he has always been this way. Things aren't like they were when we grew up. Convicted child molesters overrun Dallas and even in this rich neighborhood, he should never be too careful.

I get out of the car and meet her in the grass, and she envelopes me with an enormous hug. "Hi, baby. Did you have fun?"

She shakes her head and takes my hand.

"What do you say we go grab pizza for dinner? That place you like down the street?" I ask, getting her into the car, and buckled.

"We had that last night."

Of course, he did. I don't let her see it getting to me, and just drive off. I know we are going to have to co-parent. I'm not naïve, but right now I just want to rip his head off every time I see his face. We are both going to need some time before we can have a conversation without cussing each other into oblivion.

"What about breakfast, mommy?"

She can't be serious? I can't go to the diner again. The waitress is going to think I never cook a meal. "How about we cook pasta tonight instead?"

"Pancakes, mama, please?" She does this thing with her voice where it goes up an octave or two.

I look out the window and shake my head because the probability that the waitress will work tonight too is high. "Fine, sweetie. Pancakes it is."

When Genie in A Bottle comes on, she asks me to turn it up, and of course I oblige. She gets into the song and knows all the lyrics. That's right. She jams out to the 90s with me and never complains.

She sings with me the entire way to the diner, and I've learned the best way to keep her occupied on car rides is music. Her love for it is as deep as mine.

"We're here!" she screams, as we pull up to the curb.

From the street, it doesn't look like they are very busy.

"It's breakfast time," I say, grabbing her hand as she skips up the curb.

The bell on the door alerts the workers of our arrival, and she runs to a booth and sits down. Sure enough, her comes the same waitress I had both times yesterday.

"Back again, sweetie?" she asks, setting down an adult and kid menu and getting our drink order.

"When the kiddo wants pancakes..."

She opens the menu, even though she knows what she wants, and pretends to read it over. The cute things she does.

"Bacon or sausage this time?"

Lily puts her index finger on her lips. "Sausage."

I nod, and then take it from her, and let her go crazy with the crayons on the kids' menu. She might not say it, but I think it's one reason she enjoys coming here. Few restaurants have things like this for kids anymore. What a shame.

"Hey, stranger," a man's voice comes from behind.

As my head turns, I see his smile and respond. "Lily wanted pancakes. They have the best."

It's too early for him to meet her, yet what am I supposed to do? Tell him to get the hell away? This isn't happening.

"And you must be Lily. I'm Jeremy." He extends his hand out for her to shake, which she does.

She doesn't pay any attention after that and goes back to coloring.

"What are you doing here?"

He leans up against the back of our booth. "Sunday is dad's Philly day. I come at the same time every Sunday to pick up his order."

I want to talk to him about everything Tessa and I discussed earlier, but right now isn't the best time. Lily doesn't need to see me moving on already, and the last thing I need is for her to mention it to Dean. He might want me to think he's moved on, but he is still in my business.

"I'll see if they will deliver his order to him at the center. That'll help him adjust, you know, keeping up with his normal routines."

He smiles. "I'll see you tomorrow when we bring him in."

Could things get any more complicated? I'm being ignorant, because Dean hasn't cared, but I like to keep Lily in the dark on romantic stuff. It's hard enough on her we aren't together anymore, and going back and forth.

"Who was that, mommy?"

"He works with your uncle at the fire department. I am going to be taking care of his daddy at the center."

She puts the red crayon down. "So, his daddy has the remembering disease?"

I nod, and she slips out of the booth and runs after him. "Sir?"

Jeremy turns around and crouches down. "Yes, sweetie?"

"I hope your daddy gets better. My mommy will take good care of him."

Jeremy looks up at me and then smiles. "Thank you. I know she will."

He walks out the door, and she sits back down and continues to color until the food arrives.

"Here you go. Order up, little one."

She digs in right away, and I just sit there and watch her. Lily knows about my job, and that it revolves around helping people that have trouble remembering things. Sometimes, she will ask me if anyone remembered today when I get home, and no matter what, I always tell her yes. It might give her a sense of false hope that I perform miracles or something. But she's a kid, so I don't correct her.

I hope Don gets better, or at least gets to have more time with his kids than they are predicting. Losing a parent is baffling and at the center it's a revolving door of grieving families. I hope it's different for the Greys.

9

JEREMY

The alarm blares bloody murder, causing me to wake up in a fit, and question the time. It shows seven in the morning, but it seems like I just closed my eyes. I fucking hate when that happens. Sleep is overrated, and it's been months since the eight hours recommended have been achieved. Nightmares seem to take over my mind once my eyes are shut, and seeing my dad pass repeatedly fucks with my head. I know it's inevitable, and everyone goes, but it still hurts every time I think about a day without my father. Knowing it's coming doesn't ease the pain.

I drag my ass out of bed and raid my closet for some shorts and my t-shirt to wear under my uniform. I don't have to put it on until I'm at the station. What if I hate it? The job isn't for everyone, and the Jacksons seem to love it. With everything going on, construction can't be my job anymore, and he deserves to have someone who can be reliable. Hazel doesn't live around here, so it falls on me.

"Hey, you awake?" my dad asks, knocking on the door.

"I'm up. Be down in a sec."

This is his last day in his home, and I'm sure it's terrifying. Hazel and Aiden are leaving tonight after we get him settled into the center. He hasn't had any episodes since Saturday, but they are inevitable. I hope my dad doesn't think we are trying to get rid of him. He's not a burden, but we have to consider what is best for his health. A part of me wants to keep him home, so that he can feel comfortable, but if one day I wake up and he doesn't recognize me, it's possible he might become violent, and then what would I do? Don would never forgive himself if something happened to me because of that. If he is at the center, that can't happen, and he is realizing that it might not be so bad.

I slide the t-shirt over my head and shoulders, slip on my Nikes and grab my duffel bag. Here's to my first day at GFD.

Hazel and Aiden are already here this morning, and it's only obvious because of her voice carrying upstairs. She is so rambunctious, and doesn't know how she can have so much energy so early in the morning. How many cups of coffee has she had?

"Calm down, sis. You might wake the neighbors up."

Dad is sitting in his recliner, enjoying a cup of coffee, and watching the news like normal with Aiden. Their eyes don't even leave the television when I walk past them to the kitchen to grab my travel mug from the cupboard.

Hazel's filling up her cup, but I don't think she needs anymore.

"Did you even hear what we were talking about? Or, were you in your own little world up there?" She asks, filling my mug to the brim with coffee.

"Nope. Too busy getting ready for work. Wasn't paying any attention."

She sits her cup down on the counter, folds her hands across her torso, and then glares at me. "When were you going to tell us you are dating dad's nurse?"

Shit, how did she find out? Aiden has a big mouth. It's my business, not his. Sometimes, Hazel gets on my nerves with this whole inserting herself into my life. For someone who lives thousands of miles away, she sure sticks her nose in it a lot.

"We aren't dating. Or, we were supposed to until we found out about her being dad's nurse. We are just friends. Not that it fucking matters. Or wait, weren't you the one running me out their door on Friday night to go to Damon's party?"

Out of all people, I didn't expect Hazel to be the one to throw shade. After everything she has been through with Aiden, you would think she knew better. Raquel is an amazing woman, and it's not like she's my boss. Why is it such a big deal for anyone? She saw this coming, and maybe she made the right choice. I respect her decision, but why should her profession keep us apart?

"I meant get out and have fun, not date our dad's nurse. Jeremy, come on." Her hands are on her hips now.

"Pretty sure I can date whoever the fuck I want to. And if Raquel ever gave me the chance, I'd take her out in a heartbeat. If you want to act like you're in high school, maybe you should join Tessa and Harper and go teach. With the way you're acting, you'd fit right in."

I don't wait around for anymore attitude, just grab my mug, and walk past everyone right out the front fucking door. When Hazel gets into these tangents, there is no talking to her, and it's only going to turn into a huge fight that I don't have time to deal with right now.

This isn't how I wanted my first day on the job to go, and now I'm in a piss poor mood. It's like she wanted to bombard me about this. Sometimes, she just doesn't know when to stay out of my fucking business.

I pull out my phone.

Me: *Hope your day is going well so far. My sister is on a tangent and knows about you. Remember, small town means everyone knows your business. Sorry in advance.*

I look out the rear window, backing out of the driveway, and heading to work. Why the fuck did Aiden even have to say anything? Sometimes I feel like he likes to start shit. I'll remember that.

When I pull into the parking lot, Damon is already waiting outside for me in full uniform. He approaches my truck before I even get out.

"Chief is already looking for you."

I look at my dash. "Why? I'm still fifteen-minutes early."

"He's saying you were supposed to be here an hour ago. You better get your ass inside."

Fuck. He told me about eight thirty. I'm not the type to be late to work, but he doesn't know that. Why does this day hate me?

I take off in a sprint to the bay door and find him. "Sir, I'm here. Eight-thirty is what it said on my schedule."

He grins and slaps his hand on my shoulder. "I know, son. Just giving you a hard time on your first day. Come to my office."

I follow him to a room, not an office, and he sits down in the chair. He motions for me to sit, so I do.

"Don't let your guard down. Sometimes, they like to mess with the new guys. Damon will show you around, and you can call me if you need anything today. Good luck," he says, extending his hand for me to shake.

"Will do, sir. Thank you."

What is this, a fraternity? Who the fuck hazes grown ass men? Maybe this isn't the right place for me, but I'm stuck here now.

Damon's waiting outside the door, posted up against the wall. "Let's check the place out."

He walks me around and shows me the sleep room and kitchen area. Most of the guys are sitting around playing cards or watching tv already. I always wondered what they do when they aren't on a call.

"It's been a fucking morning, bro. Hazel is on my damn case about Raquel."

"Oh yeah, I remember you talking to her at the party. Heard she is going to be taking care of your dad."

Jesus, the word gets around fast. Even Damon knows.

"Yeah, but we are just friends. She doesn't want to lose her job over it, which I respect, but damn. The first girl in a while and she's off limits. Go fucking figure."

He laughs, and sits down at one of the round tables, and picks up a stack of cards. "Sit down and play. This might be an uneventful first day for you."

I let him shuffle the cards while I read her reply.

Raquel: *Great. Wonder if my brother knows, too.*

My eyes go wide, and fight myself to look around the room. Is Eli here today? I'm not even sure what the guy looks like, and I left before they could introduce me to him. The last thing I need is drama here too.

Damon deals out the cards, and I hurry out a reply.

Me: *Not sure. Haven't seen him yet.*

A couple of guys stroll into the kitchen and open the fridge. Is one of them Eli? It's not like I can just ask Damon. One of them grabs a Styrofoam container and sits down at the table next to us, but we lock eyes. That has to be him. I try to keep my focus on the game, but it's hard when someone is staring you down.

"Hey, what's up? I'm Jeremy."

He leans back in his chair and chews his food before speaking. "Yeah, I know. Heard you're trying to bang my sister."

Look, I'm not the confrontational type, but if someone starts some shit, I'm not afraid to finish it. That is one of the good things that came out of being in foster care, learning to defend myself early on against the older kids wherever I was. It is something that happened at every home.

"We are just friends. She's going to be taking care of my dad," I say.

He scoffs. "Yeah, well, stay the fuck away from her. Everyone here knows she's off limits. You aren't the exception, new guy."

Deep down, I want this guy to keep up and try something, because the need to knock him down a peg is on the forefront of my mind. Yet, it's my first day and already there's drama. It's not Raquel's fault, but it seems like shit is coming from every direction. Nobody wants us to have a shot. I try so hard not to get smart back, but I can't help it.

"If your sister wasn't taking care of my dad, then there would be no reason for me not to be with her. I could give a fuck less if you think she's off limits. She's a grown ass woman."

The guys in the room are staring at us now, both standing up, and only about three feet apart from each other. All I'm waiting for is for him to make a move so I can deck him in the face. Please. Come closer, draw back, something.

Damon stands up and pushes us apart. "Come on, what are we, five? Grow the hell up."

I fix my eyes on him, and even though I know it's a bad idea, I say one more thing.

"Your sister might be scared of you, but I'm not."

He lunges toward me, almost knocking Damon over, which takes some force considering he is a strong man, and then we tousle to the floor.

"My sister's name better not come out of your mouth again. You fucking hear me," Eli says, wailing on me.

I let him get a couple good punches in, so he can look like a badass and take my turn. Raquel can't get mad at me now. Her brother threw the first punch and I've been raised to defend myself. So, when it comes time to punch, I give him a nice right hook, knocking him on his back.

"Are you fucking serious? Starting a fight because I'm friends with your sister. You're pathetic. I'll date who I want, and you can't fucking stop me," I say, walking out of the room and then stepping outside.

Sure, Raquel is going to hear about this, especially with the way things spread in this town, but at least I didn't start it. How can she get mad at me? Eli needs to back the hell up, and learn that he might have been big in high school, but we are grown and he doesn't get to go around talking to people like that, especially me. Not going to fucking happen.

The door opens and shuts, and around the corner comes the chief. "What the hell is going on? Already causing trouble in my station, boy?"

Damon comes out and has my back. "No, Eli just doesn't know when to quit running his mouth. Jeremy just didn't back down, and good for him. That boy needs to learn he ain't in Kansas anymore, chief."

They both look at me, and I wait to see what his reaction is going to be. If I had been the one to start the fight, then I could see why he would get mad at me, but fuck.

"Better not happen again. Don't care if he hits you first or not. This drama shit isn't tolerated here." He raises his voice and uses his pointer finger, scalding me like a five-year-old.

The door slams shut, and Damon knocks me on the shoulder. "Don't let him get to ya. He doesn't like Eli that much, but he does his job. I think we are all glad to see him knocked down a few pegs. Good job, newbie."

I'm not even an hour into my shift and I've already been in a fight, called to the principal's office, and I just don't know how the day could get any better than this.

Seize the day, I guess.

10

RAQUEL

*A*s soon as I walked in the door, things have been going awry, starting with Arlene having a stroke while knitting with the girls, and then Paul having a heart attack in the common room. Days like this drain me, because this might be just a job for some people, but bonds are created, and when my residents get hurt or pass, it affects me. All I can do for them, and is make them comfortable, and give them a friendly face every day. Some are doing worse than others, but they all seem to care for one another, like a big family. I'm quite surprised how little there is drama here.

It's Jeremy's first day at the station, and hopefully, my brother will not be an ass. After the comments he made at the party, I'm sure he isn't happy, but we aren't dating, so he can cool it. You see in movies and tv shows all the time, the push for two people to be apart, and the people trying to cause a rift, but this is the first time I've experienced it myself. Why can't people just mind their own damn business? Eli shouldn't have any say so in who I have a romantic relationship with, and my boss shouldn't either, but do I want to risk losing my job?

My phone vibrates in my jacket pocket, and Eli's name shows up on the notification list. What the hell does he want now?

Eli: *Are you screwing around with him? That motherfucker hit me! Stay away from him!*

He thinks that telling me this will push me away from Jeremy, but it only entices me to kiss him. No one has ever had the balls to stand up to my brother, and it's nice to hear someone did it. It's hard enough finding someone decent nowadays, but how could I ever be with someone that my brother hates? And after today, Eli will never be okay with me and Jeremy being together.

Me: *Maybe if you weren't in our business... Good for him. Like I've already said... you don't get a say in that. Fuck off.*

We have a complicated relationship, always have, and one thing I won't stand for is the way he talks to me. He's almost controlling, but he's always been that way. When we were younger, there was this boy in the eighth grade who wanted to ask me to one of the school dances, and when Eli found out, he pummeled him. Almost the same situation one as with Jeremy, except we are adults now, and not teenagers. One thing I've always wondered is why he has such horrible anger issues? I don't remember him being that way before Junior High, but maybe it just never came up before then.

Eli is your typical jock type with an enormous ego, and he doesn't have friends, only those that bow down to him and do what he wants. Maybe that's why his circle of close friends has dwindled down to just the guys at that station, and I think that's only because they work together. If they didn't, none of them would see each other but in passing around Grapevine. Hell, I can't say I blame them though. Who the fuck wants to be talked down to?

Is it bad that I'm counting down the minutes until Jeremy shows up to get Don settled in today? Will his sister say something about us "dating"? Why is everyone making such a big deal out of this? It kills me we had an amazing time at Damon's party, and then, just like that, we are forbidden from seeing each other. Maybe we should both just say screw them, and do it anyway. I might talk about a big game, but some rules I just can't break.

My cell vibrates again and I roll my eyes, wonder what Eli wants now, only to see it's my best friend.

Britt: *We still on for tonight? Future hubby is going to cook us dinner.*

Ugh. Why did I have to agree to this dinner? Something still seems very suspicious about this rushed engagement, and I'm going to get to the bottom of it. I love her, but she's not the marrying type. She has said that herself too many times to count, and now she's engaged? No, sorry, not falling for it. Even though I don't want to go, I have to, because that's what friends do.

Me: *Of course I am. Give me an address. His place, right?*

When she gives me the address, then I can do some digging. I'm sure there is plenty to know about her future husband, and the internet will tell me everything. He might not have good intentions either. Maybe he has to get married to gain his inheritance or some crap. Brittany doesn't need to get her heart broken, especially if she is in this for the right reasons. But I'm still not sure that's the case. Seeing them together tonight will prove how she feels because I'm known her for a long time, and can tell when she's being fake.

Brittaney: *3604 Plaza Drive*

My cell hits the desk, and I smack my forehead. That's it. She's in it for the money. Plaza drive is like multi-million dollar mansions. I don't care how much money a guy has, it's not a reason to jump into a marriage. Money can't buy love, and Brittaney will realize that, but not before she walks down the aisle. She is very materialistic, and money can provide a certain lifestyle she has always wanted, but at what cost? A loveless marriage is depressing, and no amount of money can't fix that.

My marriage with Dean started off good. We both made decent money, and didn't struggle at all, but once the honeymoon phase wore off, things went downhill quick, no amount of money would have fixed that. I don't want Brittaney to regret her decision, but as her best friend, do I express my concerns or just let her conclude herself?

Things have slowed down at the center, and most of the residents are taking their afternoon nap before dinner is upon us. Kristen is on break, so here I am, manning the front desk in case anyone calls or needs anything. On the cameras, I see Jeremy's truck pull up, and my stomach flutters. He makes me feel like a teenager again, when you would wait for them to pick you up for a date. Except that's not going to happen. He is off limits and even though I want to screw his brains out, we are just friends. Get it together.

"Hey, there. Ready for your new favorite man to move in?" Don says, walking through the double doors with a smile.

He looks much happier than the last time I saw him, and it must be because he knows that I'll take good care of him. "Wondered when you were gonna show up. Your room is ready to be decorated and put together."

He puts out his arm, and I hook mine in as we walk toward his room together. "We are gonna have a good ol' time together. Mark my words, darling."

I laugh as we approach his door, and the others are right behind.

Hazel gives me the stink eye before walking inside his room, but Jeremy stops for a moment.

"It's been a crazy ass day. Did your brother..."

I put my hand up. "Yes, and good for you. He's an asshole. I'm not mad at all."

He sighs. "Good. Didn't want you to hate me. I'll talk to you later?"

I nod, and leave him to help Don decorate his room and get settled.

My day is over, and I've got limited time to get over to his place for dinner. I refuse to go over there in my work clothes, so they might just have to deal with me being a little late.

I check in with Kristen before clocking out and heading home. The babysitter, Tiffany, is sitting on the couch when I walk in, doing homework, and she closes her notebook and starts packing up. She is amazing with Lily and has a brilliant head on her shoulders. When looking for referrals, Tessa recommended her. Tiffany is a pre-med student, and one thing I can relate to is how stressful the med program is, not to mention how expensive it is, so when I found out that, she's the first person I called.

"Any problems today?" I ask, pulling out my wallet from my purse.

"Nope. An angel, as always. Her homework is done, and there's a paper that you'll need to sign in her folder for tomorrow."

I hand her sixty bucks, and she slides it into her back pocket. "Exams are killer this week. I don't know how you did it."

"It's worth it. Just keep pushing through. See ya tomorrow."

The front door shuts behind her, and I go to Lily's room. "Hey, sweetie. We will leave for Aunt Britt's soon. She wants us to meet her new boyfriend. I'm just going to change real quick."

I don't have enough time to take a shower and make it over to Plaza drive, so I just change out of my scrubs and into some black jeans and a black blouse and head right back out the door.

"Come on, Lil. We don't wanna be late."

She runs out of her room and straight out the door to the car. It's been a while since she's seen her, and it's every Saturday night. I'm surprised she hasn't asked where she's been.

Brittaney isn't the type to want kids because she is way too focused on where she wants to be in life. I think her exact words were, "I'm not mother material." And I get it. Not every woman wants kids, but they are such a blessing. Maybe she will change her mind later on. After meeting the right guy and settling down.

This guy though, I'm not so sure it's going to be long term and then she will crawl back under a rock, and be anti-relationship again. I hope he doesn't break her heart, and they are both in this for the right reasons. Marriage isn't a joke. Yet, so many people treat it like it's not supposed to be a lifelong commitment. My parents raised me to believe you should only be married once, and believe me, did they have some things to say when Dean and I split up, but infidelity isn't something I can overlook.

The sudden change in her attitude toward relationships is what gets me. How does one go from never wanting to settle down to being engaged in, like, three months? I could understand if they have been together for longer, but she hasn't even known this guy that long, and he could be a fucking serial killer or something. Not to mention, my irritation about the fact they moved in together and not once did she even mention it to me.

What are best friends for, if not to share good news with? Yet, I didn't even receive a damn text about it. Practically just ghosted me for almost three months with a text every once in a while, and only because I'd ask if she is still alive. I try not to make such a big deal about it, but it hurts.

I want her to be happy, and I might be a bitch about this situation, but for valid reasons. She could have fallen in love with this man, it happens, but to already be engaged and living together is insane. That shit only happens in movies, not real life.

What if I hate the guy? Or, he hates me? I need to play nice tonight, because if she goes through with this wedding, I'll be stuck with him. So, we need to get along for her sake. Here is best behavior, Raquel.

Pulling onto Plaza drive almost makes me cringe, seeing all these three story mansions, and knowing that I have to have dinner at one. I don't hate rich people, but the ones I've met are obnoxious and so self-obsessed that I wouldn't ever want to carry on a conversation, let alone have dinner with them. Brittaney better give me brownie points for tonight.

Lily is out of the car before I am, and at the door to give Brittaney an enormous hug.

"I missed you, sweet girl. Are you excited to meet Chad? He's cooking us a special dinner."

She gestures us inside, and we follow her through one of the biggest living rooms I've ever seen to the kitchen where he is standing over the stove.

"Sweetie, this is Raquel and her daughter, Lily."

He puts the utensil down and smiles. "It's nice to meet you. She talks about you all the time."

A fake smile is all I can muster, but try to focus the attention on him. "So, what you got going there?"

"It's a surprise. She doesn't even know yet. You ladies go chat and it should be ready in about ten minutes."

He is the epiphany of a rich boy living off his parent's money. What the hell is she thinking? The man is wearing salmon colored board shorts and a white polo with boat shoes. His hair is slicked back with way too much gel and a perfect set of teeth.

She takes us back to the living room and hands Lily the remote before pulling out a binder and handing it to me.

"So, I picked out a venue. The Haddonfield Mansion," she says, flipping it open. "Chad's parents have agreed to pay for the wedding, not that they needed to..."

She has printed out pictures and pasted them into the binder. The name is forthcoming, because it looks like it has fifty bedrooms or something, and has a good amount of property.

"Here is a picture of where the ceremony will be. They have an arch already for outside weddings, and if we need to have it inside, god forbid, then we will do that, too."

The nosey part of me wants to know how rich Chad's parents are to be able to afford a place like this. It must be at least a hundred grand or more to rent this out for a day. And then you have to add catering, suits, dresses, and everything else.

"Don't you think you should do something more modest? These venues are for people who want huge weddings. How many people are you inviting?" I ask.

She slams the binder shut. "Chad has a huge family, and his side will be a hundred."

I try to hide my sheer shock at that number, and move on to the next subject. "Okay, so when are we going dress shopping? For you, that's the most important part."

Chad comes into the room, and interrupts. "Dinner is ready, ladies."

Brittaney, without skipping a beat, gets up and follows him into the kitchen. Did I ever act like this when I first met my ex-husband? It's creepy. She's like a stepford wife, all put together.

At least I will get to see them interact with each other, and that will help me understand their relationship.

When Lily and I get to the table, the meal isn't something special, just spaghetti. I don't know why he felt so secretive about something like that. I dig in, and try to keep my mouth full so the conversation doesn't have to happen, but it doesn't help.

"So, she told me you work at a facility for Alzheimer's patients. Do you enjoy it?"

I finish chewing the food in my mouth. "Immensely."

He takes another bite, and nods.

"So, what do you do?"

He puts down his fork, and clasps his hands together. "I'm an investment banker. Family business. Tried to get out of it, but my dad didn't give me an option."

So, it's got to be about the money. I never took Brittaney to be a gold digger, but this isn't looking good. Can she be okay with marrying someone just because they have a huge bank account? Not that he's bad looking. I'll give her that. The way he dresses is a deal breaker for me, though.

"Wow. That's pretty cool. Do you have to travel a lot?" I ask, only to see how much time he will be away. The statistics around men who travel a lot being faithful aren't so great. Not that it's the woman's fault.

"About once a month. Sometimes more depending on the clients. Britt's going with me to San Diego next weekend. I'll be going there for a business dinner, but then we are going to make it a brief vacation since she's never been."

Okay, brownie points for Chad, for including her on his business trip. Maybe he isn't so bad after all.

"So, are you excited about getting married at the mansion?" I ask, trying to gauge his persona by his reaction.

He nods. "It's a beautiful place. My brother got married there a couple of years ago. It's becoming a family tradition, my mom says."

Oh god, he's a parent pleaser.

"Well, when you guys get back, we'll need to get a head start on some wedding planning and go dress shopping. It might take you a while to find the right one, so we wanna start soon."

She looks at Chad, and then down at her plate. "I'll be wearing his grandmother's wedding dress. It has been passed it down, and means a lot to the family."

Her not making eye contact with me while saying that tells me she is only doing it to make Chad happy, and that infuriates me. It's her wedding day, and she should get to wear the dress of her dreams. I get that being in a relationship and marriage is about compromises, but a woman's wedding dress is something you look back at for decades, and I think she is going to regret doing so just to please his mother.

I want to stand up and call bullshit on this whole situation, but spaghetti is stuffed into my mouth, and I just keep my cool. She seems happy, and no matter what I think, it's her decision. She has not asked my opinion for, so I'll wait until she does.

Dinner is delicious, but we don't stay long after that. Lily has been on a schedule and if she isn't in bed by nine o'clock, the mornings are hell.

"You know how she is if she ain't asleep on time. Talk to you later, girl."

Brittaney shuts the door, and we walk hand-in-hand to the car.

"I like Chad. Auntie seems happy."

She gets into the car, and I back down the driveway, and turn on some Boyz II Men for the drive home. Lily doesn't even make it five minutes before she's passed out in the back seat, and I have to wake her to get inside.

"Come on, baby. We'll skip the shower tonight," I say, laying her down in bed and giving her a kiss. "Goodnight."

The door shuts behind me, and it's time for some quiet. This day has been exhausting. I turn the water on and get some pajamas together before checking my phone.

Jeremy: *He's all settled.*

I smile.

Me: *Good. He's going to like it there. I'll stop in and see him in the morning on my rounds. See how he is adjusting. First nights can be hard.*

No matter how wrong it is, Jeremy always crawls back to the front of my mind, and it kills me. There's nothing wrong with fantasizing as long as I don't go through with it, right?

11

JEREMY

Smoke is billowing in the sky, able to be seen from blocks away, letting us know the fire is out of control. This is my first response since beginning at the department, and everyone has their eyes on me to see how I do in the middle of panic. Coming around the corner of Garrison Avenue, it's a gated community, and residents are staying away from the building with Police and EMS already on the scene. The fire has compromised most of the structure already, and we need to get it under control before it spreads to the surrounding buildings.

The chief parks the truck and we jump out to start assembling the hose to start taking down the fire, but Eli has a different approach. Two birds, one stone is my thought. Yet, he is only using this as a competition, and I'm not letting him bait me. It's one thing to fuck with me outside of work, but when I'm on the job, I have to focus. All eyes are going to be on me, and I can't make any mistakes today. I'm not losing my job over some petty shit with Eli. Guys like him get off on superiority. They need to be on top, and have everyone cower, but I'm not that guy. He's mistaken.

Damon, Liam, and myself get the two hoses prepped, and let the water hit the structure, trying to diminish the fire. But this one is hefty. How long did they wait to alert someone? Usually, it takes a solid amount of time for it to get to this point. After about an hour, we get it put out.

"Have all residents been accounted for?" I ask the police officer.

He shakes his head. "No deceased either."

A death on my first call isn't something I want to go home with on my conscience.

"The new boy seems to know how to handle a hose pretty well. You have a lot of practice with something hard in your hands?" Eli asks, turning to his buddy James, and laughing.

"No, but I know who wants to be next."

Right after it comes out of my mouth, I feel like a fucking douchebag. Why do I let him bait me? Raquel doesn't deserve that shit, and I know he's going to run and tell her what I just said. Fuck.

Eli pushes his chest out and starts flexing his knuckles, but he won't start a fight here. He might hate me, but he loves his job. Would he risk it just to punch me?

"Come on, boys. Let's get back to the depot," Chief yells.

On the ride back, I text her.

Me: *Been a rough day. Hope yours is going better.*

James is trying to look at my phone, and I hold it up for him. "You wanna read the messages? Go ahead."

He shakes his head and leans back in his seat.

The three dots show up, and I wait for her message to come through, but then they disappear. Maybe she is busy. Our dinner went great, and honestly, I plan on just being patient until we can give us a chance. Nothing good ever comes easy, so I just need to be calm and collected. Eli might pose a threat, but Raquel seems to be a very independent woman, and I doubt her brother will have much say on who she gets to date.

Back at the station, everyone swarms in the break room after getting out of the gear and pulls out snacks.

"How was your dad's first night at the center?" Damon asks, stuffing his face with pretzels.

I sigh. "I'll find out after work. Haven't talked to him yet."

On my side, the night was shit, and I couldn't stay asleep. The house was too fucking quiet and ominous. I'm used to it being me and my dad, and without him, it feels empty. How the hell am I supposed to sleep in this fucking house all by myself?

Hazel and Aiden are gone out of my hair, which means I don't have to worry about them being all up in my business, but they will still find out about everything. Never fails with the Jackson's.

Raquel: *What's this about being hard in my hands? What the hell is Eli talking about?*

Already? He didn't even give me time to explain myself, and now she thinks I'm a jackass. Why am I letting him screw this up? Just don't engage in anything he says, and he can't use it against me.

"What now?" Damon asks, seeing me pissed off.

"Eli has a big fucking mouth," I respond, showing him the text.

Damon is like the grandpa in the group, and he tries to keep things civil, but he wants no part of any drama. In fact, he's been that way for as long as I've known him. He's a no nonsense type of guy and that's what I like about him. He's a good friend to me and never put me in a bad spot.

Me: *I'll explain later. Be in for a visit after work.*

I want to call and try to talk myself out of the hole now, but Eli is in the next room. Why is he being such a dick? Does he not want his sister to be happy? The dude doesn't even know me, yet he is trying to make my life a living hell. I think about having a real conversation with him, man-to-man, but with his personality, it wouldn't end well. He is the type of person that needs to be in control and have all the say. Maybe that's a big part of why he is still single. Sure, he says it's because he likes a revolving door of women, but at his age, he should be thinking about settling down at some point. He's never going to get a lady with his attitude.

The conversation with Damon continues, and I tell him about how much of a change this is going to be for me, too. My days before this consisted of getting up, making breakfast for both of us, going to work, and then coming home and taking care of my dad. Now, he's at the center, so after I leave there for my daily visit, I'm all alone. The nights are going to get lonely and even though I've found who I want to spend my time with, she insists on not moving any further.

It's not that I blame her, because she has valid reasons. Sometimes, I just think the universe has it out for me. Why bring me and Raquel together if we don't even get a shot at making each other happy? Her job wouldn't fire her for going on a date with me, would they? Then there is a matter of my sister and her brother. They both seem very against us dating, but why?

"Listen, Raquel is a nice girl, but is she worth all this drama? Eli is going to make your life a living hell until you give up."

I think about it for a minute. She's intelligent, beautiful, can make me laugh, and has a deep passion for helping others. There is still so much left to know about her, but already I know she is worth it. Now, I just need to convince her to give me a shot. All bullshit aside, I know she loves her job, but I'm not petty like the guy that did her boss dirty by going up to her job. Break ups happen, and there's no need to end someone's career over it.

"Then go for it, but remember my warning." He gets up from the table, but then pauses. "Don't forget about Emily's birthday party this weekend."

Most of us exit the depot and head for our vehicles, and I'm excited to see how my dad is doing. Did he have a rough night like me? I don't know how I'm going to get used to being in that house by myself?

As I pull into the center, Hazel's name scrolls across my screen on the radio, and I want to push reject but I don't.

"Hey, sis," I answer.

"How's he doing?"

I turn off my truck and switch to my phone. "Literally just pulled up. I'll have him call you. He has his phone."

"Alright, bye."

Well, damn. She doesn't even ask about how I'm doing. Something is going on with her, too, but I don't have the patience to question her about it right now.

The automatic doors open and Raquel is standing to greet me as I enter.

"How's he doing?"

She bounces her eyes to the left and mine follow. He's sitting with the knitting club, chatting up a storm, and after a second I hear my mom's name. My dad is still in love with her even after she's gon,e and he's always said there are no other women for him.

"He's being telling them stories about him and his late wife. The ladies are loving him."

We stand there, enjoying seeing him engaged with others, and not having such a hard time adjusting to the different surroundings.

"So, listen. About that thing with Eli..."

She shakes her head. "Just please don't do sex jokes about me with my brother."

It's not like I can lie and say I haven't thought about her hand around my shaft multiple times, her lips sliding up and down, with her looking up at me. Men fantasize about shit like that, and sometimes we have relief ourselves. Seeing her in that white coat, hair up in a high messy bun, only makes me want to take her against her office wall right now.

"Shift is over. See ya."

She walks to her office, takes off her coat, and heads out the door.

It's my fault for saying it, and believe me I regret it, but I can't take it back. Eli is going to do anything he can to keep his sister away from me, and I hope to god it doesn't work. Something has got to give.

I watch my father conversing with these ladies, and it's so nice to see him socializing, and not being depressed about being here. He needs friends and people to talk to. I wish I could be a fly on the wall to listen to all the stories he's been telling them tonight.

My dad finally sees me and comes over.

"Hey, son. Just telling the ladies about your mom."

I embrace him and pat him on the back. "I heard. Just wanted to stop by and check on ya. See how your first night went," I say, leaning up against the wall.

"Oh, it was fine. Didn't sleep very well, but the breakfast was excellent. Margaret and I played a couple of card games, and then we started talking about our significant others. I'm gonna be just fine, son. Don't worry about me."

He doesn't seem like he wants to stand around and talk. Instead, he keeps eyeing the ladies, and I take that as a signal that he wants to go back.

"I'll come back tomorrow. Go hang out with your friends. Love you."

He nods, and walks back over to the chair and sits down, jumping right into the conversation again. Maybe we should have brought him here sooner. He looks happy.

I find someone to let me out of the front door and head to the car. Hazel will be happy to hear about this.

When I pull out of the parking lot, heading east toward the house, I call Hazel.

"What's up?"

"Dad's enjoying himself. You might not hear from him tonight. He's gabbing with a bunch of ladies about mom. He didn't even want to stay and visit. Can you believe that?"

She laughs. "Are you offended, Jer? That's good. He's making friends. He's only had us for a while now, remember?"

Hazel's right. After our mom died, he dedicated his life to raising us and never went out and made any friends. If we weren't around, he was at home, all alone.

"Okay. I get it. Talk to ya tomorrow then," I say, before hanging up.

The dread of going back to the empty ass house and sleeping tonight makes my stomach tense. I should've taken my sleeping pills hours ago, but it slipped my mind. I didn't think the visit with him would be so short.

I leave my truck on and sit in the driveway for a bit, thinking about everything. My new job. Raquel. My dad. Maybe this is when things start to look up for me.

Me: I am sorry about what I said to your brother. You shouldn't be involved. Do you hate me?

She has every right to be upset. I need to think before I open my damn mouth next time. Obviously, Eli is going to run and tell his sister. We have enough things keeping us apart without helping the cause. From now on, I'll steer clear of her brother. It's in both our best interests. If we do get to take a chance on us down the line, it's not going to help if her brother despises me.

Raquel: No sex jokes to my brother, especially involving me. I don't hate you, just a little caught off guard. Friends don't make sex jokes about each other.

Doesn't she understand that I want to be more than friends? The lingering eyes she has when I'm around and her deliberately staring at my ass-- I know she wants more, too. She is just afraid. I can't forget that she is only recently divorced, and with the way that ended, she is probably guarding her heart like Fort Knox. I just need to make her realize that I would never hurt her like Dean did.

I take the keys out of the ignition, walk to the door, and step inside. When it's just me, I can hear every little movement, and it just makes the environment that much creepier. The keys are set on the table and I head upstairs to get ready for bed.

Maybe the thoughts of Raquel's silky skin against mine will help me fall asleep tonight.

12

RAQUEL

The breeze whips through my hair as we sit on the bench watching Emily and Lily play. Grapevine recently updated the playground and the girls have been dying to test it out. Tessa's company is needed right now, because I'm lost with Jeremy. I want to give him a chance, but between my job and my brother, it proves to be harder than I expected.

"Do you think I'm crazy for turning Jeremy down? Be honest."

Tessa crosses her legs and places her palms on her knee. "I think you are playing it safe. And after what Dean did, I can't say I blame you."

"Dean has nothing to do with this."

As the words come out of my mouth, I know that they are true, but then it gets me thinking. Am I pushing Jeremy away because of the way my marriage ended? Could it be that I'm scared to be with anyone after he clearly cheated on me and made me out to be the bad guy?

"Don't get mad. Just remember, Jeremy isn't Dean. As far as I can tell, he is an honorable man who just wants to get to know you. The man hasn't asked a woman out in years. So Damon says."

Knowing this tidbit of information helps me. The heart break of being cheated on fucks with me every day. In the back of my head, there are a million questions. Did I not satisfy his needs? Truth be told, our intimacy took a hit when I started working longer hours, but that's part of the job, and if anyone understands that, it's Dean.

Things have been escalating between Jeremy and I. I have to keep myself from pushing him up against the wall and having my way with him. The connection we have is real, but what if it's only because everything is pushing us apart? Once all these obstacles are taken away, will we still feel this way? This pull?

"I'm thinking about giving him a chance. Why should I let my job or brother choose who I get to be with? My happiness is my own."

Tessa nods and screams at the kids. "It's time to go."

They have parent-teacher conferences tonight. Ours are scheduled for next week.

Lily and Emily hug each other and we go our separate ways to the car.

Talking things out with Tessa always seems to help me get a better perspective on a problem. She isn't one to lie, and usually she makes it short and sweet.

My phone rings, and my mother's name scrolls across the screen.

"Hey, mom. Just heading home from the park with Lily."

I hear Eli talking in the background. "Are you free for dinner?"

Why didn't they tell me about coming to visit? Of course, my brother knew and didn't tell me. He is their favorite, but it's always been that way. I think it has a lot to do with being good at sports, and making a name for himself. My parents loved that.

"Yes, where should I meet you?"

Eli yells in the background. "Diner. See you there."

My mom doesn't even say anything, just hangs up the phone.

Lily jumps around in the backseat. She hasn't seen my parents in about two years, and as much as I wish they would visit more often, it's not one-sided. They haven't seen me since the divorce, and I'm sure my mother will have lots of questions about that. They are traditional in the sense that they believe you should only be married once.

Infidelity or not. Somehow, I am supposed to just forgive Dean and make it work. And this might have worked decades ago, but no woman wants to stay with a man that doesn't make them happy.

I make a U-turn and head back toward the diner, knowing that tonight will not be pleasant. My game face is on, and if it goes anything like the others, Eli will take up most of the night talking about himself. Maybe it will keep mom off of my back. Fingers crossed.

My Kia Soul whips into a parking spot right in front, and I get out to help Lily.

"How long are they staying, mom?"

I unbuckle the seatbelt and assist her out. "Not sure, sweetie. Guess we will find out at dinner."

She takes my hand, and we make our way inside to spot them sitting by the door. Eli is already talking about a recent fire they worked on, and every story he tells, he's the hero. It's like nobody else had a hand in helping put the fire out, or saving someone from a building. I think he embellishes many of his stories.

"Grandma!" Lily screams, running up to the booth and jumping into her lap.

"Look how big you've gotten."

She has never been that much involved in my life since I left home. And if she is, it means that she doesn't approve. My family loved Dean, so when they found out we were getting a divorce, they weren't happy. The first thing that my mother asked me was if I upset him? At first, it pissed me off she would think it was something I did, but then I realized that marriages when she was my age and in today's world aren't anything similar.

We ended up on the phone for almost an hour while she gave me tips on how to save my marriage. Cater to your man. Fulfill all his needs every day. Don't let him come home to a dirty house. This is the 21st century. Why is it the woman's role?

"Have a seat, dear. Your brother was just telling us about work yesterday."

"Of course, he was," I mumble.

He glares at me, and I wave over the waitress to order a breakfast platter for Lily and me.

I spend most of the evening listening to Eli and after I eat my food, I can't keep my mouth quiet anymore.

"We have been here for almost two hours and not once have you asked how I'm doing? Or Lily? Did you want to see us, or just Eli?"

She turns to look at my father, who has been silent the whole night. "You don't seem to be in a good mood, honey. Maybe we should meet up after some rest."

That's just like her. Make me seem the out of control one.

"Rest will not make me want to sit here and listen to these preposterous fucking stories." I grab Lily's hand and step out of the booth. "Pleasant visit, mom. See you in two or three years."

Usually, I stay collected with my parents, but the way they are treating me is absurd. I'm not some red-headed stepchild.

"Why are we leaving?" Lily asks.

"Mama's tired. Let's go home."

The drive isn't silent, but me listening to Lily cry most of the way. I shouldn't have been selfish. She deserves to see them, even if they drive me fucking crazy.

Once we get home, I pull out my phone to see my mother called three times, but have no urge to call her back. She must see how rude she is to us? Eli always gets the attention, but what about her granddaughter?

I scroll through the notifications I missed and see a text.

Jeremy: Can we grab lunch? I don't have many people to talk to about my dad's condition. Not having him around is fucking with me.

He is going to have a hard time with this, and it takes some time to get used to not having family around. The transition can be rough, but Jeremy is a strong man, and he is doing what's best for his father. That's commendable.

Me: Sure. I take lunch around noon. Anywhere but the diner. Coffee shop, even.

I know his favorite place to go, but I'm getting sick of that place.

After I get Lily off to bed and lay my head on my pillow to shut my eyes, Jeremy takes over my thoughts. Pleasant dreams are headed my way.

13

RAQUEL

My mother doesn't seem to get my point from last night. Instead of egging it on, I just let it be, and invite them over for dinner tonight, without Eli. If this is going to go well, he doesn't need to be present. If she expects me to apologize for my outburst yesterday, it's not happening.

The front desk clerk is typing away on her phone and looks up at me as I come back from making my morning rounds.

"What did you do yesterday?" she asks.

"Dealt with family. You?"

She shows me her hand. "Holy crap. Congratulations."

I don't want to stay in the same room with her for too long, because I'll have to hear about wedding planning for the next decade, so I make up an excuse of needing to check on a resident and get out of there. It's not a total lie, because I plan on checking on Don, anyway. I'm sure Jeremy will ask how he is doing when we meet up.

Knock. Knock. Knock.

"Come in!"

Out of all the residents I've had the pleasure of overseeing, I think he has had the easiest transition of them all. This could be because he didn't have any socialization besides family since his diagnosis.

"Just wanted to check in on you. Jeremy and I are meeting up for a coffee and you know he's going to ask about you."

He shoots me a funny look. "Are you and my son dating?"

I cross my arms. "No, just friends. Nothing to worry about."

"I'm not worried. You seem like a nice woman, and Jeremy would be lucky to have you."

His father doesn't seem to have a problem, and it puts me at ease to know that. I'm surprised Jeremy hasn't mentioned our meetups at all to him. Did he think his father wouldn't approve?

"Well, I'm heading out for lunch. I'll tell Jeremy you said hi."

I don't meet up with people to talk about their problems, but with Jeremy, it's different. I'm a part of this ride now and if I can use any of my knowledge to make this difficult time in his life any easier, then I will do it tenfold.

I wave to the clerk and walk out the door to the coffee shop down the street. It's not always had the best food, but with the new management, the sandwiches are decent.

"Glad to see you could make it. I know you have better things to do on your lunch than be stuck here with me," Jeremy says.

I smile, and stand next to him in line to order, while trying not to stare at him. He is in his uniform, and some women aren't able to keep their eyes off of him. Not that I can blame them, but here he is, standing next to me in all his glory.

"Work treating you well today?" I ask, just trying to make conversation.

He leans into me. "It's work. Been slow. You?"

I toss around the idea of mentioning his dad's comment, but decide to wait.

"Welcome to MoJoe's," the barista says.

We both order a turkey club and a caramel latte, and then find a seat until they call our names. He stares out the window, almost with sad eyes, and I can tell something is bothering him. The fact that he talks to me about these things says something. He trusts me.

"So, what did you want to talk about? I'm all ears for the next forty-five minutes."

Jeremy half smiles, and expresses his concerns about Donald. The fear of losing him too soon, and how life is going to be without him. "I just don't feel like I have a purpose anymore. You know, with him, he depended on me every day, and now it's just me. Idle hands have never been my strong suit."

The transition to having the patient out of the home is hard on the family members who were taking care of them. They question if it's the best place for them, but Jeremy knows I'm taking good care of Don.

"Maybe you should find a hobby. Something to keep your mind busy while you are home," I suggest.

He rolls his eyes. "Like what?"

My only response is to shrug my shoulders. A hobby might not be the right answer. Most of his problems and concerns are stemming from his father's absence in the house and his passing. What is he going to do then? He needs to cope with this now, so that way when it happens, it's not so much of a life shock.

"Have you thought about going to therapy? They have support groups I can recommend."

It's a tricky subject, but it might help him cope. There are three that gather and just talk about what they are facing, before and even after losing their loved ones.

"I don't need therapy. That shit doesn't work. A stranger doesn't need to listen to my problems and give me some psychobabble."

To be honest, I'm not a fan of therapy either. So, I tell him about my experience. When Dean filed for a divorce, my mother talked me into trying out couple's therapy before finalizing it. She thought it would help us work things out, but it just made things worse. She kept telling us to speak our truth, whatever that was, and Dean mentioned many things that irritated me to my core. Things that he has never once mentioned to me, or complained about. Our sex life has gone downhill, and I never seemed present during the act. What a joke. The kicker was when he told the therapist that he felt like I stopped trying, and didn't want to put in the work it takes to make a marriage successful.

"She told me I needed to work on pleasing my husband's needs. Can you fucking believe that?"

The barista calls our names, and he instructs me to stay while he goes and gets our lunch. Should I even be discussing my past with Dean with Jeremy? Is it making him uncomfortable talking about my ex-husband?

"You only have fifteen-minutes left before you gotta be back. Sorry I took up so much of the time," he says, taking a bite out of his sandwich.

"I'll be fine. Don asked if we were dating? I mentioned we were going to lunch."

He puts his sandwich down and wipes his hand on a napkin. "If everyone thinks we are, then why aren't we? I mean, you know how I feel."

His eyes lock on mine, and in that moment I want to lean over and kiss him, but I don't. Something is keeping me from giving in. Doubts or fears?

A woman approaches our table and stands next to me, looking down at Jeremy.

"I notice you didn't have a ring. My name is Amber, and if you are ever free, I'd love to go to dinner." She slips a piece of paper on the table and walks away.

What the hell was that? Why can't I just say yes to him?

"Sorry about that. Seems no one wanted me until I found you."

He takes his sandwich back in his hands and continues eating. The Amber girl is watching us, and I want to give her the bird, but that's not ladylike and I don't want Jeremy to think that made me jealous.

It's silent until we are both done eating, and then he takes my hand in his, sending electricity up my arm. "I only have eyes for you. You're worth the wait."

Jeremy stands up, thanks me for lunch, and walks away.

Just give in already. Or you could lose him.

14

JEREMY

*H*eading back to the depot, things have shifted between Raquel and I. I have made my intentions clear, but she still doesn't seem to want to be with me. Damon thinks I should just move on and stop wasting time on someone who isn't interested, but everything in my being tells me she wants to be with me. Sure, there are obstacles in the way, but we can get through them together. If she would just let me in.

"It would be one thing if she has told you she wants to be with you, but she hasn't, right?"

I shake my head.

"So, maybe you need to tell her you want to be with her, but if she doesn't have any feelings for you, then you can move on. I don't want you to get your heart broken. Tessa might be good friends with her, but I'm looking out for you."

I want to listen to him, but my heart is telling me something else.

My phone vibrates and I see it's the center.

"Hello," I answer, my heart sinking.

"Mr. Grey, we need you to come down as soon as possible."

"Is my father okay?"

"He's been in an altercation. Can you come down now?"

"I'll be there in ten-minutes."

I get up from the table, go into Chief's office, and explain the situation. Nobody at the depot knows about my father's condition besides the Jacksons. I've been trying to keep it to myself.

"Get out of here, boy."

I race out of the depot, to my truck, and floor it to get to the center. Before dad went there, he hadn't had an episode in a couple of days, but was already showing symptoms of forgetting things. This is common in Alzheimer's patients in the later stages, and it progresses fast after that. In the last three days, he is having multiple episodes a day, which only leads me to believe that this condition is worsening and will not get better. This is the landslide the doctors have been warning us about, but even after being told to prepare for this, no one can.

When I jump out of the truck and rush inside, there are screams echoing off the walls. I rush down the hall to see what's going on. I find my dad on the floor with blood on him, and a nurse putting a needle in his arm.

"What is that?"

"A sedative. We didn't have a choice."

After he fades away, two of the orderlies help get Don back into his bed. I wait until they are gone before I question Raquel.

"What the hell is going on? Who's blood is that?"

He had an episode and punched one of the other residents after he asked where he was, and all he would say is, where is my wife? She didn't have a choice but to sedate him, to calm him down.

I run my fingers through my hair, distraught. "He came here so he wouldn't attack anyone. If he finds out about this, he'll never come out of that room."

This might be the best place for my father, but his episodes are getting worse. What would have happened if this happened while at home? I shudder at the thought.

"Your father is not himself. His episodes have become more

frequent, and it hinders his cognitive ability. There's a good chance that these might be his last few times where he will recognize you."

I drop to my knees, and tears fall. "I thought we had more time. So did he."

Raquel squats and takes my hands in hers. "Right now, you need to spend as much time as you can with him. My recommendation is for Hazel to come back if she can."

I nod. "Can I see him?"

"Of course."

He might not be awake, but it doesn't feel right being here and not coming in. What am I going to do? This is the countdown of a horrible event and I'm not ready.

His eyes flutter open. "Who the hell are you? What are you doing in my room?"

"I thought you sedated him?" I look back at Kristen.

"I did. He shouldn't be awake."

"I don't know who you people are. Where's my wife?" He is screaming and flailing on the bed. "I want my wife, damnit."

My heart drops to the floor, and I try to leave the room, but my feet won't move. Raquel tugs on my arm and removes me.

"I know this is hard. Right now, we have to wait for him to come out of this and be patient."

I swat at her hand and walk toward the doors. "Let me out. I need some air."

Situations like this rarely go well, and it's a lot for anyone to handle; let alone a guy who is trying to do everything by himself. Sure, I have Hazel, but she lives halfway across the country.

She scans her badge, and I walk out the doors, pissed off at the world. Why did this have to happen to my father?

The center doors close behind me, and I'm furious. Not at him, but at everything.

What am I going to do? How am I going to tell Hazel? I know she is still upset with me for keeping it from her, and I need nothing else to come in between us. She hasn't been back in Massachusetts for very long, and things are going great for her there. This is going to shatter her world.

I punch my car door and start pacing around the parking lot. All this rage and anger is bottling up inside me, and it needs to just come the fuck out. I know the doctor told me to prepare myself for this, but how do you do that? It's my father; the man that had confidence in me, when I had none, and I wouldn't be the man I am today without his guidance and support. Losing him is going to be the darkest day in my life, and I'm not fucking prepared for it. Never will be.

I get inside my truck and start heading back to the house. Right now, there is nothing I can do for him, and the nurses can handle it. My presence is only going to upset him more, and they don't need that.

My father is not a violent man, and I know this disease can alter him, especially if he doesn't know where he is. It still doesn't make it any less of a shock when he doesn't recognize me. I'm his son, and it's just heart breaking. I don't want him to become that way with any of the staff, but someone trained them on what to do in that situation. So if anyone can handle it, it's them.

Final stages. Raquel is being upfront with me, and I appreciate that, but hearing those damn words is like a stake in my heart. I thought we had more time, and now I know that isn't true. This is when things go downhill, and I'm not mentally prepared for it.

I'm not an idiot, I know the moment we are born, we are counting down the days until our death, like a clock ticking, but one thing is my dad has lived a wonderful life. He found true love, loved teaching, and two kids that adore him. Not everyone gets that lucky. It still doesn't make losing him any easier, and in fact, it reminds me I need to be living my life. True Love is something I have searched for, but it's never worked out. Maybe it is 100% the time to stop putting it on the back burner and get out there.

Raquel has been very helpful during this transition for him, and I know she only wants what's best for him. He didn't know he would progress this fast, and not being able to bathe or go to the bathroom himself is frightening. When he comes to, he will not enjoy being doted on, and that's a fact. What person wants to have someone else wipe their ass or give them a sponge bath? It signifies you are getting older and can't do things yourself anymore.

My heart breaks for him, knowing how he is going to react to this, and not having his freedom anymore. When he didn't recognize me tonight, I thought he would snap out of it like last time, but he didn't. My father acting like I'm a stranger. It's fucked up. Why did this have to happen to him?

The driveway outside of his house seems eerie. I haven't been sleeping the best since he moved to the center, but who likes to be in a big house alone? The memories alone are what fuels me to keep this house in our family. It is what my dad would want, and has explicitly asked for me to do, and I won't ever go against his wishes. Still, the thought of going inside and staying another night alone makes me shudder. I'm all alone here, and I want all the things he has. Maybe one day.

I can't put it off any longer. Hazel deserves to know. What am I going to say? Her chance to get partner is upon her, and she might lose her chance, but I know our father means more to her than some job.

The phone rings and rings. I pull it away from my ear to hang up and then hear her voice.

"Whatcha doing?" I ask, trying to ease into the conversation that I know is going to tear her apart.

I can hear Aiden in the background singing, and it sounds like she's at home with her new dog. "Well, we need to talk about dad."

Her playful demeanor changes. "What's wrong? Is he okay?"

My hesitation worries her, and rightfully so.

"Just fucking tell me, damnit. This silent shit is going to make me have a heart attack," she yells into the phone, and I can hear Aiden asking her what's going on.

"He's been having episodes more frequently, and today he didn't recognize me again, except this time, it's lasting longer."

Hazel doesn't respond, but Aiden asks if she is okay, which lets me know she's crying.

"He's in the final stages, isn't he?"

"Yes. Raquel says he is also having trouble with his speech, which is a sign before he has to have someone help him in all aspects of his daily life. Bathing, going to the bathroom, everything."

The sounds of her wailing into Aiden's chest breaks my heart. I remember the day she left to go to Harvard. Our father was over the moon for her, and that's one thing he was always good at, making us aware of how proud he was of our accomplishments. Before she left, Hazel always talked about paying off the house, getting him settled in, so he wouldn't have to worry about paying bills, because he should be able to sit back and enjoy life.

"I know it's a lot, sis. Take some more vacation and come back down. We both did our research and the last stage happens quickly, and we need to spend as much time as we can with him before he goes."

My eyes water, just saying that out loud, and knowing that one of these days, my father will not be around anymore. He is the epitome of an amazing father, and he didn't even have to be. He took Hazel and I in when no one else would, and made us a family. After years in the system, going from home to home, neither of us thought we would ever find a family, and the Greys proved us wrong. Everything that Hazel and I have accomplished in this life is because of his generosity.

Aiden picks up the phone. "She will be on the first flight out in the morning."

No one can blame us for being optimistic, especially when advancements are being made for many diseases, and maybe they would have a breakthrough for Alzheimer's. Neither of us wants to imagine a life without him in it, but today is the knife in the heart. Our father is going to die, and there's nothing we can do about it.

I stare at the front door, knowing that he won't be waiting for me inside, relaxing in his recliner watching action movies anymore. There will be no one to share meals with, and binge the latest show. When the center became his best option, I didn't take into consideration how it could change him. It shouldn't affect me like this, but it does.

One thing is for certain; I am not upset about having to take care of him, because that's my duty. Since his diagnosis, we have become much closer, and it is nice to spend my nights with him, laughing and watching his favorite movies, or hearing stories about when he was younger. These are things I'm glad he got to share with me before the final stages. Before he forgets me.

Tracks run down my face, and it's wet, but I have to go inside. I can't sit in my truck forever. Of course, listening to myself, I get out and walk to the front door, hesitating to put the key in to unlock it. Maybe I should think about this a different way. When I find my person, my partner, this will be where we raise our kids. It's an honor for my father to hand this place over to me.

I put the key in, and step inside, laying them down on the entryway table, and walking straight to the kitchen, turning lights on as I pass the switches. At night, this house is a little eerie in the dark, and for right now, I want it lit up.

I need to eat something, and my body is sending me warning signs. I haven't eaten since yesterday, and that makes me want to go to a buffet and eat everything there. I open the refrigerator to see what we have, and there isn't much. The cabinets hide some ramen noodles and I go for that. Quick and simple to make because I need to get some sleep. Figure out how we are going to do this with Dad and I've got to be strong for Hazel. She has Aiden now, but I don't know how well he is going to do under pressure like this.

My phone buzzes, and right now I don't want to talk to anyone, even Raquel. This day has been the worst on record and I just want it to be over. I know it's going to hit me when I see him next, and there's not much I can say to make the situation better, but knowing I have very limited time with him now, it makes me want to spend every waking moment with him.

Hazel is coming out on the first flight out tomorrow, and I hope I can hold it together when I see her. She is going to be a blubbering mess, and it's my job to be a rock for her. Is Aiden coming? On one hand, I think he would never let her go through this alone, but then again, nothing would surprise me at this point. She loves him, but I just don't know if they are end game material.

The water comes to a boil, and I put the block of noodles in the water and let it sit for three minutes. It's not the best for you, but it'll get something in my stomach fast, so I can close my eyes and escape to a new reality even if just for a couple of hours.

15

RAQUEL

This entire ordeal with Don is heart-breaking, and I checked on him to see if he came out of his episode, but he hadn't. When I left for the day, he was still very confused. If this episode continues, we will have to explain to him what's going on, but that means he could become violent again. It's hard when you don't know what's reality is anymore.

Lily is with her dad for the weekend, and Tessa is meeting me at the diner for dinner. We have become close since my moving here, and Brittaney is in her own little world with the wedding plans. She doesn't even know about Jeremy, and that she never once asked how I was doing, or what was going on in my life when we had dinner, just shows that she's too self-involved right now. Better to leave her to it.

The interstate has cars whipping in and out of lanes, trying their damndest to get to their destination faster, no matter if it's dangerous to others. That's just Dallas for ya. Jeremy hasn't answered my texts, and I'm getting worried. He's going through a lot right now, but he needs to be talking to someone. Bottling all of this up inside is only going to make matters worse.

As I get off the exit to Grapevine, my phone rings and it's Jeremy.

"Hello?"

When his voice comes over my speakers, my heart drops. "I saw your messages. Not been in the mood to talk to anyone."

I just want to pull him close and hug him. "I understand. When you are ready to talk, I'm here."

The line goes silent for about twenty seconds. "Can you come over?"

I stare at the screen on my dash, and wonder if I just imagined that. "What?"

"Or, do you already have plans? That's fine."

"No, no. I mean, I have dinner plans with Tessa, but I can swing by after."

The car comes to a stop in front of the diner, and I turn it off waiting for his answer.

"Just text me before you leave and I'll give you the address," he says, before he hangs up.

He doesn't need to push me away. After all, I work with those that have this disease every day, and I might help him cope with things that are going on. No one ever thinks this is going to happen to someone in their family, but sometimes it does.

My shoes hit the pavement as I close the car door and venture inside the diner where the bell rings above my head, alerting them to my arrival. Tessa is already sitting in our usual booth, and has a smile on her face.

"Hey, girl. I ordered your usual."

Grapevine is a place where people can remember my order, whereas in Dallas, that never happens. They see too many people every day, and it's not as cozy in this place.

"Today has been a fucking nightmare."

She takes a sip of her coffee. "Tell me all about it."

I'm not sure if she's ready for me to unload on her quite like this, but not going to turn down the opportunity to get everything out. So, I start with the Jeremy's situation, and the fact he got into a fight with my brother. She didn't seem to know about that, which is surprising. The only part I don't discuss is the events with his father because it's not mine to tell.

Tessa must have something to tell me, but she has been tapping her fingers on the table the whole time I've been going on about Jeremy and my life. I'm not one of those friends who only thinks about herself.

"So, what news do you have?"

Her excitement takes over, and she digs into her purse. "This happened today."

She hands me something and I open it. "No fucking way. Are you serious?"

"We have been trying, and Damon has always wanted to be a father. You are the first person I've told. I'm telling him when I get home."

My ass slides out of the booth and gives her a huge hug! "This is amazing. Congratulations!"

Tessa raised Emily by herself for many years, and then Damon stepped up. And there's no doubt in my mind that they are wonderful parents.

Our food has arrived, and I don't waste any time digging in. I never ate lunch today, so my stomach has been growling for over two hours. I don't eat at the diner this often, but it's the most chill place in town with good food.

"Well, Damon is going to be ecstatic. Emily, too. This is great news."

The conversation goes silent, and we focus on eating our food. She is excited to get home to tell her husband. When I found out I was pregnant with Lily, I didn't know how Dean was going to react. He always talked about wanting to wait to have kids. I set up a t-shirt with Future Dad on the kitchen table, and he found out when he got home from work and called me. He thought I was joking, and didn't take me seriously until he saw the confirmation paperwork from the doctor. It took him months to come around and be excited. He's a good dad, and loves Lily, but he should've been more supportive of me.

After our plates are empty, I drop thirty dollars on the table, and she is quick to leave.

"I'll let you know how it goes. Night, girl."

She hustles out the door, and I wait a minute, letting Jeremy know I'm fixing to leave so I can get the address. He doesn't respond right away, and I know it's already nine o'clock, so maybe he is asleep. I shrug my shoulders, get in the car, and start going down Main.

A text message comes through my car, reading it to me. Thank god for these newer cars that have this function, cause I hate texting and driving. It's his address, and it asks if I would like to pull up the GPS to the location. What a dumb question.

I'm not sure what to expect going over there, but I want to be there for him. These last moments with his father are going to be something he will remember for the rest of his life, and I don't want his anger or frustration to keep him from that. I've seen it too many times with patient's families and he will regret it.

The GPS takes me to a cute little home, reminds me of my parent's house when I was little, and I get out and approach the front door. I have to remember this is an overwhelming emotional time for him right now, and give myself a pep talk before I knock. When he comes to the door, he looks awful. His face is red and blotchy, and he is in grey sweatpants, hanging just off his hips.

"Thanks for coming. I don't have many people I can call."

I walk inside, and place my purse on the entryway table, and follow him to the couch. Most men would never let a woman see them like this, and it's nice to see Jeremy is different. From the moment I met him at Damon's party, I knew he wasn't like the others.

"What am I going to do?" he starts to cry. "How am I going to function without him? Live in this house? Take on the world without him?"

Death is a very scary subject, especially for those that are left behind by a loved one, and it gets us thinking about things we would want to do differently. The famous saying: Act like each day is your last, it is so true. We just never know how much time we have left, and everyone wants to make their mark on the world and be remembered after we are gone. I know Don has touched many people's lives and he will not be forgotten.

There isn't anything I can say to him, so I just scoot closer and let him lay into my shoulder. Right now, he just needs someone to listen while he gets this all out. I'm grateful he trusts me to be that person.

"Hazel will be back tomorrow. If you think I'm a mess, wait until you see her. When she arrives, I can't be like this. I need to be strong for her, but I don't know if I can."

His lips graze mine as I pull him in for a hug. At first, I pull away, not knowing if this is the right time or place for this to happen, but the way Jeremy looks at me, lost and lonely, I lean back into him and let it be. Even if he is only kissing me to take his mind off of all of this. He tucks his hands on my waist, and I move over on top of him. The heat of the moment kicks in, and I don't even know what I want.

He stops kissing me and leans his head back on the couch. "As much as I've been dreaming of this happening, I don't want you to regret it. Let's pick this up another time."

Most girls would be irritated, but it makes me respect him even more. He doesn't want pity sex, and neither do I. If and when we get to enjoy that side of each other, it should be a happy time.

"You might not know this, but my grandfather had Alzheimer's. It's not something I go around telling everyone, but it's another big reason I'm in this industry."

He cocks his head. "Really?"

"Yeah, he was a wonderful man, but it changed him. As kids, it was hard to bond with him, because at a certain point, he couldn't even recognize his kids, so he had no clue who we were."

His eyes water again. "It's the most awful feeling. Wanting to spend time with them, but not even being able to share that moment because they do not know who you are."

I lean in, close to his face, and kiss him. "These aren't the only memories you will have, Jeremy. Think of all the things you and Don did together over your life. They might not be picture perfect, but at least you have them, you know?"

My grandfather's death caught my parents off guard. Doctors can tell someone all day to prepare, but it's just not possible. How do you prepare to lose your loved ones? We know at some point any of us could leave this Earth, but that doesn't mean we are ready for it.

His diagnosis shook my dad to his core, and he wanted to do everything he could for him, but once his memory went, it's kind of hard to do that. At our request, he still took us to see grandpa, but sometimes he wouldn't even introduce us. We would just go to the center and talk to him. He told us it would be better this way, so we didn't upset him.

"How do I say goodbye to my father if he can't even recognize me? I can't explain to him how much he means to me, and I appreciate everything he's done for me. All the things I want to say, I can't."

I take his hands in mine, and he looks into my eyes. "You can tell him whatever you want. He might not understand now, but I promise you that man, your father, he knows."

16

JEREMY

Freshly brewed coffee is something I love waking up to. I can see Raquel pouring into two mugs, and when she sees I'm awake, she smiles.

"I didn't mean to fall asleep here," she says, taking a sip. "It just got late and I guess we were both tired."

She doesn't have to apologize. Last night is going to help me get through today. Raquel has made some obvious points, and she's right. I need to buck up and spend what time I can with my father, even if I can't be me. Hazel is going to have trouble and until she experiences it, I don't think she will understand how frustrating and confusing it is for our father not to recognize us. When someone walks in and says they are your kid, and you know you don't have any kids, then it can disrupt their state and overwhelm them.

"When is Hazel getting in?" she asks.

"Honestly, I do not know. She took the first flight out of Massachusetts, so I would assume in the next couple of hours. She should text me."

I put on the news just like I would if my father were here, and enjoy my coffee before dealing with everything that is happening today. Raquel is snuggled up to the arm of the couch, and I figured she would have bailed the moment she woke up.

My phone buzzes against the coffee table, and Hazel's name is sliding across the screen. I look at Raquel.

"Morning, sis. Catch a flight?"

She sounds like she's driving. "Almost to your house. Got a taxi."

"I would've come and got you."

She can afford to take one, but why spend the money when you have someone who can pick you up? Sometimes, I just don't understand her.

"Didn't know if you were still asleep, and didn't want to wake you so early. Chill."

Fuck. Raquel can't be here when she shows up or Hazel is going to flip. Yeah, I know I'm a grown ass man, but we have enough to deal with today, and don't need to add anything to our plate.

"Alright, see you soon."

I hurry off the phone and jump up. "Sorry for this, but you have to go. Hazel will be here any minute and she's made it clear not to date you. Well, dad's nurse. I'm so sorry."

Her expression seems genuine. "I understand. Gotta get ready for work, anyway."

She grabs her purse, keys, and walks out of the door.

I take her coffee cup into the kitchen and wash it before Hazel gets here so there is no evidence, and open the front door waiting for her to pull up. She's either going to be a mess or overly happy. One thing I've learned over the years, Hazel does not deal with grief very well. When we lost our foster mother, her entire world crashed around her. For both of us, it was the first time we had both a male and female role model that didn't want to throw us out like garbage.

A black car comes rolling down the street and then pulls into the driveway. That's her. I walk toward the trunk to help with her bags, and when she gets out, I'm shocked. Here she is wearing sweatpants, an oversized shirt, and tennis shoes, hair in a messy ponytail and no makeup. I'm not mocking her for it, but this is a rare sight. She is usually very well groomed and dressed, especially if she's out in public. This tells me she is not holding it together.

"Let's get you inside," I say, following behind her and closing the door. "I'll take these up to the spare bedroom. There's fresh coffee if you want some."

I'm trying to pull myself together because usually she would be the one keeping me organized and where I need to be. It looks like that's going to be me for now. So, I need to put my game face on, and be strong as fuck, because Hazel is going to lose her shit when she sees dad.

"Alright, I'm gonna have another cup of coffee and make some toast before we head over to see dad. You want any?" I ask, going down the staircase and notice her already laying down on the couch.

"Coffee would be nice. I haven't slept at all."

I would never say it out loud, but the dark circles under her eyes give it away. "So, Aiden decided not to come?"

She sits up on the couch and stares at me. "He is flying in later today. An event was scheduled for the bookstore. I told him to stay."

And see if that was me, and the person I was in love with was in this situation, I would drop everything to be there for them. So, I have my doubts about Aiden and if he is the right person for my sister. Who the hell lets their girlfriend come to something like this alone? That's just an asshole move, no matter what work crap you have going on.

I slide two pieces of bread in the toaster and pour myself more coffee. She doesn't seem to want to talk, so I leave it be. We are each going to deal with this in our own way, and I can't get mad at how she is acting. I have to remind myself that last night I was a fucking mess, and I would be right now if I didn't have to put on a poker face for her. Big brother rules.

Once my toast is done, I garble the first one down and tell her to get up and head to the car. We can't sit around here all morning. She is here to see dad and we can't put it off. Under these circumstances, we shouldn't waste any precious time. The optimistic side of me hopes he has come out of his episode and will recognize us because I don't want her to feel even one ounce of the hurt I did yesterday.

The entire ride over is silent. She doesn't speak a word, and when we pull up and park at the center, she stops me from opening my door.

"What if he doesn't recognize me? I knew I shouldn't have flown back last time. Dammit." Her eyes water and it's never going to end. She can't go in there looking like this.

"We knew this was coming. He might not recognize us, but he is still our dad in there. Even if it's just keeping him company, that's better than not visiting at all, right?"

She wipes her face up, nods. "We can do this."

This prepared neither of us for what is coming today, but we shall face it together. Lean on each other during this difficult time. Such as family does.

The doors open, and Raquel hurries toward us, not mentioning a word of what transpired last night. Although, that is what's best for both of us right now. My feelings for her have not wavered since the moment I laid eyes on her, yet things continue to keep us apart. Sometimes, that makes love far greater indeed.

"Can we see him?" Hazel asks, taking one last deep breath before our visit.

She nods and leads us down the hallway to his room.

"I must warn you, he has gotten worse," she says, before opening the door.

Our father is laying in his bed, watching, as always, some action movie. That part of him still exists, but he does not recognize us. I can tell by the way his brows raise.

He strains trying to talk to us, but it's clear that his trouble speaking is only going to get worse.

"Don, I just wanted to come visit and see if you needed anything today?" I ask, holding onto my sister's hand.

He shakes his head, and wavers us out of the door, and points to the bathroom. The nurse nods and helps him out of bed.

We never envisioned that he would decline so fast, and right before our very eyes, but we knew the consequences of this disease. All I wish is that I could have just one more conversation with my father, but I will not get it.

"What are we supposed to do without him?" Hazel asks, tracks running her face. "I won't even get to tell him how appreciative I am for everything he has done for me. Without him, I never would have gotten this far with my life. I just wish he knew."

I embrace her, and understand a great deal about how this is affecting her, and how much our lives are going to change after this. Will we even be able to see him? Will our presence cause discomfort to him?

To know that his swift decline in health could take him from us today, tomorrow, next week is too much to think about right now. It is my duty to stay strong for Hazel and for our family. He was clear on what he wanted, and how proud he was of us every single day. We can't forget that.

We must take some time to process, and he would not want us to see him like that. However, it doesn't change the fact that I want to be there with him until the end. Yet, how do I do that, but as if a stranger to him? He will never know who I am anymore, and that's heartbreaking.

"We should go," I say, nodding at Raquel on the way out the doors.

I hoped that he would be himself today, just to give Hazel a chance to say her goodbyes, before it was too late. Time was not on our side.

The car ride home is unimaginable. Hazel cries the entire way, and I try to console her, but she does not want it. Aiden should be here, but he is back in Massachusetts tending to his business, like that's more important than being here during this difficult time with my sister. I'm enraged that he would even think that's appropriate.

"What are we to do now? If he does not know us, do we visit him as someone else? Pretend not to know him?"

There's our dilemma. Right now, we need to get home, drown our sorrows, and come to terms with reality. Things will not get better. This is the downward spiral the doctors have been warning us about and trying to prepare us for, but we are not ready.

How does one prepare for losing a loved one, even if they have the knowledge beforehand?

17

JEREMY

It might only be early afternoon, but liquor is giving us a bit of solace right now. We are not heavy drinkers, but today seems to be something different. The circumstances around it have changed, and trying to figure out how to still be close to our father, without causing his discomfort, proves to be more difficult than we thought. We can't tell him who we are anymore, because it will only make him become agitated and confused. No one wants to pretend to be someone else in the presence of their loved ones, but this is our only option at this point. Drinking this tequila is how we are dealing with that right now.

Aiden should show up at any moment, but Hazel hasn't mentioned him in hours. Are they still doing okay? Are things not going good back in Massachusetts? I would hope she would confide in me if that's the case, but what do I know? Something seems amiss when he didn't come down with her. Or maybe, I am just reading too much into it.

She has been going through the old trunk our dad put together almost a decade ago. His parents left a little behind for him to remember them, and he didn't want that for us.

"Have you looked through this yet?" she asks, a tequila bottle in one hand, and pictures in the other. "There are pictures all the way back to when dad was a baby."

I get off the couch and join her on the floor of the living room, digging through the trunk. Memories are sometimes just what you need on a bad day, and who knows what is inside here? The first thing I see a notebook of sorts, and when I opened it, it didn't stay that way for long. It is our late mother's diary, but Hazel grabs it from me and begins reading it.

"Would she want us reading this? Isn't it personal?" I ask, feeling icky about it.

"Diaries are something that women keep to look back on in our lives. If anything, she kept this so she could remember. Aren't you the least bit curious? What was she like at a young age?"

Regina was someone who cared so much for others. Her role in the world was to become a mother, and there's no doubt she would be deeply rooted in our lives if she were still alive today. Their marriage seemed like one that had been tested many times, with cruel words from their families, but they loved each other. Nothing was going to come between that, and they didn't let it. Sometimes we forget how much outside forces can affect our lives and our decisions, but they never let it impact their marriage.

Listening to Hazel read the pages aloud makes me want to see her just one last time. Even though she is not my 'real' mother, she has been more of a mother in the short few years than my birth mother was in my entire life. She took a chance on both of us, and without that, we would have bounced between homes until we aged out. When kids age out of the foster care system, the statistics show most end up on the streets, and end up resorting to jobs that land them in jail or prison. Not all, but again just a statistic.

Don and Regina gave us a chance when no one else wanted to keep us, and then became our family. They welcomed us with open arms, and we did not make it easy the first couple of months. But when you are thrown into yet another home you don't expect to stay at, how do you act? When you are used to being thrown out like garbage or giving to someone else like a secondhand dress, you learn to not exactly get attached to anything. With them, they made it clear from the very beginning their intentions were to keep us until we become adults, and it took us some time to see they were being serious.

"Are you even listening?" Hazel says, and is staring at me.

"Sorry, zoning out. What'd I miss?"

She hands me the diary, and I read it over myself.

Things have not been going as we hoped. We wanted a family by now, and things have not been on our side. I don't want to be old-fashioned, but my whole life I have wanted to be a mother, and some women don't need that to live a fulfilled life, but I must admit it's eating away at me. I never thought this would be an obstacle Don and I would have to tackle, but it's now presented itself. We might not have kids naturally, but we are exploring other options. We have a lot of love to give, and there are plenty of children out there that need the care and attention we can provide. Don and I have talked about adoption, but becoming foster parents seems like a better serving role for us. These kids need someone who cares for them, and can show them what it is like to have a family. The social worker told us today that many are going to a new home every three to six months, and that's just absurd. How can one have any type of stability in a life like that? After a long conversation, we have shifted gears and welcome two tweens into our home. Some might think it's weird for us to ask for older children, but they are the ones that seem lost in the system. My heart broke when the social worker asked if we would house them. She almost seemed shocked that we agreed so fast. Age doesn't matter to me, it's getting to make a difference in someone's life that truly needs it. These kids have been bounced around for years, and have never stayed in a home longer than a couple of months, all moved on to bring in younger children. These kids need someone like us in their lives, and I cannot wait to show them what a true home should be like. I hope they like us.

Reading this from her mind helps me remember what a wonderful woman she was, and how she didn't care about trivial things. Things like this prove that she is one of the most unselfish human beings I've ever had the pleasure of knowing and we need more like her in this world.

A knock sounds at the door, and Aiden walks in.

"Looks like you have been hitting it a little hard, babe. Should I order some food?"

I try not to pay attention too much because the liquor might cause me to say something I will regret.

"Food sounds amazing. Let's go to the diner," Hazel replies, standing up and putting her shoes back on. "Wanna come?"

"No, I think I'm good. You guys go."

Being in the same room with Aiden right now just isn't a good idea. So even though I'm starving, it's best for me to stay here. I need to give the liquor time to purge from my system, and find something to put in my stomach.

They leave, and I start a pot of coffee. If anything is going to help speed this up, it's caffeine. Work has been very accommodating with the situation, but I still feel bad for having to miss when I've only been there for a short time, but it's not like I expected it to happen this quick. Hell, none of us did.

While waiting for the coffee to brew, I pick up all the pictures off the ground and put them back inside the trunk, wanting to put it back in the closet before making something to eat. So many of them together, and they were so damn happy. When will I find mine?

A knock on the door startles me a bit, not expecting any company, and when I open the door to find Raquel, a smile appears. "Hey, what are you doing here?"

"I figured the day was rough, and wanted to bring you guys an early dinner." She peers inside, and sees it's just me.

"Hazel already left? Is that liquor I smell?"

Things are complicated between us right now. She knows how much I like her, and I've made that clear since the moment I saw her, but last night, something shifted, and when our lips met, it's like my heart knew what it wanted. Her. The timing, however, is not correct. She deserves way more from me than trying to screw her while grieving the situation with my father.

"We drank a little. Wanna come inside?" I offer.

She steps inside and walks straight to the kitchen and sets the bag of food on the counter. "I know your sister is in town so I won't stay long, but you weren't answering my calls or texts, and got worried. Knowing the situation."

I walk into the living room and grab my phone. "I turned it on silent when we walked in the door. Had enough to deal with already, and didn't want to talk to anyone."

Our eyes meet, but only for a second, and then she looks down at the floor. What happened last night has changed something about us, but Raquel doesn't seem to know what to do.

Things have been a whirlwind, but life is short and things have a way of falling on a backburner, and instead I need to make some priorities. From the beginning, before everything impeded us, we agreed to go on a date, and then we had to go our separate ways because of the society built around us, but why should we let them control our happiness?

"So, I brought stuff from the diner. Didn't know what your sister liked, so there is plenty of food in here for you to eat for days."

I glide behind her, placing my hands on her hips as her back is toward me. "Thank you for dinner, but I'm sick of playing this game. If I've learned anything, it's living life and not to let things deter you from what you want. Raquel, it's you. I fucking want you next to me when I go to sleep, and every morning when I wake. I'm done worrying about what everyone else thinks."

She turns around and stares up into my eyes. "Events like those in the past couple of days have a way of causing people to decide... as much as I would love to believe everything you are saying, how am I supposed to know you feel this way?"

"I knew from the moment I saw you at Damon's party that I needed to get to know you. If you hadn't been my dad's nurse, we would have gone out on that date, but life has a way of throwing curveballs, and instead of taking my shot, I just let it fly right by me, but not anymore. I want my shot with you. I don't care what Hazel, your brother, or anybody else says. We deserve to be happy, Raquel. You are what makes me happy."

Things have been hard, but it's shown me to not put my life on the backburner. I need to fight for what I want, and that's her. She needs to know that I'm serious.

"You make me happy, too, but it isn't the right time. I'd love to just be happy, but sometimes that luxury doesn't apply. Happiness isn't always permanent, and with the impending circumstances, you are going to have a lot to deal with, and I'm more than willing to help you, guide you through them as I can, but my heart can't get broken, Jeremy. Grief is a terrible thing, and I have seen it consume lives, so I'll be here, but romantically we should wait to decide until later. Feelings are not always as they seem to be."

She takes out the to-go containers and starts sitting them on the kitchen table.

"In six months, I'll feel the same way, you'll see. Now, let's get to eating, because the smell is making my stomach growl already."

18

RAQUEL

*H*is declaration last night has come to a head, but how do I know that's not just the emotions of the circumstances swaying his decision? In times like this, people don't want to be alone, for good cause, but it's not the time to make rash decisions, and even though I know we both have feelings for one another, it's best to wait until things have settled down before discussing this again. Jeremy already has enough on his plate, especially with Hazel now back in Grapevine, and falling victim to rumors and gossip will not help their situation.

Jeremy might not like the way I handled last night, but it's the right thing for me. Same way, he doesn't want anyone else to be able to control his happiness. I don't want to be the person that jumps into things too fast, and keeps her heart broken after just getting divorced. This isn't just about him, and I have to watch out for myself, too.

The coffee pot beeps, and I pour the golden liquid into my mug and then add a bit of vanilla creamer to give it a sweet taste. Today is a new day and all I want to do is make the most of it. As much as I want to open my heart up for him, my gut tells me it's not the right time, and no matter what, I have to trust my instincts.

Preparation for the day ahead leads me to believe I might need a couple of cups before leaving, but there just isn't time. I shouldn't have stayed over at his house so late, but he seemed to really need someone, and Hazel never came back. I might not want to be with him right now, but I'm not just going to leave him when he is having a hard time dealing with all the tragedy he faces in his life. I'm not that type of person.

As I sip on my coffee, trying to drink it fast without chugging it, I think about how he is going to take the visit today? We discussed his fragile state of mind, and how Don is not going to recognize either of them, but they insist on still visiting. That's a good thing, but it's hard to pretend to be someone you are not. Emotions run high, and the last thing Don needs is to become violent and confused. He will make sure Hazel is in agreement and come up with their ruse together.

My last sip is taken, and then my phone rings. Brittaney? Why the heck would she be calling me? I haven't spoken to her in several weeks since she invited me over to dinner to meet her fiancée. I don't know why I'm so surprised considering she can go weeks or even months without contacting me, but when something goes wrong, I'm the first person she calls.

"Hello?"

She is crying and begging me to come over. "I can't. Gotta work today."

"Please. I seriously need you, girl."

It's funny that she says that, but she doesn't ever just call to catch up anymore. What happened to us? It's obvious that something has gone wrong with them, but I'm so sick of being called upon by people who don't give me the same luxury. Would she come running if I called her crying? Now, a couple years ago, she would have, but something has changed since my divorce. Honestly, I thought with me being single, it would actually bring us closer together, but in fact, somehow it has pushed us farther apart. I don't even run through her mind anymore, and that's the catalyst. Why should I put someone else as a priority when I don't even make their list? A friendship should not be like that.

"Sorry, Britt. Gotta pay bills."

Is it wrong of me to want more? I don't think so. It's not like I'm expecting her to call me every day, but when it's constantly only when something happens to her, it gets old quickly. We both have lives and I get that, but being my best friend for many years, I know she has always been very self-centered. That will never likely change.

I put my cup in the sink, grab my keys, and head out the door. Why do Mondays suck so badly? It's not like we don't already know it's a work day, but it's the first one after a weekend away from the place, and they always seem to go terribly.

The drive is peaceful, not a lot of cars on the road since most of the traffic is parents dropping their kids off at school and it's after eight-thirty. When I pull into the parking lot, Jeremy's truck is not there, which means, I still have some time before they show up, and that gives me ample time to get another cup of coffee in me. No doubt, this is going to be a hard day for them, and I need to show my support. Hazel might not like me for whatever reason, but that's not going to deter me. I am positive she will like me once she gives me a chance, but today is all about them.

When the automatic doors open and I see the overnight nurse scrambling around, my heart drops. She is only like this when something has happened.

"What can I do? Who can I call?"

She looks up at me. "We need to call Jeremy."

My hand flies to my mouth. "No, it can't be. He was just... what happened?" I sit down, barely able to stand, and with what feels like a brick on my chest. How the hell am I going to tell them? They are set to be here at any point to see him. This is going to crush them.

"Very well. I will reach out to Don's next of kin. Leave that to me."

She nods, and I take out my phone. Not even deep breaths are going to help me in this situation. I don't want anyone to see me crying. I hit the dial icon, and it starts to ring.

"Good morning," he says, answering.

"Hey, Jeremy. I have some terrible news. Don passed away early this morning."

My head shakes, knowing this is going to change his whole life, and I did not want to be the person to have to break the news to him, but maybe it's better this way. Tears start to fall from my eyes as the words come out of my mouth. The only response I get is hearing the phone hit something, and I scream. "Jeremy, are you okay? Hello, Jeremy?"

The nurse runs into the office and is staring at me, eyes wide. "What's going on?"

I hear a voice from far away, and can't quite make out what she is saying until she gets closer. "Jeremy? Wake up."

I scream into the phone, hoping she can hear me, and she does.

"Hello?"

"Hazel, it's Raquel. Is he okay?"

"He's not answering me. What did you say to him?"

After his reaction, how the heck am I supposed to tell her? "Your father passed away early this morning."

She screams at the top of her lungs, and starts balling, and at this point, it's not appropriate to stay on the phone. Instead, I hang up and call an ambulance to his address. They will be able to properly check him out and make sure he is okay. This is an extremely emotional situation and sometimes can wreak havoc on the body. Stress can be difficult for the body to handle.

I'm worried about Jeremy, but there are things that need to be handled for Don. The nurse seems to be overwhelmed, and that's when I find out Don was not the only resident we lost while I was gone. The worst thing about this comes with the territory of the field I work in. We lose residents often, and I know our bosses will tell us not to let it affect us, but it does. We spend eight to ten hours a day in this building and some of these residents become almost like family. To feel nothing when someone passes seems disrespectful.

When my eyes opened this morning, I knew something was off about today, and I should have known something horrible was going to happen. We knew he didn't have long, but I didn't think it would be that soon.

There is nothing I can do for the Greys right now but give them their space. This day is going to be hard enough, and now Jeremy is in the hospital because whatever happened there, I will not reach out to him. Some might find that weird, but I think it's proper. After losing someone, the first few days are filled with crying and grief, and honestly, the last time it happened to me, I didn't want to talk to a single person, family or otherwise. The worst of it all is everyone checking up on me and telling me how sorry they were for the loss. Hell, I remember locking myself in the bedroom and not coming out for almost a week. Jeremy and Hazel may very well do the same.

19

JEREMY

*W*hite walls and alcohol crisp air are not how anyone wants to wake up. Yet, I do, and it freaks me out. I sit straight up, and see Hazel in the room's corner, turned with her back toward me on the phone.

"What the hell happened?"

She hears me and hangs up the phone. "I didn't know you were awake. Let me go get the doctor." She slips outside.

I grab my forehead, which is pounding against my skull, and then it hits me. The news about our father that caused me to collapse in the kitchen while Hazel was upstairs. Tears are already collecting in my eyes, and my chest gets tight. My hand gravitates to it, and Hazel is talking, but I can't hear a word she is saying. She rushes next to the bed, puts her hand on my shoulder, and then runs out the door. I close my eyes and try to steady my breathing, one at a time, in and out. After a couple of sets, I open my eyes to find a man and my sister staring at me.

"Hello, Mr. Grey. I'm Doctor Carlton. How are you feeling?" he asks.

"Like shit. I think I'm having a panic attack." I close my eyes again, trying to steady my nerves. "Our father just died and I kinda have other places I need to be. When can I go home?"

"Jeremy, you suffered a heart attack. After some tests, it appears you might have some blockage that is causing your heart to only function at seventy percent of its capacity."

I've had no health problems in my life. "What the hell does that mean?"

"Well, you will need to be scheduled for a heart cath. This will help us get rid of the blockage and put in a stint to help rejuvenate the heart back to its full capacity. Or so, that's our hope."

Doctors and hospitals aren't my favorite place to be, and I'd just like to be back home. There are too many things that need to be taken care of with my dad's passing, and I can't do that if I'm stuck in this fucking hospital.

"How long will the heart cath take? Can I go home after that?" I ask the questions going through my head, because staying the night here is not an option.

"As long as everything goes well, you will go home tonight. A heart cath is an outpatient procedure."

I nod, and he leaves the room.

"What can I do?" Hazel asks.

There are no words to describe the pain in my heart right now. Knowing that I can never hear his voice, talk to him, or just hang out on the couch watching action movies ever again. He's gone forever. How am I supposed to come to terms with that?

This isn't the place to be right now, and I want to be back in my house in my own fucking bed. I just need to remain calm while I'm here, and get this operation done and over with, that's all.

Hazel walks over and puts her hand on my shoulder. "Let's get this operation done and then we can deal with the loss. Right now, here, I have to keep myself together."

Hazel has always been a pretty reserved person with emotions, and sometimes I think it's going to affect her negatively. If she would just open up and let them out, this is going to go a lot smoother. I'm the prime example of not letting things bottled up inside you, or something like this happens.

"He was a good man, sis. I promise you he knows how thankful we were to him, and how much we loved him."

I know she doesn't want to talk about it here, but I need to. She needs to hear this. I know what she's doing. Beating herself up because she didn't stay longer the other day, and that's only going to make things worse, and guilt is not something she needs on her plate right now.

"I'll take care of the arrangements. Dad left us instructions. Leave it to me, okay?"

She nods, and even though she is not crying, I know this is affecting her more than she is leading on. I remember how she was when she arrived back in Grapevine. The coming days are going to be rough for all of us, but the arrangements still have to be made, regardless. Planning your parent's funeral is not something I ever planned to do, but you don't always get it your way. At least, I know he lived a happy life, with a wonderful wife, two kids who adored him, and a job he loved. Many people strive for the excellence our dad achieved, and sometimes never find it.

I don't want to end up alone and unhappy, but right now I need to focus on the things my father left for me. Hazel might be acting like she's okay, but I know better. Things aren't going to get done by themselves.

20

RAQUEL

Grief comes in many forms, and Jeremy hasn't reached out to me since his father's passing. I had to call Tessa to get word if he was okay after the phone call incident. He is going through a rough time, and I don't want to overstep boundaries, but he has answered none of my calls or texts.

He is supposed to be by to get his father's thing today, but he might not be ready. With it only being a few days, he may need more time. There has been no word on the funeral arrangements, and I hope he will reach out to me to let me know. I might not have known Donald long, but being there to pay my respects means a lot to me.

My eyes keep peering over to the doors, waiting for him to arrive. What do I even say? There are no words to express my sadness for the Grey family. I hope Hazel is helping him, and not letting him bottle everything up inside. If he would just talk to me, then maybe I could help.

"Hey."

Jeremy is standing in front of me, disheveled. It looks like he hasn't showered in days, scruff on his face, and is still in sweats.

"I'll go grab his things for you," Kristin responds, giving us a moment alone.

"I've tried reaching out."

He runs his hands through his hair and then tugs at his shirt. "I don't want to talk to anyone right now. It's just too much. Going through his things, dealing with the life insurance and will. And planning the funeral. I just want to be left alone."

His eyes don't meet mine, but I can see the tears dripping onto his shirt. I want to embrace him, and let him know I care, but there's so much distance between us.

"It looks like there is a couple of boxes. Would you like us to help you carry them to your vehicle?" Kristen asks.

He nods, and takes the first box from her, and I badge him out, holding the second box in my hands. Even by the way he walks, the depression has started, and it's going to take some time to deal with it.

"Here is that card, if you change your mind." I slip a card into the middle console of his truck and touch his shoulder.

No response from him. He just gets in his truck and leaves.

Tonight is dinner at Tessa's, and maybe they can shed some light on Jeremy for me. I don't want to pry, but he needs someone on his side. Leaving him alone can cause more problems. Is anyone helping him with arranging these things? Where is Hazel?

Once my shift is over, I head over to the house to relieve the babysitter. Upon walking in, Lily is already dressed and ready to go.

"Give me a minute to put on jeans, baby girl."

I go to my closet and slip on some dark jeans and plain white t-shirt. "Okay, now we can go."

Tessa and I usually get together once a month, but she invited us over for something special tonight. She didn't have to tell me over the phone, I could just tell. Good news, I hope.

Lily sings to the radio the entire way to Tessa's and then runs inside without even so much as knocking. I've taught her better than that.

"Sorry about her. You know how she gets when she's excited."

Damon shakes his head. "She's family at this point. No worries."

I walk past him and take a seat next to Tessa. She is resting while the potatoes are boiling.

"Girl, you look great."

"No need to lie. I feel like a beached whale."

She takes my hand and puts it on her stomach, asking to see if I can feel the baby kick. It's always a miracle when you think about it. How do our bodies grow a living thing inside of it?

"So, did he come get Don's stuff today?" Tessa asks.

I nod and leave my hand on her belly.

"He hasn't been to work, which is to be expected, but he hasn't answered one of Damon's calls. Aiden said that Hazel hasn't gotten out of bed since Jeremy got home from the hospital."

Maybe I should just go over there and check on them. I know he doesn't want to see anybody, but there could be something I could do to take something off his plate. He needs to grieve without having to deal with all the extra stuff. Hazel seems to be no help from what Tessa is saying.

"You mind watching Lily for an hour? I'll be back for dinner, just gonna run over to his house and check on them. It'll make me feel better knowing that they at least have food and stuff."

Tessa nods, and I get back in my car and drive over to Jeremy's.

From the outside, it doesn't look like anyone's home besides his truck being in the driveway. All the lights seem to be off. I knock on the door, but get no response from anyone inside. So, I pull out my phone and dial Jeremy. No answer.

Me: I'm at your front door. Please let me in. Just for a minute.

I wait for the three dots, but they never show up. Footsteps are coming down the stairs and then I hear the door unlock.

"What do you want?" he asks, grimacing at the light from the sun.

"Can I come in for a minute, please?"

He opens the door, and I slip inside. I want to give him a moment, but I throw my arms around him and hold on tight. He needs someone to be there for him.

"Raquel, I don't want you to see me like this." He pushes me away, and turns around with his back facing me.

I grab his arm and pull until we lock eyes. "I will not let you go through this alone. You hear me."

His eyes water, and he embraces me. He sobs into my t-shirt, and I let him. If he doesn't let these emotions out, then it's going to eat away at him. Depression is nothing to fuck around with.

"Your father was a wonderful man, and he was proud of you and your sister. Never doubt that, Jeremy. He talked about you guys all the time to the residents."

He continues to cry, and I tell him about the brief service they had at the center for Donald. Residents talked about what they will miss about him, and some even talked about how he had impacted their lives, telling them to reach out to their estranged kids.

"The funeral is tomorrow. I haven't been able to tell anyone. Every time I pull up a number, I start fucking crying."

I take his phone and the list he has sitting on the counter. "I'll make the calls. You go lay down and get some rest."

He nods and saunters up the stairs to his bedroom.

In this very moment, I love Jeremy Grey. He is a handsome, caring man who never puts himself first, and maybe it's time for that change.

Put yourself first.

21

JEREMY

*N*othing could have prepared me for today. I long for just one last conversation with my father. I don't know how to move on without him. Parents raise us to be independent and a person of society that they can be proud of, and I hope I became that person.

I don't want to get out of bed, but with the funeral happening soon, I must. Am I up to hearing everyone's condolences? No, but my father deserves to have a nice sendoff surrounded by people who loved and cared for him.

Today is going to be the hardest of them all. It's the last time my father will be above ground, and I know people visit their loved ones, but I've always found that to be weird. Preference, I guess.

A knock sounds on the door, and for a minute, I forget Raquel stayed with me last night. About two in the morning, I went downstairs to get a drink, and she had fallen asleep on the couch. Many would run at a time like this, but she pushed through my walls and wanted to help me. I commend her for that.

"You up?" she asks, through the door.

I open it up and smile. "Good morning. You didn't have to stay."

She takes my hand and leads me down the stairs and to the kitchen table. "I made you breakfast. You'll need energy. Eat up."

Raquel sits down next to me, and we enjoy each other's company while eating our meal. My eyes peer over the kitchen, and I notice that she has removed all the idle things on the counter and did the dishes. I'm not proud of how dirty the house became, but I couldn't bring myself to do anything but lay in bed.

"You are coming today, right?"

Her fork clanks against the plate. "I wouldn't miss it. You know I cared for your father."

What if no one shows up to the funeral? I shouldn't have waited to get the word out, but couldn't bring myself to call anyone. Now I know why people have someone else doing it in the movies. It's tougher than you think.

"I'm gonna go get dressed, and then I need to call Hazel and check on her."

She nods. "I'll go home and change. The babysitter should be there to watch Lily. Damon and Tessa have agreed to keep her after the funeral if you need company."

I want to push her away and just wallow in my grief, but she is a good woman who is doing everything to make me as comfortable as possible during this difficult time. She hasn't asked me how I'm doing, says she's sorry, nothing. It's refreshing since that's all anyone has been saying since his passing. I'm sick of hearing it.

I pull my black slacks up over my waist, and then a button-down navy shirt around my shoulders. The anxiety of having to be in front of who knows how many people today is overwhelming. I've never been the guy to cry in public, but today might be a different story. It's the last goodbye.

I look at the clock and it's a quarter to noon, and I still haven't heard from Hazel or Aiden. She must be up and moving around by now. The phone rings, but no one ever picks up. Fuck it, I'm going over to Aiden's.

I rush downstairs, pick up my keys, and rush out to my truck, knowing we only have an hour until the funeral. Hazel can't pull this shit today. We have to get ourselves together because people are going to be in our face all day, and we are going to need each other today more than ever.

Aiden's truck is outside his house, so I know they are home, but when I knock nobody comes to the door. What the hell is going on? I turn the knob and it's unlocked.

"Hazel? Aiden?" I say, announcing my presence before walking into the house itself.

I hear them in the bedroom, and it sounds like they are fighting.

"Get dressed. We are going to be late," Aiden says.

I walk closer to the door, and he jumps a little when he sees me. "What are you doing here?"

"I knocked several times, but no one answered. Got worried."

He nudges me into the kitchen. "Your sister won't get dressed. I've tried. Your turn."

Maybe this is hitting her heavier than me, or maybe I just haven't begun to fully deal with his death yet, but she is going to the funeral. She is sadly mistaken if she thinks I'm going to be there by myself.

"It's time to get your ass up and put on some clothes. They are expecting us at the church in twenty-minutes," I say, pulling back the covers and forcing her out of bed.

She does a low growl and walks to the closet, pulling out a black dress and flats. "How are we supposed to smile and nod at people all afternoon?"

Hazel needs to remember we are doing this for our father, not us. This is what he wanted and said so in his will. We are to respect his last wishes. "We just do. You can lock yourself in the house after today, but attending is not optional."

I leave the room to give her some privacy to change and sit down next to Aiden on the couch. He must have a hard time dealing with Hazel. This could be a test in their relationship. and how he handles it will determine whether they are together long term.

"Okay, I'm ready. Let's go."

I go back out to my truck and lead the way to the church. With only a day's notice, I do not know what to expect today, and if people will even be attending. My father was a good man, and he touched a lot of lives.

When we get to the church, there are already people standing outside, and I brush past them to meet with the Pastor. I don't know if we are supposed to go over anything beforehand or not.

"Good afternoon. Did you need anything from us?" I ask, just wanting to start the ceremony.

"No, sir. Everything is ready to go. If you and your sister would like to have a seat, we have someone to usher them inside to the pews."

I wave at Hazel and Aiden to come inside, and we go to the front pew, which has a sign that says Reserved for Family. My nose burns, and I can feel the tears ambushing me, but I push them down.

Hazel takes my hand, and she is already balling and trying to compose herself before they open the doors.

"It's me and you. We will get through today together, okay?" I say.

A gentleman opens the church doors, and people spill in, more than I could imagine. By the time they shut the doors, almost every single pew is filled with residents coming to say goodbye to our father. Most of them I do not recognize.

"Would you like me to sit next to you?" Raquel whispers in my ear, from the pew behind us.

I nod, and she makes her way next to me and takes my other hand. The overwhelming sense of support from her during this time is something I could never imagine. One can only hope that Aiden is providing Hazel with support as well.

The pastor welcomes everyone to the service.

"We are here today to pay our tribute and our respect to a man of God, our brother, Donald Grey. Many have come who have respected Jeremy as a teacher and friend. We are here today to show our love and support for Donald's family. Our hearts ache over this situation and we are not too proud to say we have come here today trusting that God will give us the strength to move forward after this substantial loss."

Everyone in the audience is nodding, and Hazel is wailing,

sending echoes across the church. I clench my teeth, trying to get mine under wraps until after the ceremony, but I fear it's going to be harder with her next to me.

"It is human nature for us to want to understand everything, and why he was taken from us so soon, but God has called him home to be part of a bigger plan. I'd like to take this time to allow anyone to come forward that would like to say something in Donald's honor."

I raise my hand and begin the walk up to the podium. You can do this. It's your last chance to say what you want to say to him. Even if he can't hear it.

"When we think of Donald, we think about the sacrifices he has made for his students, his children, and most of all himself. He was a honorable man who would give anyone the shirt off his back if they needed it. He volunteered for many years at the soup kitchen at this church, and this is something he wished he could continue to do once they diagnosed him."

I keep my head down, staring at the podium, and not looking out into the foyer because if I do, I might not finish.

"He devoted a good portion of his adulthood to his marriage with Regina. He loved her deeply and even after she passed, he couldn't bring himself to be with anyone else. It is our human nature to want to understand why this happened, but I hope that he is somewhere looking down on us, reunited with Regina, and having the time of his life."

Everyone claps as I sit back down next to Raquel and bring her hand into my lap. The pastor asks if anyone else would like to say any words, and a man raised his hand.

"Donald Grey has always been an idol in my mind. You might not know me, but I can assure you that I would not be here standing before you today with my success if he had not believed in me. When my grades started slipping after my mother's death, he took it upon himself to nurture me, tutor me, and make sure that I did not fail his class. Most teachers wouldn't give up their free time, but Mr. Grey wanted each of his students to succeed. And because of that, I am now the CEO of a major pharmaceutical company. My prayers go out to his kids, but need I remind you, your father was a remarkable man and one can only hope that we will continue to honor his memory for many decades to come."

The pastor says some final words, and Hazel couldn't wait to get out of there. She rushes out before anyone else leaves, and I do what the Pastor tells me, stand at the back of the room, and shake hands as people leave.

"Are you ready to get out of here?" Raquel asks, looking around the room. There are still many people left waiting to talk to me, and right now, I need some fresh air. I take her hand and escape outside, closing my eyes and just letting the sun hit my face.

Things like this make you realize how little time we have, and that putting things off or not taking control of your life can be detrimental to your happiness. I might have thought I couldn't pursue a relationship while taking care of my dad, but that wasn't it. Deep down, I've feared getting my heart broken or torn to pieces. You can't find love that way. Guarding my heart, and making excuses is only going to make matters worse, and prevent me from finding my true happiness.

It might not be the best timing, but I need to be straightforward with Raquel and put my heart on the line. It's time to put myself first and start planning for my future. If this has taught me anything, it's that life is short, and I don't want to be alone anymore.

She is standing next to me, just letting me calm down for a moment, but I don't want to wait. I might sound crazy, but I'm going for it.

"Can we talk?"

She nods and gives me her full attention.

"You know we are both attracted to each other, and that was apparent at Damon's party, right? You wanted me to make sure that the way I feel isn't because of the situations going on, and they aren't."

"Jer-,"

"No, Raquel. You can't talk me out of it this time. I'm sick of tiptoeing around the fact that I'm madly in love with you. The only person I want to get through life with is you. Nobody else. We both deserve happiness, and that's our future. If only you would say yes to going out with me for real this time, and we can start our happiness today."

She stays quiet for a few moments, which scares the ever loving shit out of me, thinking maybe she isn't ready. So many things have kept us apart, but it's time to move those things out of the way. I want to make her happy.

"Yes. A thousand times, yes."

22

RAQUEL

My chest rises and falls, trying to decide what I should wear. It's our first official date, and I want to wear something super sexy. He is taking me to some fancy restaurant, and I only have a couple of dresses that will even work for that type of establishment. So the question is: red, black, or purple? Which one would he like better? I take the red one off the hanger and step into it, zipping it up the side, and turning in the mirror. This is the one.

Tessa arrives back in the bedroom carrying a shot glass. "Drink up. It'll cut the nerves."

I tilt my head back and take it like a champ. "Thanks, girl. I appreciate you watching Lily for me."

"You forget that I'm here for you. Plus, I'm sure I'll need you to babysit for Damon and I once this little munchkin makes their debut into the world."

Tessa has always been quite forthcoming with the fact she wants more kids, and Damon too. It's a pleasure to see him around Emily, and how he treats her like his own. For the longest time, I didn't know that she wasn't his, but Tessa told me all about his first wife and their struggles.

"I'll babysit anytime. You know I love kids. I wouldn't be opposed to more."

She sits on the bed, while I line my eyes, and then laughs. "Have you guys ever talked about kids before? Like, does he want them?"

Good point. I remember kids coming up in a conversation, and he said he would love a family. I still guard my walls in some respect for that subject though, because I wouldn't ever want to make another child grow up in separate households. It's hard enough for Lily. Not that I think Jeremy would ever do to me what he did.

"He wants a family."

Tessa and I are always having conversations about our lives, and our futures, and that's one thing that we can agree on. Not the perfect family, but a happy family unit. We want better for our kids than what we had growing up. Our parents were horrible, but we went without a lot, and I never wish that upon my kids.

"Also, I just want to say I told you so. They made you and Jeremy for each other. All other obstacles would move aside, and you guys would get your chance. Not to say more won't pop up, cause they will, but you guys will get through them."

Emily and Lily are sitting in the living room playing some blocks game while Tessa helps me get ready. She picks out some black wedges, not too tall but not so short, and hands them to me.

"Comfortable yet sexy. Are you still nervous?" she asks.

"Yes, but in a good way."

Who isn't nervous about a first date? The difference is Jeremy and I know each other, and it's not like it's a blind date or set up. The chemistry is off the charts. We are both looking for someone to settle down with, and have a family. Our goals are mutual, and that makes this even more exciting. There is no guessing or awkward first date questions because I already know the answers. All we have to do is enjoy each other's company.

The doorbell rings, and the girls run. "Let Tessa get it, Lily. You don't open the door for anyone, remember?"

She nods, and Tessa opens the door, and Jeremy steps inside.

"Hey, ladies. He hands all three of them a single rose, and then walks over to me and gives me a tulip. "This one is for you."

Jeremy is killing it in those black pants and blue button up. The muscles in his arms almost busting out of the shirt. It's getting hot in here. I fan myself. How did I get so damn lucky to have this man vying for my attention?

Lily walks up to Jeremy and hugs his waist.

"What was that for, sweetie?"

"Sorry about your daddy."

He hugs her back and lets her get back to playing their game. Tessa winks at me, and I say my goodbyes before heading out to Jeremy's truck.

"Don't have too much fun!"

His hand stays on the small of my back until he opens the door for me to get inside and closes it behind me. I don't know how I'm going to keep myself from jumping his bones tonight. The pants aren't too tight, but I'm happy to say the outline of his cock is visible, and it's not helping the situation. Good thing I won't be able to see that since we will sit at a table. It will keep it out of sight, keeping my dirty mind under wraps.

"I'm glad you could find someone to watch Lily tonight. Do we have a curfew?" he asks, laughing.

"Midnight."

"That gives me four hours to enjoy the night with you. By the way, don't be surprised if all the men at the restaurant are staring at you tonight. Hell, I almost pushed you into your bedroom when I walked in."

I smile, and inch a little closer to him, being careful not to hit the shifter in between our seats and whisper in his ear. "I'm up for dessert first, if you are."

His eyes meet mine, and then his footsteps on the gas, make a right turn and before I know it we are in his driveway. I didn't think he would deter from eating dinner first, but I'm not one to complain.

He walks over and opens my door, extending his hand to help me out, and then walks to the door. Jeremy takes out his key, twists it and opens the door, leading me inside.

"Don't worry. No one else is here." He locks the door, cups me in his arms, and carries me upstairs.

I laugh as the nervousness sets in. It's been way too long since I've had someone touch me, and what if the chemistry doesn't uphold in the bedroom? Shouldn't we wait a bit before going this far?

He opens his door and sets me down. "Are you sure about this?"

Fuck it, I'm a grown ass woman who has needs, and I will not turn down a man that looks like him. I nod and unzip my dress when he pushes me up against the wall, mouth on mine, and his hand inches up my thigh. *Fuck.* He moves my panties to the side and starts rubbing my clit with his thumb, and electricity shoots through my body. I arch my leg up on his hip, and he uses his other hand to hold it there. I try to hold back, because I don't want to come too fast. Hell no, I want to enjoy this moment for as long as I can. Foreplay is my favorite part of an evening.

"Tonight is all about us, Raquel. You tell me what you want, and I'll oblige. Happily."

His thumb goes faster, and I'm spilling over, so I pull him toward me, kiss him, and then whisper in his ear. "Eat me."

He smiles, and crouches down, my dress being held up around my breasts as he inches my underwear down around my wedges and I step out of them. My hands are on top of his head and the anticipation of feeling his tongue has me on edge, but first he bites my inner thigh and makes me cry out. "Fuck it! Never mind."

I pull him up, undo his belt, and drop his pants. As much as I'd love for him to take me over the edge with his tongue, all I want is him deep inside me, making me beg for more.

"I thought you'd never ask."

He pulls his boxers down, hikes my leg, and inches inside me, almost making me combust right there on the spot. His lips are on my neck and he starts out slow, but I'm not someone who likes it slow and steady. I rock my hips faster, and he just stares into my eyes, looking deep within my soul while we help each other reach the top.

He fills all of me, and as much as I don't want to move, I know how I want to finish. So, I push him off of me, walk to the bed, and get on all fours, giving him the best view of my ass and all its glory. He doesn't move but strokes himself, and enjoys while I wiggle my ass in the air for him.

"Like what you see?" I ask, looking back at him.

"Shit, I don't even want to move right now." Jeremy pulls out a condom from his bedside table and slips it on. "But it's not gentlemanly to keep a woman waiting, now is it?"

He slams into me with force, making me cry out again. He grabs my hair and tugs on it as he crashes into me. "Never thought you would be a doggy girl. I have to admit your ass is my next favorite thing after your eyes." He slaps it, and it sends me over the edge, throwing me into a whirlwind of ecstasy, and he continues slamming into me until I feel him still.

I don't know why I doubted our chemistry. This has been the best fucking sex I've ever had.

He rolls over and lays down on the pillow, pulling me into him. "I'm not sure how I'm supposed to not want that every night now. Fuck. You are all I need."

I lay there in his arms, relishing because we could have been enjoying this weeks ago, but we let others sway us away from each other. Never again.

"So, not that I wouldn't love to lie here until midnight to recuperate, but I'm fucking starving now," he says, kissing the top of my head.

"Let's go eat. I think we earned it."

23

JEREMY

The view of her ass in the air as she crawls to the edge of the bed and gets off is spectacular, and if I'm lucky enough to be with this woman for the rest of my life, I'll count my blessings every fucking day. Tonight is just a little taste of our lives together, and I can't wait to show her more.

She zips her dress back up and searches for her underwear, which somehow ended up across the room. I might have gotten a little too excited when she whispered in my ear, but what man wouldn't? Especially, someone that hasn't touched a woman in almost two years. One-night stands aren't my thing, and once dad was diagnosed, I never had time to pursue anything romantic.

I put my boxers and pants back on and look at her. Her curls are all disheveled, and you can tell we just made love. I'll enjoy being able to relish that fact over dinner tonight. Did I have any clue that the evening would start like this? No, but it exceeds my expectations and now I am going to daydream about it all the time.

We head downstairs and out the door, ready to replenish our bodies and fuel our energy. Passion is something hard to find, but most overlook it because they are so caught up in sex. Passion and chemistry make the intimate act of sex so mind blowing, and can take it to a whole new level. Raquel and I have wonderful chemistry and that's how I knew that our sex life would be off the charts. We are comfortable with each other, and have already built an emotional connection before jumping into bed together. I prefer it that way. Call me old-fashioned.

"So, do you think you'll be staying in Grapevine now?" I ask, knowing she had tiptoed around the question last time.

"I'm not going anywhere."

This puts my mind at ease, and grabs her hand for the rest of the drive over to the restaurant. It's time to take my life into my own hands and allow myself to find happiness.

When we arrive at the restaurant, we missed our reservation, but it doesn't seem too busy. So, they allow us to get a table, anyway.

"This place is beautiful. Didn't even know it existed."

"Most people don't. Not a lot of fine diners in Grapevine besides for anniversaries."

The waitress takes our order and we decide on the steak and shrimp. Hell, you can't ever go wrong with steak, right? I order a bottle of Chardonnay, which Tessa informed me is Raquel's favorite wine.

"Here's to our first date of many."

We clink glasses and take a sip.

Things have been hard since word of my dad's passing, but I'm doing what he would've wanted. He was a big believer in true love and always said it would present itself along with obstacles and we just needed to be level-headed enough to fight through them. At first, with her brother and my sister on our case, it seemed like they took our chance from us from the very beginning, but I knew our love story was going to prevail. As weird as it is to say, the moment I laid eyes on her in that backyard, I knew she was the best me for me. As much as I have always been against love at first sight, it only seems fitting it would happen to me. Make me a believer, and now here I sit in front of her, just had one of the best nights of my life, and we have chosen each other. Any obstacle that stands in our way from this day forward, we fight through and always come out on the other side stronger than before.

"How's Hazel managing?"

She is heartbroken. Her bosses aren't very pleased, but they will get over it. She has given up a lot to win them cases, and they need to recognize that. It's all business for them. Raquel doesn't seem to like that, and it's a fair assessment.

"Has Aiden been helping?" she asks, looking at me while chewing her steak.

"He's gotten better. I think the loss of my father also dredged up his father's death, and it put them both in a dark place."

Things have been difficult and I can't expect Hazel to be at the top of her game. The only man that had ever believed in us is gone, and that's something that is going to hurt us every day, but we must continue to live our lives and make him proud.

I still lay awake at night in that big empty house, just waiting to hear him call out my name, or hear explosions downstairs from the latest action movie he would have on, but it never comes. Just the silence, which makes it unbearable sometimes.

Raquel takes my hand and grabs my attention. "I know you are going through a rough time right now, and I'm happy that you wanted to go out tonight, but don't push the grief deep inside, please?"

I nod. "I've been having trouble sleeping, and not sure if I'm ready to go back to work next week. This last week has just been a lot to take in."

"Jeremy, you are a strong man, but losing a parent is as tough as it gets, and everyone will understand if you need more time. Don't rush yourself."

Tonight is not supposed to be sad, and we are approaching subjects that might make me cry, and I'm not a fan of doing that in public.

"Let's hurry and finish so we can get out of here."

I raise my hand to get the waiter's attention for our check, and drop a hundred-dollar bill inside the billfold.

She gets up and follows beside me. "I didn't mean to upset you."

"You didn't. Just talking about him... it makes me emotional, and being like that in public. I'm just ready to be out of there."

I take her hand and help her into my truck, but before opening my door, I let a few tears out. No one can expect me not to be emotional right now, and that's the only reason I felt comfortable taking Raquel out tonight. She knows what I'm going through, and will understand if I break down.

She tells me to pull over, and I do as she asks. "Look at me. You don't have to be strong for me. It's my job to be there for you right now, and I can't do that if you are holding everything in."

I keep my eyes locked on hers, contemplating whether I am going to contain myself long enough to drop her off, but I can't. The tears flow, and as embarrassing as it is, it feels right. I shouldn't feel this way about grieving my father, because he was a good man, who would have done anything for us, and all I can hope is that one day, I can be half the father he was.

"You never have to hide how you feel from me. Ever. For this to work, we have to be open and honest with each other in all aspects of our lives. Okay?" she says, cupping my chin and looking into my eyes.

I nod, and lean into her, and just let myself cry. Sometimes, I don't think I've ever felt this comfortable with someone, and it only solidifies the fact that she is my person.

"I love you."

The words come out of my mouth before I have a chance to think about the impact it could have on our relationship. She didn't say it back the first time I said it, and maybe it's because we were caught up in the moment, or she just isn't there yet, which is fine. It doesn't change the fact that I'm madly in love with her, and I shouldn't worry about telling her that.

She kisses my lips. "I love you, Jeremy Grey."

SAVOR ME

BOOK 5

1

VANESSA

$\mathcal{T}$he wind whips my hair around as Sherrie gets out of the car. Sweat drips down my forehead, and I take in the other houses on the block, hoping this is a good neighborhood for my daughter. The light blue cottage with white shutters and a black front door isn't what I would've picked, but it's all my budget affords. My daughter and I are starting all over, and until recently I never had to worry about things like paying rent, buying groceries, or making a car payment. I'm not some spoiled rich girl that comes from money either.

Sherrie has expressed no concern over us moving out of her dad's house, but I'm sure it's coming. The first night is usually the hardest, and I'm not prepared to answer any questions. Standing here, though, it's official. The last ten years are behind me, and I'm single again. It scares me to even think about it. Starting over, moving into this little two-bedroom house with Sherrie is making things surreal. I never would have pictured myself as being a single mother, but sometimes things don't work out how you want. Life happens and throws us curve balls. It's up to us to forge our own path.

Leaving a long-term relationship is always difficult, no matter the circumstances, but ten years is a long time to be with someone. It will be an adjustment getting used to being alone, but it offers up far more opportunities. There are many things I need to work out about myself and why I let a relationship go on ten years without speaking up for myself. That's the kicker.

The moving truck roars down the street and pulls over on the street. There isn't enough room in the driveway. Four men get out of the vehicle and the driver goes to the back and discharges the ramp.

"Are you ready for us to start, ma'am?" he asks before removing anything.

The white gate around the house opens when I unlatch, and Sherrie and Tina follow behind. The front yard isn't huge, but it's decent, with a walkway up to the steps that lead up to the porch. The man is standing at the back of the truck. I'm going to move at my pace. Tina and I saunter up the stairs, and then put the key in the door and twist. Sherrie pushes the door open and runs inside.

"Don't run!"

There is no decor on the walls, and it's hardwood throughout, from what I can see. I prefer no carpet. After watching a video one time with a microscopic image of how much nastiness they leave in carpets, even after cleaning them regularly, I want no part in it.

Not even seventy-two hours ago, the entire course of my life changed with just one conversation. Lee isn't a bad man, and it's not all his fault. I'm adult enough to admit we are both responsible for our relationship falling apart. What concerns me the most is how Sherrie is going to take it? Lee and I plan on sitting down with her tomorrow to explain the situation. Our only concern is for her to be aware that it's not her fault. I never hoped to have my child grow up in separate homes.

Staring at the empty beige walls in the living room reminds me of a blank canvas, just waiting to be turned into a masterpiece. Everyone envisions their house differently. Some say I have an eye for design, but I only dabble. Time just never allowed me to make it a career. My priority is Sherrie and always will be.

The built-in shelves for an entertainment center are perfect and that's one thing marked off my list to buy. Once all the furniture is in place, the list will dwindle down.

The movers start bringing things in, and we try to stay out of the way. Tina is clearly enjoying the view, and can't say I blame her. It's not a sin to stare, but she would never cheat on her husband. They have had their fair shares of problems, but doesn't any couple? The only thing matters is they are happy.

"You can put the kitchen boxes on the island," I say.

The house has top notch Stainless Steel appliances and a nice sized granite island. It's the centerpiece of the kitchen that really makes it pop with speckles of blue and gold, and compliments the backsplash while bringing the entire room together.

At the previous house, I spent a majority of my time at home in the kitchen, on a humongous island, baking goodies for Sherrie's softball fundraisers or school parties. I wouldn't say I'm the best baker, but Sherrie enjoys helping. It's something we bond over and have a little bit of fun. It is one joy of being a mother. Getting to be the one to put a smile on your little one's face. "Which room is mine?" Sherrie asks, standing at the end of the hallway, with a door on both sides of her.

"The one on the right, sweetie."

I walk down the hallway, and open my bedroom door, and imagine a king sized bed against the far wall, and the window letting the natural light in as I wake up every morning. Tina walks in after me, and takes it in. It's smaller than I'm used to, but it'll do. The attached bathroom has a tub and a shower, and the closet has built-ins for all my clothes and shoes. The closets are my favorite thing about this house other than the windows.

Tina follows me back outside to finish bringing boxes in from the car, and putting them in their respective rooms. It's going to take a couple days to unpack, and get everything where it belongs. I moved around a lot as a kid, to a different house every year, and hope I manage to keep this house for a while. Sherrie needs a stable living environment and I plan to give that to her.

Tina hasn't once asked about the break-up, but it's coming. A ten-year relationship has ended, and we didn't take it lightly, but I need to be careful what I say around Sherrie. The problems between her father and I are just that. Kids always think it's something they've done to tear their parents apart, and Sherrie will need reassurance that she is not the cause.

The house we lived in with Lee across town is similar to this one, except it had more bedrooms and square footage. Lee did offer to help me, but I think of this as a fresh start and want to do it by myself. It's one thing if he wants to help with things involving Sherrie, but putting a roof over my head is not acceptable.

Like I said, he's a nice guy, and doesn't want me to struggle, but maybe I need to. Being attached to him for so long has caused me to lose touch with the world. So many people struggle to make ends meet, and from a young twenty-year-old, Lee has always taken good care of me. It's time for me to learn how to be independent.

Lee and I spent too many years being complacent towards each other, but like many other couples do, we stayed together for our child. Complacency isn't something I want in a relationship. The minute you stop speaking your mind, and fighting for what you want, is the moment things are going to start downhill. Relationships take work and compromise. Finally, we agreed that we both deserved better. Too bad it took ten years. Lee isn't the person I'm meant to be with, but now I have a chance of being happy with someone else.

I head back outside to grab another box, and Tina is leaning up against the car.

"What?"

She crosses her arms. "Are you going to tell me what's going on? What happened between you two? This is insane."

After being best friends for almost fifteen years, we talk about almost everything, but discussing my relationships with her isn't typical. So, it makes sense this is a shock. Tina always said that we were #couplegoals. I guess we are just very good at putting on a show for others.

The separation gives me the opportunity to process what I want out of a partner and it's important that I do so before engaging in a conversation with Tina. She is trying to look out for me, and it's sweet, but right now I don't have all the answers.

She grabs a box and follows after me. "I'm just saying. You just had dinner with Aaron and I two weeks ago, and you guys were fine."

I let the box fall out of my hands onto the hardwood. "Stop asking me. I don't want to talk about it right now. Please. Give it a rest."

Tina's eyes get big, and she sets her box down. "Sorry, I'll stop. Just concerned."

I note her concern, but right now I need some time and space. It's not like he cheated on me, or abused me. We just fell out of love, or never really were. Love is something that can't be measured.

The movers continue to bring in furniture, and I direct them where everything goes, and that takes a bit more stress off my back. Lee let me take some of the furniture that I picked out when we moved into our original house when Sherrie was born. At first, I told him I didn't want to take anything, but he made a good point. If we were married, I'd be getting 50% of everything.

Lee won't use half the money he earns in his lifetime. With us gone, he will probably work until midnight and never find someone else if he doesn't change. His work has always been a big component of our issues, but it also let us have a certain lifestyle.

When Sherrie was first born, he took two weeks off of work, and helped tremendously, but once he went back, things shifted and never got better. He worked constantly, no matter if we were on vacation or sitting at home. The firm had taken over his life, and we were just background pieces for him to move around.

It doesn't mean he's a negligent parent, and someone might be okay with being in the background, but I'm not. I want someone who wants to rush home from work to be next to me, not come home at midnight, give me a kiss on the cheek, and go to bed. We were more like roommates than anything.

"Anything else you need, ma'am?" one mover asks.

I shake my head, hand him some money for a tip, and he closes the door behind him.

The living room is not big by any means, maybe 400 square feet, and the loveseat fits snugly against the wall. It just leaves just enough room for my cherry oak side tables that were passed down to me from my mother. The size is adequate for just Sherrie and I. We don't need anything extravagant.

This new lifestyle will take some getting used to, because before now I never paid attention to my bank account before swiping my card. Sherrie depends on me now, and things like groceries, utilities, and rent are now at the forefront of my mind. I barely bring home two grand a month. Hairdressers aren't exactly rolling in the dough, but I have loyal clients.

"That's all the boxes," Tina says, taking a seat on the couch, catching her breath.

"I'd offer you a drink, but we have nothing in the fridge yet," I say.

"Why don't we go grab some lunch and then do some shopping?" Tina suggests.

I know I've worked up an appetite and Sherrie has never been one to turn down food. "Come on, sweetie. We're leaving for a bit."

She comes running down the hall and straight out the door. "Can we go to the diner? Pancakes, please?"

Grapevine is a nice little town that I've grown to love, but when I was a child, I dreamed of living in a big city. The schools here are fantastic, and there isn't a lot of crime. It's a place where the kids can walk to the bus stop without getting abducted. In a big city, not so much. Lee tried to talk me into moving to Dallas a couple of times, but it wasn't the best decision for Sherrie.

"The diner it is."

Am I worried about how my daughter is going to handle the move? Yes, but at some point I have to be honest with myself, and leaving Lee is the best decision I made. Now, I have a real chance of finding someone who will give me what I want and more. Sherrie might not understand it now, but in the long run, it's best for both her mother and father to be happy, even if it's not with each other.

Sometimes staying in a relationship for the children does more harm than good.

2

BRODIE

A dispatcher alerts the crew of an emergency on Stratford Ave and the alarm blares inside the station. I shove my feet into the fire-proof steel-toed boots, and snap the suspenders against my shoulder as I pull on my fire retardant pants. Thick gloves slide over my calloused hands as I rush to get all my gear on. Heavy boots run across the floor to get into the truck as Damon jumps in the driver's seat, and the engine rumbles alive. Echoes bounce off the high truck bay walls, and then the bay door opens. He turns the sirens on and pulls out onto the street toward the address.

It's about four in the afternoon, and the roads are crowded. We have to be careful with slowing down at intersections so as to not collide with any other vehicles. Most drivers slow down and move over, but there is always that one asshole that doesn't. It's like playing a game of chicken, and they do not want to get into a crash with a fire truck. They build them strong and will demolish any vehicle.

As we pull on Stratford Avenue, the cloud of black smoke is billowing in the sky, and flames are already consuming the structure. There are no police on scene yet, and no one standing outside. There must still be people inside. Normally, we always assess how badly damaged the structure is before going on, but with indication of possible civilians inside I don't wait, but proceed with extreme caution.

"I'm going in," I yell to Damon as he and Jeremy prep the house.

"Me too!" Tristan yells, following after me toward the crumbling house.

Entering the house, smoke is drifting at the ceiling and sliding under the doors. Flames are licking the walls, bits of curtains are crumbling, and we split up to check the rooms. We need to get in and out as fast as possible to avoid the roof caving in on us.

"Anyone in here?" I yell, but with my mask on, the echoes of debris falling around the house mutes me. So, I just keep yelling, hoping someone will respond. Every second inside this house is putting us in danger.

The kitchen table collapses as the legs turn to charred stumps, and I rush through to get to the bedrooms. The door is unlocked, but no one appears to be inside. I check the closet to make sure and move on to the second bedroom. I bust it down to find a young child, around six years old laying on the floor. There is a vase broken on the floor, and cracks on the window.

"Sweetie, are you okay?" I ask, but receive no response.

There is no time to assess her, because this structure will not hold up much longer. I sweep her up into my arms, and navigate through the debris in the living room to get her outside to protection. EMT and Police are now on scene, and they rush over to me and take the little girl.

"Where's Tristan?" I yell to Damon, and he shrugs his shoulders.

I run back inside, and start yelling, going straight to the remaining rooms, and there he is on the floor, trying to get two adults to wake up. They are unconscious, but still breathing.

"Let's get them out of here. This place is about to fall."

I sling the man over my shoulder, and Tristan follows behind me, treading lightly until we are back outside.

"Still has a pulse but shallow breathing. No obvious injuries," I tell the EMT while placing them on a gurney.

"All clear inside." I say to the police officer and Fire Chief.

Each call is different, and we can't foresee what is going to happen, but we do our best to make sure everyone is out of the house. Once the fire spreads, smoke inhalation kills people.

After thirty minutes, the fire is out, but it has compromised the entire structure This family has lost everything. They wouldn't have survived this fire if we didn't respond so quickly. They train us to be on scene within five minutes. Fires get out of control fast.

"Good job, bro. I couldn't leave them behind."

He acts like I would just leave him there. The reason we work well together is because we have a long history and have each other's backs. He might not be my brother by blood, but that doesn't matter in my book.

After the others have wrapped everything up, we head back to the station for shift change. We are about an hour overdue for shift change, but emergencies take precedence. Being a firefighter doesn't have guaranteed hours because anything can pop up and it's up to us to be there. Sometimes, it's hard to make plans, especially on a day with a shift because it could turn into a fourteen hour shift if a bad fire breaks out. It's not like other jobs where you can just say you don't want the overtime.

After that call, I wish I could get out of this date tonight, but Tristan has been pushing me hard core to do this. He's a great friend, but this online dating crap just isn't panning out for me. Hell, I would much rather go home and sleep than sit through another horrendous date with someone who can't have a conversation. Intelligence is something I find extremely attractive in a woman, and up to this point, none of the girls I have matched with have any.

"I think I'm gonna cancel the date for tonight. After this, I'm exhausted," I say, walking into the station.

"Hell no. Just go. She could be the woman you have been waiting for, Brodie. Give her a chance."

Tristan has been hounding me to get back out there, and honestly most days I keep myself from thinking about how lonely I am. The chances of me finding the woman of my dreams through this is highly unlikely and I'm getting sick of wasting my nights meeting women who aren't being truthful.

That's the biggest thing. No one fact checks them. So they can lie and say they are a doctor and no one would be the wiser. So, I have to take their profiles with a grain of salt, and hope for the best. Sometimes, this is frustrating.

"Fine, but if this one doesn't work out, then I'm done. Online dating isn't working and frankly, it's burning a hole in my pocket."

I take off my gear and change into my black slacks and blue button up. We are supposed to be meeting at LA VI in twenty minutes, but I might be a few minutes late. She should understand once I explain why. It comes with the job, and any woman that dates me has to understand that.

"Alright, I'm taking off. See ya tomorrow at the field."

I grab my keys and head out the door to my truck. There is a pleasant breeze making the ninety degrees a bit more bearable. The first thing I do is roll all my windows down, and take off.

When I pull up to LA VI, my chest tightens and anxiety sets in. First dates are nerve-wracking and then there's the useless small talk you have to get through. When you are on a date, you are on your best behavior. Is it possible to skip all the bullshit and get down to the nitty gritty?

The restaurant is dark, utilizing lighting to brighten it up, setting the mood. There are candles on the tables, and a vase with flowers. There are only two restaurants in Grapevine that are date worthy, and Tristan said that if I take a girl to the diner, they probably wouldn't show up. Why does it matter? It's just food. If they are truly there to get to know someone, then where it shouldn't matter?

The hostess is standing at a podium with a tablet in her hand, and I stand in line, waiting patiently for my turn. I notice a young woman sitting on the booth by the podium.

"Denise?"

She takes a once over of my body and smiles. "You must be Brodie."

First impression is that she is pretty, but with her short green dress showing off her long legs, and black heels that must be at least six inches. We aren't going to the club. Her profile says she is thirty-two, but she appears to be younger than that. She gets up and stands next to me while we wait for the hostess.

"I was doubting, like, if you were going to show up. Online dating isn't exactly fool proof and they have stood me up before."

My hands clasp together, and I try to be nice, even though I didn't want to be here. First impressions are everything, and she is not for me. Is it wrong that I prefer a woman that doesn't wear bodycon dresses and six-inch heels? Some men might find that sexy, but I prefer jeans and a t-shirt type of girl.

"I had a call that took longer than expected. My job doesn't afford me the luxury of being off at a certain time every day."

She just glances at me and goes back to playing on her phone.

This bothers me. *Why aren't you giving me your undivided attention?* It's so damn rude to be on your phone while being on a date, especially with someone whom you have never met. I keep my mouth shut and try to stay positive. We make it up to the stand.

"Reservation for two. Brodie Hill."

She grabs the tablet and swipes twice. "Okay, follow me, please."

The hostess takes us to a table in the middle of the restaurant, and hands us the menus. Denise takes off her jacket, exposing her bare shoulders from her strapless red dress.

"So, your profile said that you were at the University?"

She doesn't take her eyes off the menu. "Yeah, I do admin work there, and like whatever else they ask me. I don't plan on staying there long. I might, like, take some time off and figure out what I want to do."

Her excessive use of the word, like, is getting to me. *Okay, I'm being a smartass now.* How is this woman in her thirties? She acts like she's early twenties at most. It's like pulling teeth to have a conversation.

"And you are a firefighter, right? That's, like, so hot."

This will not work out, and staying here will not make matters better. If she says like one more time, I'm going to gag. I should've canceled.

I refuse to sit here for the next hour or two and listen to this woman talk. Is she unable to go two sentences without using the word like? She must be lying about her age, because normal thirty-year-olds do not speak in this manner.

"I'm going to use the restroom," I say, scooting my chair out, making a bee line for the bathroom and then sneaking out the front door.

Online dating is a nightmare. I'm done with it. Tristan is going to get an ear full tomorrow.

Why is it so hard to find someone good-looking, intelligent, and wanting to settle down?

3

VANESSA

Sleep is something I've always had issues with and couple that with sleeping alone in a bed for the first time in a decade, you get my drift. Going our separate ways is the right decision, but it will take time to get used to it. My days are different now. Normally, Lee's alarm would go off around six in the morning, and would wake me up too, but I forgot to set my own alarm, so I pop out of bed around seven. He would get Sherrie up, and feed her while I get in the shower and get ready for work and then we would switch. Now, I get her up and feed her. My morning showers are gone and replaced with doing them at night, so we aren't running late.

I knock on her door and then turn the knob. "It's time to get up for school. Rise and shine!"

Sherrie gets up the first time I wake her, which is unusual and heads straight to the kitchen to sit down at the island. I don't have to ask what she wants because it's routine. So, I put the grounds in the coffeemaker and switch it on, while I put two pieces of bread in the toaster for her.

"How did you sleep, princess?"

She smiles. "My new bed is amazing. Didn't wake up once."

Lee and I agree to her bedroom remaining the same at his house, and he bought the bed for her new room. I was against it at first, but it's for Sherrie.

The toaster pops, and I take the bread out and place it on a plate.

"I'll get the butter and cinnamon." Sherrie says, excited to make her own breakfast.

She grabs the butter out of the fridge and the cinnamon out of the drawer. Lee always reminds me to monitor her or she will put way too much on there and then she's wired for the rest of the day.

"That's enough, sweetie."

She takes the plate back to the island and begins eating, while I pour the fresh coffee into my mug and add a little creamer. I have no energy, but regardless I have appointments today, and can't miss.

The responsibility is all on me now, and that means getting as many appointments booked so the bills are paid. Before, I usually only work four days a week, but now I'm going to open my schedule to service more clients. It's common sense. The more clients I get in my chair, the more money I make. So, I'll be reaching out to my clientele about the change in hours. The weekends are at my discretion only because I'd like to keep that as family time for Sherrie and I. Her softball games once the season starts will be on Saturdays and it's important to her for me to be there.

I sit down next to Sherrie, and check my calendar for today. My last appointment is at two-thirty and then I'll have enough time to pick her up from school, and then she has her first softball practice of the season.

"Are you looking forward to meeting your new coach tonight?" I ask.

She nods, and continues eating.

Lee always convinced her to try out different sports, and it's always been softball. She has come a long way since her first year, and she is always excited about the start of a new season. Her old coach moved away after last year, and I hope she doesn't end up with a coach that screams at the girls like it's college softball. Not everyone is cut out to teach little kids.

When I was her age, my whole life was softball. I played for a long time and always found it almost therapeutic. It's a good way to be social and understand how to work as a team. Every kid should try at least once. I think it's helped Sherrie bond with the other girls on the team.

"Let's get ready. We gotta leave in ten minutes."

We get up from the island and go into our rooms. The one thing I like most about my job is the ability to dress how I want. Usually I'm in jeans and a nice blouse with converse. Being on my feet most of the day, it helps.

Sherrie comes out in a pink dress and white flats. "I'm ready, mom."

I smile, spin her around, and then grab my keys.

"Let's hustle. Mommy can't be late for work."

Dropping her off is always fairly easy if everyone follows the rules, but there is always one person that doesn't understand how the system works or that's what they claim. If both lanes constantly move, then it takes around ten minutes, but right now there is some woman holding up the line. I try to take a deep breath and calm myself, but being late as the boss is disrespectful.

"Come on. We have jobs to get too!" I yell out my window and the lady rolls her eyes and gets back in her car.

I pull up to the front doors, Sherrie gets out, and I blow her a kiss before heading out of the parking lot. I've got about ten minutes to get to the salon, but Tina is most likely already there getting set up. I'm not one of those people that think just because I'm the boss, I should get away with things. My employees are aware of what I expect, and they want the same from me. It's a respectable thing. Traffic isn't too bad, and I make it with a couple of minutes to spare.

"Hey, girl."

Tina is at the front desk, messing with the computer, and rearranging the display case with hair accessories before the start of our day. I take a seat in the waiting area on the leather couch, and pick up a magazine.

"How was the first night?"

I roll my eyes, and lean my head back on the couch. "Got no sleep. Not used to being alone."

She puts together her station with combs, a water bottle sprayer, and bowls and brushes for mixing colors. "It'll get easier."

Why does everyone say this? No matter why a relationship ended, there is still an adjustment period. When you are used to sleeping next to someone, being in a bed alone is weird. It's not him that I'm missing, it's just the company.

"It was mutual. We are both moving on with our lives."

Tina's face scrunches up. "I find that hard to believe. So you guys both decided to break up? I just don't get it at all."

People on the outside don't always sense when things are wrong. Lee and I have had many ups and downs in the decade of dating. He is a wonderful man, and never did anything wrong, but we couldn't stay together for Sherrie. Happiness is something that everyone should get to enjoy.

"Did you guys stop trying? Our therapist tells us we have to make time to do things as a couple."

I love how this is the first time she has mentioned them being in therapy. Maybe she doesn't tell me everything. "Our relationship hasn't been going in the right direction for years. We stayed together for Sherrie and then one year turned into seven."

The person I end up with shouldn't be a convenient roommate. Sure, we slept in the same bed, but we were rarely intimate, and the conversations stopped. I think there came a point where we were both too scared to say anything.

"We sat down and had a long talk about us, and we were both very honest with each other. Staying with someone just because you have kids is unhealthy for the children. They take their parent's relationship as a guide for what to expect, and Sherrie needs to know that her happiness is important. Lee and I barely talking or spending time with each other doesn't provide a good example for her."

"So you broke up for Sherrie?"

Sometimes Tina doesn't quite understand things. It's like she doesn't listen fully. "Yes and no. We both want to be happy and show

Sherrie how she should be treated. By staying with each other, we were setting a bad example for her."

Tina doesn't have kids yet, and so it might be hard for her to understand. As a parent, our kids rely on us to show them things and we can't take that lightly. Even at a young age, they are picking up on how we talk and interact with people. We are their role models for many things in life, and we need to be careful what we are teaching them.

The bell on the door jingles, and my first client of the day is here.

"Morning. Have a seat."

I glance over at Tina, who is still putting together her cart, and get to work on Samantha's hair. After two hours of pulling and poking, her hair is spiked with foil. "Go ahead and sit under the dryers. I'll be right over."

I go to the waiting area and grab a stack of magazines and drop them in her lap and flip the switch. "This should give you plenty to keep you occupied for the next hour."

Beauty school is something I started when I was a senior in high school, and when I graduated, I worked two jobs to help save up to be able to open my own salon. When Lee and I became serious, he surprised me with the building. Of course, I wanted to do it on my own, but at that point, I didn't have a choice. The building would have sat empty, and the first year being paid up allowed me to be able to get in the green a lot faster. Most new businesses stay in the red for the first one to three years depending on their opening success. The best thing about it is most of my clients came over to my salon from my previous employer.

I try to stay focused throughout the day, but running around on no sleep isn't healthy. My clients pick up I'm not my usual chatty self, and many asked what is going on. Talking about my personal life or problems with my clients is stepping over the line for me.

When I'm finished with my last client, it's a couple minutes after three, and I have to try to cut the conversation short, so I'm not late picking up Sherrie from school. She's a chatterbox and would stand here and talk for the next half hour.

"Alright, I'm headed to pick up Sherrie. You still coming over later?"

Tina nods, and I rush out the door. I try to get a head start before the traffic gets heavy with everyone heading to pick up their kids, but today is a no go. It takes me almost twenty minutes to get up to the front of the pickup line.

Sherrie gets in the car, and we rush back to the house for her to change into shorts for practice. I would love to just jump in bed and doze off, but motherly duties never cease.

I hope the coach isn't a total asshole.

4

BRODIE

$\mathcal{M}$y truck door slams behind me as the dirt crunches underneath my feet. The sun is in full force today, and there is nothing but the dug out to provide much needed shade. The dugouts are rusty, but at least the field has been marked up and provided new bases.. Baseball has always been a passion of mine, even if I never made it to the professional league. Being on the mound, having everyone silent waiting for you strike out the batter to win the championship game, it's exhilarating. Nothing like it.

"I still can't believe you talked me into this," Tristan says, sneaking up behind me as my eyes take in the the ball field.

"You're the only person with any experience. You could've said no."

He shakes his head, and leans back onto my truck. No one else is here yet, and so I take my time reminiscing over the blood, sweat and tears that I've put onto this field. There were so many nights, we were out here, even if it was raining, practicing to get better. Funny enough, we got put on the same little league team and have been good friends ever since. I always pitched, and he was the catcher. Trust is important on any team, but especially between those two positions. They need to be in sync, and be able to communicate without saying a word. That's us. Even now, sometimes.

"This place brings back so many memories, doesn't it?" I ask.

Tristan steadies his eyes on the field.

Our dream was to make it into the professional league, but that didn't work out. Instead of sitting around and being upset about it, we joined the Fire department. It's nice to be back here again, even if we aren't playing. The girls will recognize our love for the sport which will help them build theirs, too. Or at least I hope.

Tristan pushes off the truck, and faces me. "How did the date go last night?"

That is the last thing I want to talk about right now. I'm over the whole online dating thing. It's a waste of time, and with taking this on, I don't have much free time as it is. Since signing up, I've been on nine dates, all of which were numbingly painful.

He laughs. "It couldn't have been that bad. Come on, man."

"She couldn't even hold a conversation. Used the word like at least a hundred times. She says she's thirty-two, but acts like she's barely legal to drink."

My expectations are high, and it's been hard to find anyone that even remotely fits. I didn't think it would be this hard, but the last girl I dated had a crazy ex-boyfriend who tried to kill me, so I'm more cautious than ever.

"Let's just say I'm at the end of the rope. Online dating is not for me. You might like it, but I'm done."

"Did you at least make it back to your house? Or was she that bad?" he asks, taking a swig of his water.

"I didn't even make it to order drinks. I told her I was going to use the bathroom and left. There was no point in wasting either of our time."

Tristan laughs into his fist. "You're kidding? No way you actually dipped out on her."

I nod, with a straight face. "She hasn't messaged me either, so I think she got the point."

Let me get one thing straight. I'm not one of those guys that take you out, buy you dinner, and then take you back to my house, only to never call you again. One-night stands aren't for me. Although, I might need to change my stance on this if my luck keeps up.

How long does a guy go without sex before his dick just stops working? Muscle memory, they say, but it's been almost two years. Way too long. At this rate, I may never get laid again.

That's the last I want to talk about online dating. It's not for me.

"I'm just waiting for the girls to show up. Practice is supposed to start in fifteen minutes," I say.

This is our first time coaching a team, but Damon came to us and asked if we would be willing to step up this season. Baseball and softball have things in common, and he didn't want Emily to have to drive to another city to play. He has a good way of talking me into things. I've always enjoyed helping others, and getting to help youngin's learn the sport is gratifying.

I might not ever get the chance to have kids of my own, but one day I would love to coach my future daughter's little league. I'm sure every parent says this, but she isn't pressured to play a sport just because I like it. She won't be responsible for helping me relive my glory days. This is so common, and it hinders the players' growth and love for the sport. They should play because they enjoy it, not because we forced them to. So many parents make this mistake and ruin the fun for the child.

"Let's take the uniforms and the cooler to the dugout. I brought waters since it's like a million degrees out here," I say, wiping the sweat from my forehead.

Even in shorts and a t-shirt, it's like I'm sitting in a sauna. It's important to stay hydrated, especially in this blistering weather, so we have to make sure the girls drink plenty during practice. I don't want to be responsible for anyone getting overheated or sick.

Tristan and I grab the two boxes from the bed of my truck, and take them to the dugout, waiting for the kids to show up. Our uniforms almost didn't make it in time. If I didn't pay for the express shipping, then there's no telling when we would have gotten them in.

You would think six weeks would be plenty of notice to get uniforms, but not for this company.

"Hey, look," Tristan says, tapping on my shoulder and pointing to a woman in the grass, getting out of her car.

"This isn't for you to pick up women. Come on."

I try not to stare, but her hair is blowing in the wind, and the shorts she has on are only drawing my eyes to her long tan legs. *Who the hell is she?* I shake my head, trying to rid myself of these thoughts, and focus on the task at hand. She is off limits.

"Now, she looks like trouble." Tristan says, still staring at her like a creep.

Cars pull up, and kids are filing into the dugout. It's nice how excited they are. I wait until all twelve girls have arrived and then we begin.

"Welcome, ladies. My name is Brodie and I'll be your coach. This is my assistant, Tristan. We are looking forward to working with you girls over this season."

I call out names from the roster, and Tristan hands them their uniforms. When I call out Sherrie's name, she steps up with a smile and then peers back at her mom.

"Welcome to the team, champ."

After I have handed the uniforms out, we have the girls play catch to warm up. It gives us time to assess them and learn what we need to work on as a team. Since it's our first season with them, we have to learn each players' strengths and weaknesses. It's almost like starting from scratch. One benefit we have is the girls have been playing together for years, so there is already a level of trust built among the team. Now we just have to build their trust in us as coaches. It's hard when a new one comes in and tries to nitpick, but I'm not that guy.

Tristan has been paying more attention to the mom's than what's going on at practice. So, I dig my elbow into his side and he winces. "Dude, let's not make this weird, okay? Stop."

He clears his throat. "My bad. I can't help it sometimes."

His attention is back on the field where it should be, but not for long. We do some drills at first base, and all he has to do is throw the ball so they are able to catch it and tag the base, but his eyes are focused on the moms in the bleachers talking. What does he see in them? A majority of them are fake blondes, with faux fingernails, and pasted on eyelashes. Who wants to be with a fake barbie? I prefer a more natural look with no pound of makeup.High maintenance is something I stay away from and avoid at all costs.

"Tristan, eyes on first base."

For the rest of practice, Tristan keeps his eyes averted and I don't have to get onto him again. I hope the whole season doesn't go this way, because there doesn't need to be any drama. If we screw this up, then it ruins our chances of being asked to come back next year. Tristan doesn't seem thrilled about it like I am, but by then, someone else will step in. Piss off the moms, and that's one sure fire way to make us not wanted on this league anymore.

"Dude, find women somewhere else. They are off limits. Got it?" I say, nudging him against the fence.

Okay, so maybe my eyes did wander a couple of times, but at least I didn't make it obvious like he did. The woman from earlier has been on her phone most of the practice. There is no ring on her finger, but that doesn't mean anything. *Fuck.* I keep telling myself she is off limits, but my eyes want to drink her in.

Her eyes come up off her phone and then she makes eye contact.

"Hey, coach!" she yells, waving me over.

Tristan glances my way, and I smile as I walk over to the chain link fence. "Yeah?"

"How much longer is practice going to be? Sherrie is supposed to be at her dad's by seven and we haven't even eaten dinner yet."

I follow her eyes trail down my body. She is totally checking me out.

"About fifteen minutes, probably. I'm Brodie, by the way."

"Vanessa."

She rolls her eyes, displeased, but even with her attitude, I still want to pull her close and kiss those pink lips of hers. It takes everything I have not to reply with a sly remark. How does she already hate me?

A beautiful woman with an attitude. What could go wrong?

5

VANESSA

$\mathcal{I}$s her coach already hitting on me? Jesus. His eyes wander over my body like he wants to pounce on me and maybe I'm enjoying it a bit. I still got it. Even after being in a serious relationship for ten years, and being out of the practice, guys are still wanting to take me home. Reminds me of my early twenties, before I Lee, and men would practically beg to take me out. I always turned them down.

I won't lie. It fuels my confidence to be desired. Sometimes we forget that when we are with someone for a long time. They stop telling you you're beautiful, and no longer undress you with their eyes. Right now, Brodie is doing just that, and it makes my heart race.

He runs back over to the kids and wraps up practice and I text Lee we are going to be late. I didn't expect this to be a long practice, or I would have made other plans.

Me: Practice is still going. Should we just do this another night? We haven't even eaten yet.

A part of me hopes he agrees to move it to another night because with the lack of sleep, I'm not exactly at the top of my game and the conversation tonight is going to be intense. I'm not ready for it, but even two days of sleep can't prepare me for tonight.

Lee: I'll order takeout. Y'all can eat here. No worries. Text me when you are leaving and I'll order it.

Damnit.

The kids are running to the dugout and Brodie approaches me again. My eyes glance in the opposite direction. He might be cute, but not my type. It'll be nice to have some eye candy for the season though.

"Your daughter is a fast runner. How long has she been playing?"

I cross my arms and scoff. "Three years. Her former coach was really great to the girls. You aren't an asshole, are you?"

His head cocks back. "Wow, you are very forward. I respect that. This is my first time coaching, but I don't think so."

"Wait, first time coaching? Do you even know anything about softball?"

So, maybe I'm being a bitch, but we need someone with experience to teach these girls, not some random dude with no experience.

"Actually, I played from t-ball through high school, ma'am. Baseball, but my sister played softball for many years too. I appreciate your concern."

He replies to me with a straight face. My stomach tenses, but it's a valid question.

I pull Lee's thread up on my phone and say we are fixing to leave.

"Any other concerns you would like to express while you have my ear?" he asks.

"Are you one of those people that yell at the kids if they mess up? This isn't professional softball, right? I won't stand for that. Sherrie loves softball and I don't want anyone to ruin that for her."

"I'll be sure to keep myself in check just for you, Vanessa. See ya."

Sherrie runs out of the dugout straight to me.

"I think we are gonna like him, mom."

I rustle her hair, glance at him, and turn Sherrie to go to the car. "We'll see."

After getting her situated in the car, I take a deep breath. Brodie appears cocky, and I can't stand men like that. Yet, him undressing me with his eyes arouses me. I haven't been single for long and I'm already drinking up men's attention. How horrible is that? Although, maybe it's healthy. It's not like I'm going to take him home and sleep with him tonight. I'm not oblivious to boundaries. How long is Lee going to wait before dating again? It's not jealousy, but a real question. Will it be weird to see him with someone else? One hundred percent, but I'll be happy for him.

I don't think I'm anywhere close to being ready to be with someone right now. The person I was when I got with Lee is not the same person I am now. I think I should take some time for myself first. With Lee, I didn't put myself and want I wanted from him first, and that's a big part of why we didn't work out. When I get into a new relationship, I want to be able to be upfront with them about what I want, and if they don't want the same things, then on to the next one. Most importantly, I need to stay true to myself.

When we pull up into Lee's driveway, my heart skips a beat. This is really happening. I'm going to have to sit in front of my daughter and explain that her dad and I won't be together anymore. How is she going to react? My head is pounding from the lack of sleep, and not eating anything today.

Lee comes out, and opens Sherrie's door, engulfing her in a hug. This transition is going to be hard on him too. I can't imagine not seeing Sherrie everyday. That's another subject that we need to tackle. He is allowed to see her whenever he wants. I'm not the type of woman to use my child to get what I want, and that might be because I want nothing from him.

Co-parenting is crucial for us. My parents split up when I was ten years old and they couldn't even be in the same room for the first couple of years. Separate households is hard enough but watching my parents made things much worse. I intend to be amicable with Lee and always put our daughter first. That's exactly how it should be.

"Hey Nessa, how did work go?" He asks, ushering us inside and into the kitchen.

"Work went by fast. So that's nice."

I mess with my cuticles, and try to keep the conversation simple. I'm a guest in his home now.

"Daddy, you should see the new house. When are you coming?"

I'd like to eat dinner before we dive into that. This headache is getting worse, and once things get emotional and I start crying, it's only going to make it worse. Food first, please!

"Daddy got takeout! I got you Orange Chicken," Lee says, pointing to the table.

She runs to it. "My favorite."

He lingers behind and his hand caresses my chin. "You look rough. Are you not sleeping?"

I smack his hand away. "That's none of your concern anymore, Lee. Don't worry about me. I'll be fine."

Okay, so maybe I overreacted, but these little moments are inappropriate, and we need to set boundaries. So, I need to make it clear.

I march over to the table, and have a seat next to Sherrie. She is already placing orange chicken on her plate and then some combination Lo Mein.

"Hey! Save some for us, sweetie."

The white takeout boxes are arranged in a straight line. Lee always goes overboard when it comes to food. As a family, we would get chinese takeout once a week, normally on a practice night, because we would get home too late for me to cook anything. It's nice for her to be able to stick to that routine.

"I got you honey walnut shrimp. Devour that yourself."

I roll my eyes and smile. On our first date, back before he got his big promotion, he took me to a Chinese restaurant in Dallas not too far from here. It was buffet style and he made fun of me for an hour because all I got was the honey walnut shrimp. Three plates worth. I admit that's probably weird, but it's literally making my mouth water right now just thinking about it.

He hands the box to me, and I dump it out on my plate. Sherrie stares, and dumps some more Lo Mein on hers, and smiles.

"So, do you like mommy's new house?" Lee asks.

I glare at him, wanting to wait until after we are done eating to get into the conversation. Why is he in such a hurry? She is going to start asking questions and I haven't even been able to take a bite yet. So, I shove four pieces of honey walnut shrimp in my mouth.

"The bed is comfy, but when are you coming?"

I close my eyes, and my breathing hitches. Here we go. The moment where her life changes forever, and she has no say in it. It makes me think back to the day my parents split up. She threw his suitcase out the door, and told him he wasn't ever allowed back. As a child, I never understood why she did that. I never wanted Sherrie to have to experience this, and now I'm wondering if we should have split up all those years ago. Maybe it would have made things easier because Sherrie would have been accustomed to us living separately from the start. Too late now.

"Well, honey. You and mommy are going to stay at that house, and I'm staying here," he says, putting down his fork and giving her his full attention. His eyes search for a reaction.

"Why? There's enough room." Sherrie turns to me with squinted eyebrows. "Did you make daddy mad?"

My heart sinks. Why does she automatically assume that I did something wrong? Seeing my little girl look at me with such disappointment makes my heart break.

"No, she didn't do anything wrong. Your mom and I just aren't going to be living together anymore, sweetie."

Sherrie shakes her head. "Why can't I live with you?"

Her eyes search for an answer from her father, but he's speechless.

"Mommy wants you to live with her."

She stands up out of her chair, and yells. "I don't want to. You can't make me."

She takes off upstairs in tears.

This isn't something I ever planned to have to discuss with our daughter, but it's the right decision. Lee and I were becoming miserable together. She deserves a good role model for a relationship and that isn't us.

"Why does she automatically assume I did something? What the hell?" I say, picking over my shrimp.

"She has always been a daddy's girl, Nessa. You didn't think this break-up was going to be smooth, did you? It never is when kids are involved."

We finish eating in silence, and after twenty minutes, I go upstairs and try to get her to talk to me. The door is locked, and she doesn't answer when I knock. I slide down the door, until my butt is on the hardwood floor.

"Sherrie, this is going to be hard for you. Please don't shut me out, baby."

Her sobs are loud, and I just want to embrace her and tell her everything is going to be okay. Maybe I should give her some space.

"I'm gonna go home. Dad will be up shortly to tuck you in."

I wipe my nose, and walk downstairs, finding Lee in the living room, his arm splayed out across the back of the couch. He waves at me to take a seat, and I lean into him, using his shirt as a tear catcher. He puts his arm around me, and just lets me cry. We might not be together, but for ten years, he was my person. He took care of me when I was sick and that doesn't all fade away.

"This is a lot to process. It's hard for me to, but you deserve someone to give you everything you need. As much as I wanted to be that guy, we just aren't right for each other. Sherrie is too young to understand right now, but give her a couple years and once she sees you are not able to wipe a smile off your face, then she will."

This transition is hard enough without having my daughter hate me. She can see her father whenever she wants and we still love her. Tonight, she needs space and that's what I'm going to do.

"I'm going to leave her here with you. Can you take her to school tomorrow?" I ask, inching away from Lee on the couch.

He nods, and brushes my arm. "It'll get better. Trust me."

I get off the couch and grab my keys off the table. "I'll talk to you soon, Lee."

Closing the door behind myself makes this situation even more surreal. This house we lived together in for ten years, it's not my home anymore.

I get into my car and turn on the ignition before texting Tina.

Me: I'm just now heading home. Rain check.

After everything tonight, I don't want company, just a bottle of wine.

Will my daughter ever forgive me?

6

BRODIE

*T*he clank of air tanks bounce off the bay walls as they are being stored away in the cabinets. Jeremy and Damon are dragging the hoses out for inspection. We didn't have any calls today, which I'll never complain. The cleaning supplies are burning my nostrils, but sometimes the Fire Chief goes a little overboard with this place. He wants everything to be clean, and in tip top shape. Once a week, we are required to do a full inspection of all equipment and clean from top to bottom. Not everyone pitches in, but it keeps me busy, so I don't mind doing it.

We have Jeremy's surprise birthday dinner tonight and I've been trying to keep my mouth shut. It's harder than you think, keeping something from someone you work closely with like this. He has no idea though, and in fact hasn't even mentioned his birthday all day.

"So, you got everything ready for the baby?" I ask, just trying to keep myself from saying anything.

There is some part of me that is jealous, but it's just not my time yet.

"Can't believe we only have two months left. Tessa has been a damn trooper too. No morning sickness, but she is addicted to sour candy," Damon replies.

Children have always been a part of my future, and once I find the right woman, everything will fall into place. I just need to stop searching, and let her come to me.

Liam and the other guys walk through the door, and start laughing.

"You guys need french maid outfits," Liam says, heading to the locker room.

Sometimes I forget that Jeremy has only been here a year, and thankfully Eli doesn't work here anymore. The constant bullshit everyone had to listen to from that guy. Sure, Jeremy was dating his sister, but this is your job. Leave that crap at the door.

"It's time for us to get out of here. No idea what Raquel has planned for tonight. She woke me up with breakfast in bed. Hell, she even drove me to work today," Jeremy says.

Don't do it. Keep your mouth shut. It's a surprise, damnit.

"Well, whatever it is, I'm sure it'll be great."

Before I slip, I head to the locker room to change into my gym shorts and t-shirt. Raquel has made it clear that we are to be there right after our shift. It makes sense she brought him to work, so she is able to control when he gets to the diner. Smart move.

"I'll see you guys tomorrow."

She is outside waiting for Jeremy. I wave and she replies with a smile. I think it's nice of her to do this for him. It's been a hard year for him after losing his father to Alzheimer's, but Raquel has been by his side every step of the way. He is truly lucky to have her.

I pull out of the parking lot, and head straight for the diner. It's Damon's job to text her once everyone is there. Does Jeremy like surprises? If it were me, I'd pass. They just aren't my thing.

Traffic isn't bad, and I make it to the diner in under five minutes, but it still appears empty. I must be the first one here. The bell chimes above me as I open the door, and Darlene greets me.

"I've got everything set up. Jeremy still in the dark?" she asks.

I nod, and walk through the diner. There are streamers and a huge Happy Birthday banner hanging on the wall. Jeremy and his father used to call in an order every sunday, and he has many happy memories here. I think it's sweet Raquel chose here for his celebration. Even though he can't be here in person, it's the perfect venue. A very nice gesture, indeed.

Damon and Tristan walk in and admire the decorations.

"She is really going all out, ain't she?" Tristan says.

He walks over and gives me a handshake before sitting down. It takes about fifteen minutes for everyone else to show up and Damon shoots her a text that we are all set.

"She's been stalling him. Filled the car up with gas, and stopped at the store to grab milk. She is hilarious. I really do think they are perfect for each other, don't you?" Damon says.

"They are happy, that's what counts. Even after the depression hit, she stood by him, and that speaks volumes to her character and loyalty. She's a keeper," I reply.

Raquel's car pulls right up to the curb and everyone crouches down so they don't spot us. Darlene acts like nothing is happening, and is wiping down the counters. How is he going to react?

"Fuck, did he see us?" Tristan says.

"I don't think so," Damon replies.

The bell above the door sings and we all jump up and yell. "Surprise!"

Jeremy jumps out of his skin. Raquel achieved the ultimate surprise, but the cracking of ihs knuckles signals he isn't too thrilled. Yet, he plays it off.

"Wow. Thanks guys!"

Everyone sits down, and Darlene makes her way around to get everyone's drink orders. She is going to make a killing tonight from this group. This is her second job to help her pay her children's college tuition. She's been here forever.

"Sorry, I'm late. I had to drop off Emily with the babysitter," Tessa says, struggling to get into the booth next to Damon.

She amazes me. From behind, you wouldn't even be able to tell she's pregnant. That girl is all belly. Damon has been nervous, and questioning whether he is ready, but we have all seen him with Emily. Damon is going to be a great father. I wish I had as much patience as he does. No matter how prepared you are for having a child, doubt will always be there for the first one. It changes your whole world for the better. He's got this #1 dad thing in the bag.

"I swear if I get any bigger, we will have to buy a bigger car."

He plants a kiss on her lips, and then snuggles into her. They have a strong relationship. No one planned on him finding someone after losing his wife to cancer. He was a fucking mess, but along came Tessa.

"By the way, the crib didn't come today. I called, and they said it'll be next week. What if I have this baby before it gets here?"

Damon rubs her arm, and kisses her cheek. "Baby, we have two months left. There's plenty of time. Don't stress about it."

There is some silence around the table, and so I bring up practice.

"Emily did great yesterday. She has one heck of an arm. You might think about grooming her to be a pitcher. If you start now, she'll be amazing once she reaches twelve and up."

They make eye contact and nod. "Actually, that's exactly what we were thinking. And thanks again for volunteering to coach. She would have been bummed if they had to forfeit the season."

Tristan and I nod and then Darlene comes back for our food order, and most of us get the burger basket except for Damon who gets the breakfast platter. They sell a lot of those here. It is their best selling item.. I've had it so many times, it's starting to get old.

"Well, we were going to ask if you were interested in doing some lessons with her. You pitched, so maybe you can help her get the hang of it. We'd pay you, of course," Tessa says.

It's never crossed my mind to offer lessons, but maybe it's something I should consider. Although with my work schedule, and now taking over the team, it might be hard to find time to be able to do that.

"Yeah. I'll try to find some time to work on that with her. But no need to pay me."

Raquel uses a fork against her glass to get everyone's attention and thanks us for coming. She hands Jeremy a big wrapped present and everyone's waiting as he unwraps it.

"I had no idea what to get you, but when I saw the idea of this, it seemed perfect."

Jeremy's eyebrows tilt and he begins to tear up. I stand up and it's a picture of Hazel, him and his dad.

"I couldn't find a recent photo of you guys, so I had someone put three separate photos together for a family portrait. We can hang this above his urn to honor him."

It's an emotional moment and everyone stays silent for a couple of minutes while Raquel hugs Jeremy and he stops crying. Once everyone starts to talk again, Tristan jumps right into softball again.

"Y'all have been around on this team for a couple years. Who do you think has catching material?"

They shake their heads, and there's a bit of a pause.

"No idea. Maybe Addilyn," Damon says.

Tristan starts talking about how practice went, and then Vanessa comes up. Why would he even mention her to Damon? Is he trying to make himself sound like a creep?

"She has this fuck you attitude, and it just makes her that much hotter," Tristan says.

First of all, Tessa comes to every practice. If he is saying this so that she will mention it to the other moms, but he needs to be careful what he says. Why is it so hard for him to keep his head in the game?

Tessa starts laughing. Apparently, she thinks it's hilarious. He isn't exactly the type to pick up women. He has no game, and hasn't been on a date in at least a year. He might try to come off as a ladies man, but we all know better.

Damon leans back in the booth, and extends his arm across the back. "Are you kidding me? One practice and you are already hitting on the mom's? Dude, no. You are asking for trouble."

He isn't wrong. We aren't there to screw the mom's. This is supposed to be about helping the team. Keeping his head in the game this season might be harder than I thought.

"It's not like I asked for her number. Jesus. Besides, it wasn't just me. He was staring at her too," he says, pointing at me.

Of course, he has to bring me into it. Sometimes Damon and

Tristan act more like brothers, and Tristan just wants to impress him. The thing is: he's married with a kid on the way and I've never seen Damon glance at another woman like he does Tessa. He's committed and Tristan might learn a thing or two from him. Plus, I'm doing a favor for Damon, and there is no fucking way I'm going to try to get with one of the mom's. That would be an epic disaster. Not to mention if anything were to go wrong, we would have to see each other twice a week for the rest of the season. Tristan might be okay with taking those chances, but I'm not. The other moms are going to be watching me, and they can have me fired from the league. No need to screw myself before I even get to the first game of the season.

"Okay, she's nice to look at, but I know boundaries. Unlike you."

Tristan swipes at the air. "Man, whatever."

Do I think she's attractive? Definitely. Do I think about pushing her up against the wall? Yes, but that doesn't mean I'm going to act on it. There are boundaries that we need to follow and I know how things like this work. My reputation with the league might be damaged, and I plan to grow with this team. So, the only way to do that is to keep my sights on getting through the season.

Plus, she reminds me of my high school girlfriend. So much attitude. She turned out crazy, so I'd rather not take any chances. So much attitude is portrayed from her eyes which leads me to believe someone has hurt her badly, and she wants to take it out on everyone else.

It's not to say I won't enjoy sneaking peeks at her this season, nothing wrong with that, but Tristan is dumb enough to try to hook up with her, and that's what has me worried.

Vanessa would eat him alive.

7

VANESSA

*T*he conversation at Lee's house has had my stomach in knots. Sherrie didn't want to come home today, and it makes me wonder if she is going to keep this up. I won't keep her from him, but she is supposed to be living with me. This break-up is going to be hard for her, I get that, and I don't want to push her but she needs to understand that what happened between her father and I isn't going to affect their relationship.

The house is silent with her here, and I keep the TV on as background noise. What if she decides she does want to live with Lee? How am I going to handle that? I don't want to have to go to court and put her through that. A custody battle is not what she needs right now. She would hate me, and it isn't like he is a bad parent. Lee is great with her, and she would be taken care of well over there, but she's still my daughter. She should be with me, but Lee should get time with her too. It's a hard pill to swallow, and us being civilized almost makes this harder.

I open the fridge and grab the microwave meal. It's hard cooking for just one person, so salisbury steak and potatoes it is. It gets popped in the microwave for three minutes, and I pace around the kitchen until its done.

Will Sherrie come home tomorrow? Lee says he is going to talk to her about everything tonight. This is messing with me, and I don't want this to strain my relationship with Sherrie. They are close, but so are we. I didn't expect this from her until she was a teenager, because it's inevitable at that age, but not now. I take the tray and sit down on the couch, trying to fake enjoying how this tastes. Home cooked meals are so much better than this crap. How do people eat these everyday?

I'm so used to having Sherrie around. When we get home, it's usually cooking dinner, eating, and then getting her showered and ready for bed. None of that tonight, so I guess I'll just watch some TV to pass some time until bed.

Just as I'm taking my last bite, someone knocks on my door, and then Tina walks in.

"I brought wine!"

She catches me off guard, and I forget about her coming over. These past couple days have been a blur, and I hope it slows down. I can't keep up at this rate. The lack of good sleep is wearing on me, but maybe some wine will help knock me out.

"Hey girl. You're speaking my language."

With everything going on, I need to talk to someone, and Tina is my closest friend. She's never judged me. This situation is draining me, mentally and physically, and I don't want to see a therapist. Hell, I can't afford it, so my best friend will have to do.

She goes to the cabinet and grabs two wine glasses and then plops down on the couch next to me. She pours the wine, and hands me a glass. Her eyes wander over my face and then tilts her head.

"You look like hell. What's going on?"

Wow, no sugar coating it, huh? I haven't told her about the things going on with Lee and I. Talking about relationship issues with others only invites them to misconstrue information. So, because of that, I've kept these things private, but tonight I'm going to let it all out. Getting it off my chest might do me some good, and then Tina might stop asking so many questions about the break-up.

"Before Sherrie came along, things weren't going great between us and we were on the verge of breaking up."

Tina's eyes grow wide. "You never told me that. Why did you guys stay together?"

"We wanted to try to make it work for the baby. And after a couple years, I think we just stayed together for her sake. Neither of us mentioned how unhappy we were, and that's the problem."

It's admirable to try to work things out when you have kids, but it doesn't mean things will get better. A child is not going to improve a suffering relationship. If anything, it will throw in some obstacles. Babies are hard, and being tired all the time, and emotional isn't going to reflect well on an already failing relationship.

"Why? You should stand up for yourself, no matter who you are with. Relationships don't work unless you are willing to say when something is bothering you."

And she's right. I should have spoken up a long time ago, and maybe things could be different between Lee and I, but I didn't. Little things turned into big things and we just aren't meant for each other. Love doesn't conquer all. That's just what fairytales want us to believe.

"Girl, we were more like roommates than a couple. We had sex maybe three times in the last four years. And I think we were both afraid to hurt the other."

She refills our glasses before responding. "That makes sense. You became complacent. It happens and a lot of relationships fall apart from it. Life moves fast, girl."

Tina doesn't even know the half of it. "So you tell your husband every time you don't like something or something is bothering you? I highly doubt that. You aren't perfect and neither is he. Sometimes it's easier to just shut up than start a fight."

This is exactly why I don't talk about relationships with people, because they always want to project like theirs is perfect. No one is perfect, and things happen. You have to pick your battles, and sometimes you don't realize it's a battle you should fight until after the fact.

"So you guys just sat down and decided to break up? I mean after a decade? That just seems crazy to me. I literally had no idea you were having problems."

Even though Lee and I weren't intimate, we became good friends and I think that portrayed the happy couple vibe. We tried to make it work, but we couldn't keep making excuses. We owed it to ourselves to find someone who made us truly happy in every way.

"Are you guys getting along? I mean most couples can't stay friends after a break-up?"

I think with us, because there is an established friendship there, and we broke up by mutual agreement, that we will still remain friends. Co-parenting is a huge deal to me, and I don't want Sherrie to witness me and Lee dad fighting. I think we have a great chance

"How is she taking it? On move in day, she didn't even seem phased by it."

I explain to Tina that Sherrie is upset with me and even accused me of making Lee mad, which is breaking my heart, but we knew this wasn't going to be easy. She is at an age where she doesn't truly understand things, and it's not appropriate to try to explain our situation.

"She loves you, girl. Don't let it question your relationship. She is going to have to deal with this break-up too. Give her some time."

Tina gets up from the couch and grabs the bottle of wine to refill our glasses, and turns on the tv. It's nice to be able to talk about this with her, and wish I would have confided in her about all the things going on with Lee.

I'm done talking about all this, and want to change the subject.

"Guess what happened to me at Sherrie's practice?"

She turns to me, and her eyes go wide. "Spill."

At first, I didn't plan on mentioning it, but this is a safe zone. Tina isn't going to spread my business.

"So, we met her new coaches. Brodie and Tristan."

She waves her hand around. "Come on. Give the good stuff."

I tell her all about the exchanges with him and how they were both undressing me with their eyes. I don't find Tristan attractive, he's just not my type, but Brodie, that's a different story.

"Holy shit. Girl! Are you gonna do anything about it? I mean you are single now."

She's out of her mind. I am not going out with anyone right now, especially my daughter's coach. My focus is building my relationship with Sherrie and figuring out what I want. I refuse to waste another decade with the wrong person.

"I mean it can just be a hookup. No one said you had to marry the guy. It might do you some good to get laid."

Tina has been with her husband for a long time, so it surprises me to hear her suggest this. He is the worst person to hook up with, and things would just be awkward. I have to see him twice a week for practice, and that's enough. No need to complicate things. He is her coach and that's it. Nothing is going to happen between us.

"I agree it's been a while, but hookups aren't really my thing. Plus, I just got out of a relationship. Don't you think I should take things slow?"

Tina shakes her head. "Opposite. You should use this time to figure out what you want, and there is nothing wrong with getting your needs filled. Men do it all the time. Why can't women?"

I laugh at her point, but it has nothing to do with me. Women are able to sleep with whoever they want, but I'm not.

Sherrie and I need to work through whatever is going on. She needs her space, and I understand, but at some point she is going to have to talk to me. She has always been a daddy's girl, and this break up just tore her whole word apart. Lee is right. She is going to need some time to process this, and I don't want to rush her. Yet, at the same time, I want her to understand that neither of us are to blame. With her age, it's hard to be able to explain anything and expect her to fully understand. That's my dilemma.

Is she going to stay at Lee's for a while? Does she not want to live with me? What am I going to do if she doesn't want to come back? Her being gone is really messing with my head. What will I do if she wants to live with Lee? It's not right for me to say no, because we are both good parents, but it's still a knife in my gut.

"She said she wants to live with her dad. How do I even respond to that?"

Tina throws her up in a ponytail and then clasps her hands together. "We know how close those two are, and it's always been like that. It's natural. Just give her some time. I'm telling you, once she has processed all of it, she will be asking to come back."

Tina is watching whatever the heck is on the tv now, and I'm stuck in my head. Honestly, I need to stop over analyzing things, and just take it day by day. Worrying about what's going to happen is going to make me have a heart attack and then what good am I to anyone?

"How long do you think Lee is going to wait to start dating?" I ask, taking a sip of wine. "Like is there a rule of thumb?"

I'm not sure why I'm asking Tina, since she was only in one serious relationship before she met her husband.

"Hell, I don't know. Are you expecting him to sit around and wait?"

Her question actually has me questioning if Lee dating would even upset me? It's hard because we have a long history, but we are better off friends. Is it weird for him to be kissing another woman? Hell yeah, but it's something that I have to get used to. And I won't cause any trouble for him or any relationships, because I want to be happy without judgment too.

The only thing I'm worried about with this is my daughter being introduced to other women. I hope Lee has the sense to keep her out of it until he is in something serious. This is going to be confusing enough without bringing other people into it.

Am I prepared for the next step? How is my life going to be as a single mother?

8

BRODIE

The blaring alarm causes me to shoot off the cot, and raid my locker to get my gear on. The lack of sleep this week has started to take a toll on me, so I tried to sneak a nap in. My flame resistant pants are maneuvered on, and I rush to the bay. Boots on the ground echo across the bay as everyone loads up into the fire trucks. Every second counts.

"It's on Meadow Brooke," Tristan says.

His parents live on that street and the worry is evident in his eyes. I think it's something we all worry about because house fires are possible anywhere. That's why it's so important to have an escape plan in place and up to date smoke detectors. You would be surprised how many homes could have been saved if they had put batteries into their detector.

Damon pulls out of the bay, and heads toward the fire, and Tristan is on the edge of his seat when we turn left onto the road. It's not his parent's house, but only two houses down. His parents were outside, talking with the neighbors. Thank god.

The smoke is billowing in the sky, and a crowd is forming in front of the house. A man is approaching the house. I don't waste any time when we come to a stop, to jump out, and stop him.

"You can't go in there, sir."

"The family never came out. They must still be in there!"

Tristan nods to me and rushes inside. They always tell us not to be a hero, but we can't stand around and do nothing. The structure hasn't begun crumbling yet, so there is still time to get everyone out safely. I yell to Damon that we are going inside to make sure it's clear while he and the others prepare the hoses. You never let a fellow man go in alone. That's our rule.

The door is already open, and the smoke is thick, without my mask I wouldn't be able to see a thing. If there are, in fact, people in here, they may not be conscious.

"Tristan?" I yell, maneuvering from the living room to the hallway. "Where are you?"

A muffled voice comes from somewhere, but can't pinpoint the location because of the low rumbling from the fire. So, I open each door going down the hallway, until I get to the last room. Tristan is trapped underneath a part of the falling debris, and the man is trying to get it off him, but not having any luck. There is a woman and two children huddled up on the bed with blankets covering their noses. This will help them from breathing in the smoke directly.

The piece of debris is heavy, and with the two of us we are barely able to adjust it off him. We need to get out of here before it starts falling apart.

"We have to get out of here now!" I yell.

"I can't walk. My leg is broken," Tristan replies.

The man helps me carry him, and the mother and children follow us closely. The fire is out of control, and if they don't get it put out soon, the whole structure will be compromised. I don't want this family to lose everything.

We move slowly through the hallway, and I keep my eye on the roof for any buckling, and we come close to getting hit a couple of times. The roof has started falling in the living room, and has taken off most of the area so there is no route to get out of the front door safely.

"Do you have another exit?" I scream to the man.

He nods, and turns us down another hallway that leads to a side door. We make it out, and around the house to the EMT's. If we hadn't gone inside, this family could have been killed.

"Thank you so much. You saved my family," he says to Tristan.

We set him on a gurney in front of the ambulance, and he is cursing from the pain. Our job is dangerous, but this is what we signed up for. To protect our community. We are aware what our job entails.

Damon and the other guys have two hoses, spraying down the structure, and he instructs me to go with him. They have it handled. I've never rode in the back of an ambulance before, and never really cared to you, but if Tristan wants me to go, then I'll do it.

"Come on, sir. We have to get him to the hospital."

I climb up in the back and sit on the ledge on the side of the cab. They attempt to put his leg in a splint or something like it to keep it straight, and take his vitals.

"Are you sure you didn't do this just to get out of being my assistant coach?" I ask, only kidding.

"Damnit, you caught me."

At least he is still able to joke around with me even when he is in pain. I am just trying to keep his mind on something else. If it is broken, he will be on leave for a while.

"Looks like I'll be coaching solo. Now I don't have to fight you over Vanessa," I say.

"We both know that you aren't one to break rules. So, I have nothing to worry about. Good try, though."

It's hard to joke around with a guy that has known me for two almost three decades. He's right. I'm not the type to break rules, and sometimes I wish I could be more like him. Tristan was always the one that wanted to bend certain rules a little bit. Nothing illegal, but when he was a teenager, he was very rebellious.

"You never know. Hell, you might come back and we will be married with kids."

His eyes go wide, and for a minute he thinks I'm serious.

"Dude, I'm just kidding. Chill."

When we get to the hospital, he is taken straight to a room where a nurse checks him out, and it doesn't take long for them to determine it's broken. His tibia to be exact. The amount of pressure pushing down on his shin, it makes sense. They set the break which causes him to scream like a little girl and then cast it. Reminder to never break mine. Screw that.

"Can I have some pain medication? This thing is on fire and making my jaw hurt."

The nurse smiles and leaves the room.

"Well, it's official. What are you going to do for the next eight weeks?" I ask.

He rubs his forehead. "Guess I'll finally be able to watch and delete everything off my DVR."

I laugh, and the nurse comes back with his discharge and medication paperwork. She explains everything to him.

"Well, let's break out of this place," Tristan says, sitting down in the wheelchair as the nurse rolls him out of the room and out the ER exit.

Damon is waiting right outside, and helps me get Tristan in, then puts the crutches in the bed of the truck.

"The chief has everything ready for you to sign, and then I'll take you home. They give anything for the pain?" Damon asks.

"Yes, and right now I can't feel a thing."

The ride is mostly Tristan talking about random things. What pain medication did they give him? He is out of it. When we pull up, the guys are outside waiting on us.

"I'll use the crutches, guys. No need to carry me around."

He goes into the office with the chief and we go to the breakroom.

"Maybe you should cancel practice tonight?" Damon suggests.

"No, I can handle it. The girls are excited for the season."

It's nice to have kids being active instead of sitting around on their devices all day. Kids don't play in the street like we used to. They are all stuck inside on the computer or their phones doing the next Tik Tok challenge. I don't want to take that away from them.

"Since you are taking him home, I'm gonna head to the ballfield."

I'm not going to lie, it's going to be difficult doing this on my own, but if it's between doing that and canceling the season, then I'll gladly take it on. That's just the guy I am.

The truck rumbling to life, and then I put it in reverse and pull out of the parking lot onto Main Street. Practices might have to be longer, but are the parents going to complain? Maybe Vanessa, but it's my only option.

Three girls are already in the dugout, getting their equipment out of their bags, and getting ready for practice. Their moms are the ones that are at school thirty minutes before school gets out so they don't have to wait in line. Never made sense to me.

"Hey, ladies. Ready to have some fun today?" I say, walking into the dugout and tapping them on their heads.

They scream, and head onto the field to warm up. I wait patiently for the other players to show up before jumping into practice. Parents sometimes bring their kids late, and it's not the child's fault. So, I don't get onto them about it.

Once all the players are accounted for, and the parents are gathered in the bleachers, I tell the girls to go play catch and warm up. I might as well get it out of the way to figure out how we are going to do this moving forward.

"So, my assistant coach got hurt on the job today and will be unable to help for at least six weeks. Since it's only me, I might need to extend practices by about half an hour so the girls can get the one-on-one attention they need to get better. Does anyone have issues with that?"

My eyes immediately glance at Vanessa who isn't paying attention.

"Okay, so practices will be two hours instead of the normal ninety minutes." I say.

"Mommy, why don't you help?" Sherrie yells.

She is playing catch with Addilyn right behind me, but it gets Vanessa's attention.

"Help with what?" she asks, putting her phone down.

"Tristan got hurt and Coach has no one to help. You played softball."

Vanessa's eyes fixate on me, and then a fake smile takes over. "Of course, mommy would love to help. I played for almost seven years."

The parents thank her for volunteering and she follows me out onto the field to assist me. Vanessa stands far from me, and must not be thrilled about our new partnership. Let's just keep this professional with no lingering glances.

This might be harder than I think. Vanessa is wearing a pair of blue shorts, and a white t-shirt. I try to keep my attention on the girls, but she is distracting. Her long legs are tan and flawless.

This might be a mistake.

9

VANESSA

Do I mind helping out my daughter's team? No, but being forced to work with Brodie, might be hard. His biceps are filling out his t-shirt nicely, and he has a perfect smile. It's so inappropriate, but I can't stop. What the heck is going on with me?

Why did Sherrie have to volunteer me? It's not like I could've said no. All the mom's were staring at me, after hearing about my experience. Plus, I didn't want to let my daughter down.

"Let's all line up behind first base. We are going to throw you the ball. Catch it and then tag the base before throwing it back to Vanessa. Okay?"

The way he says my name, it's almost like it just falls right off his lips. Being in close proximity to Brodie is going to be hard. If he wasn't the coach, then maybe in a couple months I might give in and let him ask me out, but that's not the case. Why did he have to be her coach? Why did Sherrie have to volunteer me?

We run the drill with every girl twice to teach them the importance of tagging the bag. It's one of the most important things when being in charge of a base. Who is going to be play the bases? We only have two weeks until our first game, and there's a lot of ground to cover.

Maybe he isn't the egotistical type. Do I have him pegged all wrong? First impressions are usually what I stick by, but it's possible I am trying to justify why he isn't a good guy. My heart might be broken right now, and steel bars around it, but he seems like a decent man. Or is it all for show?

After practice, he pulls me to the side in the dugout. When his hand touches my arm, a bolt of electricity makes my hair stand up.

"So, we should talk about the party. It might make more sense to have it at your house. Tristan and I weren't going to have one, but since you have joined the team, I figured why not. Sherrie mentioned you like to bake?"

Of course she has been talking about me to Brodie. I don't think she understands what she is doing.

"Yeah, we usually have the start of the season party at my house ever year. You want to have it this weekend? I can talk to her dad and make sure he doesn't have a problem with her missing a couple hours with him."

Lee wouldn't have a problem, but the right thing to do is at least ask. This co-parenting thing is only going to work if we work together.

"That would be great. Saturday? Just let me know the time and what you want me to bring."

Brodie retreats to his vehicle and I take Sherrie's hand and head for the car.

"What were you and coach talking about?"

I tuck my hair behind my ear. "The season party. You love it every year. Now we have to come up with treat ideas."

She screeches, and gets into the backseat. "Is he going to come?"

"Of course. He's the coach, sweetie."

Sherrie likes him, and that's a good thing. It's not like she hated her previous coach, but something tells me she likes Brodie more. It could be that he is more hands on with them, and doesn't get frustrated when they mess up.

I get in the driver's seat and start the car. "I say we stop and get some ice cream before dinner. Our little secret?" I say, peering in the rearview mirror.

"I won't tell."

We stop and get some cookie dough double dips and then go back to the house. I let her watch some TV while I make some spaghetti for dinner. They should make half pound boxes of noodles for smaller households, because I hate to throw away half a box of anything.

Someone knocks on the door, and the peephole shows Tina on the porch.

"What are you doing here?"

Tina walks inside, face red and puffy. "Sorry for just showing up, but I really needed to talk to you."

She sits down at the island with her head in her hands. Something happened. I grab two glasses and a bottle of wine.

"Here. Maybe this will help."

She pushes the glass away. "I can't have alcohol."

Why? Tina is a wine-o.

"I'm fucking pregnant. Like what is Todd going to say?"

Aaron is aware of the risks of having unprotected sex. Would he really be a dick about this?

"I mean you guys have talked about having kids, right? What's the problem?"

They have been together forever, and at one point they were trying to conceive so maybe she is overthinking this and he will be ecstatic.

"About three months ago, he told me that he didn't want to have kids. Our lives were going perfectly. He is so focused on his job, and god - what am I going to do?"

I embrace her, and let her cry on my shoulder. Todd is not an asshole, and I have no doubt he will be happy about this. Her emotions are getting the best of her.

"Try to calm down. You can eat dinner with us."

She closes her eyes and takes some deep breaths. "Okay, I'm fine.

Seriously. My husband loves me, and I'm gonna be a mom. After all those years trying... this is a blessing."

I nod, and smile. "You will be a wonderful mother. No doubt in my mind."

She grabs a bottle of water out of the fridge, and starts chugging until there's no more left. "So, let's talk about something else."

I move around the kitchen, putting the sauce in the small pan on the stove, and stirring the noodles. "Guess what happened today?"

"Today was practice, right? Did he ask you out? Please tell me he did."

I laugh. "Nope, but the assistant coach got hurt, so Sherrie volunteered me to help out. Can you believe it?"

Maybe it won't be so bad. We won't have to spend any time alone, and we always have an audience. It'll help keep me in line. But damn do I want to rip his clothes off.

Tina is enjoying this news.

"If that isn't fate telling you to take a chance, then I don't know what to tell ya."

Who believes in fate? The first person I date after Lee can't be my daughter's softball coach. Is it weird that I think Lee would be pissed? Probably a bit. I would think it's weird if he started dating his assistant.

"I've been single for less than a week, Tina. I'm not denying he's hot, but a relationship isn't in the cards right now."

Do I think I'm trying to make excuses as to why I can't be with Brodie? Yes. There are so many reasons why it's not the right thing to do, especially now. Why couldn't he have come into my life later on and not as her coach. If he would've asked me out then, my answer would be yes. However, that's not the case and so I have to tread lightly.

"Do you think he's the relationship type? Maybe he isn't. Maybe something no strings attached?"

I love how Tina mentions this, like it's just a natural thing. I've never gone home with a guy from the club or bar. Every single man I've ever slept with has been my boyfriend of some time. How does she expect me to just sleep with someone without knowing anything about them?

"Friends with benefits isn't my sort of thing. I'll pass," I say, turning off the stove and grabbing three plates out of the cupboard.

I dish out some on each of them and then walk over to the table. "Time for dinner, sweetie."

Tina wants to think I'm ready to move on already, but I'm not. It's just too soon. Is it weird that I want to talk to Lee about this? The last thing I want to do is move on too soon and get hurt.

"So, what do you think of your mom being your coach?" Tina asks, spinning the noodles onto her fork.

"Cool. I know she misses playing," Sherrie responds.

She's right. Softball was something that helped me become social when I was a kid, and a bond was formed with my teammates every year. Sometimes, I miss that comradarity. It was nice to be a part of a team.

"Well, I'm glad you thought of me."

I end dinner on a high note, and send Tina on her way to talk to her husband. He's going to be happy.

As for me, maybe coaching won't be so bad.

10

BRODIE

*H*ow is it already Saturday? I've got so much to do before I go to Vanessa's and help her with the team party. Of course I'm the person that pushed off grabbing everything for it until a couple hours before, and I still have to swing by and check on Tristan. How is he handling being stuck at home? How many shows has he already binged?

I grab my keys off the entryway table, and head to Tristan's. He is going to ask about the team and how things are going. He might try to act like he didn't want to help me, but I'm not fooled. His love for the sport is as strong as mine, and if Vanessa wouldn't have been there on the first day, he would have had fun with the kids. I have no doubt about it. I can't get mad at him for being distracted, because so was I, but we have to do our jobs. He didn't need to be so obvious about checking her out. What if it made her uncomfortable and she complained? Thankfully, she was too busy on her phone to notice.

I pull up in his driveway, and head to his door, knocking once and then opening it.

"I've brought you pizza. How you doing?" I say, sitting it down on the coffee table in front of him.

"This is so boring. How am I going to survive weeks of this?"

He opens the box, and puts a slice in his mouth. "How did practice go? You never called me back."

I take a seat on the couch, and start laughing. "It went well, but Vanessa has stepped up and helping me."

He sits his slice on top of the box, and glares at me. "You've got to be fucking kidding me? She wouldn't do that. No way."

I run my fingers through my hair. "Dead serious. Matter of fact, she is hosting the team party at her house in just a little bit."

Tristan is jealous, and I get it. He wishes it was him getting to stand next to her without appearing to be a creep. It makes it easier on him.

"Well, you are screwed now. She definitely isn't going to get with you."

I scoff. "You were the one trying to get with her. Not me."

He rolls his eyes, and picks his pizza back up. "Sure, keep telling yourself that, bro."

The attraction is there, but I'm more about connecting on a deeper level. Looks fade over time, and I want to be with someone who I will love fifty years from now. Personality is important for me. Vanessa has something bothering her right now, and drama isn't something I want to be caught up in. So, I plan to stay away from her.

"Don't worry. Nothing is going to happen. Anything else you need before I head out?" I ask, getting off the couch.

"Already leaving?" he asks.

"I still have to pick up everything for the party and it starts in almost an hour. Don't think it would look good for me to be late."

He smiles and tells me to get the hell out of his house, jokingly.

I jump in the truck and head to the grocery. Once inside, I pull up the list that Vanessa sent me, and start throwing juices and snacks into the cart. She is baking all of the dessert items so that's one less thing for me to have to buy.

The girls have been adamant about having their annual party. It's something they look forward to every year, and I didn't want to take that away from them. As their coach, it's nice to witness them bonding as a team. A team only works if they trust each other, and parties like these build relationships.

After checking out, and loading them into the truck, I plug her address into my GPS. I'm shocked to find out she only lives a couple blocks away from me. When I pull on her street, I see her car and pull in the driveway.

"You made it!" Sherrie screams, coming off the porch and down to my truck. "Do you need help?"

I nod and hand her the two lightest bags, and take care of the rest myself. Vanessa is standing on the porch in a royal blue summer dress that comes down to her ankles.

"Told you I wouldn't be late. Fifteen minutes to spare," I say, following her inside and setting the bags down in the kitchen.

The island has softball-shaped cookies, marshmallow bars, and cupcakes on it. All this sugar is going to get them wired up. These next few hours should be fun.

"Let me show you the back yard," Sherrie says, grabbing me arm and pulling me to the back door.

"Do you think we can all fit in the pool?"

"Yes. You girls are going to have some fun today, huh?"

She nods with a smile and then runs back into the living room.

"So, what do you need help with?" I ask Vanessa.

She motions to the fridge, so I take the juices out and stick them in the fridge, and put the snacks on the counter. She put a lot of time into this party.

Cars begin to arrive, and Vanessa and I greet them outside.. We must be very brave taking on twelve girls for the afternoon. Vanessa is capable of doing this herself but I have no experience babysitting children.

"You'll have to give me some pointers. This is out of my comfort zone," I tell her.

She laughs. "Better get used to it. There are many of these parties throughout the season."

Vanessa is a little more laid back today. Maybe whatever was bothering her is gone and she found an outlet for all that attitude.

I follow her outside, and the girls get into the pool. It's only four feet so everyone is able to touch, but we still keep an eye on them.

"Hope you are good on a grill," she says, opening up a tupperware.

A grin crosses my face, and I start it right up. "You can call me master."

She shakes her head, and walks away. Okay, maybe that was too much.

Jokes aside, the only way I'll be helpful today is by knowing my way around a grill. She did all the baking, and all I did is bring some snacks and drinks. It's not like I'm trying to impress her or anything.

I keep my eyes on the girls, making sure they are okay, because the last thing I want is to have to explain an accident to any of their parents. That is quickest way for them never trust me. No, thanks.

"So, what made you want to become a coach?" she asks, walking up behind me.

"My friend Damon, Emily's stepdad asked me. He knew that I used to play, and didn't want them to have to forfeit the season."

She crosses her arms. "So you got roped into it?"

"No, it's not like that. Baseball was always an outlet for me, and a majority of my childhood was spent on that same field. It's nice to be back there again, teaching them to be better."

I can't tell if she liked that answer or not, but it's the truth.

"Honestly, I haven't played in so many years, but Sherrie took to it quickly. It's nice to see her have something to keep her occupied. She's got a lot going on, and it'll help."

Should I ask? It might be private, and I don't want to overstep my boundaries with Vanessa. She scares me sometimes with how forward she is, but I ask anyway.

"Anything I can help with?"

"No, her dad and I broke up and she's not taking it well. It'll take time for her to adjust for both of us."

Well, hot damn, that's why she has been so full of attitude. I can't blame her.

"Well, if you guys need anything, let me know. I only live a couple blocks over."

She nods, and turns her attention back to the girls.

"My parents split when I was young, so I get where she is coming from. It's difficult, but you seem like a good mother, so I'm sure she is going to get through it with your help."

When my parents split up, my whole world plummeted around me. I didn't see it coming, but I don't think kids ever do. Things don't always work out, and going back and forth between their houses was a pain in the ass. They fought over holidays and birthdays, and all I wanted was to spend those days with both of them. Even now, you won't find them in the same room. Hopefully Vanessa and her ex get along well enough to co-parent, because mine sure didn't.

"If I can say one thing from experience, the thing I hated the most was going back and forth. Even though you guys aren't together anymore, try to keep it on a stable schedule. My parents fought all the time about who had me on what weekend."

Vanessa tilts her head back. "Right now, we are both just trying to give her some space to deal with it. If she wants to go to her dads, I let her. We are still friends, and that's the best thing we can do for our daughter. She is my priority."

It's nice to have someone talk about their kids in that manner, which just concretes the fact that she is a great mother. Some parents are selfish and put their own needs or wants above their kids, and that's not how it should be.

"Sherrie is lucky to have you."

Our eyes lock for a moment, and then we pretend to be doing something. Nothing is going to happen, but that means we don't have this undeniable attraction. It's almost hard to deny. I think about giving in, and just pulling her aside and confronting her about it, but I stop myself. She just got out of a relationship.

When she is ready, she will have any guy she wants. Her luscious lips, and beautiful eyes. There's no doubt she will have an abundance of men asking her out.

Why do I want that guy to be me so badly?

11

VANESSA

A squirrel runs across the fence, and stops. It leans up on its hind legs and nibbles on its fingers, chittering. Sometimes it's nice to take in animals in their territory. The kids are laughing and squealing playing games in the pool. Normally, the party would be at Lee's house, but I didn't think it would be right to ask, and it's no longer my house. The girls don't mind, and I didn't know if the back-yard would provide enough space but it's adequate.

The charred scent of the barbecue envelopes around me, and I breathe it in. It reminds me of all the times my dad would grill when I was younger. Such good memories before our family went to shit.

Brodie is handling that while I keep an eye on the kids. We might have had a moment but that's over. He grew up with divorced parents, we share that in common and our love for sports. Maybe he isn't so bad after all. I keep telling myself there must be something wrong with him, but I could be trying to keep myself at a safe distance.

Brodie steps over and nudges me with his shoulder. "You okay?"

There are so many things that are sloshing through my mind and having him this close isn't helping. I want space, but at the same time, his arms would feel good around me. What is wrong with me? I've never felt this pull to someone before, and it scares the shit out of me.

"Just a lot on my mind. You can imagine. Just trying to get through this party," I reply.

Why is it so hard to let someone in? Even as a friend? Tina always questioned why Lee and I didn't get married, and maybe she is right. We have commitment issues. It's not hard after both our parents went through painful divorces and spent our childhood fighting. It doesn't exactly make me believe in a happy married life. Holy shit. I'm scared to end up like my parents.

"Can I ask you a personal question?"

He nods, pulling the hot dogs off the grill.

"Your parents being divorced, doesn't it ever make you think that marriage isn't worth it? Like there is no happily ever after?"

He turns to me, places his hands on my shoulders, and stares dead in my eye. "Sure, my parents hated each other, but that doesn't mean my marriage will be like theirs. Don't let them ruin your chances at being happy. There's someone out there for you, and once you find him, he'll make you believe in happily ever afters."

Why didn't I ever question this with Lee? We were together ten years and never got engaged? Yes, we were only together two years before we got pregnant with Sherrie, but we were already having problems. If we hadn't had Sherrie, we wouldn't have stayed together this long. Is it possible I close myself to the possibility of really letting someone in?

Brodie tells the girls to get out of the pool and eat. He puts the hot dogs on the platter and places the condiments and buns on the long picnic table. The girls grab their towels and take their seats. With all the swimming they have been doing, I'm sure they have an appetite.

Brodie and I sit at opposite ends of the table, and I try not to glance at him. He had some of the same obstacles as a child, and surprisingly he has been a gentleman.

The girls start talking about the other teams, and how they think the season is going to go, and Brodie just watches and listens to them. Their confidence in themselves and the team is high and that's a good thing. The team enjoys having Brodie as their coach, and as long as he keeps calm under pressure, this season should go wonderful.

The girls get back in the pool after eating, and I grab my phone.

Me: You still coming over?

Her offer to help is nice, but a part of me thinks it's a way to give Aaron some space. I know he isn't upset about her being pregnant, but there is a lot of things that he will need to change before it gets here. He might have to step back a bit on his career path, but that's what you do for your kids. Tina doesn't want him to give up anything, but he's stubborn and will do it anyway.

The girls yell at us to join them, but I'm not wearing a bathing suit in front of him. Ten years ago, I wouldn't have had a problem, but my body isn't as toned as it used to be. Kids will do that to you. I shouldn't care what he thinks, but I do.

Brodie walks up the ladder, and gets in. I am hoping he is going to take his t-shirt off, but nope. What a shame. Although, it's probably more appropriate with the kids.

"Hey..." she says, coming out the door and stopping dead in the tracks. Her eyes land on Brodie in the pool, splashing the kids, and having a good time.

She walks down to me, and takes a seat. "Wow, he's hotter than you described. If I was single, you'd better your ass, I would be under him so fast."

"Tina! Shut up, there's kids."

She laughs, and scoots her sunglasses from the top of her head over her eyes to hide the fact she is obviously staring at him.

"Come in, mommy."

I shake my head, and Brodie gets out and practically drags me. "The kids have spoken."

He doesn't even give me time to take off my dress before I'm underwater. It can't be flattering how the dress is stuck to my body when I come to the surface.

"Seriously, what is wrong with you?" I ask, wiping the water off my face.

He starts laughing and splashing me with water. "Live a little. Have some fun. It won't kill ya."

That's when the fight begins, the girls and I start splashing him non-stop, and everyone laughs. He's right. I've been wound up so tight, that I've forgotten how to have fun.

"Oh, you're in trouble now," he says, slinging me over his shoulder and then dunking me underwater again. "That'll teach you to mess with the Grill King."

When his hand touches my ass, I think he might move it, but it stays and he dunks me again. His grip is tolerable, and thank god he doesn't catch my grin.

Tina is enjoying herself from the sidelines, her sunglasses on the edge of her nose, smiling. Oh, god. She's not going to shut up about this once everyone leaves. I try to get her to come in, but she refuses, so I get out and sit back next to her, and leave Brodie in there with the kids.

"Girl, he's perfect. Good with kids and smoking hot. Why you are so against it? You can't tell me you don't think about how nice it would feel to have those arms around you?"

"Nope, never."

"Bullshit, I'm thinking about it right now. I'm married, but you aren't. Have some fun."

Tina is never going to stop pushing me, but at the same time, I don't want to do something I will regret.

Brodie gets out of the pool, rips off his t-shirt, while Tina and I gawk over him. I want to run my hands down his chiseled chest, and around his muscular shoulders.

"So, what are you ladies talking about over here?" he asks, taking a seat and drying off.

Tina glances his way, smiles and replies. "How cute you are. You are single, right?"

He hesitates for a second. "Unfortunately. Girls only want the guys that just want to string them along, so I'm over it."

Interesting. Is he being genuine or putting on a show?

"So, you don't string girls along?" Tina asks.

"I might not have the best example of relationships from my parents, but I would consider myself a good guy. I don't believe in wasting time. If I like someone, then I'm all in."

Tina glances over at me, and nudges my shoulder.

"Do you think Vanessa is attractive? Just wondering why you haven't asked her out yet?"

I jump out of my chair, and put my hand on my hip. "Stop trying to set me up. Don't answer that."

"Of course, she is, but it's clear she isn't interested."

Brodie's eyes linger on mine, and it makes my stomach flutter. Why am I so opposed to letting this gorgeous man take me out on a date? Oh yeah, because I've been single for less than a week.

"Brodie, don't mind Tina. She just wants me to find someone, but I'm not ready to date anyone right now. It's not you."

He shakes his head. "That's what they all say."

Brodie walks off, and asks the girls to get out of the pool since six is approaching. Their parents will be coming shortly to pick them all up and they haven't even had any of the cookies. My island is covered in junk food and I don't have enough room to store it.

"Grab a towel and dry off before going in the house and grabbing some sweets," I say.

Brodies pulls a dry shirt from his bag and throws it on, and marches inside with the kids.

"Seriously, stop. You made me insult him for god's sake."

Tina shrugs her shoulders and follows me inside where the kids are gathered around the island stuffing their faces before their folks arrive. They are going to go home sugared up, and I'm glad the only person I have to worry about is Sherrie. Lee will be here to pick her up, but I'm glad he didn't mind me keeping her for the party.

Brodie doesn't even make eye contact with me, and if Tina wouldn't have stuck her nose in my business, this wouldn't be awkward. I love her to death, but sometimes she needs to learn to keep her mouth shut. She only made matters worse for me.

I get ziploc bags out and start stuffing treats inside for the girls to take home. They didn't even make a dent, and I only have so much space.

Cars start pulling up, and the kids head outside with their bags.

"Don't forget to take some of these home with you. Share with your parents or siblings."

The girls avalanche over until all the bags are gone. Brodie helps me round up the kiddos when their parents arrive, and by six thirty, they have all been picked up.

Sherrie is inside packing her bag, and Brodie just stands around with his hands in his pockets next to me. Is he scared to talk to me now?

"I'm sorry about that. She means well..."

He shakes his head. "No need to apologize. Rejection sucks, so let's not harp on it."

Lee pulls up in the driveway, and Sherrie comes running out, and straight to the back door.

"This is the coach. I'm sure Sherrie has mentioned him," I say.

Brodie shakes Lee's hand.

"I'll pick her up tomorrow if you need. Just let me know."

Brodie and I go inside and help Tina clean up the madness that ensued from the back door to the kitchen. Water is tracked throughout the house, but I expected that.

"It's tricky since we are co-coaching, but one date wouldn't hurt. If you despise me afterward, then Tina will leave us alone."

He turns to me. "Are you kidding?"

"Not in the slightest. She is going to harp on this for weeks and I don't want to hear it. So, I'm agreeing to one date. You game?"

He stops at the door, and turns his head. "Pick you up tomorrow at 6?"

I smile, and Tina shakes her head. "Should've just listened to me from the jump."

It's only one date and then we will put this behind us.

12

BRODIE

I'm beyond surprised to be going out with Vanessa tonight. She is one of the players' moms but I can't overlook the pull. When she's close to me, I just want to pull her close. So that has to count for something. It's one date and if it goes horribly then we will put it behind us, but what if it goes great? Am I ready to be in a relationship with someone who has a child? Someone who has ties to another man for the rest of her life? How is their relationship? It crosses my mind that he will be in here life forever. I'm always said I didn't want someone with baggage, but maybe that's my problem. I need to throw all that out and start over.

I knock on Tristan's door and he calls out for me to come in. He is going to be mad, but I owe him the respect to tell him.

"How's it going? Whatcha watching now?" I ask, plopping down on the couch.

"Don't ask. Same bullshit. How did the party go? Kids drive you nuts?"

When I don't answer right away, he turns his attention from the TV to me.

"It went great. Kids were a blast."

He nods, and glances back at the tv.

"Vanessa and I are going out tonight."

He slaps the couch, and scoffs, but doesn't respond. He cups his face.

"Listen, I'm a hypocrite but her friend showed up at the party and asked if I found her attractive. Did you expect me to lie?"

He nods enthusiastically.

I'm the one that told him not to flirt with the moms and here I am going out with one. I have to at least go out with her. Online dating has been a monumental mess, and she's the first girl I've met in person that has piqued my interest, and I have to go with my gut.

"It's one date. Her friend pushed her, it's unclear if she actually wanted to go out with me or she only did it to get her friend off her back."

A part of me hopes she is excited. She has only been single for a short time, and I will be careful. When kids are in the picture, we have to tread lightly.

"You needed to hear it from me, but I'm a grown ass man and don't need your permission to go on a date. You are the one that has been pushing me to do this, maybe not with her, but with strangers."

Tristan has a right to pissed off, but that doesn't mean I'm going to cancel with Vanessa. We agreed to one date and I plan to make it enjoyable. Maybe she will want to go out again.

"I gotta go get ready. See you later, man."

He will get over it. There are plenty of women, and it's not like he had eyes only for her.

I text her before backing out of the driveway, and heading to my house to change.

Me: want to make sure we are still on for tonight?

She might be rethinking this, and it won't surprise me. Vanessa doesn't have to go out with me just to please her friend. I have seen the way she looks at me, and she might not want to admit it, but she wants me too. Vanessa is not good at hiding it.

My truck comes to a stop in my driveway, and I jump out and walk inside to get ready. Tonight isn't supposed to be romantic necessarily, because she hasn't expressed she has feelings for me, so I want to take her somewhere casual and friendly. It will help take some of the pressure off the night. Tonight, I just want to get to know her better. Cut the bullshit, and give me the truth. A peek at the real Vanessa.

I throw on a pair of jeans, and a green striped button up. Is she going to dress up? Tonight can't be any worse than the dates I have been on from online. There have been some doozies.

My phone buzzes against the bathroom sink and I brush my teeth.

Vanessa: Yes.

The one word response throws me off. Is she not looking forward to our date? Or is she just playing hard to get? Either way, she isn't backing out, and that gives me the opportunity to show her the kind of man I am.

It irks me how women are always complaining they are no good guys left, but they purposely gravitate toward the men that don't give them the attention they need. Meanwhile, I'm over here just waiting for my queen and nothing. Bad boys are trouble, and usually it ends in heart ache, so why not just trust the good guys? I'll never understand.

I gargle some water to clean out the leftover toothpaste from my mouth, and then grab my keys. Her house is only a couple blocks away, but I like to be early, even if it means I have to wait.

The truck backs out of the driveway, and turns on Sycamore and then her street. There are two cars in the driveway, and my guess is Tina is there. Vanessa is probably regretting saying yes and she is trying to talk her into having a good time.

I'm not one of those guys that pressures women. First dates are typically how you get to know someone, and I don't expect anything else. Vanessa is going through a lot and it might be beneficial to be the person she can talk to. Everyone needs an outside sounding board, right?

I open my door, and gracefully walk up to her door, and knock. Tina opens it, and gestures me inside to sit on the couch.

"Fair warning. She's a mess. Give me five more minutes."

Their voices are going back and forth inside, but they aren't loud enough for me to make out the words. Vanessa has a screech to her voice, and Tina has her hands on her shoulders, trying to comfort her. Is going out with me really this bad? Maybe this is a bad idea and we should just call it off. My head falls into my hands.

"Ready to go?" Vanessa says, grabbing her clutch off the island and standing by the door.

Her eyes aren't puffy, but she is wearing a lilac dress with a jean jacket and black wedges. The dress gives me full view of her long legs, and the color compliments her beautiful eyes.

"You look beautiful."

She opens the door, and I walk out and open the door for her. She laughs, and shuts the door herself. When I get in the driver's seat, she clears her throat.

"Something the matter? If you want to cancel, I'll understand," I say, before backing out of her driveway.

"Let's get out of here. Tina is still watching us from the living room window like a creeper."

Does her friend usually meddle in her love life? If she didn't push Vanessa, we wouldn't be going on a date right now so I thank her.

The ride over is pretty silent, and she is very fidgety. Is she nervous? I'm not the type of guy she has to be nervous around.

"The diner, huh? This must be the staple of Grapevine," Vanessa says, unbuckling and getting out before I'm around the car to open her door.

The bell rings above our heads as we step inside and I let her choose the booth. Her ass is perfectly round in the outfit, and I try not to be obvious.

She sits down, clasps her hands together, and stares out the window.

"Are you scared to look at me? You haven't made eye contact with me once since I picked you up?"

She begins to pick at her fingers. "It's been a long time, okay? And I'm not even sure if I'm ready to be on a date."

"But here you are."

Darlene takes our drink order, and I try to start a conversation.

First dates are notorious for basic questions and I'd rather not do that.

"So how long were you and your ex together?" I ask. Okay, so maybe talking about ex's isn't the best conversation starter but might as well get it out of the way.

"10 years. But it wasn't all sunshine and rainbows. We had our troubles and in the end we had to split up. We weren't happy and we both deserve better."

Holy shit. Ten years? That's one hell of a relationship. It makes sense why she isn't ready to date yet. Breaking up with someone is hard enough, but after a decade, their lives are intertwined, even more so with Sherrie in the picture.

"Good for you. Some women will stay and be complacent. It says a lot that you wanted more for yourself."

I have plenty of guys at work that are with their wives, but they aren't happy. Divorces are be brutal and with kids involved, it's a hard battle. If they filed, their concern is if they would be able to see their kids. That shouldn't even be a worry. They are good fathers, and that shouldn't be hindered because they didn't want to stay with the mom.

"How is Sherrie handling it? I went through the same thing around her age."

My entire focus is on her as Darlene sets down our drinks, and walks away.

"Lee and I sat her down and explained it. Worst night of my life. She didn't come home for three days. One day at a time right now."

Sherrie is a good kid, and something like this is going to crumble her perception of reality. No longer seeing her parents together. It's a mind fuck, but she is smart.

"What about you? Why are you single?"

She takes a sip of her drink, but her eyes focus on me. Finally.

"Well, Tristan had me doing that online dating crap. FYI don't waste your time. I did, and I'm over it. If I'm meant to be with some-one, I'll find her a different way."

"That's not what I asked but online dating isn't an option for me.

Too many sickos out there. Can't have that with Sherrie. Anyway, tell me about your ex?"

I hesitate at first, but I'm an honest person. So, I tell her about Cheryl. The first few months were amazing, and things were going great until her ex-boyfriend showed up at my house and threatened to kill me. Apparently in his mind, they were still together, and I am not one to tolerating cheating. So, I kicked her to the curb, and explained my side to the man. I don't think he believed me, but my conscience is clear.

"Wow. Who does that? If you aren't happy, then break up, don't go out and cheat. The grass is always greener. It just appears that way because it's fresh and new. I don't think people understand how real relationships work."

I'm interested in hearing more about this. How does she think relationships work? What does she try to avoid? Everyone has their hard passes, and it's better to see if we are compatible now besides on an attraction level. She's fucking gorgeous, but sometimes that's a red flag for crazy. I've had enough crazy in my life to last a lifetime.

13

VANESSA

I'm trying to keep myself from giving in. Brodie is decent, but some guys are good at hiding their true selves. It's tricky and I have to be careful. Keep my impenetrable walls up. I'm not opposed to getting to know him, but I'm not ready to be in another relationship so soon. It took me ten years to stand up for myself and it's important that I don't just jump into something. I'm not scared to be alone, and that's a good thing.

Darlene comes back and takes our order. She has eyed me a couple of times, but we aren't ready yet. His reaction to certain things help me gauge if he's putting on a front.

"So how do real relationships work?" he asks.

Listen, I'm not an expert, but some people aren't in it for the long haul. They give up when things get tough, or just don't want to deal with it. That's called being a damn coward. When you truly love someone, you fight against the obstacles, not each other. You fight to be next to that person, and don't just run away when things get hard. My parents weren't necessarily happy, and from the little that I do vaguely remember from back then, they did fight a lot. It was always over stupid things like not taking out the trash, or forgetting to put the dishes away. Now that I'm an adult, it's obvious they were not upset about those actual things, it's the little things that turn into bigger issues.

"You sure you want my answer?" I ask, getting his confirmation before I lay it out. "A real relationship is work. Sure there is a honeymoon phase, but that will pass and then the real work begins. You don't get with someone to change them, and you don't have to like everything about them. Everyone has flaws. Communication is key. If something pisses you off, say so. Irritated, say something. Little things turn into monumental ambushes and that will ruin a relationship."

Darlene approaches just as I'm finishing my sentence and sits the plates in front of us. This conversation is getting interesting.

"The only thing I would add to that is personal time. If I'm in a relationship, it's nice to be able to get out and do things by myself, without having to feel bad about it. Just because I want to go without you doesn't mean I have an ulterior motive. It's healthy to spend some time apart, no matter how long you've been together."

He is speaking my language. I'm all about curling up on the couch and watching a movie together, but sometimes I just want to go out to dinner with a friend. Lee always used to have a problem with that, almost like I didn't want to spend time with him. In his defense, he worked all the time, so when he was home, he wanted to spend time with us. I can't fault him for that, but I still need me time. That shouldn't be a problem in any relationship.

"Okay, we are diving in head first. While we are here, what's the thing you hate the most? Like deal breakers?" he asks, digging into his country fried steak and potatoes.

This is a hard question, because there are so many things that I learned in my past relationship that I never want to deal with in the future. Is it going to sound like I'm just bitching about my ex? That's a major turnoff.

"So, I'll say this. If you have the need to check my phone, then we shouldn't be together. Or you shouldn't have a problem with me checking yours. Don't be a hypocrite. Also, intimacy. Let's just say that sex isn't the only form, and I need more than that from whoever I'm going to be with and they should expect the same."

I search his eyes for a reaction, and a smile tugs on his cheeks. "Hallelujah! Preach it, because one of my ex's was all about getting in bed, but didn't want to touch me otherwise. I agree with you that trust is a relationship killer. So is communication."

Our outlooks on relationships are similar or he's just telling me exactly what I want to hear. Why am I so quick to think Brodie is lying to me? Maybe I do have some type of trust issue when it comes to this. He is sexy, caring, good with kids, and knows exactly what he wants. Any other woman would be jumping at this opportunity and I'm still so hesitant.

"Can I ask why you think you aren't ready to date?"

I don't have an answer.

"I've been single for less than a week."

"That's not an answer. Sometimes things come into our lives at the right time, and honestly I find it mind blowing that you walked onto the field the day I told Tristan I was going to stop. As soon as you pulled up to the field, I wanted to ask you out, but being the coach complicated things."

It still does. What are the other moms going to say? What is Lee and Sherrie going to say? Tina wants me to move on, but Lee is still in the back of my mind, screaming at me to wait. But why should I?

"I'll admit that when I noticed you checking me out, it gave me a confidence boost. Don't you think it's too soon?"

"Do you think there's a length of time you have to wait before you can be happy? Personally, I've been waiting to find my person, the one that I can talk about anything to, and fall asleep with every night. If you want to wait before continuing, I won't say no."

Brodie is chipping away at my walls, and a part of me wants to let him in. Why should I want to be happy? Whether it's him or someone else? After being in a failed relationship for way too long, I don't want to waste any time. I just didn't think it would happen so soon. Brodie makes me feel sexy, but shy.

Being with someone new is always exhilarating, not knowing what to expect. I'm unable to anticipate his moves like I could with Lee. It's actually refreshing.

"I don't know what I want. Can we not label it? Just have fun and see where it takes us?"

Without the pressure of calling it dating, maybe it won't overwhelm me. If we weren't calling this a date, than I wouldn't be anxious because I have no idea what's coming next.

"I'm gonna be honest, here. We don't have to label it, but there's one stipulation that's a deal breaker with me. We can't sleep with other people. Not saying you have to with me, but I can't handle another man putting his hands on you. Can you handle that?"

Excitement tingles inside me, and my mind rushes to Brodie fucking me right here on the top of this table. He just pushes the dishes onto the floor and takes me. People fantasize about sex, so why should I be ashamed?

"Actually, that's perfect."

We both smile and go back to eating our food, and somehow it dawns on me that I just agreed to continue seeing him. Maybe things will work out this time. I've been wrong about Brodie, and he might be one of the last good guys out there. I'd be stupid to let him get away, especially when his eye is on me.

"What next?" he asks.

I grab my phone and text Tina.

Me: Is Sherrie home? Can I stay out a little longer?

Tina is going to be ecstatic to know I haven't walked out on him. She thinks fate brought us together, and he is the perfect man for me. How can that be if we barely know anything about him? How can he be my perfect match?

Tina: She's home and in the shower. Girl, I got this. Enjoy yourself ;)

I send a quick reply and put my phone back in my clutch. "Whatever you want to do."

He leaves forty dollars on the table, grabs his keys, and usher me out of the door.

Once we are inside his truck, he asks if there is anything specific I want to do. Yes, fuck me right here.

"I'm game for whatever. Let's go."

He pulls out of the parking lot, and onto Main street. We appear to going back to my house, until he turns on a different street. He pulls into the driveway and shuts the truck off. This must be his house.

"Come on. We can watch a movie. Your pick."

I jump out of the truck and admire the landscaping. There are beautiful healthy flowers in the garden by his porch. He opens the front door, and when I step inside, it's not at all what I expect.

The house is well-decorated, and things are tidy. A bachelor usually has stuff laying around, dishes in the sink, but not him. I glance around his house to see if there is any indication a woman has been here, but not a trace.

He sits down on the couch, and hands me the remote. I flip through until I find a Romantic comedy that I haven't seen a thousand times and press play. My shoulders tighten.

"We can do something else if this makes you uncomfortable?"

I shake my head. "No, my shoulders just hurt."

He maneuvers himself behind me on the couch, and he starts to massage them. I almost tell him to stop, but it almost makes me cry from the pressure. The last time I got a massage was over six years ago. Here we are, on our first date, and already he's noticing my needs.

I want to run for the hills, but something about Brodie keeps me calm. He doesn't scare me, at least not in the traditional sense. Getting close to someone so fast is bound to get my heart broken and it terrifies me. Yet, he is so blunt about what he wants, and that thrusts me toward him even harder. I like that he didn't beat around the bush and just told me how he feels.

His hands work their magic, relieving the tenseness and leaving me relaxed. He asks me to lay down on the couch, and then begins on my back.

"How do you know where to apply pressure? I've never understood that?" I ask.

"By the tenseness of the muscles. Normally it's rock hard and you just have to knead it out."

When his hands rise off of me, I sit up and gaze into his eyes before kissing him. His mouth opens up for me, and I don't stop to think about what I'm doing because then I will overthink it.

I move on top of him, straddling him, and he cups my ass firmly while my hands work through his hair. There's so much passion. Something I have been missing for a long time. My mind is telling me to stop but everything else tells me to go for it.

I pull my dress over my head, and for a second his gaze is stuck on my chest, until he notices I'm not wearing any underwear.

"What a naughty girl."

He unhooks my bra. Brodie takes them in my his mouth, giving them the attention they deserve, and his hands slide around my back. I throw my head back, moaning as he flicks my nipples with his tongue. Holy fuck, it's been too long.

I pull his shirt over his head and throw it on the floor, running my hands up his torso, enjoying every muscle. Our eyes meet and the desire is clear. I start to unbuckle is pants, and his puts his hand on top.

"Are you sure?"

It's nice of him to ask, but I wouldn't try to take his pants off if I wasn't ready for him. My body is on fire and I need a release now!

I unbuckle his pants and he helps me get them off, and then I take him in my mouth. His hands spread across the back of the couch, and he's taking me in. I look up through my lashes and maintain eye contact as I continue until his head throws back. He is getting harder, and I just want him inside me.

He grabs his wallet out his back pocket, and pulls out a condom. "Get up!" he growls, pulling me up to a standing position, and then picking me up with his hands cupping my ass. I kiss him, and he shoves me against the wall.

He holds me up with one hand and uses the other to pin my hands above my head as he inches inside me causing me to gasp. Fuck. He starts slow, and then works his way up to a steady pace. I tug to get him to lower my hands, but he tells me not to resist. He's fucking hot when he takes charge.

He pounds into me, while biting my neck, and I moan. It turns me on when he growls, and I come, but he doesn't stop. I want to show him he's not the only one that will take charge.

I remove my hands from his grip above my head, and he eases me down. "Sit down!" I've never been so forward during sex but he makes me want to break out my shell. He obliges, and I straddle him again, this time easing myself onto him, and taking exactly what I want. My hips swivel on him and I'm already on the brink again, but this time it's his turn.

"You feel so fucking good. I want you."

It's like a primal instinct and he grabs my ass, and starts thrusting up into me, and he gazes into my eyes without ever wavering. His mouth makes an O and we don't stop. I want to fulfill him. He leans forward, and bites my shoulder as he slows down.

"You are fucking magnificent, Nessa, but I'm not done." He pulls the condom off, and then flips me onto my back. "I want to taste every inch of your body."

His head dips in between my legs, and it leaves me breathless when his tongue nips at my clit. Where the fuck has this man been? And why did I try to resist? The euphoria of having this hot as fuck man giving me exactly what I need is orgasmic itself, and it's been so long since I've had someone else touch me, that it sends shivers up my spine. He bites the inside of my thigh, and then works his up over my stomach, breasts, until he reaches my lips.

"Tell me exactly what you want," he whispers in my ear.

"You."

"Tell me. How?"

I flip over with my hands on the back of the couch, and my ass pointed up. "Just like this."

He grants my wish, and puts another one, and slams inside me. My breathing hitches, but I want everything he will give me. I don't want it to ever stop. I'm on top of the world.

"Harder."

He takes my hair into his hands and smacks my ass. "I might just stare at this ass all night."

I grip the couch as my release approaches, and sends me into convulsions, but he keeps going.

"I don't think I can handle much more."

"Trust me, you are about to have the best orgasm of your life," he says, slapping my ass again and picking up the tempo.

It builds and builds until I cry out and my body starts locking up. This is the best fucking release I've ever had, and I just want to keep going. He is someone who takes care of my needs, and his pleasure comes from seeing me come. I'm sensitive, but he pulls out, and then lowers himself underneath me, and his tongue starts to circle slowly.

"Are you trying to kill me?" I ask, trying to get away from his tongue.

"Don't you want that again? They get more intense. Let me help you come one more time."

He puts his hands around me, keeping in place, while his tongue circles around my clit, causing me to moan louder than I ever have. The build up is almost instantaneously since I haven't come down from the last one, and my toes start to curl.

"Oh my god, don't stop. Get me there. Fucking get me there!"

He goes faster until I literally fall on top of him from the over-whelming release.

I roll over, letting him sit up, and i fall into his chest. "Holy shit. Where have you been all my life?"

"Have you never had an orgasm before?" he asks, eyebrows furrowed.

"I have, but nothing like that. Of course, we usually are done after the first time."

He laughs. "Where's the fun in that?"

Brodie is someone I want to sleep with again, and he's a gentle-man. It's about time I find someone who will treat me good and fuck me right.

14

BRODIE

*V*anessa's phone rings and wakes us. She sits straight up. "Oh fuck!"

Apparently we wore ourselves out last night and ended up falling asleep. She grabs her phone from her clutch, and answers.

"Hello?"

Her voice isn't loud enough for me to decipher her words.

"I'm on my way."

She hangs up the phone, and starts crawling around picking up her dress and bra.

"Are you in trouble? I didn't expect us to fall asleep."

She shakes her head. "No, but not Sherrie is going to ask questions. We have to be more careful next time."

So, she plans on there being a next time? A smile reaches my ears, and I stretch out on the couch.

"You should really put some clothes on. I can't be distracted," she says, throwing my pants.

She clasps her bra, and then pulls on her dress over her head. I pull my pants back on, and then go to my closet to grab a different t-shirt. "Last night was amazing. If you would still like to see me, I'm game."

Vanessa isn't as innocent as she might portray, and I like a little kink in the bedroom. Vanilla sex is nice, but it's predictable and sometimes it lacks passion. I want to hear Vanessa beg me for more, to go harder, to fuck her.

"We'll talk about this later. Can you take me home? I've got to shower and change to get her to school in like thirty minutes."

Okay, so maybe I shouldn't have kept her out all night, but I don't regret it for a second. If she wasn't in such a hurry, I would surprise her with a quickie before I take her home, but that's out of the question. Bummer.

I grab my keys, and follow her out to the truck where she gets in and doesn't say a word for the three blocks to her house. Tina waves at me through the living room window.

"You are entitled to have a little fun. See you at practice."

She walks up to the front door and slips inside.

When I get back to the house, I glance across the living room and daydream about last night. Sex is a natural thing, and I refuse to be embarrassed about it. I might not sleep around, but when I'm with someone I like, it's easy to show them. Vanessa has proven that it is more than just an attraction between us, and even so, if this does work out, our sex life is going to be healthy. How does she feel about exploring? Without knowledge of her past relationships, she is a closed book, but I don't like to get bored. Is she willing to try new things? I'll add this to my mental list of things to talk to her about later.

After taking a shower, I grab my bag and head to the station. Jeremy and Damon are already pulling equipment out, and the chief is watching them.

"Hey, bro. How was your day off yesterday?" Damon asks.

"Perfect."

Damon squints at me, and then starts following me into the locker room. "Perfect, huh? Did you finally find a girl? You have a cheesy smile on your face."

Damnit. She doesn't want me to tell anyone. So, I need to respect her privacy and keep it to myself. Otherwise, I would be shouting it

from the rooftops. Normally, I'm not really one for secret relationships or hook-ups, but Vanessa's situation is tricky. I need to be
understanding toward her situation.

"I did, but it's still new. Don't wanna jinx it."

Some of them make fun of me for not just going out and finding a
woman to scratch the itch. They might be okay with sleeping with
random strangers, but I'm not. First of all, I'm not a fan of catching
sexually transmitted diseases. Sleeping around will ruin your life.
Plus, it just doesn't compare to being with someone you have feelings
for. When there is a deeper attraction there, it makes it more
passionate and that's what fuels my fire. Vanessa and I have things in
common even going back to our childhoods, and she is able to relate
to the issues I am facing with my parents. Even when it comes to relationships, we see eye to eye on almost everything, which means this
could be the girl of my dreams. I'm not saying I love her or anything
but there is a reason she has been brought into my life, and if she
wants us to play a secret game until she's ready, I'll happily oblige.

Damon just stares at me as I put my bag into my locker, and I
close it. "Seriously. Let's get to work. Chief doesn't like us standing
around idle when there are things to do."

If we stand around, he is going to start asking questions, and I'm
not a good liar. If he asks about Vanessa, then he is going to know.
She will kill me, so I walk out of the locker room, and into the bay.

While I'm doing inspections, Vanessa is clearly on my mind. I've
been wanting to settle down and have a family for a couple years, and
then this crazy woman walks into my life and puts me on my ass. She
has admitted she likes me, but doesn't want to jump in head first.
After everything that happened with her ex, it's understandable that
she wants to take her time and see if this could work, and I'm all for
that. I just wonder if she is going to lead me on and then dump me? I
don't want to get my heart broken, so I need to keep my walls up, and
protect myself. It's the smart thing to do.

As much as I want to just open my heart fully, it's difficult when
the other person guards their heart. No matter the reason for it. I have

to spend more time with Vanessa. As long as she stays honest with me, then this will work out.

I pull out my phone and text her.

Me: Listen, I just wanted to check on you. Last night was amazing and I hope you don't regret it. We can go about this at whatever speed you want, but don't lead me on.

Things are different with her, and normally I stay far away from women with kids because of the issues that arise, but not with Vanessa. There was a pull that gravitated me toward her at that first practice. I couldn't take my eyes off of her.

Vanessa: No regrets. No man has ever done that for me. I have to admit, I'm thinking about it right now. Are you?

She is a dirty girl, and it's nice of her to open up toward me more and more. Even at the party, she was so closed off and now she is being playful. I adore this side of her.

One thing that works in my favor is she just got out of a decade-long relationship. She is willing to fight for her happiness or she would have stayed with him. She deserves better, and I'm going to go show her I'm the person to do that.

Me: Why just think about it, when you can have the real deal?

Daydreaming about Vanessa's lips around my cock is getting me hard, and I'm not going to be standing around the depot with a boner. So, I try to keep my mind busy, by inspecting the hoses.

Vanessa: Only if you promise to make it worth my time =)

She has no idea what she is getting herself into talking to me like that. I don't half ass anything, especially sex. Watching a woman succumb to an orgasm is better than having one myself. I think that's why I'm intrigued by her. She started off with an attitude, but honestly she just needed someone to give her a release. Being pent up will damper your mood, but I'm willing to help.

Me: I'm a good listener. All you have to do is tell me exactly how you want it.

Damon keeps staring at me, and I notice I've been on my phone a lot so I go and put it up in my locker so she won't distract me anymore, but my mind just fantasizes about being inside her again, and hearing her moan into my ear.

How am I supposed to think about anything else when she is baiting me? She wants me just as bad, and can't wait to get my hands on her again. I took it easy on her yesterday, but next time, I'm going to make her see just how amazing sensory deprivation is. This might be her first experience but I want to experiment. If she thinks the orgasms from last night were mind blowing, she's in for a real treat.

A tentative man is perfect when it comes to being in the bedroom. Exploring and finding new things sexually with someone is a bonding experience. Think of it as a trust exercise.

I'll fulfill all of her darkest desires without hesitation.

15

VANESSA

*B*rodie has me daydreaming about last night all day, and it's distracting. I haven't been thoroughly fucked like that ever. The way he asked me what I wanted, and did it without hesitation makes it even more enticing. What else does he have up his sleeve?

Tina hasn't stopped asking me for details since I got home this morning. She isn't stupid. We slept together.

"Girl, did you enjoy yourself? I'm not slut shaming or anything," Tina says after my last appointment of the day.

"It was fucking phenominal, okay."

It's weird talking about my sex life with her since her husband is so close with Lee.

"I knew it. He just looks like he would know his way around a woman's body. But not in a douchebag way."

She isn't wrong. Brodie read my body language, and was one step ahead of everything I wanted. It's not all about the sex. The conversation went well and we have the same views on many things that are important in a relationship. I'm finally figuring out that I need to stop letting Lee effect my life. We aren't together anymore, and if Brodie brings me happiness, then I shouldn't be scared. It didn't matter how long it's been since we broke up.

Tina playing matchmaker might have worked in my favor this time, but I'll never tell her that. Plus, what is her husband going to think when he finds out she set me up?

My phone vibrates and pick it up thinking it's Brodie finally messaging me back, but its not.

Lee: So, you stayed out all night?

How the hell does he know that? Why is it any of his business? I slam my phone down on my table. "Did you tell your husband I was out all night?"

"What did you expect? I had to have an explanation on why I wasn't able to come home."

So he ran and told Lee and now I'm going to have to explain myself. But why should I? We are not together and if I want to stay out all night, it shouldn't be any of his business.

Me: I did. We aren't together so I'm not sure why you are even concerned?

"Now, I'm going to have to deal with Lee. This is why I didn't want to go out with him."

Tina is my best friend but sometimes she truly doesn't think things through before she opens her mouth, and this time it's going to bite me in the ass. Lee didn't need to know about last night, and now it's going to make things awkward.

Lee: Wow. Ten years and you are already seeing someone? I guess I'm just shocked. Guess things were even worse between us than I thought.

Is he acting like things weren't bad between us? Why is he even saying this shit right now? We haven't been in love for years, and I refuse to feel bad for enjoying myself. I'm free of him, and if I want to see someone, then it's my prerogative.

"I think Brodie is just what you needed. Even if it was just sex. You are glowing today."

I don't want to talk to Lee about it anymore right now.

Tina's final appointment walks through the door, and she has been coming here for years. She's very open about her life, and she treats Tina like a therapist sometimes. Always complaining about her problems.

"My hair is a mess. Fix me!" Denise says, sitting in Tina's chair.

I've never really liked her. She loves drama, and I try to stay far from it. The last time she was here, all she talked about was her ex-boyfriend who she left because he didn't make enough money to support her lifestyle. Why is it his problem to support her lifestyle? Get a job and support yourself. Girls like her give us a bad name. It truly pisses me off when she speaks. She always leaves Tina a good tip so she sits there and listens to her gripe and tells her stories.

"Girl, I have to tell you about a date I went on last week."

Tina obliges, and stops. "Come on. Give me the dirt."

She goes on to tell her that the guy shows up late, and then he ditches her before they were even able to order drinks. She sat there for almost thirty minutes waiting for him to come back before she left.

"Can you fucking believe it? I'm a catch and he just left? Why are guys such assholes?"

Tina gives her some speech about how nice guys are hard to find, and that she will find her perfect match someday and to be patient. Denise doesn't take it to heart.

"I think I want to go up to the fire station and give him a piece of my mind. Is that crazy?"

Tina nods, and goes back to cutting her hair.

Does Brodie work with the guy Denise went out with?

"What was his name? The guy I'm seeing works there too."

"Brodie. Tell the girls to stay far away from him. He's hot but an ass."

Holy shit. She went out with Brodie? I can't imagine him going out with someone like her. He said Tristan made him do some online dating, and it didn't work out for him. I never expected to run into someone he went out with at work.

"Did he give off any vibes that he wasn't interested in you?"

Asking her questions about it might be bitchy and Tina keeps peering at me. She is probably wondering why I'm asking her about it and is wanting me to stop.

"I mean, my friend kept texting me. We didn't even really get to have a conversation."

My head shakes, and I finish cleaning up my station..I can't be mad that Brodie went out with someone else. He has been upfront with me about things this far, and it's not like he is purposely hiding that he has gone on dates with other women. He's an attractive man.

"See you later, Tina. You coming over tonight?" I ask, grabbing my purse before heading to the school.

"See you around six thirty. You going to see boy toy tonight?" she asks, winking.

"Maybe."

I walk out the door, and get into the car before saying anything else. A part of me wants to bring this up to Brodie, but then again does it make me look jealous? I don't want him to think I'm crazy or anything? I back out of my parking spot and head down the street to pick up Sherrie.

When I arrive at the school, the pick up line has died down, and Sherrie is waiting by the curb and a smile displays when I pull up. She gets into the car, and I take off toward the house. I hope she doesn't bring up me being gone last night. She isn't ready to hear that I'm seeing someone. Will people judge us if they find out? The moms will probably have a field day, but they will be jealous.

"How was school, honey?" I ask, grabbing her backpack off the set, and shutting the car door behind her.

"Long. Can I have a snack and watch tv?" she asks, walking up the stairs to the door.

I put the key in, and open it. "Of course."

I spend the next hour thinking about last night and wanting to do it again. Why has it been so long since I've had great sex? I'm young! I don't feel bad one bit for wanting it. I bite my lip, imagining Brodie pushing me against the wall and crouching down between my legs. That man has some magical hands.

My phone vibrates and it's him. He must have just gotten off work.

Brodie: how was your day? Apparently I had a ridiculous smile on my face and the guys wouldn't shut up about it.

This is why Brodie stands out to me. Most men wouldn't even be reaching out to me. They would play games and wait a couple of days. I like that he isn't doing that and checking in on me. It shows he is interested.

Me: Tina wouldn't stop asking me for details. You know how she is. We gotta be careful next time. No more sleepovers.

Although, I would be lying if I didn't want to wake up in his arms, curled up on the couch.

Brodie: Did you tell her I made you come five times? I don't know how much girls share with their friends. You might make her jealous, so probably better to keep that between us ;)

I laugh and Sherrie glances at me. Her gaze only stays on me for a couple of seconds before she goes back to watching tv.

The sex is magnificent, but I have to make sure he is someone I have a possible future with before I get to wrapped up in the cycle. I refuse to be in a relationship that won't go anywhere again. I learned my lesson with Lee.

So, what do I want? An important factor is Sherrie and he does well with kids. The softball party didn't phase him and that's a definite plus. A major problem is going to be how he handles co-parenting. Even though I am not with Lee anymore, it's important we maintain a relationship for our daughter. Will Brodie have a problem with that? To me, that's a deal breaker. I don't want conflict between my boyfriend and my child's father. That's unnecessary chaos. It's too early to bring this up right now, but it's something that's going to be in the back of my head.

Me: Tina could tell but I'm not into discussing my sex life with others. Too personal. Please tell me you didn't tell anyone?

We agreed not to label this.

Brodie: Tristan knows, but only because you didn't tell me before we went out that you didn't want anyone to know. But besides him, no one else knows. You were very adamant about not telling anyone. I haven't told a soul. Pinky promise.

A knock sounds at the door, and Tina walks in.

"What are you ladies doing?" She joins me at the island and glances at my phone. "You are already sucked in, aren't you? A good night will do that to you."

She's careful about her words with Sherrie in the room but her wink says everything.

"Do you mind watching her for an hour while I run an errand. All you have to do is preheat the oven and put in the lasagna for about forty-five minutes."

Okay, so I want to go talk to Brodie in person. Maybe I shouldn't waste away a good opportunity. Take my life back.

She nods, and I pick up my keys and head out the door. Why am I going over there?

When I pull in his driveway, his truck is outside and he isn't expecting me. So when I walk up to the door and knock, I don't expect him to answer.

It takes a couple of minutes, and he opens the door in just a towel.

"Do you normally answer the door like this?" I say, crossing my arms.

"I saw you through the peephole. Are you complaining?"

I push passed him, and he shuts the door.

"So, one of your dates came into my salon today. Does the name Denise ring a bell?" My back is turned to him.

"Yeah, I actually went out with her the night before I met you. Why?"

"She seems to think you are an ass and women should stay away from you."

He comes up behind me and wraps his arms around me, and then whispers in my ear. "And what do you think?"

He starts kissing my neck, and my eyes close letting the heat travel down my body. I try to keep myself from giving in, but when he grips the hem of my shirt and his fingertips graze my abdomen, the ecstasy of his touch is too much.

He slowly raises my shirt up over my hand, and I turn around gazing into his eyes. He doesn't take them off of me as he unhooks my bra and my breasts spring free.

"I think it's only fair since I'm naked."

His towel has fallen to the floor and his cock is at attention.

It's taking over my mind all day, and I've been daydreaming about being with him again. It's like a craving.

I lean in, kiss him, and then unbutton my pants and maneuver them down to the floor and step out of them.

"There. We're even," I say with a smile.

He picks me up off of the floor, gripping me by my ass and carries me into his bedroom and lays me on his bed gently

"You can stop me at any point, but I think this is what we have both been thinking about all day."

His lips touch my abdomen, and it sends a sensation downward. It's like I'm sexually charged and I'm reliving my later teenage years again.

His opens my legs and dips down in between them, nipping at my inner thighs and then hos tongue touches my clit and my back arches. Fuck! His tongue is magical.

"Want me to keep going?"

I nod, and continues. Moving in circles around my clit, and sending me into spasms. When he adds a finger, and then another the pressure sends me into ecstasy. He uses his tongue and fingers in harmonious sync until I tighten around his fingers and grab the sheets.

"Fuck. Yes."

He waits for me to sit up and stare at me before asking me. "What next?"

I just sit there and stare.

"Tell me what you want."

His eyes dance over my body.

"I want you to fuck me until I can't take it anymore."

Where did that come from? I'm not normally so forward like this.

"How? You want me like this?" He slips inside me, kisses me, and then flips me over on my stomach. He pulls my hair and slips inside from behind. "Or like this?"

I bite my lip, and don't respond. "This only works if you answer. Tell me."

"Let's not limit ourselves to one position. You can have me however you want."

He growls and slams into me, making my head thrash back and moan. What is it about this man that makes me want to stay in this bed and never leave?

His hand reaches around and starts running my clit as he continues inside me and the build up is steadily building and makes my head spin.

"You are going to drive me crazy. Aren't you?" I ask, breathily.

"As long as you let me. It'll be my pleasure, babygirl."

He asks me to sit up and picks me up. Nibbling on my neck, and pushes me up against the bedroom wall.

"Personally, there's something sexy about having you up against this. It makes me go deeper, and you can grind against me while I hold you steady."

I rock my hips, riding against his hard cock, claiming every inch of him. He fills me and I don't want to stop.

My alarm goes off and I stop.

"I told Tina I would be back in an hour." I stare into his eyes.

"Well then let's finish," he says, carting me back to the bed and thrusting into me steadily while massaging my clit.

"Don't come without me. I'm almost there!"

He speeds up faster, sending me into a frenzy and I can't hold off much longer.

"Come for me!" I yell.

Just as I say it, he pumps one last time and stiffens.

"Fuck, babygirl. I'm never gonna be able to get enough of you."

He slips beside me, and I lay on his chest.

"So, let's keep this between us just for another week. And then you can tell your friends. I just want to enjoy this before everyone else knows our business."

"Understood. Whatever you want," he says, kissing my forehead and stroking my hair.

He is showing me what I've been missing for ten years and I never want to go back to a loveless relationship.

I deserve a man that treats me well, has enough respect to listen when I speak, and that fulfills my desires.

So far, Brodie checks all the boxes. He may very well be the answer to my prayers.

16

BRODIE

The surprise visit from Vanessa last night is just what I needed. She has disrupted my life, but in a good way, and I can't get enough of her. She's like a drug, and I crave her constantly. As much as I like her sex drive, there's more that I need. A relationship based purely on sex will fail but I don't think it's all we have. Sure, we have already discussed some of the important things like what we expect in a relationship and our deal breakers, but I need to know her on a deeper level.

Sexual chemistry plays a role in a healthy relationship, and we have established that this won't be an issue. In fact, something tells me she is going to be a woman who is turned on by exploring new things. Vanessa has a side to her that I'm not sure she has shown anyone else before, and that makes it even more fun. She has come out of her shell and it's beautiful to witness.

Me: Are you free tomorrow night?

I want to take her somewhere just the two of us. No fancy restaurant. No bed. I'm not kidding myself. In the past I have overlooked things because I liked a girl, and I can't do that again. Especially with what I want. My future involves having children. Is that something she is even considering in her future? If she doesn't want more kids, that's a deal breaker for me. I've always dreamed of having two or three kids running around.

Vanessa: *I'll see if Tina can watch Sherrie. See you at practice.*

It's easier to get this stuff out of the way early so I don't fall for a girl that I can't have a future with and end up breaking my own heart. As much as I crave her, it wouldn't be fair of me. No one should have to settle. Not on something like this.

I put my phone back in my pocket and give my attention back to the poker game.

"How do I always whoop your ass?" Damon asks, throwing down a royal flush.

"You cheat. That's how. No one has that good of odds."

Why do I even play against him anymore? Poker is not my strong suit, and I'm not much of a gambler. When there are slow days, and we have nothing to do, it's about all we have.

"So, will you be going out with her again?" Damon asks, taking a sip of his cherry pepsi.

"I hope so."

"Whoever she is, you're happy, and that's what I care about."

Things have been going well for us, this far, but it's early. I'm scared shitless, because I want to open my heart to her, but there's this doubt that she might not be ready. I'm not privy to everything that happened with her ex, and she might still have feelings for him. The timing of us meeting together did come at a difficult time for her, but maybe that's exactly what is supposed to happen. Yet, I want to keep myself from falling for her.

I want to text her throughout the day, but she might not want to be bothered. Some women like the constant contact and others despise it, so I need to figure out which one she is. There is still so much to figure out about her, and peeling back her layers to reveal her true self.

"Quitting time. See you at practice, tonight."

Damon catches me off guard because Tessa usually brings her, and he might be able to tell a shift between Vanessa and I. If so, then the cat will be out of the bag. I don't want to give her a reason to run from me, but she does want to keep it a secret.

I grab my bag out of my locker, and head outside to my truck. It's nice that practice is almost right after shift ends, so I go straight there. Will Vanessa act differently toward me with everyone around? I'd love to be able to call her my girlfriend, but in due time. I respect her wishes to keep it private. The pressure from others might be detrimental to a relationship, and she might have a point.

My truck grinds against the gravel in the parking lot, and then comes to a stop. I get out and grab my drink from the middle console. A couple of the kids are already here in the dug out so I join them.

"Hello, ladies. Ready for some drills?" I ask.

They nod, and go back to gabbing.

My eyes waver over the parking lot waiting for Vanessa to get here, because I don't want to start without her and Sherrie, but then a black Audi pulls into the parking lot and she jumps out. Did Vanessa get a new car? I maneuver my sunglasses over my eyes, and a man gets out. He puts his bat bag on her shoulders, and takes her hand.

That must be Lee.

I try to play it cool. He comes over and introduces himself, and then takes a seat on the bleachers.

"Where's your mom?" I ask Sherrie.

"A client made her late so daddy had to pick me up."

I pull my phone out.

Me: Where are you?

"Alright ladies, line up behind first base. Your job is to catch the ball, tag the bag, and throw it back to me as fast as you can."

The last thing I need to do is bring any attention to myself. Her ex-boyfriend is sitting in the bleachers watching my every move, and I'm sleeping with Vanessa.

Her calls pulls into the parking lot, and she jumps out of the car in black shorts and a blue t-shirt. She stops and talks to Lee before stepping on the field. They are amicable, which is good for Sherrie's sake.

"Sorry, I'm late. Client took longer than expected."

She steps in for me, and I stand off to the side, letting her run this drill. I try to keep my eyes to myself, especially with the audience behind me, but it's hard as fuck. When the ball rolls on the ground, she has to bend over, and it kills me when her long legs flex.

I take over, not wanting to stare, and the only way is to keep myself busy. Let's split up into two groups. Half of you go to third base."

If we separate, then we aren't close to each other and maybe it will help us stay professional and keep our eyes to ourselves. She has been checking me out and someone is bound to catch on.

I keep myself busy throughout practice. If we are going to keep this a secret, then I need to get my act together. It's hard when you have feelings for someone.

When practice is over, Lee is gone. So, when I find Vanessa away from the girls, I approach her.

"Did you get a hold of Tina?"

She nods. "Yeah. Pick me up around six?"

I smile, and head to my truck, not waiting to cause any attention. Something tells me the moms might be on to us.

My truck pulls out of the parking lot and heads toward Tristan's house. I haven't seen him in a couple days, and it's clear he's upset about my date with Vanessa. Women aren't something to be owned, and it's not her fault that she agreed to a date with me.

I stall in his driveway. A woman is not coming between our decades long friendship. He's had a hard time finding someone too, but it shouldn't affect my love life. He's got to understand that, but it's not worth losing a friend over.

He opens his front door, and stands there with crutches. "What the hell are you just sitting out in front of my house for?"

I get out of the truck, and walk inside. "You still mad at me?"

He laughs. "I'm over it. There are plenty of women out there, and I'm not going to fight you over a girl. Not worth it."

I'm glad he is finally seeing the light and has decided to drop it.

"By the way, how'd it go?"

I leave out some of the details on purpose. Vanessa is aware he knows, and she can't be mad as long as he doesn't run his mouth.

"Well, I'm glad you found someone, bro. It's about damn time."

We sit around his living room for about an hour, just watching some crime show, and then I leave to go home. I still need to eat and take a shower after the long day.

I pass by Vanessa's house on the way home, and Lee's car is outside. A part of me wonders why he's there? It's like eight at night. So, I turn around, and pull in the driveway. I have a perfect view through the living room window. Lee, Vanessa and Sherrie are sitting around the table, laughing and eating. Is there more to their relationship than she is telling me? I've never seen someone so cozy with their recent ex? Does it bother me? Yes, but if I want things to work with Vanessa, then I can't be jealous towards Sherrie's father. He will always be in the picture.

So, I back out of the driveway, and head home without letting them see me.

Don't ruin a good thing before it even gets going.

17

VANESSA

Sherrie joins me at the dinner table, and we talk about practice, when someone knocks on the door and then comes in. I expect it to be Tina, but it's Lee.

"Daddy!"

"Hey, baby girl. Eating dinner?"

She nods, and he comes and sits at the table. "Room for one more?"

I nod, and make him a plate.

"Sorry, I couldn't stay for the whole practice. I had to take care of something."

His eyes glare at me, but I try to stay chipper for Sherrie. I refuse to fight in front of her for whatever he is mad about and he shouldn't be walking into my house either. Is he still upset about me going on a date?

Sherrie tells him all about practice, and Lee listens, but his eyes keep glancing at me.

"Are you enjoying coaching? You loved softball when you were younger. I think that's where our daughter gets it."

"It's nice to teach them about the mechanics, but it's been years since I played. Sherrie enjoys having me engaged in her experience, so when she asked, I couldn't say no."

Once Sherrie is finished eating, I ask her to go get in the shower and ready for bed. After she leaves the room, his fork drops against his plate and both elbows bang down on the table.

"How long have you been messing around with the coach?" he whispers.

Did Tina tell her damn husband about Brodie? She's supposed to be my best friend, and what I tell her should stay between us.

"Excuse me?"

He swipes at the air. "Oh, don't play dumb. Everyone saw the way you looked at each other today. Our relationship wasn't the best, but you couldn't even wait a month before getting into someone else's bed?"

This conversation is crossing a line. Why should I wait until he deems appropriate to find someone? I spent ten fucking years of my life thinking about others, and now I'm finally doing what I want.

"Lee, I'm going to stop you right there. You hadn't touched me in almost three years. I don't know if you were getting it elsewhere, but that's not healthy. I deserve to be desired, and touched. Brodie is a good man, and has been upfront about everything. Why is it my problem that you aren't dating yet?"

I get up from my chair and slam my plate down in the sink.

He follows me and then gets real close. "I fucked up, okay. That's obvious, but I still love you. Seeing you with someone else is killing me, and I thought maybe being apart would help us get back to way things used to be."

He is not pinning this break-up on me. We were both unhappy and expressed that. Why would I ever go back to someone I spent ten years with after being miserable? Lee is a good man, but not someone I want to be with, and he's clearly mistaken.

"We are not right for each other. So, sitting around waiting for me to come back to you is pointless. I was trying to keep things between Brodie and I quiet for a while but now there's no point."

Sherrie walks out into the living room, carrying her pajamas, and stops in the living room. "Are you guys fighting?"

I pop my knuckles. "Oh no, honey. Everything's fine. Go get in the shower. It's almost bedtime."

Once she has left the room, I turn back toward him.

"I think you should leave, and from now on, you need to respect my privacy. Don't just walk into my house. You don't pay the bills here."

He steps onto the porch, and I slam the door in his face.

After everything, Lee comes to my house and says shit like that? He is fucking insane. He should have worked harder on our relationship when we were together, not after. I refuse to be pulled into his rollercoaster ride anymore, but maybe he's right about one thing. Brodie and I should slow things down.

I might be moving on too soon, and even though Brodie is amazing, I have to be careful. The fear of being alone isn't the reason I run toward him, and I barely have taken the time to get used to being single.

Sherrie comes out and hugs me before going to bed, and I text him.

Me: Can you come over?

We need to talk about this now, and as long as I'm being honest with him, he'll understand. From the beginning, I have told him I might be moving on too soon. I don't have feelings for Lee anymore, but I should be taking time to really figure out exactly what I want. For way too long, I put the needs of Sherrie and Lee above my own, and that has to come to an end.

Brodie: Sure. see you in 5.

The plates left on the table are washed and put in the drainer before he arrives.

Brodie: Here

I step out the door, and sit down on the porch and he joins me in gray sweatpants and a white t-shirt. He's fidgeting with his fingers.

"What's going on? Is something wrong?" I ask, laying my hand on his arm.

"Why was your ex over here?"

"He came by to apologize for not staying for Sherrie's whole practice. He hadn't eaten so I made him a plate."

He clicks his tongue. Does Lee scare him?

"Can I ask you a question?" he asks, looking me straight in the eyes. "Do you still have feelings for him?"

I scratch my head, and then pat my knees. "If you are asking if I'm still in love with him, or want to be with him, the answer is no. He is, however, Sherrie's father."

He shakes his head and stands up. "That's not what I asked. Do you still have feelings for him?"

"No."

He sits back down next to me, and his arms encompass me. It's normal for someone to be jealous of an ex, especially if seen having dinner with the girl they like, but he has nothing to worry about between Lee and I. That's over.

"So, why'd you ask me here?"

He isn't going to like this after he just questioned my feelings for Lee.

"Lee knows about us, and I think we should take things slow. Not that I'm complaining, but I'm just getting used to the idea of being single again, and I'm already dating someone."

His eyes follow me as I continue to pace, but his nostrils flare.

"So Lee shows up, and suddenly you think we are moving too fast?"

Things just are moving too fast, and I'm being swept up into this whirlwind.

"Listen, I don't normally do secret relationships, but you were the one that agreed to that first date. You asked me not to tell anyone and I did, even though that's always been a red flag for me. Now, suddenly your ex-boyfriend finds out about us and you want to slow things down?"

He storms off to his car, and backs out of my driveway.

"Please don't leave!" I yell.

His car goes down the street, and my heart drops. Why is this so difficult? Either I want to date him or I don't?

What the hell do I want?

18

BRODIE

*W*hy did I let myself fall for her? She isn't being honest with herself, and I refuse to put my time and effort into a relationship that isn't going anywhere. I deserve better! It's one thing to want to wait but when you clearly are upset that your ex found out about us is a red flag. Why should she care what he thinks? From what she has mentioned, he didn't treat her well, and definitely didn't give her enough attention.

I knew better than to get involved with a woman with baggage because she obviously still has feelings for her ex or she wouldn't be doing this. His opinion shouldn't matter on anything but stuff involving Sherrie. I let my guard down, and now I'm kicking myself in the ass.

I sit in my driveway for a second, trying to calm down. Vanessa is a wonderful woman, but she needs to figure out what she wants. It's impossible for me to give her everything unless she lets me in.

Things are going downhill, and I didn't want to sit around and end up yelling at her, because that would ruin everything, so I left. It gives me time to calm down.

Me: I really like you, but you are letting your ex-boyfriend influence our relationship. You might not realize it, but you are. If he knows, then there is no reason to keep this a secret anymore.

Normally, it takes a lot to get me upset but Vanessa is going back and forth and I can't keep up. Do I want to lose her? No, but I'm also not going to play games. Finding the girl of my dreams has been my goal, and I won't sit around and waste time if it's not her. The fact of the matter is I want a family, and sitting around in my late thirties and casually dating isn't something I want. My forties are approaching and I want to be able to have fun with my kids, and I don't want to be old and gray when they are toddlers. Time is of the essence and I have to be careful about who I waste my time away with, and right now Vanessa isn't wanting to be in a relationship.

I get out of my car, and walk inside, going straight to my bedroom and getting under the covers. Something about this has me on edge, and I don't like it. My father said something to me once that has always stuck with me. A woman can build you up, but that same one can tear you down until you feel like nothing.

I've always considered myself a good man, and someday I will find someone. Waiting around is difficult but I have to keep my faith that there is someone out there for me. Whether that's Vanessa or someone else.

Vanessa: We have been moving fast. Hell, I normally don't sleep with a man without going on a couple of dates, yet here we are. I'm scared I'm jumping into something with you because I'm scared to be alone, and that's not fair to you.

She is scared to get hurt so now she's making excuses. Why can't she just give me a damn chance to prove to her that I'm what she needs? Alone or not. No one wants to be alone in life, if they say that it's a lie. As human beings it's only natural to crave companionship, and there is nothing wrong with Vanessa searching for a man. Lee might have a problem with it, but once they broke up, he should have no say so in that part of her life. Why won't she just let me in? Stop making excuses, and follow your heart. She wants to trust me, but something is holding her back. The fear of other people finding out about us is overshadowing everything else, and it shouldn't.

Me: Scared to be alone? Whether that's the case or not, you need to think about what you want. Do you want me to be with me? Do I make you happy? I literally wake up thinking about you, and you're on my mind all day. Can you say the same?

I deserve someone who wants to be with me, and as much as it hurts, maybe she isn't the right woman for me.

Vanessa: Yes

Sometimes you have to let someone go, and it's for the best. Maybe she needs some time to figure out what she wants without Lee butting into her life. Tina is the one that pressured her into going on a date with me. Vanessa needs to figure out what she wants, and then tell me. I can't do this back and forth.

Me: Then what's the problem? I get you're scared, and so am I, but I've been clear about not leading me on. And right now, it feels like that's what you've been doing. I deserve better than that. So you need to make up your mind.

I want to curl up in bed and let everything out. Why is it every time something is going good, someone else has to come in and ruin it? Something has to give. I shouldn't have to be a complete dick to get someone, but the bad boys seem to not have a problem. Good guys like me are hard to find, yet when someone finds us, it's like we have to work twice as hard. How does that make sense? Do women not want to be treated well anymore? They want to be the ones chasing after a man?

I need to stop before I'm up all night. After switching with Liam, I have an early shift, and it's not safe to be without sleep. So, instead of going back and forth, I turn off my phone and go to bed hoping that she comes to her senses.

FOUR IN THE morning comes too soon, and I roll over to shut off my alarm, and then throw the blankets back over me. Why did I ever agree to switch with Liam? It's too damn early to be up and working.

The bed is comfortable and my eyes start to close, but I sit up. If I'm late the Chief will kill me, and I can't afford to get written up. The thought of having to get up and deal with what happened last night is weighing on me, and honestly I just want to start my morning out with some coffee before I even turn on my phone. Did she even reply back last night?

She likes me, that's clear, but the timing isn't working out. A part of me thinks we should have waited to go out, and maybe this would have worked out better. Tina pushed her to go out with me, and if we had waited, maybe we could've had a better start.

I leave the light off and throw on some clothes before grabbing my bag, and heading out to the truck. The ignition rumbles and I back out of my driveway, and maneuver the eight blocks to the station. The only person at the depot is Damon.

The door slams behind me, and Damon looks over his shoulder.

"What are you doing here?"

"Switched with Liam and regret it," I answer, slumping into a chair, and laying my head on the table.

"You look like shit. Everything okay?"

I shake my head. "Honestly, I have no fucking clue. Would rather be anywhere but work today."

He waits for the coffee to be finished, and places a cup in front of me. "Drink up. We got a long day ahead of us. Calls or not."

After it's halfway gone, I turn on my phone and her text messages start coming in.

Vanessa: I swear that's not been my intention. Listen, I like you, but it just feels rushed.

Vanessa: Hello?

Vanessa: I think it's best if we stop now. You don't deserve this, but this was a bad idea.

Is she fucking serious? It's bad enough I have to work alongside her at the field, but she is taking the easy road out. She has feelings for me, and she's just too scared to admit it. My fist slams down onto the table.

"Bro, you okay?"

I want to run over there, but she has made her decision. If she wants to push away a man that will treat her like a queen, then so be it.

"Let's just find something to do, okay?" I say to Damon, while typing out a text.

Me: If that's what you want, then fine. All I did was try to treat you good and if you want to let your ex get in the way, and influence your decisions, then so be it. I really tried.

At least she didn't lead me on any longer. Vanessa is clearly not the one for me and my heart will remain protected.

19

VANESSA

Things have gone downhill. Lee is fucking with my head. Brodie is amazing, and I want to let him in, but everything is pushing me to say it's too soon. He doesn't deserve to be used, and I don't want to jump into a whirlwind romance right after getting out of a ten-year relationship. Brodie has been nothing short of amazing, but I have doubts. What if he isn't the guy for me and I get my heart broken? What if things go great, he gets close with Sherrie, and then disappears? My fears are more based on protecting my child than my own. Is it normal to go through this?

Practice tonight is going to be awkward, but we will keep it professional. Our issues should not affect the team, and I plan to keep it that way. I haven't texted him back since his response this morning, which is still stuck in my head.

Lee is not the reason for me backing off. There are no romantic feelings toward him anymore, and he has to remember that I spent ten years of my life with Lee. Brodie walked into my life when I was just getting out of a serious relationship, and wants me to jump right back into one. My life hasn't even calmed down from the previous one, and Sherrie is not going to be okay with me dating someone else so soon.

It is ridiculous to let my daughter influence my decisions, but her happiness matters to me, and I'm not the only that gets hurt if things go south. I have to take that into consideration no matter what I want.

The entire morning I've been in bed, trying to figure out how to get over him. How can I feel this deeply after only a week or so of knowing him? My heart is being pulled out of my chest.

Tina is cleaning up station when I walk in, and the dark circles under my eyes already tell her the story. She frowns, and gives me a hug. "Trouble in paradise already?"

"Sorry, I couldn't be here this morning. Brodie and I broke up or whatever," I tuck my hair behind my ear, and sit down in my over-sized t-shirt and leggings.

"What did he do?" Tina asks, sitting down next to me. "I'll kill him."

When I tell her it was my decision, her eyes bug out.

"Why in the hell would you break up with him?"

She only knows what I have shared, and maybe she's right.

"I don't think I've ever seen you as happy as you have been since going out with him. You might not listen to me, but you are making a mistake."

Right now I am stuck in this push pull situation. I want to be with Brodie, but then something in my gut is telling me to stay away. Which one do I listen to?

"I wouldn't even be in this situation if you didn't push me to go out with him. I wasn't ready.. Now, I can't stop thinking about him."

My intention isn't to be harsh to Tina, but it's the truth. If she didn't open her mouth at the softball party, than things would be normal. I wouldn't have to push him away. Why is he the only one I want comforting me right now?

"If you want to blame me for finding someone who made you happy, so be it, but you are the one running away," she says, walking out the salon and leaving.

Fuck. Now she's mad at me too. Why do I keep screwing up? Maybe it's better for me to skip practice today, but honestly I'm worried that if I send Lee with Sherrie, he will start drama. Brodie doesn't deserve that.

I lock the salon up, and head to get Sherrie from school. The team can't suffer because of our issues outside of it, so I have to go and put on my best smile for the kids.

It's easier said than done, when I pull up at the ball field and Brodie is standing there. He doesn't look the best either, and probably had a long night like me. This is screwing with both of us, and I need to figure out what I want.

"Hey coach," Sherrie says, running into the dugout.

Brodie exchanges a quick smile, and then goes back to staring at his clipboard.

What? He can't even look at me now?

"So what is the plan for today? Batting drills? Outfield?" I ask, hands on my hips.

He nods, without even looking up. He isn't in a place to talk to me right now. Neither am I, but I'm here.

"Can I talk to you for a second?" I ask, touching his arm, and his eyes stare blankly back at me. "Please?"

He walks out to the parking lot, and people are walking passed us. I wait until they are by the dugout and bleachers before I open my mouth.

"Listen, we are having problems, but let's not take it out on the team. The girls don't deserve us in a bad mood. Can we keep this professional while we are on the field?"

Brodie runs his fingers through his hair, and his jaw tightens. "I'm trying, okay. What do you expect when you make me fall for you and then you just run away?"

My jaw drops, and I can't speak. Fall for me? He starts to pace, and then he lowers his voice down to a whisper.

"Vanessa, you are the one that needs to figure things out, not me. I know exactly what I want. You have known that from our first date. Please don't play around and act like I am at fault for any of this. Now, let's go get practice started. We are already behind."

He walks off to the dugout, and I'm left in the parking lot with a million things going through my head. Brodie is falling for me? A tear falls and I wipe it right up. This is not the place for this, but he's right.

Why am I pushing away a good man?

Practice is rough, but we get through by staying on opposite sides and running drills with the girls separately. Lee has called me a couple of times, but I haven't answered. He's probably still upset about Brodie and I. I don't want to give him the satisfaction of us breaking up after he left last night. He's a coward, playing tricks with my mind, and I think Brodie is right.

I'm done letting my life fall apart and putting myself second. Lee has no say so in who I date, and when. His mind trick of still having feelings for me is fucking with my head, and I won't let it happen anymore. He had ten years to make our relationship work and he failed.

When Sherrie and I arrive at home, Tina is waiting on the porch for us, a wine bottle in hand. We can't stay mad at each other for long, and I need to apologize.

"Go inside and take a shower," I tell Sherrie as I approach her. "Listen, I'm sorry about earlier. You're right. I'm pushing him away and sabotaging my own happiness."

She smiles, and follows me inside to grab two wine glasses. "I knew you would come to your senses. Men like him don't come around often. You have to give it a chance."

A car pulls into my driveway, and Tina peeks out the window. "Were you expecting Lee?"

My head tilts back and I scoff. "Nope, but he would just show up at my house like he owns it."

I walk out, and put my hands on the door when he tries to open. "You aren't welcome here right now. Go home."

"We need to talk, Nessa. About what I said last night."

"Actually, you told me you still had feelings for me, after you found out I was seeing someone. Why are you trying to manipulate me?"

He forces his door open and grabs my arms. "I love you, Nessa. Maybe it took me seeing you with another man to realize it, but it's the truth. Just give me one more chance before you start dating someone else, please?"

I look him dead in his eyes. "I do not love you, Lee. You just don't know what to do without us. In due time, you will find someone who will make you happy, and then you won't think about me at all."

He tries to pull me close, and I fight him off. "Don't make me cause a scene. Sherrie will be out of the shower any minute, and she doesn't need to witness this. Go home."

His eyes are wet, and his hands are on stomach. "Are you really just going to throw away ten years?"

I stand my ground, with my arms crossed, and nod. "Go home!"

Lee stares at me for a second, and then gets in his car and drives off.

Tina comes out, and hugs me. "Are you okay?"

For the first time in a long while, I stood up for myself. This marks the time in my life where I fight for what I want, no matter what others think.

"Can you watch her for a bit?"

She smiles, and hugs me again. "Go get your man."

20

BRODIE

I stop by Tristan's on the way home from practice. He is the only one to talk to about this. He will probably laugh at me for falling for her so quickly.

"So, what brings you by?" he asks. "You look like hell."

I go to his fridge and pull out a beer before joining him on the couch. "Vanessa pushed me away, man. I really thought she was going to be the one."

His head cocks back. "The one? You knew her for what a little over a week? Don't fool yourself, bro. She's hot, but bad news."

Even after everything, I want to punch him in his mouth for talking about her like that, but he's already hurt so I refrain. Some of it has to do with me going out with her and not him. I must remember that.

"You don't get it. I literally think about her constantly. I've dreamed about our future, and I've never done that with anyone. Ever. I want to fight for her, but it's hard to do if she doesn't want anyone to know we were ever together. I'm backed into a fucking corner that I can't get out of.."

Instead of responding, he just listens to me ramble, and honestly that's all I need right now, someone to let me vent, and get it out of my system.

"You know what, you aren't going to understand. Thanks for listening, but you can't give me the advice I need," I say, walking out of his house.

Tristan has been in maybe one serious relationship, and he isn't the person I need to be talking to about this. If anyone should hear my pleas, it's Vanessa. Maybe she wants me to fight for her, show her that I'm in this for the long haul.

I race my truck to my house, and rush inside to take a shower before reaching out to her. It doesn't have to be tonight, but she needs to hear me out. I have to tell her everything and get it off my chest before she walks away from me for good.

The hot water beats down on my skin as my hands are against the wall, letting it flow down my body. Tonight has been a shit show and something has to give. Vanessa is stuck in my mind, even after her pushing me away, and it's killing me. I refuse to let her walk away from me without a fight. What kind of man would I be if I just let the woman of my dreams walk away?

I wash the sweat of my body with my blue loofah and body wash before turning the nozzle off and grabbing my towel. There is no way I was going over there smelling like death. The towels tightens around my waist, and I walk to my closet to find some clothes, but then my doorbell goes off.

Who the hell is that?

After crossing the living room to the door, I look through the peephole.

"What are you doing here?"

Her eyes avert to my chest, and she pushes me inside and shuts the door with her foot. Her lips are on my chest, and I'm caught off guard.

"Wait, what the hell is going on? You said you didn't want to see me anymore. Why are you being so hot and cold?"

She doesn't even listen to me, just continues down until she's on her knees, with me in her mouth. My hand cups the back of her head, and as confused as I am right now, the way my cock is hitting her throat is shifting my focus for a second.

"Okay, as much as I love this, we need to talk before this goes any further. You know my rules, I don't just sleep around. Okay?"

Vanessa stands up, and takes off her shirt. "I'm trying to apologize, but let's make it a game."

My eyes drop down to her breasts as she unhooks her bra and they spring free.

"I'm done letting other people make decisions for me." she says, and then unzips her jeans and then they fall to the floor before she steps out of them and kicks them across the room.

"Okay, I wasn't forcing you to be with me," I say, but she puts her finger to my lips.

"From now on, I am going to do what I want without worrying about what anyone else thinks. Like the fact that you make me so fucking happy, but I don't want my heart to get shattered into pieces."

"I am not going to hurt you, Vanessa. Just let me prove it to you," I say, pulling her close.

She pulls her underwear down to her feet. "That's why I'm here. I'd rather get my heart broke into a thousand little pieces, than to walk away from you and regret it for the rest of my life."

"Are you saying that we don't have to keep this a secret anymore?"

She nods, and I pick her up, cupping her ass and lay her down on the couch.

"Then I know exactly how we should celebrate."

Her legs spread, and I dip in between them. Her back arches, and she gets wetter. My tongue circles around her clit as I slide two fingers inside, warming her up for me.

"I just want you, Brodie."

My dick stiffens hearing her say those words, and I hover over her. "You can have me anytime you want, day or night. I'm yours."

21

VANESSA

My thighs cramp up as I try to get out of bed. I'm playing hookie today. After spending hours at Brodie's house last night, Tina left around two in the morning. Finally doing something for myself, and not to please others has open my eyes to what I really want. Happiness. Instead of letting fear stop me, I'm going to embrace it, and use it to propel me forward. Brodie deserves a chance and letting things like my previous relationship or having a child get in the way of that is absurd. Single mom's date all the time, so why should I let that stop me? Sherrie deserves to seem me happy, and not allowing myself to have that will only make my world a sad, dark place.

"It's time to get up for school!" I say, knocking on her door, but then she's already in the kitchen eating her toast. "What are you doing up? You sleep okay?"

Sherrie nods, and goes back to eating. She knows something is going on with me coming home late twice in the past week, but right now isn't a good time to tell her. Brodie and I are still new and she doesn't need to be involved for at least a couple of months. We have to spare her heartache, even if I'm giving mine over to him.

Brodie is the first man that has been honest with me from the start, about everything. He made it clear on our first date that he wants something long-term. He wants a commitment, and eventually I think I will be able to give that to him.

Even with Lee, things always felt out of place, like he just wasn't the right man for me, even though I loved him. It took years for me to figure out that love isn't everything. Sometimes love will conquer all, but only if it's with the right person.

We experience love right out of the womb, and our parents show us what love is, and then we grow up and branch out into the world. It's then that we find out that love can also hurt. I've been in love three times in my life, and of course, each time I thought we would sail off into the sunset together, but obstacles were presented and it ended up in flames. So, I have to remember that love is a powerful thing, and we have to fight for it.

I pull a pair of leggings from the closet and a black t-shirt and throw them on before hurrying Sherrie out the door. To be honest, I don't feel like going to work today, and I'm entitled to have a sick day every once in a while.

Me: I won't be coming in today. Hold down the fort.

Tina has been there since the day the salon opened and knows just as much as I do. She has her own set of keys and I trust her.

Tina: I got this. Enjoy your "sick" day.

So, maybe Brodie is off today and it's just an excuse to get to see him this morning, but whatever. The high coursing through my body right now is intense, and I want to ride it for as long as I can. The empowerment of choosing myself has made things clear. I've wasted too much of my life making other people happy and putting myself on the back burner, but not anymore. That ended yesterday.

I am a new person today, and the promise I make to myself is to always think about myself first. Now, that doesn't mean Sherrie isn't taken into consideration, but how can she be happy if I'm miserable?

When I pull up the curb in the drop off lane, Sherrie hesitates to get out.

"What's wrong, baby?" I ask, turning to the backseat.

"Is daddy picking me up today?"

"Of course. But we have your first game this weekend. So, make sure you get rest."

She nods, and gets out of the car and heads inside.

Something is bothering her and when she gets back from her dad's, we'll talk about it.

Me: So, any plans this morning?

He might not even be awake yet. We had an eventful night and I'm wore the hell out. Maybe, I'll just go home and hop back into bed. I'll watch some tv and jut relax the day away.

When I pull up in the driveway, my phone beeps.

Brodie: Laying in bed trying to recuperate from last night. How are you feeling today? If I'm sore, then I know you must be. ;)

I smile and roll my eyes

Me: Don't flatter yourself. I'm playing hookie if you want to join me in bed? Doors unlocked.

The three dots appear, but then they stop. It will be nice to spend one more day until everyone in the world knows about us. The outside pressure is overwhelming, but I'm not going to let it get to me. Outsiders' opinions don't matter to me, and don't have any say so on my happiness with Brodie. It's only him and I.

I go inside, and head straight for the bedroom. It's nice and cool in here so I wrap myself in the blankets and turn the television on. When's the last time I got to watch anything during the day? Heck, probably at least a couple of years. I stop when I find Criminal Minds reruns. Derek Morgan is the walking embodiment of how men should treat their girls. The way he treats Penelope is magical.

The font door opens and closes, and then Brodie walks in.

"Morning, beautiful. Couldn't turn down the chance to cuddle in bed with you all day," he says, laying down on the bed and then kissing me.

He pulls me into his chest, and we watch the show together, just enjoying each other's company without a care in the world.

"What are your plans for tonight?" he asks, kissing the top of my head.

"Nothing at all. I'd be happy with this," I laugh.

There is something that pulls me to him. They have these movies about love at first sight, and no one ever believes it will actually happen, but something happen on the field that day. I couldn't take my eyes off of him, and ever since I have found myself thinking about him. Now, I'm going to embrace it, and enjoy being close to his warmth, where I feel safe and at home.

"Instead of me going to the gym later, how about if I get a workout right here?" he says, flipping me on my back and caressing my cheek.

"I think I can help you work up a sweat."

He gets off the bed, and walks out of the room. When he returns he has an ice cube in his hand.

"What exactly do you plan to do with that?" I say, leaning up on my elbows, and he scares me with a wicked smile.

"Whatever you let me."

He pops the cube in his mouth, and crawls up to me.

"Lay down."

I do as he asks, and he lifts my t-shirt, trailing the cube down my chest, in between my breasts, and then down my stomach until he leaves it in my belly button. He moves down to pull my leggings and panties off, and then take it back in his mouth, and continues trailing down until it's on my thigh. He takes in between his fingers and rubs it on my thigh as he dips in between my legs and runs circles around my clit. I arch my hips at the hot and cold sensation. Fuck!

"It's so cold!" I scream, so he takes the ice cube on my clit and focuses with his tongue. I will never get enough of him, how he can read my body so well.

What the hell is he doing to me and how have I never tried this before? The shift between hot and cold sensations is driving me to the edge, and toes begin to curl.

"Yes, please. Don't stop," I yell, grabbing his head and holding it in place as he starts moving his tongue faster making my thighs shake. "Yes! Yes!"

He comes up with a smile, and kisses me. "Never done that before?"

I shake my head.

"Well, we will definitely have to do that again. Anything else you haven't done, you'd like to try?"

I get off the bed, and walk over to my closet, grabbing two red silk tie. When I come out with it, his eyes twitch and so does his cock.

"You sure are a naughty girl, aren't you? So you have never been tied up before?"

I put my wrists near the bed posts and smile. "Always a first time for everything."

He takes the ties and notches them around the two posts, leaving me enough slack so that I don't get marks. Smart thinking.

"Do you know why women like to be tied up?"

I shake my head.

"It's a thrill. You can't put your hands on me, which means I can do whatever I want, and that means you have to trust me. Do you?"

That's a loaded question, but I nod.

He kisses me and trails his kisses from my chin to my belly button and then stops. I find myself watching his every move. He spreads my legs, and inches inside of me. My hands pull at the ties, wanting to touch him, but I can't.

"I will never hurt you, Vanessa. However, I'm down to give you pleasure in every way imaginable if you let me. We will start small, and work our way up."

Honestly, Brodie is unlocking some kind of hidden trap door inside my body because I can't imagine ever being sexually intimate with anyone else. He is able to read when my body wants more or less, and he switches course.

He uses his right hand to keep himself steady, and the left gently trails down my neck to my breasts, and takes my nipple in between his fingers, making them hard. His hands aren't calloused like you would think, but quite smooth. My breathing hitches when he gets down to my clit and begins to rub in circles, all while his eyes are dead set on me.

He smiles, moves up to kiss me, and then thrusts into me hard.

"Ugh!"

Brodie cups both my breasts as he moves fast into me, forcing me to watch his every move, without being able to move. When I get close, I want to pull him closer to me, and run my fingers through his hair, but the ties prevent it. So, I thrust my hips up, and put my leg around his ass, forcefully pushing him deeper inside me.

"Come with me," I say, almost out of breath.

A sexy growl erupts, and he speeds up even faster, until my walls close around him, and he stills.

"You have no idea what you do to me, do you?" I smile, and lay my head back on the pillow, as he unties me, and pulls me onto his chest. "How am I ever going to get enough of you?"

You never will...

22

BRODIE

This is exactly how I want to spend my day off, snuggled up with Vanessa. I'm so happy we were able to work things out, and get through our fight. Is it crazy for me to be falling for her so fast? After years of searching for my future wife, Vanessa walked onto that field, and it's hard to walk away. Sure, she had an attitude and things going on, but I couldn't just stand around and let her pass me by.

Her body curves with mine, and we continue watching some reality show she has put on that I have no interest in. My eyes start to close when she says there is something we need to talk about, and those words always scare me.

"Did I do something wrong?" I ask, sitting up on the bed.

"No, but we do need to make sure we are on the same page for certain things."

I nod, and my chest rises and falls, waiting for the subject.

"First, a family. You want one, right? Here's the thing, I'm not opposed to having more children, but I want to make sure the person I have another one with is going to be my husband. It's important we make sure this is going to work before we bring someone else into the mix, even Sherrie."

Vanessa and I once again agree on something. Having a child with someone is a huge responsibility, and you are counting on them to be there. Kids are ripped apart because relationships don't work out, and I wouldn't want to put my kid through that.

"I think that's just as important to me as it is to you. Our histories. You will make an amazing mother. Look at Sherrie."

We are taking things slow on that front, and if she asks about us, we won't lie, but she needs to have time to still get used to her mother and father not being together, and I don't want her to resent me for being with Vanessa. Children at her age are very vulnerable when it comes to families splitting up, and she needs to be able to take that in at her own pace.

She leans in and kisses me.

"Second, we need to talk about Lee. He is Sherrie's father, and isn't going anywhere. Promise me you will be civil?"

"As long as he doesn't pull that crap again, then I'll be fine."

I don't agree with how Lee has conducted himself since I have come into the picture, and manipulated Vanessa to get what he wanted from her. Co-parenting is important for Sherrie and I would never come in between that, but he has to understand his place. He has no say so in Vanessa's life, and as long as he doesn't cross the boundaries set, then we should all be fine.

Things don't need to be heated between us, and I'll make sure to stay out of Vanessa's way when it comes to Sherrie. They are her parents, and even if I don't necessarily like it, they must communicate. I always wanted this for my parents when they broke up, and Sherrie deserves for her parents to get along when it comes to her. Plain and simple.

This is new territory for me. I have never dated a woman with children, and in fact, up until Vanessa, I never planned on doing so. Sometimes, plans have to change accordingly. If I wouldn't have been open to the idea, then I wouldn't be laying here next to this beautiful woman right now.

Things are a little different, since we coach Sherrie together, and eventually she is going to notice that we are acting differently toward each other, but we want to try to keep things strictly professional on the field. I don't want any of the parents thinking I'm playing favorites. I will treat Sherrie the same as anyone else on the team. That's just the type of coach I am.

Will Sherrie be okay with me dating her mother?

MY HAND REACHES BESIDE ME, but the bed is empty. Vanessa isn't able to stay over right now, because we haven't told Sherrie about us. I'm not pressuring her at all, considering she is still trying to get used to her father not living with them and that's enough for her to process for the time being. I won't lie though, a part of me wishes we could be at her house snuggled up in bed again all day today, but being an adult comes with a price. Bills. So, I mosey myself out of bed, letting my feet hit the ground, and then wrestle with my hair. It's all over the place, and a shower might do me some good.

The clock shows it's almost seven which means this has to be quick for me to be able to make it to work. Liam agreed to work my second half of the shift for our first softball game today. Are the girls are ready?

I turn the nozzle to hot, and go to the closet to grab a pair of shorts and a t-shirt to put on afterward. I get in, and the water hasn't heated up fully, so I back myself out of the water, and grab my body wash in the meantime. Once the steam starts to fill up the shower, I use my loofah to wash all the sweat off my body from yesterday, letting the water run over my body. Normally, I would enjoy a longer shower, but there's a time crunch so I turn the knob off, and wrap the towel around my waist.

Vanessa is supposed to have lunch with Tina today, and I'm sure I'll be the topic of conversation. Normally, I don't like when people meddle in my business, but without her help, we wouldn't be together. She nudged Vanessa to go out with me, and that set things in motion sooner than I anticipated.

I step out of the shower, and emerge into the bedroom, pulling my boxers on and then my shorts. My phone buzzes on the nightstand.

Vanessa: Have a good day back at work. See you at the game this afternoon.

I set my phone down and let my t-shirt slide over my shoulders and down around my torso.

Me: Wish we were still in bed. Why do we have to be adults?

The swoosh alerts me that the text has been sent, and I grab my bag and keys and rush out the door to head to the depot. Vanessa and I aren't keeping things a secret anymore, and I'm excited to tell Damon. He has been wondering what's going on, but I couldn't tell him. He's not usually someone I keep secrets from, but I did as Vanessa asked.

After I pull into the parking lot, Damon is getting out of his truck, and meets me walking in.

"How was your day off? It was boring around here without you."

My mind recalls being in bed all day, and that's probably not what he wants to hear. "It was good. Girlfriend and I hung out all day."

"Girlfriend, huh? So, things are working out, then?"

My mood has shifted, but I'm happy now. There is no hostility toward Vanessa for thinking things through. I needed her to be sure she wanted to be with me, and not because her friend was pushing her to. A relationship can't be based on a lie, and even though our attraction and chemistry was very real from the beginning, she was having a hard time.

"Vanessa and I are doing well. Hit a bump, but worked through it."

He stops as we enter the locker room, and turns around. "Vanessa?"

This is going to come as a shock to some, but really if they paid enough attention, they could have figured it out.

"Yes, but I can't let what others think stop me from being happy. You of all people know how that goes."

I throw my bag to the bottom of the locker, and shut it. Damon just smiles at me, and asks if I want to play some poker. Honestly, I'm in such a good mood, maybe this time I'm clear headed enough to beat him.

"Sure, why not."

We head to the break room, and I put the coffee grounds in to make a fresh pot. How would I survive without coffee? There are some days when I end up on so many calls that I don't get to go home for an entire day, no matter what time my shift is supposed to end. When duty calls, we are expected to be ready. Caffeine is a big component of that.

"So, are you and Vanessa going public? Can't wait to see what the softball mom's have to say about that. They are vicious. And you being a good-looking single man. Well, they were probably taking bets on who could get you first."

My head cocks back. "Are you serious? That's ridiculous. Do they not have better things to do with their time?"

Damon laughs and then goes into this big spill about how things have been in the past. A lot of the moms aren't faithful to their husbands, and they might seem like they are trying to screw me, but they definitely are. Apparently, their first coach got kicked out of the league for sleeping around with the mom's.

"He wasn't only sleeping with one of them, but like four. And one day at a game, they were talking about their weekend, and that's when they put the pieces together and found out they were all sleeping with him. Isn't that the shadiest shit ever?"

Well, they don't have to worry about that with me. Vanessa is the only mom I'll be sleeping with, so they can back the hell off. I'm not one to create drama, so if they want to start something then I'll put an end to it real quick.

The coffee machine is ready to go, and I pour into two mugs for Damon and I.

"Do you really think people are going to have a problem with us dating? I mean, we are adults."

He shakes his head. "There is always someone, but I wouldn't worry about it."

Damon shuffles the deck, and just before he starts to deal, his phone rings.

"Hey babe," he answers. "What? Right now? Okay, I'm on my way!"

He shoots up out of his chair, and starts crying. "Tessa is on the way to the hospital. She's having the baby. I gotta go."

"Get out of here. I'll tell the chief!"

Today is a great day to bring a baby into the world, and I can't wait to be an uncle. It's one thing to hold someone else's child, but when it's yours, it's the most beautiful thing in the world. And one day, I will experience the joy.

The day wastes away, waiting around for news from Damon. The last time I talked to him Tessa was almost fully dilated and the search engine says that means she was close to having the baby.

Emily is with Raquel because she couldn't go to the hospital with them and we have our game today. She is ecstatic about having a baby brother, and it will probably take over her mind, but I'm not going to worry about it.

Two o clock comes fast and it's time for me to get out of here and get to the field for our first game. The girls are going to do great, and I'm excited to start the season.

Vanessa: it's almost game time. Do I need to pick up Emily for the game?

She is truly an amazing woman, and I'm lucky to have her as my co-coach. The girls have two adults that love the game and don't have to worry about winning. We have made it clear that it's about them having fun playing the game.

Me: Raquel will be bringing her. See you in a bit.

I grab my bag out of my locker and get to the truck. This is going to be our first game that we aren't trying to hide our relationship from everyone. Sherrie's dad will also be at the game and I'm hoping we can keep it civil.

Vanessa didn't keep things from me, but when I found out he tried to get back with her, it did piss me off a little bit. He had his chance over ten years to make her happy, and he failed. Now he just can't stand her being happy with someone else. Unlike him, I'm going to make sure everyday Vanessa knows how much she means to me. She deserves that and so much more.

Today is our first outing as a couple, and it might come with some turbulence, but we will get through it because we have each other to lean on. We can't let outside influences ruin our relationship.

Will we be able to get through today without pissing anyone off? Will Lee be able to keep his feelings to himself or will he make a scene?

23

VANESSA

The diner is empty when I walk in. Sherrie is with Lee this weekend, so he is bringing her to the game later. He has only texted me in regards to our daughter and that's how it should be.

I sit my purse down in the booth next to me and Tina starts in.

"You are glowing. I'm assuming you are feeling better today?" she laughs.

So what if I played hooky from work? I haven't missed a single day since we opened, and honestly it's time for me to take a vacation. It's been on my mind. Maybe Sherrie and I can go somewhere just the two of us.

"I laid in bed all day."

"Oh, I'm sure you did," she winks.

The waitress brings us some coffee, and I put two creams and three sugars inside.

"But really though? Are you happy? I haven't seen you perky like this in years. Brodie is just what the doctor ordered."

Honestly, I have Tina to thank for this whole situation. If she wouldn't have pushed us together, then I wouldn't have taken the chance of going out with Brodie.

"We are in a good place. Got our first game with the girls today. Lee's going to be there."

Tina's eyes go wide. "Wonder how that's going to go?"

Lee better stay in his lane and not cause any drama. Why is he so upset about this? He had ten years for his chance. Don't come running to me now. I never would have guessed Lee would act this way, but it goes to show people always surprise you.

"Do you think he is going to say something to Brodie? He seemed livid at the house, and unfortunately he is the coach of his daughter's team, so he is gonna have to get the hell over it."

I take another sip of coffee and ponder her question. "If he can't be a man, and accept the fact that he missed out on his chance, then that's on him. Brodie shouldn't be treated badly because of his mistake. I hope Lee will be an adult about the situation, but only time will tell."

The game starts in less than an hour, and honestly my nerves are all over the place. Not only because it's our first game of the season, but with Brodie's and I's relationship evolving, we don't want to it affect the team in a negative way. We want to remain professional on the field.

"Are you coming to the game today? Didn't know if you had clients coming in this afternoon?"

She replies. "Yeah, two color clients. So I can't make it, but I'll be at the next one cheering her on."

I put a couple dollars on the table for the coffee, and say goodbye to Tina. I can't be late for warmups, and typically the coaches are the first people there.

My tires crunch on the gravel as I pull into the parking lot at the softball fields. The other team is already warming up. What time did they get here?

Sherrie has already been worrying about the game, and wants to win. This is exactly what I don't want. She doesn't need to worry about that, but instead focus on her love for the game. These girls need to get out there and enjoy themselves. They are too young to have that in their mind but some of these parents engrave into their kids that that's the only point of playing sports. And that's exactly why they aren't coaching.

When Sherrie showed interest in playing softball, Lee and I agreed that we would only let her join a team that didn't have a coach as a player's father or relative. They are many reasons and one of the biggest ones if you lose coaches a lot because of that. When their daughter moves up, so do they, and they leave the team behind. Or they show favoritism toward their child, and someone else who is better fit for a position gets overshadowed.

Our team doesn't have to worry about any of that. We have their backs, and even if their parents push them to win, we are the ones in the dugout with them, and as long as they have fun and do their best, then it doesn't matter the outcome of the game.

At this age, it's more about learning the fundamentals of the game, than actually playing itself. When they get into their teenage years, the coaches will pick kids that understand their fundamentals over someone who plays a good position but knows none of the rules. I want to shape these girls, and push them to learn more about whatever position they plan on continuing on.

Lee pulls up, and Sherrie jumps out of the car. She has her bag and her jersey on ready to go. He doesn't get out, so I take it he might not actually watch the game. Please tell me he is not going to let this keep him from seeing his daughter play. I have half of a mind to walk over there, but with the team starting to show, I can't focus on him.

Parents are already taking their spots on the bleachers, and girls are getting their equipment ready to go.

"Who's ready to play today?" I ask.

They all yell in unison.

Brodie is running a little behind because of work, but he should be here any minute. We have about twenty until game time and it's time to get the team warmed up.

"Alright girls, go out on the field and play catch until Coach gets here, then we will do drills."

The girls run onto the field, and pair off to warm up. Now, Lee gets out of his car, and his eyes bear into mine, and he doesn't look happy. I haven't talked to him in person since he showed up at my house, and honestly I think it's a waste of time for me to beat around the bush.

"How is she? First games are always hard on her," he says, lacing his fingers through the chain link fence.

Okay, so maybe he isn't going to be a complete douchebag today? Softball means a lot to his daughter and his issues with me shouldn't overshadow her game.

"She's excited. Better coach this season," I reply.

He scoffs. "Oh yeah, I forgot Brodie is the best fucking coach ever."

Lee walks away, and takes a seat on the first set of bleachers.

I hear Brodie's truck pull in, and he darts out of the truck and into the dugout.

"I'm here!"

He rushes past me and onto the field. "Girls, it's game day. Are you ready? Do you have any questions before we start?"

A couple girls ask which position they are going to be playing today. Once they are informed, they are excited and ready to play.

Lee is giving him the stink eye from the bleachers, and Brodie can take care of himself, but there shouldn't be any hostility. It's insane how this is playing out, and now I wonder if Lee only broke up with me, to see if I would come back to him. So, when he found out about Brodie and I, it pissed him off.

The girls start running drills until the umpire calls the start of the game.

"So, how is it going?" he asks, arms crossed.

"Amazing. The girls are ready. Today should be a good first game," I reply.

"I meant with Lee being here. He won't stop staring. We can't have drama here," he says.

I nod, and peer over my shoulder at Lee. It's one thing to have a vendetta against us, but if he causes a scene, both of us could be removed from coaching and the girls would have to forfeit the entire season. Surely, he's not dumb enough to pull anything.

The umpire hollers at us, and the four coaches stand around him. We get to bat first, and the girls start getting their helmets and bats ready. I post the line-up on a dry-erase board and erase the names as they bat so it's easier for the girls to keep track.

Sherrie goes up to bat, and she gets two strikes, but on the third ball, she knocks it good, and it goes straight passed the pitcher, the second baseman and into the outfield.

"Go, baby, go!" I yell.

She drops the bat, and gets to first base, and Brodie is telling her to run. So she takes off and just barely makes it to second base before they tag her.

"Safe!"

The rest of the game went smoothly, and our girls paid attention and played well. Game is almost over, and we are tied. We have one girl left to bat, and if she hits the ball and brings the runner on third home, then we will win the game.

"I'm nervous!" Kaylin says, before walking out of the dugout. "It's all riding on me. That's too much pressure."

I put my hands on her shoulders. "You just go out there and do your best. I promise none of us are going to be mad. You've got this."

Kaylin steps up to the plate, and gets into her stance. She looks at her mom, and nods to the umpire that she is ready. The ball goes toward her and without hesitation she knocks it into the outfield. She takes off running and makes it to first, but the runner from third slides to home.

The umpire yells. "That's the game folks."

All the girls start jumping up and down. They have worked hard, and it's amazing to win, but it's not required.

Sherrie runs up and hugs me, and then Brodie. "You guys are the best coaches ever."

I don't turn around to see Lee's reaction because I know it's probably shitty.

"You girls won the game, not us. Let's celebrate!" he yells, going into the dugout, and opening the cooler filled with ice cream pops. "You are all winners in my book, regardless."

After the girls eat their ice cream, and start to file out of the parking lot with their parents, Lee is still sitting on the bleachers. Can he not at least come over here and tell his daughter good game? He isn't acting like a child. Most of the parents have left, so I approach him, keeping my voice low.

"Your daughter is ready to go. Don't you think you should congratulate her?"

She stands up, and gets close to me. "I don't want to be anywhere near the two of you right now. So, better if I keep my distance, tell her I'll be in the car."

The way he is acting isn't going to hurt me, but it will affect his relationship with Sherrie and he can't blame that on me.

I will not let him ruin my day.

Brodie is standing in the dugout, waiting for me. I hate that he has to see Lee acting this way. I don't know what his problem is, but it's time to get the hell over it. I've moved on, and now he needs to. Plain and simple. Why he thinks that I would ever "date" him again after the catastrophe of our previous ten years experience is fucking astronomically naive. The fact that he is acting this way toward me in front of our daughter is going to be a problem, and our problems don't need to leak gas onto the fire. Sherrie has enough to come to terms with right now, and I don't need him making things worse. And if he does, I will not be the "Nessa" he has known for a decade. Mama bear will rage out and claw his ass. He better tread lightly.

"It's been a day, but I was thinking we could go to a nice restaurant for dinner, you know, a proper second date? Or do you already have other plans?"

My knees are aching, and my skin is on fire from being in the sun all day. Honestly, my plans were to go home, run a bath, and relax. Yet, going out with Brodie sounds tempting.

"We can go tomorrow," he says, shrugging his shoulders.

"No, tonight's great."

Sherrie starts walking toward me, so he excuses himself and starts walking to his truck.

"Is Dad feeling okay? He's been acting weird?" Sherrie asks, lugging her equipment bag on her shoulder, walking through the gravel parking lot to Lee's car.

"Don't worry about it, sweetie. He'll be fine once you get back to the house. Call me if you need anything, okay? Love you."

When we get to the car, I don't say a word to him, but only shut the door behind Sherrie, wave, and get into my own vehicle. I don't even want to give him the option to say anything snarky.

It surprises me how different he has been acting lately. Lee hasn't shown this side of him for the decade I've known him, and I want to know how he hid it from me? If he doesn't get his shit together, the next girl is not going to put up with it. He has another thing coming.

Brodie, though, is not cut from the same cloth as Lee. He knows exactly what he wants, and he isn't afraid to tell me. It's refreshing to meet a man who is as vocal about his wants and needs. I might have only met him a short while ago, but I've never been more sure of a man in my life. Goosebumps travel up my arms, and the hair on the back of my neck stands up. I think I'm falling in love with him.

No, I love him.

24

BRODIE

*R*omantic comedies don't depict real life. Sure, people fall in love everyday, and under the weirdest circumstances, but sometimes they don't show the real struggles we go through to be happy. Why do they want us to believe that love comes so easily?

I put my truck in drive, and head home. After the blistering fire of the sun, I'm no doubt covered in sweat. Nothing a shower won't fix.

It's time to take Vanessa where we can enjoy some wine, and some decent conversation. She is nothing like the girls from that online dating site. Vanessa is authentic, and sure she has flaws, but don't we all? No one is perfect, and I plan on spending the rest of my life showing her how amazing she is. That's what she deserves.

Lee might have a problem with her seeing someone, but now I'm confident she will keep him out of our business. He almost ruined our relationship once, and I bet she won't let him do that again.

As my truck pulls onto my street, I see my mother's car parked in my driveway. What the heck is she doing here? I haven't seen her in five years. She isn't the type to call before coming for a visit, she likes to just show up on a whim. My truck barely comes to a stop before she is out of the car and at my window.

"Where have you been? I've been sitting here for almost two hours and you didn't answer your phone."

Between work and the game, I haven't really checked my phone, and didn't expect any company. "Work and a ball game. Next time leave a voicemail or text me. How was I supposed to know you were here?"

My mother and I are not close. Our relationship changed after she kicked my father out. As an adult, I'm not upset with her for leaving him, but she could have let me see him more often. A parent should never use a child as an incentive and that's what she did. If he wanted to see me, then he would have to give her money. If my father would have gone to court, he would have paid a hell of a lot less than he gave my mother.

I open the truck door, and he steps back a bit, giving me room to get out. She just stares at me, like I'm a stranger. It has been five years. "Let's go inside."

She follows me to the door as I unlock it and open it for her. "What hotel are you staying at?"

"I figured I'd stay here tonight. Is that a problem?" she asks, taking a seat on the couch.

She is not the type to give a warning before her arrival. Could she have shown up at a more awful time? Vanessa and I are back on good terms, and I promised her a fancy date tonight, and now this.

"I need the house to myself tonight. I can get you a hotel, though."

Her head practically spins a 360 and then she glares at me. "You would make your mother stay in a hotel? I'm only here until tomorrow afternoon. Why don't you cancel your plans and stay home with me?"

She just shows up and expects me to drop everything to accommodate her? It leaves a sour taste in my mouth, and reminds me of what she used to do to my father. Let's just say she is vindictive and manipulative. She will do anything to get her way.

"Sorry, you should have given me some heads up and then I wouldn't have made the plans. I'll call the hotel and get you a room booked for tonight."

Advanced notice would have made this situation a lot easier for both of us. Vanessa is too important to me to just cancel on her, good excuse or not.

I'm running out of time, and the odor from being out in the sun is getting worse. So, I leave her in the living room while I take a shower. The warm water drifts over my pecks, and down my body, soothing my aching muscles. My loofah lathers me up with body wash and the water washes it away. After turning the water off, I wrap the towel around my torso, and head to the closet. LA VI is more fancy than where I normally go so I choose the blue striped button-up and some black slacks.

When I step back into the living room, she is watching tv. I use the towel to dry my hair, and sit down with her.

"Listen, I gotta leave. Do you want to come back in the morning? We can go to breakfast before you leave?"

She rolls her eyes. "I wouldn't have wasted my time coming if I knew you weren't going to be free. You're right. Next time I'll call you."

Without hesitation, she gets off the couch and walks out my front door.

I close my eyes, take a deep breath, and let her leave. There is no reason for me to feel bad for this. She didn't call, end of the story.

There is no time to waste, so I slip on my dress shoes, grab my keys and head out of the door. The truck starts up, and I mosey over a couple of blocks to her driveway. Tina's car is there and I should've expected her to be present. She has a way of planting herself in people's business.

I sit in my car for a couple minutes, giving her time to finish getting ready, because she doesn't appear to be in the living room. Tina isn't someone I want to sit around and have a conversation with, and not in a rude way, but she likes to meddle. She has made that crystal clear from the start. I don't want her getting into my business, so I'll steer clear of any opportunity of being alone with her for a conversation to spark.

Tina comes to the windows and sees me. He hands waves to me. Guess it's time to knock now. Hopefully Vanessa is almost ready to go.

"She's almost ready. I heard the girls won today. Good job, coach."

I nod, trying to keep the conversation short and to the point without being rude. "They did all the work."

Tina goes back into the bedroom, and I remain in the living room, waiting on Vanessa. It's normal for women to take longer to get ready and I've learned you always make the reservation for 30 minutes after you are supposed to arrive.

The bedroom door opens and she steps out in a floor length red dress, with a slit up the side to her mid thigh. *Fuck.* How am I supposed to not stare at her magnificent body? She's bringing her A game, because now all I'm going to be thinking about during dinner is what I'm going to do to her later on in my bed.

"Let's just go to my house. We don't need dinner, do we?" I say and then grin. "Just kidding, you look gorgeous though. I like you in red."

She says goodbye to Tina, and we walk to my truck, and I hold the door open for her.

Vanessa has me wanting to skip the romantic candlelit dinner and go straight to dessert. As much as I want to, this is a special night, and my stomach is already growling. This doesn't stop me from imagining myself between her legs, dress still on, but with no panties. The things this woman does to me.

The slit in her dress is riding up, enough for me to know that she is not wearing any underwear, and that just forces my dick to jump. Her hair is in curls falling against her back, and it's the first time I've seen her with a face of makeup.

I keep my eye on the road, but lay my right hand on her exposed thigh and her breathing hitches. She has no idea what she has in store for her later. Things are going to get hot and heavy. She did great with the silk ties, so maybe we can kick it up a notch, if she'll let me.

The truck pulls into the parking lot, and I hop out to open her door, extending my hand. Once she is on solid ground, I touch my palm to the small of her back as we walk to the door and go inside.

"Reservation for Brodie Hill," I say to the receptionist.

"Right this way."

We follow her to the corner of the restaurant, and the dim lighting sets a romantic vibe. Once she shows up to our table, there are candles lit, and a bottle of wine chilling in ice for us.

"Well, I wasn't expecting this. Wine and candles? The whole shebang," Vanessa says.

I would like to take credit, but this is all the restaurant's doing. They must put a bottle of wine for all their guests to encourage them to open it. It puts the man on the spot, but in the back of my mind, the bottle could cost hundreds of dollars. I never splurge, so what the hell, I open the wine, and pour it into the glasses sitting in front of us.

"To us and our future together," Vanessa says, clinking hers to mine.

The fact that she sees a future with me is wonderful, and I hope this works out. The pull to her is magnetic and I don't want to start over. Vanessa needs to be my happily ever after.

She takes a sip, and then smiles. "I have been looking forward to this all day. I've been on a high. Still can't believe we won today. Sherrie was so excited."

An inkling of me doesn't want to hear about Lee, but it comes with the territory. He isn't going to push me out of their lives, but he will try. It's inevitable. The only reason he would act that way is if he still has feelings for Vanessa. Why he let her get away is beside me, but I'm not dumb enough to let her out of my sight.

The waitress comes over and we pick up the menus. I've been lost at looking at her, there's been no time to look it over.

"So what are you thinking?" she asks, not looking up from the menu.

"You can never go wrong with steak. That's my motto," I say, closing my menu and ordering it medium well.

She laughs at me. "You want it with no flavor? Live a little." She turns to the waitress. "I'll have the same, but medium rare."

The waitress laughs, and I change mine to appease Vanessa. I'll try anything once.

"So, I have an honest question. Since we are talking about futures already. Where do you want to be in five years?" I only ask because even though I can't take my eyes off of her, she needs to be going in the same direction as me. It's important. Vanessa takes my hand on the table.

"Well, hopefully I'll be sleeping next to you every night, but also in my own home. Oh, and Sherrie will have adapted to the change between Lee and I. She's still struggling, and it kills me we are putting her through this."

No mention of kids, and that's huge for me. If Vanessa keeps me around, I'd love nothing more than to be a stepdad to Sherrie, but I've always dreamed of having at least two kids. Is she down to have another one? This isn't something that I can budge on. No one should have to settle on things like this. Obviously it is different, if you get married and find out one of you can't have kids, but that's not the case here.

"Kids?"

She crinkles her nose. "I'm not opposed to having more, but don't want to rush. Things need to be airtight between us to bring another kid into the mix."

I think we can both agree on that note. After our childhood experience with growing up in separate households, neither of us want that for our children. The fact she is already dealing with this for Sherrie means it is in the forefront of her mind. The difference is from what I've gathered, her relationship with him had never been that great. I think showing her who I am, and giving her all the love and support she needs will help her see the difference. I'm father material, and as much as I don't want my child to be raised separately, things happen.

I take a moment to just gaze into her eyes, taking in her beauty, and how strong she is. There are many women and men that stay in bad relationships because of children, and as much as I'd like to say that would never be me, I've never been in that situation. Sometimes, you don't realize how bad a relationship was, until you find someone who gives you that instant spark and shows you what you deserve.

I'm hoping that I am that person for Vanessa. Leaving Lee isn't something she should ever regret.

The wine is good, but my stomach needs something substantial soon. The energy is draining from my body, and my blood sugar is crashing. I forgot to eat lunch before heading to the field, so I haven't eaten anything since seven this morning.

"You're pale, and quiet. Everything okay?" Vanessa asks, reaching across the table to tilt my face up to get a good look. "Do I need to take you to a hospital?"

I shake my head. "Just need to eat."

The waitress walks over with our plates in tow, just in the nick of time. "Two seats, both medium rare. Can I get you anything else?"

We shake our heads, and I grab my knife, not wasting any time, and stick a piece of it in my mouth. Vanessa watches me as I shovel my sides into my mouth in between the steak.

"Slow down. You're going to make yourself sicker."

My energy level is coming back up, and I start to notice a shift. "I'm going to be fine. Just haven't eaten since early this morning and didn't even realize it until now."

Vanessa continues to eat, but keeps her eye on me.

The fact she is worried about me is endearing, but we have too many things I'm looking forward to tonight, and if she thinks I'm under the weather, she might not want to come back to my place. That just won't do.

25

VANESSA

*W*ho forgets to eat? Especially someone with his job? How dangerous. I keep my eye on him while he finishes eating.

"Maybe you need to set a reminder on your phone. Something to make sure you don't do this again?" I suggest.

"It's not like it happens all the time. Don't worry about it. I'm fine now."

The color in his face is back, and a smile sweeps across it. There's the man I know. Maybe he's right. He just needed to eat and get something in his stomach.

I lay my hand on his, while the other one is still maneuvering the final bites of his meal into his mouth. How the heck is he able to eat all of that? My plate is still half full and I don't think I could put another bite in me.

"So, what are your plans after this?"

The fork clings against his plate, and he uses the napkin to wipe his mouth. "Dessert." He puts his hand up in the air to get our waitress' attention and she brings him the check.

I hope he knows that I am not the type of girl that needs fancy restaurants. Honestly, I would have been just as happy staying at home and cooking something for him.

"I like the sound of that," I reply.

It's been hard to keep my eyes off of him tonight. The way his biceps are begging to be free from the long sleeve dress t-shirt or the way his pecks are practically bursting out. Am I ever going to get enough of Brodie? He's like a drug, begging for just one more taste, one more hit, and then I'll be okay for a while.

He hands the black book back to her with his credit card inside, and his legs bounces underneath the table as he licks his lips. Is he thinking about me? All I want is to have him wrap his big fucking arms around me, pick me up by my ass, and slam me into a wall. He knows how to read my body and give me just what I need, without me having to beg. Sometimes I think he enjoys it when I beg, but who wouldn't? My skin tingles knowing what's coming, and gets worse with every passing second of sitting here.

"Here you go, sir. Have a great night," the waitress says, sitting the book on top of the table. He whips out the pen, puts a tip, and signs and then nudges his head toward the exit. "It's time for dessert. Let's get the fuck out of here."

He playfully chases me through the restaurant, using his fingertips to tickle my ass every time he gets close enough to me, and then I dart ahead a little until we are outside again.

The aroma of fresh daisies hits me as soon as I take that first deep breath, and I stop dead in my tracks. I close my eyes to take in the smell, and a smile takes over.

"What is it?" he asks, taking my head.

I open my eyes. "Daisies are my favorite and Sherrie's too. When my mom invited us down a couple summers ago, she spent three hours outside in my mama's garden picking them."

He scoops me up into his arms. "It's time to get a move on, unless you want me to take you right here in front of the restaurant." My head shakes, and he walks me over to his truck and puts me into the passenger seat.

Something Lee never gave me. The time of day. Now, that's something I never have to worry about with Brodie. He has never once cut me off, ignored me, or talked down to me. Hell, most of the time, he asks why I don't talk about myself? It's a habit I need to break, and he's the one that will push me along to do that. There are so many things that I didn't even notice I needed until Brodie walked into my life.

The entire ride home his right hand is on my thigh with my hand on top of it. He talks about work today, and then the subject of his mother comes up.

"Do you not want me to meet her?" I ask, a little offended. "Do you think she won't like me?"

Maybe I'm in my feels a bit, and sure we haven't been together very long, but the only thing I know about his mother is that she kicked out his father and made it hard for them to see each other after that. Do I think I'll like her? Not likely, but I'm his girlfriend and putting on a fake smile with her is my duty if he wants me to.

"No offense, but she would eat you alive. She is very overprotective, or so she wants everyone to think. Here's the thing, I had no idea she was coming, and was at my door when I got home today from the game."

Does he not think I can handle myself? I'm not over here jumping for joy to meet the woman that made his childhood hell, but maybe he needs someone by his side while she's here. My mother isn't much different, and for once he has someone who completely understands what he would be going through every step of the way.

"I'm just saying, if you want me to meet her, I will. You don't have to shield me from her. I'm a grown ass woman who can handle herself, remember?"

His eyebrows almost lift off his face as he peers over at me, instead of keeping his eyes on the road.

"Wow, miss attitude is back. Where's she been? Keep it up and I'll have you over my knee when we get inside," he says, pulling into his driveway.

He turns the engine off, gets out of the truck, and comes around to help me out. As soon as my feet touch the ground, he pulls me in, and plants a mouth watering kiss on my lips. He's getting right to it. Not that I mind. AT ALL.

"Let's get inside first. You got neighbors, remember?" I say, pulling away from him and edging toward the front door. "You plan on joining me, or do I need to take care of myself?"

I sway my ass walking to the front door and step to the side so he can unlock it. It's like someone else comes out and takes over my body when I'm around him and thinks get heated. I want to talk dirty, explore, and sometimes take complete control. He brings this whole other side of me out and it's been an adventure.

He turns around to shut the door behind himself, and I grab his hand, moving to graze up my thigh and then he is reminded that I'm not wearing any panties. I am staring into his eyes, and at that moment when he can feel me, how excited I am, and his face goes dark, almost makes me burst.

"Where would you like me tonight?" I ask, his fingers still lightly moving around downstairs. "You still look a little hungry?"

He laughs, gets on his knees, and props my right foot on his shoulder. "Don't fucking move a muscle."

My head shoots back as soon as his tongue hits me, and I try my best not to move. I run my fingers through his hair, and tug on it. Yes, yes! I have never been able to get myself to the edge this quickly, but Brodie is a pro. Within a couple minutes, he has my thighs spasming, and moaning his name while he takes me over the edge into a fucking bliss. He doesn't stop there.

"I'm not done with you yet," he says, picking me up and carrying me to his bedroom. He lays me on his bed slowly, and makes it a point to strip slowly, locked on me, and I drink in every single second.

Brodie stands butt naked in front of me, and I'm in awe. How the hell am I so lucky to be with him? I want to run my fingers down his chest, and put him in my mouth to show him my appreciation for everything he does for me. I haven't felt like alive in over a decade, and he has this way of bringing out a new side of me, or maybe it was just laying dormant under the surface from lack of intimacy.

Brodie starts to crawl up the bed toward me, and I giggle as he gets closer, but instead of getting on top of me, he pulls me into his chest. His fingers go through my hair, and his breathing slows down.

"Let's just stay like this. Even though I want you so fucking bag, we haven't enjoyed a night without sex yet. You know I want more than just pleasure from you, right?"

I lift my head up, and turn toward him so I can see his eyes. "Of course, but I'm not sure after that if I can stop thinking about you slamming into me all night. You give me a strip show and then tell me we aren't having sex? What a tease."

My finger starts at his peck and slowly moves down his chest to his torso. The closer my hand gets to his dick, his breathing starts to get faster. He wants me, I can tell, and why should we have to refrain from having sex tonight?

"Are you really not going to let me take care of you?" I ask while my hands close around him and start moving up and down. "You need this just as much as I do. What do ya say?"

His eyes close, and his arms go behind his head, and I hear no more words from him.

There isn't a chance in hell I'm going to let him leave himself high and dry after the orgasm he has just given me. I pump my hands, and don't look away from him. His mouth curves, and when he becomes stiff, his eyes open.

"How did I get so lucky?" he asks.

I lean in to kiss him, and speed my hand up, wanting him to get his release and allow myself to watch. It's exhilarating watching a man tip over the edge because of you. His hand curls around my head and pulls me in for another kiss right as his body tenses, and he groans.

"Holy fucking shit. I'm never ever letting you go. Might as well get used to me."

I place one last kiss on his lips, and lay back down on his chest, knowing that this is it.

EPILOGUE
BRODIE

*E*veryone in the stands is silent, as Sherrie steps up to the plate. We are at the bottom of the last inning, and we are down by one point. If we can get this hit, and bring our runner on second base home, then we will win the Championships. *A first for our team.*

A bead of sweat drips down onto my nose from my forehead, but my fingers are interlaced into the chain link, not wanting to take my eye off of her. I've been in the position before, where it's all riding on one player to hit the ball good enough for the team to win. I don't envy Sherrie right now a bit. She is nervous when she bats anyway, and now to put this extra pressure, let's hope she can focus. Deep breath, eye on the ball, and follow through.

Vanessa is standing on first base, biting her nails, and cheering Sherrie on. Last night, she was so nervous that she couldn't even eat dinner, and this isn't going to help either. I wish she could believe in herself like we do. She has the skill and the drive, but the one thing she needs to work on is confidence.

The umpire takes his position as Sherrie's shoulders rise and fall and her bat goes to position.

That's Right. Deep breath.

The pitcher winds, and her bat doesn't move, or it's an automatic strike. *Good girl.* Pitcher winds again, and she hits it, not waiting a single second to drop her bat and take off to first base. The ball is up in the air, and lands in the outfield, giving our runner a little bit more time to get home, but Laurie gets to third base and stops.

"Keep going! Run!" I yell, trying to get her over the home plate before they get the ball here.

Laurie runs and her eyes are locked on me as I wave her in. As she slides into home plate, the ball misses her by milli-seconds.

"Safe!" The umpire yells.

The girls run out from the dugout to celebrate their victory, and parents come on the field, rushing to their daughters. This team has evolved so much in the last two years, and have shown their dedication to the sport. I will not steal their spotlight, not as a coach. They are the ones that are playing the game, and putting in the work to get better. We are now champions.

Vanessa runs to Sherrie and envelopes her in a hug. "You did it! We couldn't have won the game without your hit. I'm so proud of you."

I give them a couple minutes before I wrap my arms around her, too. "Look at you, champ."

Vanessa and I retreat to the dugout and let the girls have their moment. Their confidence coming into this game wavered, but this should prove to them they are worthy.

"Good game, Coach. Looks like we will have to go out and celebrate after the party finishes out there," she laughs.

Now is the time.

"You have proven to me that happily ever afters do exist, and that soulmates are real. Never in a million years did I think that the woman with an attitude in this very spot almost three years ago would have been my future wife, but that's the thing about love. It can happen anywhere, and when you least expect it." I drop down to one knee, and open the black box. "Will you do me the honor of becoming my wife and giving me the chance to show you everyday just how much I love you?"

Her hand flutters around, and water sprouts from her eyes. I see Tina out of the corner of my eye. She has calmed down a lot since she had Max.

"Say yes, already!" she screams.

"Yes, Yes, a million times yes!" she jumps into my arms, kisses me, and then I slide the ring on her finger.

Tina pushes the stroller into the dugout. "It's about damn time."

The crowd on the field is now starting to dwindle down, and Sherrie runs over to pack up her equipment. When she sees the ring on her mom's finger, her eyes get big, and look over at me.

"You finally did it? I can't believe it!"

She hugs her mother first, then me. "Thank you for making her so happy."

It might have taken a while for her to get used to the idea of her mother dating me, or anybody, but it was my job to show her that I made her mom happy. Sherrie wasn't oblivious to the issues her parents faced while together.

"I say we go to the diner and celebrate. Breakfast for dinner sounds amazing right now," Vanessa says, not taking her eyes off the ring.

Honestly, it feels like my life has just come together so nicely since Vanessa made her appearance. Sure, it was rocky at first, but anything worth a damn doesn't come easily. The wait was horrendous but now I have her by my side, and she will be my wife. I'll spend everyday showing her how amazing she is, and comforting her through all the trials and tribulations that come with life.

My life is now complete...

RAVISH ME

BOOK 6

1

LESLIE

A voice comes over the intercom system, alerting us to a fire on Atlanta Avenue, and the alarm blares to get everyone's attention inside the station. The cot squeaks as I sit up and poke Angela next to me. Of course, a call comes in right as I'm about to doze off. *Just my luck.*

"Get up. Let's go!" I yell, knowing every second makes a difference.

She wipes her eyes and looks around and finally hears the alarm. "Shit!"

Working overnight shifts suck, but we sneak in a nap every chance we can get. Sometimes, it's non-stop and other nights we don't get a single call. We never know what we are going to get, but are always ready to go. It's part of our extensive training. Not to mention, our father is the chief, and he expects more from us than the other firefighters.

The men try to treat us like we're equal, but sometimes it's hard not to notice when they don't. They barely speak to us, except Damon and Tristan. It's like we don't exist until we are on a call and they need our help. *Isn't that funny?* So what if we're females? We can handle our own because our father raised us to be good firefighters. You can't imagine the crazy things our father has had us do before we started here. He wanted proof that he wouldn't have to worry about us out in the field. Here we are, years later, and he has never had a complaint.

We run to the locker room, and I pull on my fire retardant pants, snap the suspenders against my shoulder, and shove my feet into the fireproof steel-toed boots. You never know when you're going to have to go inside and save someone. It's better to be prepared in gear.

Damon is yelling at everyone, telling them to hurry up. The dispatcher says the fire is spreading quickly and they need a quick dispatch. That's understandable, but we can't get on-site without protective gear.

Thick gloves slide over my hands as I rush to gather all my other gear. Heavy boots run across the concrete bay floor as the rumbling of the engine echoes off of the walls. Angela opens the high bay doors and jumps in the truck just as Damon turns the sirens on and pulls out onto the street.

He isn't normally on this shift, but with a new baby at home, he tries to help his wife out as much as he can during the day. Why he would give up his day shift is beyond me? Hell, if they gave me the opportunity, I'd stick with it for the long haul. Everyone wants to work the day shift. For some weird reason, it's where the least amount of action happens. I assume because people are at work, in school, or whatever for most of the day.

"How's that baby doing? Sleeping better at night, yet?" I ask.

He shakes his head and hands his wallet back to me. "That's the newest shot of her. It's my first time being there since birth. Emily isn't legally mine, so I missed all the newborn and toddler stages. Tell me it gets easier?"

Damon doesn't take his eyes off of the road, so he doesn't see me shrug my shoulders. "I don't have kids, so how would I know?"

We pass an accident on the way, but can't deter from the fire. They will have to find someone else to respond. It looks pretty bad with a car flipped upside down and two smashed vehicles.

My stomach always drops when we get a call, because in the course of my career, I have discovered more dead bodies than I'd like to admit, and it never gets easier. The consequences of a slow response is engraved into my brain, and I never want that on my conscience.

As we approach the scene, the billowing smoke doesn't look good, but there are people lined in the streets when we come to a stop. The police are already on scene and trying to keep bystanders away.

"Everyone accounted for?" I ask.

"The neighbor says there is a family inside, and the car is still in the driveway," he says, pointing to the silver Toyota Camry.

Angela and I look at each other, and run toward the front door of the home, where smoke is sliding underneath. We put our masks on before entering. Flames are licking the walls and a haze coats the room.

"Hello? Anyone in here?" I yell, turning around to signal to Angela that I'm going to head to check the bedrooms and she follows me.

"Divide and Conquer, sis."

The bedroom at the end of the hallway has smoke coming from under the door, and when I turn the knob and push it open, it hits me in the face. I swipe at the waft of smoke trying to see, and that's when my eyes set on a young girl, maybe seven, lying unconscious on the floor.

When I scoop her up in my arms, there is no response, but there's a pulse. If she doesn't get clean air soon, she might not make it. I rush through the home, trying to shield her as best I can from any flames.

"Female. Around seven-years-old. Unconscious and needs oxygen now!" I yell, as the EMTs take her from me and I go back inside.

The fire is spreading quickly, and the entire structure is unsecure. Angela runs out of the second bedroom and waves at me to follow. I enter and there are two bodies, one male and one female, on the floor. I squat to check their pulse and nothing.

I look up at Angela and shake my head. "They are gone, but we need to get them out of here."

Removing them from the scene before they get burned might save the family some agony when it comes to a funeral and identifying the bodies later.

We use teamwork to get the woman out first, and then the man.

The little girl is awake when we get to the firetruck, but then the EMTs announce there are no pulses, and the little girl bawls.

"Daddy? Mama?" she says, trying to run to them, but the EMT stops her.

I nudge Angela and walk over to the little girl. "You need to go to the hospital, sweetie. Do you have a family member that lives close?"

She shakes her head and wipes her eyes. "Are they going to be okay?"

I can't bring myself to lie to the little girl, but her parents are gone. My heart breaks thinking that she might have to go into foster care because of this.

Angela, Damon, and Tristan work to get the fire under control without me, while I try to calm the girl down. She's too young to understand what this means for her. Without parents, she will be going with DHS workers tonight until they can find someone in the family that might take her. And if they don't, the poor thing will end up in foster care. I try to hold the tears back, but it's harder when her blue eyes are looking up at me. Her life has just changed drastically and there is nothing I can do about it.

"Why can't I ride with Mommy and Daddy? I don't want them to be alone," she says, trying to push passed me as they shut the back doors of the ambulance.

"That's not possible, sweetie. You have to ride on your own."

She looks up at me through her lashes. "Will you ride with me? I'm scared."

Normally, this isn't something we do, but the circumstances call for it. She is all alone, and I don't want her to think no one cares about her. She shouldn't have to go through this alone.

"I'll be right back," I say, and then nod to the EMT waiting to take off.

Damon and the others are fighting the fire, and even though my job is to stay here, he might understand. He is a father, and can feel for this little girl.

"She wants me to ride with her. She's scared," I say.

He nods without hesitating.

Damon is someone I admire because this profession runs in his family for generations, too, but sometimes we have to bend the rules a bit. We are human after all.

I kneel in front of the little girl. "I can ride with you, but once we get to the hospital, they will take you to a room to be examined. They won't let me go back with you, okay?

She shakes her head, and gets into the ambulance. The workers seem impatient, and it starts to bother me because they need to show this little girl some respect. How would they feel if this happened to them? They don't have to be jerks to her.

They lay her down and secure her on the gurney before taking off because it's required by the law. She is coughing up a storm, but her voice is starting to sound better, not all scratchy. I let the workers do their job while I try to keep her breathing into the mask, and not fighting them.

I tell her a story my father used to tell me at bedtime about a fearless King and Queen who would do anything to protect their kingdom and their children. It keeps her occupied until we pull into the ER ambulance bay, and they remove her. The nurse asks for her vitals and they whoosh her away to a room for observation and tests.

I don't want to leave, because she is going to be all alone, and soon Child Services will show up to take her to a group home until they can reach out to anyone in the family that might take her in. However, in my line of work, I know that in most cases, the child ends up in foster care.

My cell phone rings, and it's Damon.

"Swinging by to pick you up on the way back to the station, okay? Two minutes out."

I know it's not part of my job, but sometimes this becomes too much. My heart breaks every time I see a dead body, or a child hurt, and unfortunately, that happens as a firefighter. Maybe that's why I'm going back to finish the last semester to get my English degree. My dad, the chief, knows that I didn't plan on staying with the department forever. So, he can't hold it against me.

Damon pulls up and I hop back inside next to Angela.

"How's she doing?" she asks, putting her arm around me.

"She's getting some tests done, I assume. They just rushed her back."

My sister knows how much things like this eat away at me, and after all these years, I need a change of scenery. Something that doesn't revolve around gas leaks, car crashes, and a lot of death. I'm sick of seeing these things.

When we get back to the depot, I take off my gear and go back into the sleeping area. I need a freaking drink after this, and before I have to focus on schoolwork hardcore.

Angela isn't like me. She can turn her brain off after a scene like that, and I wish I was more like her in that aspect. My parents always tell me I have an enormous heart, and sometimes it's not a great thing with a profession like mine.

Honestly, I didn't know what I wanted to do with my life after high school, and my dad has always been my hero, so until I had a plan, he said I should just get certified and work at the station. Angela and I liked it at first, you know, seeing as there is a stereotype against women in this profession, but as we handled more calls with DOA's, it slowly started bothering me. The emotional distress from these calls throws me into a depression. Seeing all that death and not knowing if we could have prevented it by being just a little faster responding to the scene, it started eating away at me.

"Shift is over!" Angela yells, and heads to the lockers with me following. "What are your plans for tonight? Anything special before your big day back at college?"

After a day like today, a couple shots wouldn't be the end of the world. "Wanna go to The Tavern? They are having happy hour tonight from seven to nine?"

My sister has never turned down going to a bar, especially if I'm the one footing the bill. "I'll meet you there at seven."

I slip on my jeans and rock-n-roll t-shirt. I can't go to the bar smelling like smoke. I've got about thirty-minutes to spare, so out the door I go to take a quick shower and change.

I never know what to expect when my sister is around. She is the prettier one, and usually has guys hitting on her all night while I'm in the corner just enjoying a beer. Sometimes, I wonder why I still agree to go with her, but then it's entertainment.

All I want to do is get today out of my head and then curl up and read an enjoyable book. Is that too much to ask for?

2

NOAH

The wedding pictures on my wall bring up the very thing I'm trying to forget. My beautiful wife, Janet, passed away some time ago and I've tried my hand at these new dating apps everyone is using, but it only leads to some very horrible dates. The women are just not as intelligent as I need them to be, and I want to find someone who shares the love of literature as much as I do. Some people might think that wouldn't be hard, but the people nowadays are more enthralled with how many likes and follows they can get on social media rather than curling up on the couch with a good book.

Honestly, I think I'm just going to give up on this whole dating thing because at this point in my life I'm working towards tenure and that is going to secure my retirement. Everyone dreams of the day that they don't have to work anymore. Where they can go out and do whatever they want at whatever time of day without having to answer to somebody else. My late wife told me before she took her final breath to make sure that I enjoy life and live it to the fullest. She didn't want me to sit in a room and be depressed. No, she wanted me to get out there and enjoy my life and do the things I want to do. And that all leads to this very point. I have to give up just a little now so I have what I want in the future. Dating isn't something that I need to do, but she wanted me to be happy. But right now it just seems like that's not in the cards for me. It seems hard to find someone mid-thirties or older that isn't focused on having a family right now or that doesn't already have multiple kids.

Don't get me wrong, I'm not saying that having kids in your mid-thirties is wrong because honestly most people have kids by now, but I'm not looking to start a relationship with somebody who will not want kids in the future. My dream with Janet was to have a huge family and be happy but her cancer took that away from us. And now I have to find someone to fall in love with again and start all over. It's almost too much because do I really want to start all over? I mean, here I am at thirty-six-years-old and a widow, and right now all I want to do is secure my future.

On Sunday nights, I usually go into my den to work on projects and sip on a glass of cognac, but tonight I've decided that I should get out of the house. There's nothing good about sitting around in your own home alone. I need to get out and enjoy life, talk with other people, and socialize instead of sitting in my den all by myself all of the time.

The last time I went to the pub a couple of months ago, there were a few women who approached me and asked me if I would buy them a drink, and honestly, I said no. If I wanted to buy somebody a drink I would offer, yet women think that it's okay to just come up and ask for us to buy them a drink even though nobody offers to buy me a drink. Why are the men always responsible for buying the women drinks? And I'm not saying that women should have to put out because we buy them drinks, but at the same time, we should not be expected to buy you a drink just so you can have a good time.

Honestly, I'm just looking for somebody who has some intelligence about her. I'm not saying she has to be a genius, or that she has to have an IQ of 130, but I want to have a conversation about things that have meaning. On the dates that I've gone on through the dating apps have all been meaningless conversation filled and how hard is it to find someone who can carry a good conversation? This is what happened when I found my wife. We sat and we talked for hours;

they physically had to kick us out of the bar when it closed because we didn't want to leave.

I touch my hands to my lips and then press it on the picture like I do every day before leaving my house. Sure my wife might be gone, but I am still going to love her for the rest of my life. She was my soulmate. She was the person that I could talk to about anything; when having bad days or when going through something awful and she always had my back with no hesitation. I need someone like that again and it's become harder and harder to find someone that can match my expectations.

I walk into my den and secure my laptop into the bag, then grab my wireless mouse and keyboard just in case and a set of headphones. I figure why not work on some things while enjoying some cognac and pretending to socialize. I mean, maybe I'll find somebody to strike up a conversation with and maybe I can find someone who enjoys literature, but most likely not. They seem to be hard to find.

My right leg eases into the car first, my left following as my ass hits the seat. The car rumbles when the engine starts and I head to the way of the pub. I've always dreamed of writing a book and hitting a list, or even just having someone downright love my work, but it's become harder now that she's gone. The drafting stage has been awful and I'm one of those people that have the feeling that they just aren't good enough. Why would anyone want to read what I write? What makes me so special? These are the questions that go on inside my head every single time I sit down to finish my book. Yet, when my late wife passed, she told me not to let anything stand in the way of what I want to accomplish. She knew how important it was for me to finish this manuscript and turn it in, and yet, since the day that she passed, I have written maybe a couple thousand words on it. I need to get this complex out of my head so that I can move forward. The only person that has read this manuscript was her, and she loved it, but none of that matters unless I can complete it. I'm about four chapters away from finally writing the end on this manuscript and maybe some liquor will provide me the courage to turn my brain off and write the fucking thing. The thing that perplexes me the most is the fact that people think that writing a book is easy and in fact it is so freaking hard. There's so many moving elements within a story that you have to work with, and perfect. This is difficult.

I've been sitting on this idea for about a decade, so when you think about it took me a decade to write 80% as a book and that's all conclusive on the fact that I have imposter syndrome. I just don't feel like I'm good enough for people to want to read or pay to read my work. But I'm sure that every novelist has come across this and has found a way to overcome diss doubt in their head. I just need to focus on getting it done, and then I can worry about making the result of the product better. It's all about getting words on the page and flushing out your idea to where you can focus on making it better. The first draft of anything; whether it's a short story, a résumé is never going to be the end result that you would give to an employer or a paying customer. Do you have to go back and revise it multiple times to tell if it's good enough? Hell, it's not almost perfect? But then I read online on the forums they say that nobody will ever be perfect. There will always be flaws, missed typos, and things that you overlook, but that's what an editor is for, to find all the things that the writer missed.

I pull into the gravel parking lot, the rocks crunching beneath my tires as I come to a stop and turn the ignition off. I grab my laptop bag and walk around to the side entrance of the pub. Inside, it's packed with patrons gathered around little tables and the bar back. I think that this might be just what I need to get rid of the imposter syndrome for one night. If I can finish even a chapter tonight, that would be a huge step in the right direction. I go straight to the bar and order my Cognac and wait for the bartender to bring me my glass. When he does, I'll leave the bar back and try to find a table for myself away from the jukebox and the front door. Even though I brought headphones, the distraction of the door opening and closing and a new song coming on every three minutes is going to make it harder to focus. Tonight is about focusing on this manuscript and nothing else. I want to keep my word to my late wife and get this project done so I can move forward with the process and make her proud.

I take a sip from my glass and set it down next to my laptop, waiting for it to boot up so I can open up the Word document and begin writing. I pull my headphones out of the laptop bag, and press the on button to connect the Bluetooth to my cell phone. I'm not one of those people that can listen to actual music while they write. For the writers that use that and say that it helps them focus, that's awesome, because I'm the complete opposite. The only thing I can have in the background as far as music goes are instrumentals. Usually, I go on a streaming site and look for something pertaining to the scene that I'm working on, whether that be romantic, suspenseful, thriller, or horror music. Instrumentals can help you set the scene and write the details for you. We all know in horror movies the intense doom of the loud suspenseful music that leads up to the killer being revealed or the person getting murdered. Music like that helps me get into whatever I'm writing and know what mood I need or how I need to set the precedence for the readers. No matter what anybody says, readers can be super picky and they want things done a certain way. There are industry standards for each genre of writing and if you don't stick to those industry standards, then the readers are going to revolt. Just going to have a devastating effect on someone's book release and can tarnish their career from the very beginning. So, I use little things like this to help me make sure I'm setting the correct scene and mood for the reader every time I sit down to write a chapter.

Being in the pub actually makes it easier because I'm in the very thing that I'm writing. The easiest way to write believable dialogue is to go out and sit somewhere and watch other people have conversations. I'll admit I've had some pretty funny things happen while people watching, and they might have made it into my book. It's always fun to come up with a new idea based on something you have actually witnessed.

The computer finally starts up and I take a sip of Cognac before putting my fingers on the keyboard. I put my headphones on and my fingers start clacking. The more of this that goes into my system, the easier it is to turn off my self doubt and before I know it, a couple hours have passed and I have written almost 3,000 words. One chapter down and three more to go before my novel's first draft is complete.

I go back up to the bar, lean, and wait for the bartender to come and take my order, but I see a woman coming over towards me with some of the most beautiful blue eyes I have ever seen. My mind doesn't go to asking her out or anything because bars are typically the best place to pick up a woman, especially if you're wanting something long term. So, I just wait for her to come next to me and ask her what her favorite book is.

And her answer surprises me...

3

LESLIE

*A*ngela might forget the instances of today, but it's still in the back of my mind. That little girl is now going to be all alone and her parents can never tell her they love her and that to me, it's just devastating. Weirdly enough, I want to embrace her and tell her that everything is going to be OK, but I can't promise her that. If she ends up in foster care, everything she has known in her life it's going to be fucked up. Sure, there are some good foster homes, but for the most part, the system is not great. People taking kids just for the checks show them no love and treat them with no respect. Some kids even enter into a home that is abusive and after everything that she has gone through, she shouldn't have to go through something like that.

My car comes to a stop outside of the pub and Angela is waiting right outside the door for me in a red miniskirt and a white tank top. Why does she have to dress like we're going to the club? Does she plan on taking somebody home tonight? Here's the thing about my sister: she can be a little provocative. She is a grown ass woman and if she wants to take someone home and sleep with them every night that's her prerogative, but I don't know if that's something that has ever crossed my mind.

Yes, I know I'm probably one of the 10% that has never had a one-night stand, but honestly, the opportunity has never presented itself and maybe it's just not for me. Especially at a bar. Most of the men that frequent this place are brooding and have an inflated ego who needs to be knocked down a peg, and normally, that's what my sister Angela does. She finds the most arrogant man in the room and makes it her mission to knock him down. She wants him to know that he has to work to get her to go home with him and usually that means ten or more shots and the bill paid for by him. Me, on the other hand, I don't need anyone to buy my drinks. I can buy my own and worry about everything myself. There's too much stigma around a man buying drinks for women in a bar because sometimes it makes them think that youare going home with them at the end of the night. But that's not the case with me. I never want a man to think just because he bought me a drink, that he may somehow get in my pants. Because I could be nothing but far from the truth.

I turn my engine off and get out of the car and Angela walks over to me.

"What the hell are you wearing? Do you expect anybody to buy you a drink wearing that?"

I love how she always just assumes that I am here to pick somebody up. My dating life hasn't exactly been the best in the last five years, and honestly, I contribute that to the fact my job is emotional and they might teach us not to let emotion get the best of us while performing our job duties, but it's easier said than done. Seeing a child stuck inside a burning building or finding someone dead on arrival isn't something that just gets erased from my mind when I leave the scene. Angela might forget that easily, but I don't.

"I'm not here to flirt with men, Angela. I'm here to blow off some steam, drink a bit of liquor, and then go home and sleep. You, on the other hand, are here to find someone to take home and that's your prerogative, but don't push that on me."

My sister flicks her wrist, walks toward the front door, and inside she goes with me following after her. As we walk in, all the men turn and stare at Angela. Go figure. That's exactly what she wants. Unlike me, who walks straight to the bar to order a drink, Angela stops and talks to one of the men, who obviously asks if you can buy her a drink and she replies yes. Doesn't she get sick of having to flirt with these men just to get free drinks? I'll never understand why she does it.

I put my elbows on the bar and yell to the bartender, but he can't hear me over the jukebox playing, Uptown Girl. The only thing I don't like about this pub is the jukebox is so loud that you can't have a conversation without having to yell.

"So, what's your favorite book?"

The man standing next to me with his elbows on the bar waiting for his drink looks over at me. But he doesn't look like the rest. He is wearing khakis with a button-up shirt, headphones around his neck, and a pair of glasses. He doesn't strike me as the type to take home women, but I could be wrong. This could be a sign that he's putting on to not look like a player.

"Great expectations has always been my favorite. You?"

"I'm more of a mystery person, so I go with Agatha Christie. Have you ever read any of her books?"

Okay, so he's definitely not like the other men here, and it's actually kind of nice to have a change of pace.

The bartender comes over and drops his glass of Cognac in front of him and then asks me what I would like. I order a vodka and Sprite and he comes back within a few seconds and places the drink in front of me.

The man has gone back to his table, which has a laptop, and his headphones are now back on covering his ears. So either he's playing hard to get, or he really didn't think that I was interested in carrying on the conversation. But, in fact, I'm intrigued by this man because instead of using some crazy-ass pick up line he just asked me what my favorite book is which tells me he cares more about meaning things than most of society. Most people don't pick up on my love for literature, but I've been an avid reader since I was seven. My parents couldn't keep up with my book purchases. They filled most Christmases and birthdays with new books for me to find my next adventure. Honestly, sometimes it's hard to find a book that you can dive headfirst into, but sometimes you just have to take a chance.

I grab my drink and pull out the chair across from him at his table and take a seat. He looks at me, slides down his headphones and smiles.

"Did you want to talk some more? Normally, people get pretty bored talking about books, but I could talk about them all day."

This man sitting in front of me is different from the others, and I like that. My vodka and Sprite is the perfect combination. I am not usually one for talking to random men at bars, but a conversation about novels seems just up my alley.

"So your favorite author is Agatha Christie. I have to know which book is favorite and why?"

He scratches his head and maneuvers the headphones from around his neck and places them on the table.

"It's not actually a novel. Thirteen Problems is a short story collection, and honestly I'm not one to enjoy short stories, but it's a real work of art. Have you ever read it?"

I shake my head, take another sip, and listen to him tell me about the collection. The atmosphere almost fades away, not hearing the loud music or other people anymore, just him and myself chatting about our favorite books. It's interesting to meet someone that has the same taste in authors as me. The classics don't get enough attention anymore, except when they are required in high school English classes. It's a shame more people don't enjoy them.

"My name is Leslie, by the way," I say, extending my glass to him.

"Noah," he replies ,and clinks his glass to mine.

This is when I notice the ring on his finger. The man is married. What the hell am I doing? I down the last of my vodka, and pop up from my chair.

"Sorry for keeping you from your work, I'm sure you are ready to finish up and get home to your wife."

He frowns and then looks down at his hand. "Sorry to give you the wrong impression. She passed, but I still wear the ring. It's a habit."

It takes me a minute to decide if I believe him. He could just be saying that, but he doesn't seem like that type of guy so I sit back down. "What happened?"

She passed away from brain cancer, and it was pretty sudden. His wife knew something was wrong, but the doctors did all kinds of tests and couldn't figure it out. After a year, they were finally able to determine it was brain cancer, and she passed within a month.

"I always wonder if she would have lived longer had they caught it sooner... I miss her every day."

The fact that he is sitting here telling me this, gives him a point. Most men would never talk about something so personal to a stranger, especially while showing actual emotions. A tear leaves his eye, and I lean over and wipe it away.

"I'm so sorry."

Noah wipes his eyes, and then places his hand on mine. "It's hard, you know. Being in this life without her. She wanted me to be happy, and not isolate myself, but sometimes all I want to do is lock myself in my den and write horror stories."

This man is broken, and he needs some guidance.

"I can't imagine or begin to understand how much that hurts... I'm just here to forget about what happened today. We can both drink our sorrows away together."

He walks over to the bar and comes back with a new vodka and Sprite. "Don't worry, I don't expect anything."

I tell him about the little girl, and he sips on his Cognac, not taking his eyes off of me while I'm speaking. It's refreshing because others would have acted like they were listening, and just nod, but he is actually listening to me.

"You had a rough day. Listen not to be forward, but I'm enjoying the conversation and your company and would love you to come back to my place."

He shakes his head, but before he can retract the offer I agree.

I'm certainly nothing like my sister, who has already left with someone, but he is the first man that has been a gentleman about it.

Hell, I could be reading more into it, and he's not even asking to sleep with me. Maybe he is just lonely.

It seems maybe it's been a while since we have been touched, and some intimacy is something that helps take my mind off everything from today.

A release might be just what I need...

4

NOAH

This is the most pleasant conversation I've had in a long time, and didn't even have to get on a dating app. Leslie has agreed to come to my home, and I almost retracted the invitation. Now, she probably thinks I just want to sleep with her. Not that I'm opposed to it, but that's not my sole intention. There is a first edition of Thirteen Problems in my den at home and I'll offer to loan it to her.

"Not to be weird, but I'll just follow you."

I laugh because having an exit strategy makes sense. She doesn't know me. I could be an axe murderer or something.

"Yeah, that's fine."

She follows me out, and waits to see what car I get into, before turning her car on and pulling out after me. I never thought I would ask a woman to come back to my place, but maybe finally finishing a chapter has given me some much needed confidence.

When I pull into my driveway, she pulls up beside me, and cuts the engine. Is she starting to regret her decision?

When she gets out and shuts the car door, she has a smile on her face, but can't tell if it's forced or not.

"If you want to leave, you can. I don't want you to feel uncomfortable," I say, walking up to the front door and slipping my key into the hole.

"I texted the address to my sister in case you end up being a murderer."

At first, I laugh but then she has a straight face, so she must be serious.

The big wooden door creaks as it opens, and I gesture her inside. I wasn't expecting company so I hope the place looks okay. I walk over to the light switches and turn them on, illuminating the living room and kitchen area.

She looks around, and I walk to the double doors of the den. "Feel free to look around. Just gonna grab that collection for you."

Instead she follows me, and takes a deep breath as she enters my office. Others would probably make fun of me because it's old-school with the all wood built-in's and the all wood desk.

"This is beautiful. You even have a fireplace." She looks around, taking the wide open space in.

My computer sits on my desk, and Leslie sits down in my chair. "You are a writer, huh?"

The printed copy of the first twenty chapters are sitting on my desk, and she starts to read the first page before I snatch it.

"Sorry, it's not ready for anyone else's eyes yet."

Her hands fly up in front of her body. "Understandable."

I go to my bookshelf and grab Thirteen Problems and hand it to her before stopping at the double doors. She is still sitting in my chair, but has opened the book to the first story.

"Would you like to stay here and read? I can go make some coffee or grab you a drink."

"Warm tea would be nice. Too late for coffee," she replies, not taking her eyes off of the page.

I shut the double doors, leaving her be, and head to the kitchen. Do I even have any tea in the house? I start going through the cabinets and find some Old English, and it's still within date.

I grab a mug and fill it up halfway with water, and then put it in the microwave for forty-five seconds. When the timer goes off, it's steaming and I place the bag in it, dipping it into the hot water.

I grab myself a beer, and head back to the den to drop off her tea, but when I open the double doors, she is standing in my office chair and trying to get something off of the top shelf.

"What the hell are you doing? You're going to break your neck."

I rush over to the desk, set the drinks down, and grab her waist until she falls back into my arms. Her eyes lock on mine, and I lean in for a kiss.

Her lips are soft, and it's nothing like I imagined. I always thought the first woman I kissed after my wife would make me feel disgusted, but there was a spark. This isn't just some random woman I met at a bar. We clicked on a more personal level about literature, and not just by attraction.

When her lips let go, her eyes opened to allow me the honor of drinking in the beautiful blue color.

"I didn't expect that, sorry."

"No, I shouldn't have kissed you. Did I make you uncomfortable?" I ask.

She gestures to the ground, and I put her down.

"Noah, with all due respect, we are grownups. We can kiss one another without feeling ashamed or awkward about it."

I grab my beer without responding, and leave the room again, shutting the double doors to the den behind me. Why did I kiss her? We only just met and this isn't like me. Leslie is an attractive and intelligent woman and she's here at my house. I'm an idiot. Why am I acting like a thirteen-year-old boy with his first girlfriend?

The doors open, and her footsteps come to the living room until she is standing in front of me. "Noah, I'd love to kiss you again."

Leslie stands there, staring down at me until I shake my head, and she straddles my lap. Her hands intertwine around my neck and she leans in. Her lips are nice, and I part my lips to give her more access. This is not how I saw my night going when I went to the bar.

My hands caress the small of her back, and my heartbeat races.

Am I ready to sleep with someone? Leslie is date material, and I'd love to see her again after tonight, sex or not.

"We don't have to do this. You can take the book and see me again sometime. No rush."

She leans back a bit, and removes her shirt. "Gentleman like you are hard to find. I'm not letting you go."

As her hips grind, I find myself growing harder and harder. My penis is begging to be set free. I unclasp her bra, and her beautiful breasts are just waiting for attention. I maneuver onto her back and take one of them into my mouth, nibbling on the nipple, and watching her head push back into the couch. It's been way too fucking long.

My right hand slides down her abdomen, unbuttons her jeans, and slips underneath her panties. She is almost ready. The wetness already accumulated helps my finger ease inside, and a slight moan erupts from her throat, so I insert a second and work them in and out until I almost have her on the edge.

Even if it's been four years since I've been inside a woman, the thrill is still there. The most attractive thing is hearing the woman moan and beg for more. I'm the one taking them to the edge and making them spill over. All the ecstasy they are feeling is because of me. Leslie will be begging for more by the end of the session.

She moves my hand, and grabs the sides of her jeans, and slides them down her legs, until her underwear and jeans are on the floor. The sight of her naked body on my couch makes my dick ache.

"Let me take care of you," she says, sitting up on the couch, but I stop her.

"All I want to do is get inside of you."

Leslie giggles and lays back on the couch as I position myself on top of her with one leg arched up on the back of the couch and the other hooked behind my ass. As my dick slides into her, it's like electricity shoots through my entire body, and I realize exactly what I've been missing. I just needed to get out of my head.

I slam into her, and she moans right into my ear. Like I can get any harder. All this time, I have been holding back, and as soon as I step away from the dating apps, I meet her. Where has she been?

She pushes me off, and leans me back on the couch, easing herself on top of me, and swivels her hips to drive me into an absolute rampage. If she doesn't stop, I won't last much longer. She is going to think I'm incompetent. So, I place my hands on her hips, forcing her to slow down.

Her nipples are hard, and I thread them in between my thumbs which causes her to speed up again, and before I can stop her, we are both spilling over the edges.

"Fuuucccckkkkkkkk."

Her hips stop, and she kisses me before easing off of me and grabbing her shirt. Guess that means there is no time for cuddling, huh?

"You don't have to hide your body from me. It's perfect."

She blushes and sits down next to me. "You have to say that. We just had sex."

"Actually, if I was a typical guy, I already got what I wanted, so I wouldn't have to lie at this point."

Leslie doesn't know me very well, but I'm not like the men her age. She can't be but maybe thirty, and from the looks of her demeanor when she first saw me staring at her, she thought I was going to try to pick her up. Everything that has happened tonight is not typical for me, but I'm liking this newfound confidence in myself.

She picks up her phone while leaning into my side, and then hurries off the couch. "Shit, I gotta go. It's already three."

Leslie takes off her shirt, putting her bra back on, and then the rest of her clothes.

"Can I have your number at least? Or did you get what you came for?"

She smiles, hands me her phone, and then gives me a kiss. "I got more than what I came for, Noah."

I plug my number in and stand up to give her a proper goodbye kiss before she walks out of my house.

That girl is going to be trouble, but I can't wait to see her again.

5

LESLIE

When my alarm blares at seven in the morning, I fly out of bed. Did I even sleep? I didn't get back to my house until almost four in the morning and don't think I dozed off until almost five. How the hell am I supposed to concentrate today? I get my ass out of bed, run to the closet and throw on a pair of jeans, a T-shirt, and some Converse. The only thing I'm worried about is being comfortable. The desks two years ago were stiff and made my back ache. Hopefully, they have made some changes.

I grab my heavy ass backpack and take off out my front door. The campus is only two blocks from my house, so I just sprint, knowing that finding a parking spot is going to make me late to class.

Noah showed me a good time last night, so I don't want to complain, but never again on a school night. I need to be more careful next time. It's not exactly a great impression to be late on the first day, and I don't need any of my professors having something against me right out the gate. These four classes are the end game for me, and after I pass them, I'll finally have my degree. Sure, I can do freelance work without it, but having a degree helps with attracting new clients. This is for my benefit.

My feet hit the pavement one after another all the way until I step onto the campus quad. There's a grassy lawn crisscrossed by side-walks with benches spaced along the pathways. It's been about a year and a half since I was here, and it looks like it has been renovated and redecorated. There's a tall building around the perimeter with libraries, lecture halls, dining halls, and probably some of the admin-istrative offices. My favorite part is the bell tower in the middle of the quad. I lean over with my hands on my knees, trying to catch my breath. The warmth of the sun is peeking out from behind the clouds causing a bead of sweat to trickle down my nose. The heavy backpack strap is pulling on my shoulder, probably leaving an indention. I'll be glad when I don't have to do this anymore.

The central courtyard has decorative pavers and a fountain. I look around, seeing all these barely adult kids, and this is their first day. Fall semester always brings the freshly graduated kids, and they all look so comfortable. Maybe I should have attended the sneak peek where someone walks and shows you where all your classes are. It would have come in handy this morning.

There are navigational signs to help the new students figure out where they're going, but all I see are students lounging on the lawn, someone handing out flyers. She tries to hand one to me, but I brush it off because I only have seven minutes until my first class starts and don't have a clue what building I'm going to. I walk over to the middle of the courtyard where there are signs that show you where all the buildings are, and find the English hall on the map. I run towards it out of breath and hoping that I'm not late, but it never fails. There is a crowd trying to get into the building and up the stairs. I try to inch through, but they are pushing and shoving me. Assholes.

This is my first day back in over a year and a half and I'm feeling the pressure. The kids are looking at me because I'm clearly older than everyone here and it's making me feel out of place. Hell, I'm old enough to be their professor. I head up the stairs to room 106. I stop outside the door, taking a moment to try to collect myself. My chest rises and falls, and I try to slow my breathing. Apparently, I need to go on runs again because I should not be this out of shape. *Okay, come on. Get in there.*

I open the door and can hear the professor's introduction, but I take a few seconds before walking inside. It's still pretty quiet and my breathing is still too loud. They don't want to hear me struggling for air.

"Welcome to American Literature. Most of you have put this class off until your last semester, but this isn't going to be a breeze."

The door squeaks as I push it farther open, and everyone turns and stares at me. As I turn to find a seat, I trip on the entryway rug and fall on my face. The sheer embarrassment is enough, but then he pauses his introduction, runs up the steps, and offers me a hand.

"Maybe you should be more careful. And on time."

My eyes travel up his body, and our eyes meet. It's Noah.

You've got to be fucking kidding me. How is this possible? I didn't know he was a professor. I thought he was a writer? Or a business guy working on his laptop last night. He didn't think to mention his profession to me? I guess I can't be mad because I don't think school ever came up.

I lean over before standing up and get close to his ear. "What the hell, Noah? Really?"

We both stand, and he clears his throat before looking away from me. Neither of us could've expected this.

Noah continues his speech. "You might try to get by my class, but if you wanna pass and graduate then put forth the effort."

The whole room goes silent as Noah makes his way back down to the front of the lecture hall and my dumbass is still standing in the same spot. This is completely throwing me off. How am I supposed to stay in this class now? There isn't another professor teaching it this semester, and I don't want to have to wait another semester to graduate? What the hell am I supposed to do?

"How about you go find your seat so I can go over the syllabus and begin class?"

The tiered seating with fold-down adjustable desktops are fancy compared to what they had two years ago. I take a seat at the first desk on the outside and pull out a notebook, and open to the first page, and click my pen to start writing whatever Noah has to say.

"If you will flip your syllabus to page two. These are the books that we will be reading, discussing, and writing papers on this semester. The campus library has eight copies in stock, so if I were you, I would just buy a copy so you don't have to wait for someone to return it."

I flip to the second page, and on the list is Thirteen Problems by Agatha Christie. Well, I already have a copy of that, so I'm good. A smile takes over my face, and as I look up, Noah is staring at me. Try not to be so obvious.

Seats creak around the room as students move around in their desks, but it doesn't break the intense eye contact between us. He smiles and begins reading the entire list of books. There are ten. I watch his lips move as he talks, and remember how nice they felt against mine last night, or how magical they were against my breasts.

"That's all I have for this class today. We will start the normal class schedule on Wednesday, and you will need to read the first two chapters of Great Expectations and be prepared to discuss them in class."

Everyone starts putting things away in their backpacks, zippers opening and shutting, and then students start to file out of the room. I stay in my seat because I need to address this. Noah is my fucking professor.

After about ten minutes of waiting for all the students to leave, there is only one lingering still sitting at a desk in the back, texting away on her phone.

I sling my bag strap on my shoulder and head down the aisle that leads down to the teaching area with a podium and a stool. His desk has a laptop, notepad and a couple pens.

"Can I help you, Ms. Haddon?" he says, not looking up from his laptop.

"So, you know my last name now?"

"You are the only Leslie in this class."

I look up to see if the girl is gone so I can speak freely, but she is still there.

"Listen, I didn't know you were a professor, and if I knew that last night, this would have never happened."

He adjusts his tie. "So, you enjoyed yourself, but now that we have discovered this, you wish it didn't happen?"

"No, I don't regret it, but I can't sleep with my professor," I whisper.

"And I can't sleep with a student."

He looks up at the double doors at the back of the classroom open up, and students start filing in. Why are they so damn early for the next class?

"Listen, we will talk about this later, Ms. Haddon."

I grip my backpack strap on my shoulder and walk up the stairs and when I reach the top, I look back at Noah. Two students have made their way to talk to him.

How am I going to sit in this classroom three times a week and not imagine him in between my legs?

6

NOAH

I'm the type of person who doesn't need an alarm. My internal alarm is enough. I am up and out of bed by five every morning, and can't remember the last time I've been late to anything. Punctuality is important. Especially, on the first day of classes.

I get into the shower, and wash off all the excitement from earlier this morning before putting on my suit. Okay, so maybe I'm the weird one that still wears them, but I like to appear professional. Others might wear khakis or dress pants and a polo, but I'm not the type.

After putting the pod into the coffeemaker and grabbing my mug, I notice a little pep in my step. I wonder what that could be from? Finding Leslie isn't something I intended to happen, but we were both in the right place at the right time.

She texted me last night to let me know she made it home. I couldn't go to sleep until I knew she was safe and sound. There's some excitement around getting to see her again that leaves me ready to get this school day over with so I can speak to her.

What if after thinking it over, she doesn't want to see me again?

I shake my head, trying to get rid of those ridiculous thoughts. We had sex. She doesn't strike me as the type to go home with random guys.

The coffee ceases pouring into the cup, and I put a couple of swigs of creamer inside before taking a gulp. Perfect. I have four classes to teach today, and then the possibility of seeing Leslie. Is it too soon to ask her to dinner? I've been out of the dating game, so I don't know what is customary. I'll just play by my own rules.

Me: *Would you like to go to dinner tonight?*

I press the send button and sit down on the couch. There are about ten minutes before I have to leave, and I need every single drop of caffeine to put up with the ungrateful students I'm about to have to teach.

This is my fourth year teaching American Literature, and most students put it off until their last semester, and then expect me to pass them for mediocre participation. Some of the professors might let this slide, but I do not.

The university has pegged me as a tough teacher. Many other professors don't take to me well because I won't let anyone get by with crappy work. Why should athletes get a C if they didn't complete the assignment and deserve an F? Why is it my responsibility to make it to where they can play? Instead, the coaches and university should pry into their brains that education is more important than winning games. If they want to play for the team, than do their homework and put in the effort. So maybe I'm a little old-fashioned when it comes to that, but I'm not changing my ways for anyone.

My phone vibrates against the coffee table.

Leslie: *I'll be free around 7.*

A smile erupts, and I send a smiling emoji back.

My eye catches the time and I have to head to campus. I place my mug into the sink, and head out the door. First days are always short. I try to let them out early, since we will only go over the syllabus today. No need to stick around and waste an hour simply talking about random crap. Most of the students like the first days for that reason. Short classes.

When I approach campus, the parking lot is packed and it takes me almost twenty-minutes to find a parking spot. We are not off to a great start. I cut the engine, and grab my laptop bag. A mustang pulling in beside me almost takes my door off the hinge.

"Watch out! What the hell!"

The kid just stares at me, and waits for me to walk away before getting out of his car. Sometimes, I wonder how people get their license. It seems like no one knows how to drive anymore.

I pull out my phone to see if Leslie responded, but the glare from the sunlight makes it impossible to see. Walking the Quad to the English hall, I contemplate the best restaurant to take her tonight. Landry's is romantic, but not so expensive that I'll have to cut back on spending for the rest of the month. Yet, I'm wondering if that will make me seem cheap. Am I supposed to go all out on a first date?

The double door entrance opens with students filing out, and I sneak in and up the stairs to the lecture hall. I'm surprised to find almost ten students after inside. Usually, most don't show up until about five minutes before and trickle in right before the class starts. Occasionally, I have a couple students that always run late and blame it on not knowing where to go. I try to cut a little slack on day one, because maybe they are telling the truth.

I maneuver down the aisle that leads down to the podium and stool, but also my desk. There is still about four minutes until class starts.

"Who wants to put one of these on every desk?" I ask, raising the syllabuses into the air. There is usually always one over eager student who wants to earn points with the professor.

"Me, sir."

I hand her the papers, and pull out my laptop, powering it on, and going to the cabinet to get a bottle of water. My eyes gaze around the room, as students continue to file through the double doors and find their seats.

When my laptop shows eight o'clock, I begin class.

"Welcome to American Literature. Most of you have put this class off until your last semester, but this isn't going to be a breeze."

The doors in the back squeak open, and a woman enters, but

doesn't make it far before she trips and falls. I rush up the stairs, and offer her a hand. Embarrassing moments always outweigh anything else. Kids will be talking about this all day.

"Maybe you should be more careful. And on time."

Her hand perks up, and when her eyes meet mine, I almost throw up. Leslie is on my classroom floor, looking up at me. What the hell is she doing here? I shake my head, not wanting to believe it. Her eyes are wide in the same state of shock as me.

She leans in and whispers. "What the hell, Noah? Really?"

Leslie gets to her feet and I clear my throat, looking out over the classroom. I can't make it obvious we know each other, because rumors travel fast here, and that would not be good for my career.

Without looking back at Leslie, I make my way back down to the front of the class to finish my introduction. The whole room is focusing on me again, instead of her, which is what I want. Except instead of her moving and finding a seat, she is just standing at the back, gaping at me, like she's seeing a ghost.

"How about you go find your seat so I can go over the syllabus and begin class?" I say, gesturing to her to sit down.

I go on about my introduction and give her time to settle in. Right now, my focus is on getting this done, and these students out of here. This blind side is aggravating, because what the hell am I supposed to do now? I slept with a student. Sure, I didn't know it at the time, but still. I could lose my fucking job.

The students barely pay attention while I talk about the novels required for this class, and once I say the word early, they all come alive, putting the papers away in their backpacks and shoving their way out of the door. A couple students come up and have questions, but they are answered in the papers, and I instruct them to read it over and then ask during next class if they still need clarification.

Leslie is still sitting in her seat, and one other student in the back of the classroom. We can't talk about this here. It only takes one student to overhear and my career ends.

"Can I help you, Ms. Haddon?" I ask, looking down at my laptop as to not stare at her perky breasts that were in my mouth last night.

The girl in the back just isn't leaving.

"I didn't know you were a professor... I know this would have never happened."

She is quite right about that. If her being a student here came up in conversation, the sex would have not happened, but that makes me think about being inside of her and I adjust my tie. "So, you enjoyed yourself, but now that we have discovered this, you wish it didn't happen?"

Please don't say you regret it. I don't, but this does mean we have to be very careful.

"No, but I can't sleep with my professor."

"And I can't sleep with a student."

The double doors at the back open up and students start to come in. This conversation will have to finish another time.

"Listen, we will talk about this later, Ms. Haddon."

The frown hurts, but I have to remain professional at this university. Tenure is important if I ever want to retire, and no one can overhear our conversations.

As she takes off up the stairs, my eyes stare at her perfect ass in the painted on jeans. How am I going to watch her walk away every day?

7

LESLIE

The rest of the day didn't go according to plan. After Noah ended class early, I went over to the campus coffee shop and gave myself a minute to process this whole catastrophe. Of course, the first guy that piques my interest in years is my fucking professor. The universe has a funny way of screwing me over, and this is just the beginning. Now, I have to sit through the whole semester, staring at him. Knowing that nothing can ever happen between us.

My next three classes only go over the syllabus and dismiss early, so I'm home by three. That's the best thing about the first week of classes, usually they are cut short, and it gives everyone time to ease back into the swing of things from having a break.

I walk in the door, take off my shoes, and sit on the couch with my backpack. The notebook with all my assignments so far this week are written down nicely according to the class and due date. This is not the semester to get behind or slack off. My focus should be on graduating and finally getting to do what I want.

My phone vibrates against the table.

Noah: So, our date is cancelled, but I can make dinner at my house. We need to talk.

My head hits the back of the couch. *Why did he have to be my professor?* I swear my luck with guys is horrible, and after last night, today was supposed to be a good day. Running into him in that classroom, fucked the whole day up.

Noah is supposed to be the guy I've been looking for, and instead, he is someone I can't have a relationship with without consequences. Life has a funny way of playing tricks on us. The forbidden men are always the ones we want the most, and Noah is someone who I can have an intellectual conversation with without him looking down on me for being a woman. That, in of itself, is a turn on.

Should I even respond? I mean, going over to his house is not a good idea, especially since I still want him inside me again. What if we end up having sex again? Sure, there is a thing called self-control, but Noah has sparked something inside me that wants to rebel. I don't want to be the girl that costs him his career. After mulling it over, going over there and talking this out like adults is going to be better than just avoiding him. He is my professor and no matter what I still have to see him two to three times a week. If I don't go, it might make things more awkward, and that's the last thing I want.

Me: *I'll be over in twenty.*

Why did I have to go to that bar yesterday? I should have just stayed at home and drank by myself. Noah would have never approached me, and this situation wouldn't exist. Yet, here I am, gawking over my fucking English professor. Pathetic. He probably gets students that crush on him all the time. It's not like he's a bad-looking man, especially when you get to know him. His intelligence just makes him even fucking hotter to me.

Good thing it's my night off, because this has been an exhausting day and after going to see him, I'm sure it's only going to get worse. What is he going to say? I can imagine it's that he can't continue this, or pursue it in anyway, and that we need to stay away from each other. What if he tries to get me to take a different class? I am not waiting another semester to take this damn class just because of Noah. It's not happening. If he just trying to let me down easy?

If it's just a talk and dinner, I'm not going to change. My jeans and t-shirt will suffice. I grab my keys and head to his house. What's the worst thing he can say? We can't see each other? Honestly, I don't see how he would want to after today.

When my car comes to a stop in his driveway and I cut the engine, the urge to reverse and just go hits me. Maybe it's better if this conversation is done over the phone, instead of in person. If Noah hadn't been my professor, I would be going out on a proper date.

The front door opens, and he waves me inside.

"I'm coming!" I yell, opening the car door and shutting it behind me.

He waits for me at the door. "You nervous about seeing me? I saw you pull up?"

I don't want to admit that I'm concerned of the outcome of this visit. It's easy to get sucked into attraction, and now that it's against the rules for us to be together, it makes it even more appealing. So fucking weird.

He shuts the door behind both of us, and I take a seat on the couch where we had sex last night. This probably isn't the best place for us to chat. Noah strides over, and takes a seat farthest away from me.

"Dinner is in the oven, but we have things to discuss." He rubs his hands together, and doesn't make eye contact with me. "As much as I would love to continue seeing you, it's unethical."

I never thought of myself as the girl who sleeps with her professor. Noah doesn't deserve to lose his job or be put in a place like this because of what happened between us.

"Listen, I know this is bizarre. I think we can both agree that if we knew then what we know now, we never would have slept together."

He nods, and runs his fingers through his hair. "Never."

"So, there is no need to freak out about this. I'm not going to tell anyone, Noah. I'm not some young student trying to sleep with you to better her grades or something. I'm a grown ass woman who understands the consequences."

As much as I like Noah, things between us are at a standstill. We can't pursue a relationship. I don't ever want to have to questions whether I made an A off my own intelligence or because we are seeing each other. Some might use it to their advantage, but not me. He's lucky he slept with me and not some other student.

My phone buzzes against the table, and I pick it up to reveal an email from the Financial Aid office. I've been waiting for them to tell me what my assignment is this semester. My mouth drops.

"Have you checked your email?" I ask, staring at my phone.

He takes it out of his pocket, and clicks it open. "You've got to be fucking kidding me."

This cannot happen. It's one thing for us to be in a classroom filled with other students, but his office without supervision? Not a good idea.

Out of all the teachers on campus, they have to assign me to be a teaching assistant for him? What kind of sick crap is this?

"I'll just request someone else. Not a big deal," he replies, clacking away at the keyboard on his phone.

"No, don't do that, please."

He looks at me, and tilts his head. "I'm sure there is another teacher that could use an assistant, Leslie."

"This is the only way my tuition is paid for, and I can't afford it out of pocket. Noah, please..."

He lays his phone down on the table and turns to me. "There are other teachers. Calm down."

"You are messing with my future. Don't tell me to calm down. What if all the assignments have been given, and I have to drop out because you couldn't handle me being your assistant. I'll never forgive you."

The oven beeps, and he gets off of the couch, and heads into the kitchen. Instead of giving him space, I follow him. He has to understand that without this, I can't continue my semester. I will be stuck at Grapevine Fire Department forever.

"I refuse to let you fuck this up for me. We can be professional. Our past does not have to affect our professional relationship in any way."

Honestly, at this point, I don't even want to stay for dinner. I'd rather go home and drink some wine. Too much has happened today that I need to process, and being here right now isn't good for either of us. Is it bad that even though he's my professor, my mind is still replaying what happened last night?

"I'm going to go home, Noah. Not feeling up to dinner," I say, grabbing my keys and heading for the door.

He yells from the kitchen. "Meet me at seven in my office. First floor of the English hall. We will discuss your role and what's expected."

Instead of responding, I open the front door and walk straight out.

Noah might not want to lose his job, but he doesn't strike me as the type to want to ruin a life either. I have one semester left to graduate and I'll be damned if anything is going to stand in my way. Being a teacher's assistant is the only way for my tuition to get paid, and even if it's with Noah, professional is all I'll ever be.

8

NOAH

*I*t's not a good idea. She should be assigned to someone else, but I can't be the one that ruins the chances of her graduating just because I want to fuck her again. The spark from last night, it's still there, and even seeing her kneeling in my lecture hall today, I wanted to continue seeing her. I know it's wrong on so many levels, unethical, but she's not a child.

This isn't an ethical boundary I ever thought I'd be faced with, but here we are. Leslie is an amazing woman, and if she is still single come the end of the semester, I would love to get to know her better, but she should've at least stayed for dinner.

It's good to know I'm not the only one freaked out about this situation. She has things riding on this also, and knowing that she is just trying to finish the semester to get her degree, who am I to stand in the way?

The perspiration has caused a ring on the coffee table from my Cognac and I go to the kitchen and grab a coaster. My wife would have a cow if she saw this. What am I supposed to do with all this food? I shouldn't have cooked anything. How could I expect her to stay and have dinner with me after telling her we can't see each other? I'm a fucking idiot.

Jaden is in town and he might be able to help me confirm that I'm making the right decision. A professor sleeping with his student is one thing, but with his assistant, that's even worse. I don't want to be that guy. Especially, after how hard I've always been on my students. I hold them to a high standard, and this would ruin my reputation.

I grab my phone.

Me: Wanna come over and catch up? Made a casserole and saw your car in the driveway.

I haven't seen Jaden in almost six months, but he's one of my good friends. He works in corporate funding so he's always traveling. Jaden is the one person that I can talk to about this situation who I can trust not to run their mouths.

Jaden: Be over in ten.

He has been telling me to get back out there, but I didn't feel like I was ready, until meeting Leslie. She is just so down to earth, and anyone that can sit down and discuss literature with me for multiple hours in a winner in my book. Someone like that is extremely hard to find. And yet, here I am, unable to see her because of my profession.

Jaden is the one that talked me into trying out these newfound dating apps, and honestly, I'll never do it again. Some people might like the blind date thing, but not me. Finding happiness with someone isn't going to be easy, especially a second go around, but I won't sabotage myself either.

There is a knock at the door, and then it opens and closes.

"Hey, man. Been a while."

Jaden only lives a couple blocks away and knows to just walk in. Hell, he's been coming over here for over a decade.

He follows me into the kitchen and makes himself a plate. It's my wife's recipe. She was the one who cooked meals normally, but some of it rubbed off on me.

After dishing our food, we head out into the living room, and I put on the History Channel for background noise. I don't plan on watching the documentary, but hate when it's quiet.

"So, how are things going with you and Evelyn? Is she still traveling with you?"

Jaden and his wife almost got a divorce last year. She was sick and tired of being home by herself all the time. He offered for her to come on his trips with him, and they have been doing that ever since. This eases her mind because she knows what he's doing. For some reason, she thought he was seeing someone else, but Jaden is the most loyal man I know.

"Better than ever. We are going to renew our vows next year. It'll be our ten year anniversary. She wants to do something special, so I'm going to surprise her."

One thing I know about Evelyn. She doesn't normally take to surprises very well. One year he threw her a birthday party, and when everyone popped out and screamed happy birthday, she thought she was having a heart attack. Maybe he should rethink that.

Jaden asks how I've been, and I try to mosey around the subject at first. Give him the rundown on the university changes, and the tenure situation, but then he asks if I've been seeing anyone. I hesitate and he puts down his plate.

"Listen here, don't hold back on me. You know I'm rooting for you to find love again. What's going on?"

How do you tell someone that you slept with a student, but even after knowing the consequences, somehow you want to go against all of that and do it again anyway? I'm a fool. I can't give up everything I've worked for.

"So, I met a girl last night. We talked about Agatha Christie, discussed our favorite books, and she came back to my place."

"Look at you. That's great. How did it go?" he asks, picking up his plate and taking another bite.

"Well it went great, until today when I found out we can't see each other again."

"Why is that? Please tell me you aren't pushing this girl away. She sounds like your type. So, what is it?"

I pop my fingers and look down at the floor. "Turns out she is one of my students. Obviously, I didn't know that last night, and neither did she. So, we can't see each other again."

He drops his fork on the plate, and starts laughing. Like uncontrollably.

"Wait, you're serious?" His eyes lock on mine as I nod. "I thought you were kidding. She's not like nineteen, right?"

I knock his shoulder. "I'm not a fucking cradle robber, J. She's in her thirties. I would never sleep with someone that young and you know it."

Sure, I could have deterred from telling him she was a student, but I knew some sound advice. And J is the only person I trust.

"Hell, if she is grown, I don't see the problem. Unless you think she might use this to blackmail you or something?"

Leslie doesn't seem like the type that would ever do something like that. Matter of fact, she seems to really need to pass this semester. No way she is one of those girls that uses sex to get better grades. Especially, since she didn't know I was her professor when we met.

"No, not her."

After all the student loans, and getting those paid off, tenure is what is going to take care of my retirement. I didn't go through all of this to have it ripped away from me. I need to be careful. Sure, Leslie seems like a wonderful woman, but I need to make sure she doesn't take away everything I've worked so damn hard for in the last two decades.

"Then I say what the hell, go for it. Trust your gut."

The crackling of the fireplace helps me zone out. Should I say fuck it and just keep seeing her? Everything inside me is saying not to take the chance. What if it doesn't work out and she causes a scene at the campus? Or someone sees us out somewhere and decides to tell the University? I'm not so young anymore, and sneaking around doesn't seem up my alley.

My only hesitation is can we wait until the end of the semester? Will she even want me after that long? A woman like her can have any man she wants, and the likelihood of her still being available in five months is unlikely.

There isn't anything wrong with pleasuring myself to her every night. And every time I do, I'll wish they were her soft hands around me...

LESLIE

*I*t's the second day of class, and honestly after yesterday, I have no excitement to go back. Maybe it's because Noah and I can't see each other anymore, but that's reality. I just need to get a grip and get through this semester. *Focus on the degree, girl.*

I throw on a pair of black shorts and a plain white t-shirt. *Simple, but cute.* You can never go wrong with Converse. I check my phone to see if my sister has text me back, but no notifications. *Seriously?* On our days off, we usually don't talk, but only because we are usually trying to catch up on everything we have neglected during our shifts or catching up on sleep.

I grab my backpack, sling it over my shoulder, and take off toward campus. The quad is full with kids running around, some yelling, and another guy playing his guitar. Is it cool to hang out in the grass now or something? See me, I would be worried about getting bitten by fire ants or something else. Who knows what the hell is in there? Why are these kids laying down in the grass and making out for? They'll regret it later.

The pounding of my feet against the concrete fills my ears, until I block everything else out. This meeting with Noah better go okay. I don't want him to second guess his decision to let me remain his teaching assistant. If he did ask for a transfer, they might not be able to find me someone else, and my whole semester would implode. So, I must be on my best behavior. No matter what. This is too important to me to fuck it up. If I don't graduate, then my credibility as a freelance editor and writer wouldn't hold the same weight. Clients want a degree. It proves that the career has been cemented and the freelancer has the background to handle the work. Firefighting needs to come to an end, and I need something else in my life. Being up all night, I feel like a fucking vampire. Sunlight hurts my eyes because I'm just not used to it anymore.

The English building seems to be the busiest no matter what time of day it is. They have a small library on the first floor surrounding offices, and there are always people going in and out. I continue to walk the first floor until I see *Mills* on one of the doors. My chest rises and falls before knocking.

"Come in!" he yells.

The door squeaks as I enter, and he is scribbling away on some paper. He doesn't even look up, but when I go to shut the door, he suddenly talks.

"No, the door stays open when I'm with a female student, Ms. Haddon."

My eyebrows heighten, and I push it back open and take a seat in front of his messy desk. Is he worried someone is going to question his door being closed? He can't possibly be worried about me? I would never be that girl. The one that uses her sexuality to get what she wants. I like to earn my way. I oblige his request and open the door all the way back up.

"So, I'm here. What do you need?"

His desk is beyond cluttered, and honestly, it doesn't seem like the Noah I know at all. I always took him as the highly organized type like his house. Of course, I'm not a professor, but I'm sure there is a lot involved that us as students don't realize. Maybe this is why professors get assistants because they have no clue how to stay organized or don't have the time. There are papers everywhere with no rhyme or reason, plus his laptop and a wireless printer. I don't know how he finds anything on this desk.

"So, I've got some things for you to take care of, Ms. Haddon."

Why is he calling me that? I'm not my fucking mother. "Leslie is fine."

Noah is typing away on his computer, and has barely even glanced at me while I've been in his office. Is this really how he is going to be? He wouldn't be this way with another student. I get that we slept together, but he needs to grow the fuck up. This is business, and he needs to stop acting so cold toward me. This is not how this entire semester is going to go.

"Are you aware of what an assistant does?"

I nod, and roll my eyes. "Let's get a move on. I'm not an idiot."

"I'll provide you with worksheets before each class that you will put on the desks before it starts. If I need help putting together presentations, then I will ask for your help, otherwise, this is basically the jist of it."

He acts like I didn't get the same damn email he did. It explained the job duties. Why is he being so cold and distant? He closes his laptop.

"You will be expected to attend every class, take good notes, help with creating or delivering learning materials and even sometimes help with assignments, quizzes or exams."

I clear my throat. "Mr. Mills, wouldn't that make it easier for me to get a better grade, if I know what's going to be on a quiz or exam beforehand?"

He looks up, and shakes his head. "As a teacher's assistant, you should be on top of things. So, inadvertently, you would know what is going to be on each test anyway. Do you plan on using this position unethically?"

His eyes are still fixed on the opposite side of the room while he's talking to me, and I'm sick of being nice.

"Are you not even going to look at me now? Stop acting like a five-year-old. I won't be treated like this for the rest of the semester."

He needs to remember that this is a professional relationship, and respect is key. What is anyone going to think if he won't even look at me for gods sakes? And then to question my ethics? Where the hell is the Noah I know?

His knuckles turn white, and I cross my arms. "Seriously, what is going on? This can't be about the other night. We have discussed this."

He cocks his neck. "Yes, we have, but right now, I'm trying to keep myself from crossing this desk and kissing you. So, yes, Leslie. I'm trying to restrain myself and not give in to the idea of taking you on this desk," he says, in a low raspy growl.

"And that is exactly what you told me to steer clear of. How am I supposed to do that with you talking to me like that?" I fan myself.

Even with him acting like an ass, my mind is still playing a daydream of him in between my legs as I sit on his desk. I won't lie; it's always been a fantasy of mine, but not necessarily at college, more like an in home office.

He hands me some worksheets and asks me to place one on every desk before class. I take them and get up from my chair. "You know, I didn't think you were going to treat me like this. You're being an asshole. Restraining yourself or not."

I turn my back toward him and start for the door, until I feel him grab my arm. It lights a spark, as I spin around to face him, looking up at him through my lashes. His stern look makes me want to get on my knees, and help relief some of his stress, but the door is open.

"I'm sorry. This is a first for me. Just trying to be professional and unbiased is all," he says, caressing my arm, but looking at the door.

"Future reference, if you are going to grab me and spin me around, you better have something better to say or do next time," I say, lightly grazing my hand on the bulge in his pants. "If you don't want to daydream about you fucking me in this office, be a little nicer, professor."

As I turn around, he leans into my back and whispers to me. "How much I would love to fuck you in my office, Ms. Haddon. Maybe in five months' time. Have a good day."

My knees become weak and I walk out of his office and up to the lecture hall. My panties are wet, and my arousal is eating away at me. Fuck! Instead of putting out the worksheets, I make a bee-line for the bathroom and take care of myself. There is no way I could handle sitting through Noah's class under this condition.

Professor Mills wants to fuck me on his desk. I can't fucking wait.

10

NOAH

What the hell is this woman doing to me? I know better than to act this way, especially when anyone could walk by and see. The bulge in my pants is noticeable, and I can't go to class looking like this. My office is a safe zone, and I can't let her get me all worked up. My mind needs to stay out of the gutter, and focus on being professional even when around her. It only takes one person to see us together, and assume the wrong thing, and my career will go down the drain.

I know she needs this assistant position, but the first day going like this isn't a good sign. Granted, it's not her fault I can't keep myself from getting a fucking boner with her close to me. Leslie doesn't deserve to be screwed over because of my issues. I think it's best if we don't meet in my office anymore. Keeping myself in line is going to be harder than I anticipated, and it only takes once to screw everything up.

I close the office door, lock it, and sit down in my chair. There is no way I'm going into the lecture hall during this conundrum. My mind still won't let her go. She takes over my dreams. It's like my mind wants what it can't have. Leslie is off fucking limits. I know that, and yet it's still hard as hell to see her here. Why can't I just push her out of my head?

The lasting effects of Leslie are still going, and this bulge in my pants isn't going to go away. There is only one way to take care of this, and I don't have a choice. I close my eyes and imagine her here again. Her beautiful body will look ravishing splayed out on my desk, with me between her legs. The moans erupt from her throat, and yell my name. *Noah!* This office isn't soundproof, but I will use my hand to muffle her, until she spills for me.

I unbutton my pants, and work myself, thinking of her soft hands instead of my own. Her lips are even better. *Fuck, Leslie.* She is a rarity, and the fact that she is able to read me from the beginning, makes it even more monumental. I continue pumping myself, daydreaming about her on my desk, against the bookshelf, and when I finally get my release and open my eyes, the hunger to have her again is overwhelming. My hand isn't enough. I need her.

Have I always craved sex this much? Something about Leslie is leaving me craving her, and it's like a drug. Just trying to get by until my next fix. Five months is a long time, and my mind can only take me so far. Eventually, I'm going to need the real thing again.

Leslie is a fucking masterpiece. She's intelligent, gorgeous, and sassy. The little bit of attitude I've seen from her, only makes me want her even fucking more. It's been a while since I have been able to indulge in my fantasies, and Leslie would look stunning in a leather outfit holding a whip. I lick my lips. Oh the things I'm going to do with her when the time comes.

I clean myself up, and then stuff my laptop into my bag, and head to the lecture hall. When the double door opens, she is walking around the room, putting the worksheets on each desk just as I asked. *Good girl.* She takes a minute to stop and look at me before continuing. She has no idea I just took care of myself.

I travel down the aisle, step down to my desk, and unload my bag onto the desk. Today we are discussing *Great Expectations*, and I'm interested to see her input. Of course, I have to make it not obvious, so she won't be the first person I call on. Hope she did her homework.

Students file in and take their seats, but don't seem happy when they find the sheets on their desks. I don't know why they think classes are easy. If anything, they get harder the closer to graduation they get. It seems no one wants to work hard in their last semester, but they have another thing coming in my class. So many people don't take college seriously, but they need to. A college degree isn't required for all jobs, but without one these days, it's hard to get a decent job anywhere. In my parent's time, college graduates were rare, and if you had a degree, that meant you were wealthy already. Now, with all the federal grants, it's easier for everyone to get a higher education, but not everyone is willing to work for it.

I like the students that are hungry. Usually, it's the ones that have everything to lose. There have been students that I have had the privilege of teaching that worked their asses off to graduate. They didn't want to be stuck in their small town, or working at a dead end job. These are the students that work the hardest. Most of the students this semester seem like the other type. The ones where their parents are making them go to college, and they don't actually have any idea what they want to do with their life, so they are just doing what they are told. So, their enthusiasm toward their grades isn't there.

As a professor, it's my job to know which type my students are, and help them succeed. Every semester is different, and sometimes I get lucky and will have more of the hungry type than the slackers. I'm not so lucky today.

"Seriously? What are we in the second grade?" a student says, picking up the worksheet and looking at it.

"Indeed, Mr. Winchester. If you can't fill out this worksheet, then you obviously didn't do your homework, and that's your first F. Congratulations," I reply.

When I give out homework, it's imperative that they do as I say, because participating in class discussions is twenty-percent of their grade. It might not seem like a lot, but when you only get C's on your papers, that twenty-percent can make or break you graduating.

There is still a few minutes left before class starts and as more students arrive the hall becomes loud. Students carrying on conversations, the door opening and closing every few seconds, and students getting their supplies out of their backpacks. I look around the room to find where Leslie is now sitting, and my eyes land in the third row. But that's not all they find. There is a gentleman talking to her, and she is smiling. I take a deep breath, because a small amount of jealousy starts. *She's a student. Remember that.*

I walk over to Amber in the second row, close enough to where I can hear their conversation, and ask how she liked the book. She replies, but I'm not listening, and instead turning my focus on Leslie.

"Would you go to dinner with me tonight?" the man asks.

Calm down. She is not yours. Leslie can go out with whoever she wants.

"I'd love to."

I walk back up to the front, and pace for a minute. Leslie is going out with another guy, and for some reason, I'm furious. My fists tighten, and I start to see red. What the hell am I going to do? Personally, I want to go over and punch the guy in the face, but I can't. We are not even an item, and jealousy isn't a good look. My fear is she won't be single by the time the semester ends, and what if I lose her forever? All because I'm too scared to say fuck the university and do what my hearts wants.

"Alright, settle down, class. Your assignment was to read the first two chapters of Great Expectations for class today. First order of business is to take the first fifteen minutes to fill out this worksheet, and then we'll do a class discussion."

I turn the timer on from my phone, and the students take out a writing utensil from their backpacks, and then the hall goes silent. I take this time to get a hold of myself, because in this lecture hall, I can't let things affect me. Especially, Leslie. This is where I need to remain professional and let her do what she wants. I can't expect her to not go out with anyone. She is a beautiful woman, and I have been clear that we can't be an item until after the semester is over. *Did I think she was going to wait around for me?* I laugh, and a couple students look up at me.

Why am I over here acting like a scorned lover? I need to stop getting jealous and let her live her life. She understands that this can't be anything but professional until after she is no longer a student in my class. So, I need to keep my feelings at bay, and under the radar. Gawking at her talking to another man isn't helping my cause.

I need to remember my goal and screwing the pooch over a woman isn't going to secure my retirement. She is free to go out with whomever she wants, and I will stand by idly and be patient. It's my only option. What would I do if the university found out? Teaching has always been a way to fill a void, and my novel still has two chapters to go before it's even got a completed first draft. No one is ever going to contract it, so it's not like I'm going to make a million dollars or anything. She helped me open myself up, and that's exactly what I need. Someone to help me realize that it's all in my head. Focus on getting the words on the page and nothing. Imposter syndrome can't get me.

I pace around the room, and notice the guy smiling at her, but she isn't paying attention. She is a good student and is working on the assignment. Will she have a good time with him? I brush it off, knowing that this man is probably going to try to take her home on the first date, and she isn't that type of girl. So, I have nothing to worry about.

The fact remains: *Leslie Haddon is off-limits.*

11

LESLIE

*M*y eyes stay on the paper in front of me, and I hunch over the desk not to let my eyes wander. I can feel Noah staring at me. Right now, we are in class and I have to act like just a student. It's hard, for sure, when my heart wants other things, but that'll have to wait.

The guy sitting next to me asked me out tonight, and since I'm single, why the hell not? Is it rude to agree when you don't actually see it going anywhere? I mean, guys do it all the time, right? Ask a girl out just to get laid at the end of the night. So, I don't know why I'm trying to make myself feel bad about it. I mean, the guy is cute, but he's not Noah.

"Alright, pencils down," Noah says, as the alarm goes off. "Pass them to the front and let's begin our discussion."

Hands fly up and he calls on someone in the back. The student stands up and looks around the room. He isn't so eager to talk now.

"Well, sir, the first chapter introduces Pip, and some other characters..." he starts to taper off.

"And what did you think about the introduction? Did it keep you intrigued to learn more about him?"

"Yes, sir."

He looks around the room, and calls on another student. "What about you?"

"Being an orphan myself, the chapter hit home for me. The quality of writing is wonderful and nothing like the books coming out today. There is so much detail, and fluff in them, that just isn't in newly published novels."

I look at Noah, and he is staring directly at me. Why? His eyes bear into mine, deep into my soul, and my panties become wet.

"What about you, Ms. Haddon? Anything you would like to add?" He crosses his arms, and leans on his right leg.

"I find it depressing that he never met his real parents, and the only information he knows is what his sister has told him. The cemetery, crying beside his parent's graves, actually caused an emotional response, which is exactly what a good written novel should do. Get you into your feelings."

Noah's lip twitches, and he leans back on his desk. "And what else?"

"The complexity and prose of this novel is second to none. You just don't find writing like this anymore, and it truly pulls you in and leaves you intrigued at the end of every paragraph."

He nods, and calls on another student so I sit down.

The discussion over chapter two emerges, and somehow I can't concentrate. Did he hear the man ask me out? He is acting weird, but he wouldn't want me to sit around and wait for him. I'm sure he isn't going to be. A man that looks like that can have any woman he wants, and the way he can fuck, they will come back for more. Hell, by the end of the semester, will he even want me anymore? Or will he have gotten his fix for someone else, and move on?

What hold does this man have over me? He can look at me and I want to fuck his brains out instantly. I've never been a very sexually active person. In fact, I'm usually the one that doesn't have sex with a man until we've been together for a while. And not ever on a first date. But Noah is different in every way. He's educated, well-mannered, great in the bedroom, and his eyes make me melt. Being around him makes me want to jump his bones every time. It's like a pull, and I can't shake it.

"Make sure to read chapters three and four. Another worksheet will be provided next class period, so be prepared. Remember participation and the worksheets are twenty percent of your grade."

Students start packing up their stuff into their backpacks, and I meander in the aisle, waiting for Noah to be free, but the man next to me is waiting for me at the door, waving me over.

"By the way, I'm Adam. Here is my number," he says, handing me a piece of paper and walking off.

I don't turn around because I feel him staring at me, and the heat rushes to my cheeks as students push past me out the door. Do people not see him doing this? He is going to get himself in trouble. I walk out the double doors, and down the stairs. How am I ever going to focus in class?

A part of me thinks I need to cancel this date because maybe it is wrong to lead someone on. I can't see myself dating anyone else right now. My head is set on Noah, and even if it's five months from now, I don't think this pull is ever going away. It's too fucking strong.

By the time I get to my front door, sweat is dripping off of me, and I regret not wearing something lighter. Black isn't the best color to wear when it's a million degrees outside. I get inside, drinking in the air conditioners, and take my shoes and socks off to let my body heat reset.

I go through my backpack taking out Great Expectations and starting the third chapter, even though I've read the book a million times. Deep down, I know that I don't need to read it again to pass any exam or discussion, but maybe I will pick up on something I missed the first few times I read it. It happens with movies sometimes. You have to watch it a couple times before you pick up on things you missed on the initial watch.

My phone vibrates, and I pick it up off of the coffee table.

Adam: So, diner at six?

The date is happening, but I don't plan on kissing him or anything. Maybe I can talk him into being just friends. I'll pay for my meal and he will pay for his. He just caught me off guard when Noah was in my head, and maybe it felt nice for someone else to want me. Adam is worried about taking me out in front of other people. Okay, so that's a dig at Noah. I can't be mad at him for not wanting to jeopardize his career for me.

Me: See you there.

I have never met Adam in my life, but he is probably close to thirty, and a non-traditional student like me. He looks like a guy that would work in finance and be named Chad. That makes me chuckle.

Around five-thirty, with little energy, I head over to my closet to find something to wear. Maybe a summer dress and some flats? I don't feel like getting dressed up, and going to the diner, but I agreed to go, so I suck it up. Who knows, maybe Adam is going to be sweet and get me out of my head about Noah. That's what I need. Someone to take my mind off of him until the end of the semester. But I'm not that kind of girl. Relationships should mean something, and not just be a fling. Adam deserves better than that. So, I decide to give him a shot.

After lining my eyes, and putting some bounce in my hair, I turn off my lights, grab my keys, and head to the diner. When I pull up outside, I can see Adam in a booth, and he is tapping away at the table. Nervous twitch. He doesn't need to be like that around me. I smile, unbuckle, and walk inside, with the bell alerting my entrance.

He turns around and smiles. "You look beautiful, Leslie."

I have a seat across from him, and pick up the menu like I don't already know it by heart. The waitress recognizes me.

"Hey girl, it's been a little bit since I've seen you in here."

I nod, and go back to looking at the menu while Adam orders a Dr. Pepper, BLT and fries.

"I'll have a Mountain Dew and the cheeseburger basket, please," I say, handing her the menu.

He wipes his hands on his pants, and then entwines his fingers.

"So, I'm new here. Don't know much about the area. This is the only place I've eaten."

"It's pretty good. Fries are the best."

My phone vibrates in my dress pocket, and I pull it out to make sure it's not an emergency. Why the hell is Noah calling me?

"Do you need to get that?"

I shake my head, and put it back in my pocket. "Where are you from?"

"Michigan, actually. My father lives here, and isn't doing too well. I moved here and decided to sign up to finish some classes."

Adam is already turning out to be a good guy. I mean, changing his whole life to move here to take care of his father. That's admirable.

"I've lived here my whole life. My family comes from a line of fire-fighters. My dad's the chief."

He chokes on his drink. "You're a firefighter?"

Why does everyone think I'm kidding when I say that? The stigma around there only being male firefighters pisses me off. "Yeah my dad, sister and myself."

I don't even mention that I'm finishing my degree to get away from it, because I'm already a little irritated.

"I just didn't think women did that. Fight fires. That's cool." He looks down at the table.

He tries to change the subject and tell me about Michigan, but honestly I just start to tune him out. Why do people have to be so sexist about things like professions? It's not the 1950s anymore.

"Is there a problem with women being able to do the same job as any man?" I ask, not being able to hold my tongue anymore.

"Well some jobs... they just wouldn't have the strength to do..."

And that's when I lose it. "Have you never heard of Camilla Parlew. She is the strongest woman in the country. Would you tell her she doesn't have the strength to do a man's job, because she could bench-press twenty of you without breaking a fucking sweat."

I leave a ten dollar bill on the table as I get up, walk out the door, and get into my car.

Why did he have to be sexist? I thought he might be a sweet guy, until that comment.

My phone starts to vibrate again, and I pull it out of my pocket. Noah has called me three times, but not voicemails or text messages. I let it go to voicemail and take off.

12

NOAH

There is going to be a spot on my rug from all this damn pacing. Why is she even out with that guy, anyway? A growl erupts from my throat, and my knuckles clench. How am I supposed to be okay with this? Maybe we can't be together right now, but I didn't think she would be dating someone new in a matter of days. *Jesus.* Or is she just doing this to get a rise out of me? I throw my phone on the couch. Why won't she answer the phone?

All I can imagine is this douchebag being someone who uses her to satisfy his needs and then breaks her heart, and even if I can't have her right now, I don't want her to go through that. I should stop calling her. Hell, I'm the one that told her we couldn't see each other anymore, and I'm over here pacing around my house like a fucking idiot, while she's out on a date with some stranger.

The thought of his lips on hers, I can't fathom it. Am I going to lose her? Leslie is making me go crazy, and throwing all my sanity out the window. Do I stop being a pussy and just say fuck it? Is being happy more important than my tenure? Or my reputation at the university?

No, I can't. It would be career suicide.

A rap at the door takes me out of my head, and I jog to the door.

"Who the hell..."

When I open the door, Leslie is standing there, cheeks flushed, and arms folded. "What are you doing here? This isn't a good idea."

"Just let me in, Noah," she says, walking right in, and straight to the couch.

She's already hard to resist in front of others, and now here we are alone. My self-control isn't what it used to be, and after relieving myself while thinking of her today, I'd love nothing more than to be inside her right now.

"Why are you calling me? You told me to stay away. Make up your fucking mind!"

I don't even know how to respond. Do I tell her that I want to throw everything away for her? Or, will that just scare her away?

"Are you even listening to me?" she says, waving her hands in front of my face.

I grab her wrists, and hold them. "Give me a minute, damnit. You just showed up at my house. Do you have any idea how much I want to push you up against that damn wall right now? Say to hell with it all, and just not care?"

I let go of her wrists, and start pacing in front of the fireplace again, running my fingers through my hair. This is insane. I'm like a fucking addict waiting for their next fix and it's right in front of me.

"I need you to tell me right now. Are we going to stay away from each other or not? We are both too old for this back-and-forth bullshit."

She gets closer to me, and I capture her cheeks with my hands. "I want so much to see where this leads. Truly, but aren't you scared someone will find out? What happens if the university does, and then they start reviewing all your work to see if I fairly assessed you?"

Leslie doesn't have anything to worry about because no matter how good the sex is, or how much I like her, she will only receive grades she has earned. I'm not that type of professor.

"I won't worry about that. Literature is my strong suit. They can check all they want, the grades I receive will be earned, Noah. Don't ever give me a grade I don't deserve."

She looks up at me through her lashes. "So which is it?"

I look deeply into her eyes, and then my lips are on hers. The will to stay away is broken, and all I want is her. Her hands lace into my hair and all my self-control goes out the window. Leslie is someone who I can't help but want to be around, and so what if she's my student. We are both grown adults and as long as we keep it under wraps until she graduates, we won't have a problem. I'm sick of fighting it.

She pushes me down on the couch and straddles me, pushing my shoulders back so I sink right in. *The things you do to me!* She brings her shirt up over her head and throws it on the floor. My eyes gaze at her perky breasts and wanting them in my mouth.

"Are you sure you want to do this?" Her hungry eyes look like she wants to pounce on me like a Jaguar on its prey.

"You are all I think about, dream about.... All I want is you."

Her lips are back on mine, and I'm rock hard. I don't know how I'm ever going to be able to think about anything else. Leslie has sparked something inside me, and usually I am not a very sexual person, but ever since I came across her at the bar, it's all I think about.

I'm going to let Leslie call the shots tonight. She wants to take charge and I'm going to turn off my dominant side and let her be in control.

There is something extremely sexy about a woman who knows exactly what she wants.

13

LESLIE

He is pressing hard against me and right now, all I want is to show him he is making the right choice. I will never purposefully jeopardize his career. He has been clear about how much it means to him, and for this to work, we have to be careful. Do I like being the mystery girl he can't tell anyone about? No, but it's only five months. How hard can it be?

His hands wrap around my backside, and start to move with me as I move my hips. Why are his clothes still on? I get off the couch, and put my hand on my hip.

"Undress for me."

He cocks his head back. "What?"

"Take off your clothes. NOW."

He grins and stands up, and removes his shirt fast.

"Slower. I want to enjoy the reveal."

My hand runs from his chin down to his belt as he undoes it, and slips it out of the belt loops. His eyes never leaving mine. As he unbuttons his pants, and then takes the zipper down, I lick my lips. There is something simply irresistible about a man who undresses for you.

His pants hit the ground and he steps out of them and then pulls his boxers off.

"What about you?" he asks, standing buck naked except for his socks.

I get a little closer, and push him back on the couch, his dick on high alert.

"Now you can watch me."

I turn with my ass facing him and hook my fingers to my sides, slowly pulling my pants down, and bending over so he gets a good look at my ass. It's my best feature.

"Fuck, Leslie. I swear you have the nicest ass I've ever seen."

I laugh and step out of my pants and kick them to the side. "It's all yours now."

He nods, watching me slowly walk over to me on the couch. I get on my knees, and spread his legs apart, maneuvering myself to a better angle. "Now, the question is do you want me to suck you dry first or ride you like I'm competing in the Daytona 500?"

His eyes go wide. "Fuck, I have to choose. I want both. I choose both. But how about you let me take care of you, too?"

I take his hand. "Where is your bedroom?"

He leads me into his bedroom, which is immaculately clean and I push him down on the bed. He looks up at me.

I get up on it, and angle myself over his mouth. "Be a good boy and make me come, hard."

His tongue immediately starts licking my clit, and I put him in my mouth. Noah is one man that knows what I want. He can read my body and know when I'm about to come.

He sucks on my clit and I moan, but he can't hear me with my mouth full. His groans tell me he's enjoying himself, and we are both working toward the common goal. The release.

I continue to move up and down on his hard cock as he sucks my clit, and then eases a finger inside me. A moan escapes and my back arches.

"That's my girl. Fuck all that. Just sit on my face and let me take you all the way."

"Hover or sit?" I say, looking over my shoulder at him.

He pulls me down on my his face, and starts going faster. I sit straight up and run my fingers through my hair. *Fuck!*

"Holy shit. I'm gonna suffocate you!"

He smacks my ass, and continues, holding my thighs apart and down on him. "Don't move. Stay just like this."

His finger moves faster and faster as his tongue swirls about my clit and I'm about to combust. It's like a burning sensation in my core, and I start swiveling my hips, grinding on his face.

"I'm about to come. Don't fucking stop!"

He goes even faster until my thighs start to convulse and I scream. "Fuck."

He does one more lick on my clit and I jump. I love how sensitive things are after an orgasm.

"You know if you push through, the second orgasm is easier to reach if you let me continue."

My eyebrows fly up. "You want to make me come again?"

He brings me back down on his face, and this time, he focuses on my clit only, and his tongue circles it, making me jerk around, but it feels good.

"You good?"

"Keep going," I say, taking my breasts into my hands, and letting myself ride his face. This man is my white knight that has charted into make sure I have as many orgasms as I want. He's not even worried about himself.

He puts two fingers inside me, and pumps them in conjunction with his tongue on my clit and it pushes me over the edge. This one is so much stronger than the first and I find myself on cloud nine. I'm so fucking sensitive that if he touches my clit right now, I might slap him.

"I told you. Have you never had two orgasms back to back before?" he asks, wiping his mouth as I get off of him.

"Let's just say most of the men I've been with are more worried about getting themselves off than me. Hell, I barely got foreplay."

He slaps the bed. "Well, you hit the fucking jackpot. I get off on making you come. Feeling you writhe underneath me because of my touch, nothing is fucking sexier."

I slide my fingers over myself, and it's still sensitive, but staring at his rock hard dick makes me want to slide inside.

He catches me and places his hands on his cock, stroking it. "You want it?"

I nod, licking my lips. "Then take it."

He lays back, and I sit down, easing him inside me. My hips start to swivel and then I pick up my tempo. His eyes close, and he groans.

"Listening to you moan and feeling you come on my fingers and tongue... I'm so fucking hard right now."

I lay down on his chest and use just my ass to bounce myself on his cock. My teeth easily sink into her chest and he groans.

"Don't fucking stop. Take me. Fucking take me, Leslie!"

I quicken my tempo, and ride him like competing in the Daytona 500 and the trophy is his cock.

"Smack my ass!"

His hand slams down, making me scream out and sends us both over the edge. We both still, taking in the overwhelming sensations, and then I drop beside him on the bed, breathing heavily.

"You know there's no going back right?"

His head turns to me. "What do you mean?"

I laugh. "After this, I'll never want another man again, Noah. You have screwed me, so just remember that."

My head falls to the bed, and I continue to try and catch my breath. I didn't know why I came over to Noah's, but good thing I did. Adam would have never treated me this way. I'll put that on the list as one of the worst first dates ever, but I did get a good ending to the night.

He pulls me into his chest, and kisses the top of my head. Cuddling isn't something I'm used to, since most men are a hit it and then do something else type, but Noah is being sweet. I like this, and can't wait to do it more often.

Are we really going to do this? Is he really ready to take on being in a relationship with one of his students? We will be careful, and never go out in public around here where we can be seen, but sometimes you can never be too careful. It only takes one person to see or interpret something wrong, and his reputation goes down the drain. That's a lot of pressure.

"What's on your mind?"

I don't respond.

"Listen, you're too quiet. I might not have known you very long, but it's abnormal, so talk to me, please."

I turn over and balance myself on my elbows. "Don't get me wrong; I want to be with you, but are you sure you are ready to take the risk? There are so many things that could go wrong, and I don't want you to resent me if something happens."

His finger lingers down my chest. "If anything, tonight has cemented my decision. The loneliness has been depressing, and for the first time in years, I have a light. You."

I blush.

"No, seriously. You make me feel alive, like I haven't felt in a long time, and you gave me the confidence to almost finish my novel. That's a huge accomplishment. So, yes Leslie Haddon, I'm sure I want to embark on this adventure with you by my side. Stop questioning it and just enjoy."

My chest rises and falls as his lips touch mine, and everything seems to be coming together nicely. The universe brought us together, and there has to be a reason. He must be the man I'm meant to be with, and I can't run away. He is my addiction.

14

NOAH

*H*er silk skin feels like heaven against my chest, and I want to know everything about this woman. What was her childhood like? What is her family like? These are things that are important in a relationship and family can be an obstacle. Not that I'm thinking about meeting her parents today, but mine, for example, are not easy people. My mother is highly protective and my father doesn't trust anybody. He's more of a conspiracy theorist and my mother, well, she doesn't think I should be with anyone else.

Janet wanted me to move on and find someone. These last few years since her death, I have done everything but find happiness. Instead, I put the focus on my career and tried to finish my novel, but everything seemed to be stagnant. I miss the way I used to feel when we would come home after long day's work and snuggle on the couch. A partnership is about having someone to share the good and hard times with and with her gone, I have been taking on everything by myself. Depression hit me like a ton of bricks, and seeing a therapist did help, but even she suggested I try to get back out there.

When I met Leslie at the bar, it was like something clicked and I knew I liked this girl. Not everybody can hold a conversation with

me, especially about literature, and she did. To find someone that
shares the taste of classics is hard these days.

"Do you have anywhere you need to be?" I ask.

"No, I don't work until tomorrow night."

How are we going to get to see each other if she's working
overnight? She will be working while I'm asleep and then spend most
of her day at the University. I'm not one to run away from a challenge.
Relationships take work, and as long as we both put forth the effort,
we should be fine. After this semester, she plans on doing freelance
work anyway, so she won't be working overnights anymore, and we
won't have to sneak around.

Leslie stays quiet, and for a minute I think she might have fallen
asleep, until she starts to rub my chest.

"What's on your mind now?"

"This might be weird for you, but I'm curious about your wife,
Noah," she says, admiring the picture of us on our wedding day on
the nightstand next to the bed.

This isn't something I usually talk about, but with her I feel
comfortable. Would anyone else be okay with the fact that I still have
pictures of her on my nightstand? The point is, Leslie is, and that's
why I'm so intrigued. She understands that just because my wife has
passed doesn't mean that she is not still in my heart.

"She was an amazing woman. Extraordinary. Very driven and
focused on her career. Basically, picture me but the female version.
We had big plans for our retirement. Travel all over the world and do
all the things we had always talked about."

Leslie sits up on her elbows, and stares at me.

"How long were you guys together?"

I stroke my chin. "Almost ten years."

The thing is they went by so fast. We were twenty-years-old when
we got together and got married within two years. I'm not typically
the one that believes in love at first sight, but that's definitely what
happened.

"Are you sure you're ready to be with someone else?"

It's a valid question. But what concerns me is that she's asking me now after we slept together twice, and I've told her I'm basically willing to risk my career to be with her. Doesn't that make it obvious that I'm ready to be with someone else? I wouldn't be sitting here with her if I wasn't.

Leslie shouldn't have to question this, and my job is to make her understand that I'm ready. Sure, my job is important, but the reality of the situation is I can't expect her to wait around for five months and not date someone else. And then what happens if any guy comes and she falls in love with him? My chance with her is now, and walking away from my chance at happiness is just slapping myself in the face.

I take her hands in mine. "Of course, I am. Why would you ask me that? I'm here with you bearing my soul, and you're asking if I'm ready to be with someone?"

She shrugs her shoulders and looks down at the bed sheets. "You are too beautiful to do that. Look at me."

Her eyes come up and meet mine.

"I'm not like those fuck boys you might've been with before. And I don't date just anybody, so let me be clear. Leslie Haddon, I'm ready to move on and be with someone as long as that person is you."

MY HAND SLAPS the pillow next to me, missing Leslie's head by a quarter of an inch, and she didn't even move. Wow, she must be a heavy sleeper. I roll onto my side and inch out of the bed, trying not to wake her up. I know she has a long day ahead of her, considering she has to work tonight and we were up until almost four in the morning. Good thing it's Saturday and we don't have classes today. My arms stretch above my head, and then I pick up my boxers and slide them on. Guess it's time to figure out something for breakfast. I saunter through the hallway and living room into the kitchen. Waking up with someone in my bed is new, but it's nice. This is one of those times where I have the option to cook an actual breakfast for more than just me. The refrigerator opens and I pull out the carton of eggs and some sausage. Something small. We used so much energy last night, and we need to replenish. I take out the coffee grounds and put two scoops into the maker before pressing start. I'm not sure how late she normally sleeps, but Leslie still needs to eat something.

I grab a skillet out of the cupboard and spray a couple pumps of PAM cooking spray so that they don't stick and then crack four eggs open and scramble them in a glass measuring cup, before pouring them into the skillet. What if she doesn't like eggs? Whatever, who doesn't like them? I swat away the thought, and grab a smaller skillet to put the pre-cooked sausage links into the pan.

While waiting for the food to cook, I grab my mug out of the cupboard and pour it half full of coffee and then get the creamer out of the fridge. Some people like their coffee black. Those are people you should run away from, far far away.

The eggs start to cook, so I use my utensil to move around the bottom of the skillet to flip them over, and let them cook all the way through, and the sausage is getting good and brown now. Janet used to make fun of me because every weekend this is what I would make: eggs and sausage. Why is that weird? It's a good breakfast with lots of protein. Her thing was oatmeal and I can't stand that stuff. To each their own, I guess.

Finding Leslie has been a godsend, and even though Janet wants to move on, I'll never forget her. She was my first love and will always be in my heart. I think that's another reason why I'm so drawn to Leslie, because she doesn't have a problem with that. It's not something I can just shut off, you know, she was my wife for a decade, and I loved her.

I turn the stove off, and scrap the eggs and sausage out of the skillets onto two plates before grabbing a mug for her and filling it with coffee in case she wants some. Probably not, considering she needs her sleep, but would like to keep her options open.

I grab the plate, a fork, and her mug and venture into the bedroom, putting them on the nightstand, and brushing her hair out of her face.

"I've made breakfast, if you're hungry. You should at least eat something," I say, sitting down on the edge of the bed while she stretches.

"You didn't have to do that, Noah."

"There's coffee, too. Or you can eat and go back to bed."

She leans in for a kiss, and then eyes the breakfast. "I'll eat, but coffee will only make it impossible to fall back asleep. I can go home and go back to sleep after I eat."

"Nonsense, you are fine right here. Eat up. What time do you need to be up?"

She grabs the fork and shovels some eggs into her mouth. "Five."

I kiss her forehead, "I'll wake you up then. See you in a bit."

There are plenty of things for me to do today while she rests. I need to work on my novel and knock out the last chapter so I can finally start the dreadful editing phase. That's my goal over the next few hours. I cruise into the den, and turn on my desktop, and wait for it to boot up. If I can just finish this chapter today, I'll call it a win.

I open the word document, and take a deep breath and I read the last line I wrote, letting it open my mind to continue and the inspiration hits. My fingers clack on the keyboard for what seems like forever, and before I know it, I'm typing THE END.

"Yes!" I scream, and pump my first in the air.

It's finished. Well, the first draft anyway, so now I have to go back through it and find the weakest parts and make them better.

I hear footsteps and Leslie is standing at the door. "What the hell is going on?"

My feet travel until I'm standing in front of her. "I finally finished it. My rough draft is complete."

She smiles and pulls me in for a hug. "That's amazing!"

I look at my watch and it's already almost five o'clock. The time passed while I wrote. "Sorry, I didn't even notice the time. Guess I woke you a little early, sorry."

She shrugs her shoulders. "That's okay. I'm gonna head home and get ready for work."

I walk her back to the bedroom to grab her things, and then move to the front door. "It was nice having you stay over. So, do you have any plans tomorrow?"

"Just catching up on sleep and working."

I give her a kiss, and watch as she walks to her and starts it. She waves to me before she backs out of the driveway.

Janet needs to hear about this. She will be so proud to know I finally finished it. Yes, it's weird that I talk about my wife like that, and that I still go and see her, but I can do what I want. I usually go and visit her once a month, take fresh flowers, and check on her gravesite.

I grab my keys, and go visit her.

When I get to the site, my emotions get the best of me. It is weird being here, in a way that it reminds me that I'll never see her again. Death sucks. When I find her headstone, I kneel.

"It's been a while. Today, I typed the end in the manuscript and even from her you have been pushing me to finish it. It's been hard, and my progress has been slow-going since you've been gone, but it's now complete. And I'll continue to work on it. Thank you for always believing in me."

I go from a kneeling position to sitting in the grass. "Your wish has come true. I stopped pushing everyone away, and fate brought me a lovely woman. She makes me smile, and keeps me on my toes. You'd love her."

I wipe my eyes. "She reminds me a lot of you, baby. She is beautiful, intelligent, and has spunk about her. I'm trying to do what you said, be happy, but sometimes it's harder than others. I love you."

15

LESLIE

The depot is quiet, as it normally is at seven o'clock. Most of us never get enough sleep, but that comes with the territory of working this shift. Everyone else is up when we are asleep, so we have to make up for lost time on our off days.

"Girl, we've got a lot to talk about," Angela says, bombarding me in the locker room.

"Can I put my stuff up and get some coffee first?" I ask, putting my bag with my clothes in it, and then walking passed her to the rec room.

She leans up against the wall by the coffee maker and just starts laying it on me. Apparently, the guy she went home with from the bar has become a regular. Angela has been with him every night since. When she starts talking about their sex life, I raise my hand.

"I don't need to know about all that, sis."

She waves me off, and continues on as I put some creamer into my coffee and sit down at the table with my laptop bag.

"How was your night? I haven't talked to you."

She has no idea about Noah since she left before me, and I don't think Noah will be comfortable with me telling anyone about us. She is my sister, but she might say something to the wrong person, and the consequences if anyone finds out are too risky. So, I just lie and say I had a few drinks and then went home.

"I just slept most of the time if I wasn't in class."

Sneaking around with Noah is going to get old, but it's only for five months. The reason we are doing this is valid and not stupid like not wanting his wife to find out. Angela has done that before.

"I totally forget about my date."

"What date? I thought you just slept."

I laugh. "So this guy from class asked me out. He was cute, and around my age so I said yes."

"And?"

"Another man that thinks that women can't do the same jobs as a man. He was almost appalled by the fact that I was a firefighter. Walked out on him," I say, laying my laptop on the table and opening it up.

"What is wrong with people? This isn't the fifties anymore. Whatever."

I turn on my wireless mouse and open up the manuscript I'm supposed to be working on for a client.

"Hey ladies. I know we just got here, but I'm wiped. The baby doesn't ever want to sleep. I'll be taking a nap if you need me," Damon says, walking through the rec room.

Poor guy is having a hard time. Black circles are under his eyes. I don't know much about babies, and never really had an itch to be a mother. I don't dislike kids, just can't picture myself being a mom.

"I'm gonna watch some TV. You get to work on your editing stuff."

I smile, and take a look at the document. If I could get by with just my freelance clients, I would be the happiest woman in the world. My father isn't happy about my decision, but the plan hasn't been to be a firefighter my whole life. I have been clear since the beginning. Once my freelancing takes off, then I will be doing that full time. Honestly, it's not like I'm doing bad right now. I make around $1200 a month doing editing, but to do it as a career, I would need to double that. The problem is - I have had clients reach out to me and ask my qualifications and when they find out I don't have my degree, they go with someone else. So once I graduate, my business should double, if not triple.

An average eighty thousand word book is around nine-hundred dollars and I can do two of those a month while working at the department, but when I quit, I can take on more projects and not have to worry about the overnight schedule. It makes me exhausted all the time no matter how much sleep I get.

The deadline for this one is in two weeks, and I'm about a quarter of the way done. As I go through and line edit, it makes me happy when I see all the suggestions and comments I've made. This is something I love, and soon I will be doing this full time. A grin takes over.

Freelancing isn't something new to me. I've been doing it for about five years now, and my client base is not huge, but repeat clients are my bread and butter. Sometimes, I have to turn them away because I don't have the time to give it my full attention. My reputation is more important than making money. If I can't give the client my absolute best, then they should go with someone else. Period. Anything more than two manuscripts a month is just too much, especially with taking on school, too.

In five months, I won't have to worry about being here, and I can wake up whenever I want to, and go to sleep whenever. I'll be able to make my own schedule, and that opens up the possibility to take on five to ten clients a month. Think about the possibilities. If I have five clients, that's $4500 a month if it is eighty thousand words. My dream is important to me, and I've always wanted to work for myself.

Now is the time to focus on what's best for me, and that's working toward my dream. Freelance is the place to be, and soon enough I won't have to answer to anyone but my clients. I can take on much or as little work as I want.

My phone vibrates and I pick it up.

Noah: The house is quiet with you here. My pillow still smells like you.

Angela looks at me, knowing no one ever texts me this late. Unfortunately, she knows me well, and I don't have many friends.

"Who is that?" she asks, turning around in her chair.

"Just that Adam guy."

Me: Believe me, I'd rather be there than here. I'm working on client stuff now. Maybe it'll be a quiet night for me.

I get a couple more pages edited, before my phone vibrates again.

Noah: You don't have long until you don't have to work until six in the morning anymore. I have to say I'm a little stoked about that. We can actually spend every night together.

Wow, he's already talking about spending nights together, and our future. Most men run at the sight of commitment and Noah is just going for it. No regrets.

Me: Well, you won't have to hide me away in a tower either. Come the end of the semester, I'm taking a vacation. It's been years since I have left Texas. Miss cabins.

About seven years ago, I rented a cabin in Arkansas, and stayed for a week. There is something about being in nature that is so peaceful and relaxing. Every morning, I would enjoy my coffee on the patio overlooking the woods, and listening to the sounds of birds chirping.

Noah. A cabin it is. That sounds perfect.

Knowing me, I'll sit here and text him instead of working, so I turn my phone off and give my full attention to the client. I can't start slacking now, not when I'm so close to finally doing this as a career.

16

NOAH

*A*s I walk on the campus, in the quad are students talking amongst each other and looking at flyers being passed out by a patron. Most are about eighteen or nineteen-years-old and they have no clue about the real world yet. The best thing about being a professor is that my class is typically taken by seniors. I am known for being a hard teacher and that means they save it for the last semester. Being such, they should have some real world experience by then, but that's not always the case. Like assignments, for instance. When I say it's due on a certain date that doesn't mean it's due the day after, or the week after. Other professors might cut them some slack, but not me. Sure it's their last semester or their last year, but frankly, they should know better by now. They've had four years to learn how college works and how assignments work, and after three and a half years, if they don't understand, I don't feel sorry for them one bit.

I push through the English hall doors and saunter into my office, opening the door, turning on the light and setting my laptop bag down on the desk. Leslie should be here any minute. I turn my laptop on and let it book up while I grab a bottle of water out of my mini fridge.

"So, what do you need me to do today, professor?" she asks,

leaning up against my door, wearing a short enough red summer dress and sandals.

Is she trying to tease me? Her legs are perfect, and the dress hits just above mid-thigh. My mind starts to wander. There is barely anyone in this building yet, since my class is the first one of the day and rarely do students get here this early before class.

I stand up from my desk, and whisk myself over to her, just close enough. "I was wondering why you never texted me back last night. Did you fall asleep?"

"Oh, I turned my phone off. Those clients have deadlines and I would've stayed up all night talking to you."

"All you have to do is tell me to shut up. I went to sleep shortly after, anyway."

Does she think I don't understand how important her freelance work is? Everyone wants to work for themselves. Isn't that the American dream? If that's what she wants to do, then I fully support her endeavors. She should have every right to fulfill her dream.

"How much did you get done last night or should I say this morning?"

"About forty pages or so. Only two-hundred more to go."

Leslie is driven like no other. How many people can hold down a part-time and full-time job, plus go to college? I don't know how she does it. This semester is going to be exhausting, but there is a light at the end of the tunnel. She will come out the other side much happier.

I go back to my desk, and push print. The worksheets for today will take some time. So I sit down and have her do the same.

"So, about this cabin vacation? Do you have somewhere in mind?" I ask, the printer being noisy in the background.

"There's one in Arkansas. It's about four hours away, but it's beautiful."

"Send me a link. I'd love to book it after the semester ends. You and me. A week in a secluded place. We won't get anything done."

This semester might be exhausting for both of us, but when we can do things together out in public, it will be a game changer. Leslie isn't the type of woman meant to be hidden. I want to show her off to the world, but not for five more months.

The printer stops, and I grab the papers. "If you'll just place one of each desk like before. See you in a little bit."

I take the next twenty minutes or so to go over what I'm looking for in a discussion of the next two chapters of Great Expectations today. Students in the past have bought the Cliff Notes version and think that is enough to get by in this class, and they are sorely mistaken. I can spot it from a mile away, because they always use the same verbiage when talking about the book, and pass it off as reading the book. They forgot how long I have been teaching this class.

Ten minutes to eight, I grab my things, and head to the lecture hall, letting the double doors open, and making my way down to the desk. There are about fifteen students already in here, and Leslie is sitting in the third row again. Her eyes land on mine, and then look away.

Adam enters the hall, and sits down next to Leslie. My fists clench, watching him closely, as he begins to take out the book and then look over at her. She shakes her head and then gets up.

"You too good to sit next to me now? Why the fuck did you just up and leave in the middle of our date without an explanation?"

He begins getting aggressive and I can't sit idly by and watch. As a professor and her boyfriend, this won't stand in my classroom.

"Adam, why don't you come down and sit in the front row today? I'll let you lead us into the discussion of chapter three and four today. Hope you read them."

He scoffs and grabs his bag, coming down to the front row, and then slams his stuff down, before looking back at Leslie who mouths, thank you, to me.

"Go ahead and start us off, Adam."

My focus isn't on the discussion, but Leslie. The summer dress she's wearing is sitting right in the middle of her thigh, and every time she adjusts herself it rises a bit higher. I imagine myself between her legs doing what I do best. Fuck. I have to remind myself I'm in a lecture hall full of students and this is highly inappropriate. Her eyes land on mine and a smile ensues. She caught me.

I walk back over to my desk and grab my phone and Adam continues his thoughts on chapter three.

Me: I can't wait to get underneath that dress after class.

Her phone vibrates and she looks down at it before typing back.

Leslie: This is highly inappropriate professor. Focus on class.

This might be harder than I thought... Especially, if she wears dresses like this all semester.

Me: But that's no fun. At least I'm the only one that can see your pink underwear. Although they won't be staying on for long.

We might be in class right now, but when I see her later, I'll devour her. She is like a damn addiction. When she is around, I just want to be near her, inside her, and nowhere else.

Leslie: What underwear?

I cock my head, and look back up at her. She has somehow removed them without anyone noticing, and opens her thighs just enough for me to see her and my dick twitches.

That's my naughty girl.

17

LESLIE

The rest of my classes don't go as well as Noah's. His eyes didn't leave my body for the duration of class, and I don't think anyone noticed. Let's just say that after seeing his eyes nearly jump out of his head when his eyes landed on me without any underwear, tonight is going to be good. Sure, we have to get through our classes first, but now it's three o'clock.

Noah: Meet me at my house. Leaving campus now.

The situation in class left us both hot and bothered, and I can't wait for his hands to be on me. Something about him brings out this side of me I've never seen before. Hell, I would stay in bed all day with him if adulting wasn't required.

Me: I'm already standing at your door. Hurry up.

The heat is intolerable, so I go back to my car and turn on the AC, until he pulls up.

"Come on," he says, jumping out of his car with his laptop bag, and heading straight for the door.

I follow after him, and he ushers me inside, drops his laptop bag, and starts undoing his shirt.

"You have no fucking idea how much I want you right now. No

underwear in class. Making me stare at your wet pussy and not being able to touch it. Evil. Pure fucking evil."

He picks me up, and slams me against the wall, his lips on my neck, and hand up my dress.

"Still no underwear, just the way I want you."

He moves us to the bedroom, and he lays me down, and before I even get my bearing, he's in between my legs, making my back arch. For the love of god!

The tension has been high all day, and I'm just as fucking turned on as he is, and within a few minutes, I'm gripping his sheets and screaming for my life.

"Now be a good girl and never do that to me again," he says, wiping his mouth.

Obviously, he doesn't understand how much fun it was to watch him squirm in front of all those other people, and not one of them noticed. What an exhilarating feeling.

"Yeah, I'll be sure not to."

I sit on the bed, and he walks over to his phone. "You can't stay long, but I'm glad I could take care of you before you go."

Noah is one of the few men that doesn't throw a two-year-old fit when it's not all about them. Sometimes, it's nice to just get a release real quick and go to work. Not every encounter has to be penetration. I'm lucky to have found Noah when I did.

"So, I've got some good news before I go."

He turns around and grips his chin. "And what is that?"

I don't have many people I can share this with because most of them are against me leaving the Fire Department. "Today has been one for the books. A client reached out to me and we have signed a contract for six manuscripts over the next six months. This means, with her plus my regular clients, I can go freelancing full-time."

My calendar is already booked up with my regulars at two manuscripts a month, and I would be a fool to turn down this contract. It locks me in to get paid $1200 a month for the next six months. So, I'll be bringing in four grand a month from my freelance contracts. This has come out of nowhere, but I'm not going to bite a gift horse in the mouth. This is the contract I have been waiting for and it's impossible for me to continue working full time, finish my degree, and do this on the side. It has to have my full attention.

He picks me up and twirls me around. "That's amazing! So, you know what that means."

I tap my chin. "More nights with you."

Relationships usually either work or don't, and with Noah, my schedule was bound to make things tough for us, but now once I'm officially self-employed, we don't have to worry about it. It gives us the freedom to find out what's between us without any hiccups. Well, besides being one of his students. I don't see that ever becoming a problem though. We are careful.

"Seriously, though I have to go. I'll talk to my dad about putting in my notice tonight. He's going to freak. Might end in tears," I say, giving him a quick kiss and leaving.

My father is one that thinks that being a firefighter is in my blood, and it's an honor to serve the community. I don't disagree, but when my dream is becoming a reality, I can't just push it away. No, it's time for me to plow head on and enjoy it. He might think I'm out of my mind, but it's my decision.

My car comes to abrupt stop, and I jump out of the car, and unlock my door. I want to get to the depot early and catch my dad before he leaves. I don't want to waste another day away. My notice needs to be put in tonight. So, I change real quick, grab my go bag, and get back into my car, heading straight to the depot.

The gravel crunches underneath my tires, and his truck is still in the parking lot. Yes. Here goes nothing.

Tristan walks out, and waves at me before getting into his car. He rolls his window down.

"What are you doing here already?" he asks.

"Gotta talk to my dad. You not working tonight?"

"My mom's in town. Gonna take the night off."

I smile and wave him off before opening the door and walking inside. Before approaching my father, I go and drop my bag into my locker, and then head into the small office.

"Hey, kiddo. You're early," he says, not getting up from his chair.

"We need to talk."

My father shakes his head. "You better not be pregnant. I told you girls to be safe. You are not ready to be a mother."

"Jesus, dad. I'm not freaking pregnant, calm down."

His hand goes to his stomach. "Good. I'm not ready to be a grandpa yet. What is it then?"

I take a seat in the chair in front of his desk, and cross my legs. "I need to put in my notice. My contracts are going to overextend me for the next six months at least, and I can't continue to work here. It's been a pleasure working under you, but it's time to let me go, daddy."

I try to play to his emotions, and maybe he won't get so pissed. It doesn't work.

"You've got to kidding me? I didn't actually think you were serious? This is a stable income. Who knows if these people are going to need you in a year? Two? What are you going to do then?"

I take a deep breath before responding. "Not that it's any of your business, but I'll be making almost twice what I make here, and I plan on keeping a portion of it in savings in case a rainy day happens. My finances shouldn't be your concern. I need you to submit the paperwork. How long do you need?"

He wipes his mouth, and scoffs. "We are overstaffed on the night shift. So, just give me a date and I'll submit the official paperwork before I leave."

Giving me the option to choose my last day isn't like him, but I'm his daughter. "Well, how about tonight then?"

He shakes his head. "You know that means you won't be rehirable, honey? Do you really want to burn that bridge? At least give us a week."

"You just said you were overstaffed, so you don't need me anyway. So, tonight will be my last night. I'll leave my equipment in the locker when I leave in the morning."

I get up from my chair and go into the recreation room, not giving him time to talk me out of this decision. He will try. And sometimes, he is good at talking me out of important things. It's best to cut the rope.

Me: *It's official. Tonight is my last night. So, I say we celebrate tomorrow.*

My phone lays on the table, and I pull out my laptop.

"What's got chief in a pissy mood? Isn't it his last night of the week?" Damon asks.

"It's because of me. Tonight is my last night, partner. You think you can handle things without me?" I ask, punching his shoulder as he sits down next to me.

"What? Everything finally fell into place for you?"

I nod. "I'm set for the next six months at least, and even then, with my regulars, I'll be fine."

He gives me a high-five and then I get up to make myself a cup of coffee. It might be my last night as a firefighter, but it's still going to be a long night.

The transition into sleeping at night is going to be weird. Besides on my days off, it's light outside when I drift off, and now it will be dark. Hopefully, I can retrain my body. Working a normal office schedule will be nice. It opens up so many things for me. Hell, maybe I can finally go and hang out at that new coffee shop that opened a couple months ago, or even go to the campus.

Once the coffee maker stops, I fill my mug, and get to work. If I can finish this manuscript in the next two days, then I can enjoy a few days before I have to start the next one. Tomorrow is going to be a celebration. A step in the right direction for me. Am I scared shitless? Yes, but if I don't take that step now, when I have the best chance at succeeding, then I'll never do it.

18

NOAH

*M*y coffee steams on the table as my eyes span over the manuscript open on my laptop, and haven't done a damn thing in almost an hour. I tap on the coffee table, and start to pace again. Why can't I read it? Every time I try to start, it's like a mental block prevents me.

When I started writing this novel, Janet was still alive, and I spent many nights on this couch with her writing while she watched her favorite show. Maybe I need to go about this a different way. I turn the volume up on my laptop and go to the review tab. There is a read aloud feature. It's worth a shot. I need to use the momentum of finishing it to get started on edits, and the longer I let it sit, the less likely I am to ever publish. Janet would want me to see this through.

A British accent starts reading my words, and it helps me catch some things that just don't hit the way they need to. Opening lines need to pack a punch. Setting the scene for the entire novel and what the reader can expect. So, I click on the comment button and type, *Make this better.* I idly stand by while it reads the entire first chapter, and I have so many things I need to tweak. A first draft is never going to be good enough to publish. At least mine. There might be writers who can write a first draft and it be publish worthy, but mine needs work. This draft was important and I need to focus on just getting words on the page, instead of taking the time to describe the setting, and develop my prose. This is what I need to perfect in my next draft, as well as fix any lingering plot holes or developmental issues that may have arisen over the course of writing this draft.

My phone buzzes. Her name comes up, and honestly, I have been trying to focus on getting some of this done this morning.

Leslie: You there?

I unlock my phone and open the thread to read her previous message.

Me: That's great! Yes, we will celebrate. We can order in. My treat.

It's funny how things have worked out in our favor, and now I can enjoy nights with her by my side. We might have only known each other a short time, but it feels right.

Things are looking up for Leslie. Some people dream about being their own boss, and working for themselves, but it's a lot of work. Not saying she can't handle it, just things like health care and 401K aren't really an option unless you set it up. With a normal job, that comes with it, and the company matches up to a certain percentage. I don't want to damper her excitement for being self-employed, but I hope she thought about these things. They might not seem like a big issue now, but come when she's sixty-years-old, it will be.

I let the British guy read the second chapter, and I make notes throughout, noticing where pacing is a little off, and wording could be better to pack a punch, but for the most part, I'm enjoying it. Why am I so hard on myself? As a Literature professor, people must think I'm like the know-it-all of English, and even I make mistakes. Fiction is an imaginative art through expression, and not every book is going to hit someone the same way.

Janet used to tell me, "Write the book you want to read, and they will come. Make your own world and do a deep dive into it to express yourself."

Clearly, she had more faith in me than I do, but that's objective. I just have to remember that I created this world inside these pages, and the only person that can tell this story is me. So, it's my job to make it the best it can be, and then share it with everyone else. Others might not like it, but there will be a portion that will, and that's what I need to be searching for.

I take the next two hours to listen to the chapters and make notes, and I have gone through the first six chapters and made extensive notes for revisions. This read aloud feature is actually quite productive. I don't know if sitting down and reading to myself would have netted these results in such a timely manner. I check my watch and it's already noon. Jesus.

The urge to text Leslie rides over me, and I shoot her a text.

Me: So, how was the last night of being a firefighter, Ms. Haddon?"

She said her dad might end up making her cry, but I hope he is more supportive than that. My parents have always been that way for me, and every child needs that. We want to make our parents proud, and some will go to great links to do so.

Leslie: Boring. We didn't get a single call. So, I just worked on a script. Got another thirty pages or so done. Hoping to finish it today, and then I'll have two days before I have to start the next one.

Freelancing isn't an easy job. Sure, everyone might think it is, but you have to be self-sufficient and be able to stay on task without having someone to hover over you. It's not meant for everyone, but I think Leslie is going to do amazing.

Me: That's great. So, what are your plans for today? Have you gotten some sleep yet?

I'll have to leave for campus any minute, and she will be there, but I still want to check on her. Once the excitement wears off, the real work begins. She is going to kill it, but it will still be an adjustment. Going from having a strict work schedule, to working whenever you want is a change. Sure, you can set your own hours, but you still have to be productive and meet the deadlines for the clients. So, Leslie still has to be careful.

Leslie: Got a couple hours, and took some naps at the depot. See you on campus, Professor.

Maybe I shouldn't like when she calls me professor, but I do. It shouldn't be this exhilarating to sneak around with a student, but I have to be honest, I'm getting off on it. The only difference is she is around my age, and it started before the semester began, so it doesn't make me feel as dirty.

My mind goes to pictures of Leslie in a school girl outfit, and I immediately try to get it out of my mind. She doesn't need to dress up in outfits to appease me, I'll take her naked any day of the week. It's all going to come off anyway.

19

LESLIE

*T*hings are looking up for me, and I'm officially self-employed. After a couple hours of sleep, I get out of bed, and ready for the day. Thank God it's a Friday on top of that. The last day of classes with week, and then I can get some stuff done. I can't blow this chance and need to make sure I stay on track. As my own boss, it's up to me to stay on task and meet the deadlines.

As far as Noah's class goes, I have already read Great Expectations a gazillion times, so I don't have to read it again to put my two cents into the discussion or fill out a worksheet, so it's left me room to work on the other classes assignments without being overloaded.

I change into some denim shorts and a Star Wars t-shirt and head to campus. The world appears differently to me now. One thing I'm looking forward to the most is not being a vampire. I can get out and enjoy things during the day, and anytime I want, without having to worry about not getting enough sleep or missing work. My laptop can go with me anywhere, and that means I can work from wherever I choose.

My feet hit the concrete, one after another, as I enter the quad and go straight to the English Hall for my morning meeting with

Professor Mills. It feels weird to call him that, but as his teaching assistant, I do need to appear professional to others.

His office door is closed, and that's not typical for him, so I knock. His voice tells me to wait a second and when he opens it, a man, probably another professor, walks out and he ushers me in.

"Good morning, Ms. Haddon," he says, looking over my shoulder to see if we are in the clear.

"What the hell was that? He didn't look happy?"

I set my bag down in the chair in front of his desk, and cross my arms. Noah just paces around his office, running his fingers through his hair, and staring at the ground.

"What's going on? Who was that, Noah?"

He starts to talk but then groans, and shakes his head. "I'm livid right now. Honestly, I need a second to calm down."

I take a step back, and look around the room for the worksheets for today. He must not have them printed yet. He unlocks his laptop and sends them to the printer.

"Sorry, I hadn't had time yet. He was waiting for me when I got here."

"Is everything okay? You're making me nervous."

"That Adam kid apparently made a complaint about me. Called me a bully. Not my fault he doesn't know a fucking thing about how to read."

Noah seems extremely frustrated, talking with his hands, and shuffling papers around on his desk.

"Well, you aren't, so case closed."

"I wish it were that easy, Les. Complaints are taken seriously here, and that's just an arrow on my back. Obviously, he knew he wasn't going to pass my class, so he had to go and do something to override the university's judgment when he fails. Go figure."

This isn't something he needs to worry about, and Adam is a dick. It's not like I can say anything, because then Adam would know how I found out. That would send out clues about Noah and me, and he definitely doesn't need that going to light right now.

"I try my fucking hardest to be a good professor, but I don't let people walk all over me like the others. They need to learn how things operate in the real world, and no place of business would tolerate the way he acts."

"Noah, take a breath. You are only talking out of anger because of the things he said to me, and then being an ass yesterday. We don't know anything about him other than that," I say, putting my hand on his shoulder and he brushes it off.

"Careful. Anyone could see us, remember?"

He needs time to deal with this, and he clearly doesn't want me here right now. "Well, give me the worksheets and I'll go distribute them before class."

Noah hands me a stack of worksheets, and I walk straight out of his office.

I'm not mad at him, because he must be freaking out. Teaching is something he loves, and to have a chance of having that taken away or having a strike on his record because some student wants to piss him off, that has to strike a hard blow. All I can do is be there for him, and try to help him through it.

I get upstairs to the lecture hall, and walk around placing a worksheet on each desk. It's empty besides a couple of girls gossiping in the back row about some party they are going to tonight.

"You his little bitch now?"

I turn around to see Adam now sitting in the front row.

"No, the university made me his teaching assistant for the semester. It helps cover my tuition."

You will not let him get a rise out of you. Take a deep breath, Leslie.

"He won't be teaching here much longer. Asshole needs to learn to stay out of my business. Yesterday, you and I were having a conversation and he shouldn't have interfered. His job is to teach the fucking class, that's all."

Adam seems to have a lot of hate toward Professor Mills and that startles me. What else is he going to do if the complaint turns out to be squashed by the university? What is Adam capable of?

"Don't get butt hurt. Just do the homework and come to class. One last semester and then you never have to see him again. Why make such a fuss?"

Students start filing in, and I just go about my business placing the rest of the worksheets on the desks. I shouldn't even be talking to Adam at all, especially after our failed attempt at a date. I don't know why he is so pissed about Noah moving him to the front. It's not like he was paying attention anyway.

"Good morning, everyone. Class is going to be cut a little short today, but it's Friday, so I'm sure no one is going to complain. Fill out the worksheet on your desk and then turn it in to me, and you may go," he says, making his way down the aisle to the front of the hall.

Why is he cutting class short? I pull out my phone to see if he texted me but nothing, so I take my seat and fill out the worksheet within the first ten minutes. Good thing I've already memorized the book at this point. I grab my bag and head down to Noah.

"Thank you, Ms. Haddon. Have a good weekend."

He doesn't even make eye contact with me, so I mosey up the aisle and out the double doors. Something is going on. What isn't he telling me?

20

NOAH

*W*ithin twenty minutes, all the worksheets are turned in and the lecture hall is empty. It's not like me to leave class early, but I've got other things to deal with. Adam might think he's coming for my throat, but I don't go down without a fight, especially when it comes to my career. I hope he's up for a battle.

I'll grab my laptop bag and the worksheets and head back to my office downstairs. Adam is waiting outside my door leaned up against the wall.

"Sup, teach? How's your morning going?"

"We are not to talk outside of the classroom, Adam. You know that. Your formal complaint is going under review and they will be watching our every move."

This guy must be an idiot. Why the hell would he show up at my office the morning that he made a complaint about me? Actually, this might work to my advantage because I can bring it up to the council and they will see that he is approaching me. So, if he is accusing me of being a bully, then why is he coming to my office after class?

"Why don't you go ahead to your next class, Adam? I've got things to work on," I say, as I shut my door in his face.

I pull up my phone and bring up the text thread between Leslie and I.

Me: *Sorry it's been a shit morning. I still want to celebrate later. What do you want for dinner?*

Honestly, I'm gonna eat whatever - I'm not really a picky eater. When Janet was alive and cooked for me every night I didn't really have a choice but to eat whatever she made.

Leslie: *We could always go out to dinner. We don't have to stay around here since we're getting out early today. We could venture out to the city.*

As appealing as that sounds, I don't know if it's the best idea. How do we know where to go and who is going to see us? And right now, with me being under a microscope, I don't exactly need to bring any more attention to myself. But I consider it to make Leslie happy. Few students come from Dallas to Grapevine to go to college, and it's highly unlikely that we will run into anybody, but to do so we must be very careful.

Me: *I can make reservations At Landry's for us and request to sit in the back away from everybody. That way we can at least enjoy ourselves without worrying about being spotted*

Leslie: *As long as I'm with you, I could get a fuck less where we go. But we should be able to enjoy a celebratory dinner without having to worry about others.*

She's right. With five months ahead of us, honestly I don't want to keep her hidden or cooped up in the house until the semester is over. The sneaking around might be a little exhilarating now, but it'll get old fast. And eventually, she's going to want to go out on actual dates and go to dinner at nice restaurants and do things as a couple, but with me being her professor we have to be extremely careful about where we go.

I pull up the search bar on my phone and Google Landrys, and dial the number to secure a reservation for six. The house just put a note on our reservation that we would like to sit in the back away from everybody if possible. She said it shouldn't be a problem.

Me: Reservation made for six. Do you want me to come pick you up from your house or you gonna meet me at mine?

I know she has classes the rest of the day, but usually the first week they let class out early and I'm the only professor that didn't do that except for today. so there's a chance she might be free before 4 o'clock today.

Leslie: I plan on getting some work done if classes get done early enough. But let's say meet you at your house around five?

It'll take us at least thirty to forty-five minutes to get to the restaurant from here, and that depends on traffic. Getting into Dallas isn't a problem, but once you are in the city, it's a fucking nightmare.

I sit down at my desk and open up my laptop trying to push this complaint out of my head. If Adam had a fucking problem with me, he should've come to me and not in the university. If he doesn't like how I handled the situation between him and Leslie, then he could've talked to me as a man, not a coward.

The problem is, this isn't my first complaint. There are many students over the years that felt like I didn't treat them properly. And most of those students were wealthy. So, they were used to getting special treatment and I'm just not that type of professor. Unfortunately, every single incident was deemed valid by the university and only because their parents contributed substantially to the university. The complaints are in my personnel file, but they told me they wouldn't count against my tenure since they had to agree with the parents to keep the donations.

What a fucking joke. We live in a society where money does the talking, and that's not how it should be. Sure, I get it; the university needs money and funding to continue running, but the morality of it was wrong. Do these people not have any morals? Here I am, a teacher at this university and I bust my ass to make sure that I'm fair, but tough. This complaint is not valid and I have not bullied Adam at all. And if asking him to sit in the front row and lead a discussion on a book he was supposed to read is considered bullying, then I must be way out of the loop.

A knock sound at my door and it opens with Professor Jones entering.

"So, I've talked with the council and they would like to speak with you if you have a moment."

"Yeah, I let my class go early so I have about twenty- minutes until my next one is that enough?"

He nods and I follow him out the English hall doors over to the administrative offices. Honestly, I probably should be worried, but I've been through this so many times with ungrateful students, that I know my opinion and what I say doesn't matter in the end. They will not listen to me, but I know I did nothing wrong.

He opens the door to the conference room and there are six men and women circling around the table.

"Good morning, Noah. We were just going over the complaint that one of your students, Adam, submitted this morning to Professor Jones. We would like to hear your side of the story."

I take a seat at the front of the table and twine my hands on the desk.

"Adam is not an exceptional student. I know it's the first week, but he has trouble paying attention and has not been keeping up with his assignments. Yesterday, he sat down next to one of my female students and was getting aggressive with her because, apparently, she did not stay for their entire date and at that point she was becoming very uncomfortable. So, I asked him to move to the front of my class and begin the discussion on Great Expectations."

I stop and pause to give them time to process what I'm saying. "I have done nothing wrong here. It's not my fault that he didn't do the homework and could not adequately talk about the chapters. At no point have I bullied him, but he might feel singled out because I had to move him to the front of the class. But that does not equate to bullying. Am I correct?"

The director glances over at the man next to her, and clears her throat. "Let me be clear, Professor. Because of the other complaints in your file, we have to take this seriously."

Fire enters my body and my hands slam down on the table.

"What do you mean, other complaints? Those weren't valid and you know it. The only reason is because their parents paid a substantial donation to this university. I was told they would not be held against me."

I stand up from my chair, and hover over the conference table. "Let me be clear, Director. If you don't remove those from my file, I will get a lawyer. My reputation and tenure at this university will not be threatened by a bunch of students who can't handle assignments. Their parents might get them out of things, but I'm not going to stand by and let them ruin my career."

I fix my jacket, walk straight out the door, out of the building, and to my car. Classes are cancelled for the rest of the day. I will not standby and idly be attacked from this establishment over something that they did. My best interest is to protect my career, and the first thing I need to do is get a lawyer.

My car door closes and I pull out my phone to text Jaden. He might have someone he can refer me to. Honestly, if I show up with a lawyer, I highly doubt they will refuse to remove them from my personnel file. It will leave them with no choice.

Me: Listen, I need a lawyer to help me get some complaints removed. Know anyone?

I drop my phone into the passenger seat, and take off toward the house. There is no way I will be able to focus on anything related to that place today, so I'm just going to call it an earlier weekend.

I go straight to the den and boot up my computer. Something needs to distract me from all this bullshit. As soon as it displays, I open up Word, and the document and press Read Aloud on chapter seven. Maybe I can knock out a few more chapters before dinner tonight.

My phone vibrates against the desk.

Jaden: Maybe Sulikowski. 785-676-9853

I put the phone back down and try to give my attention to the manuscript. After listening to the first six chapters from this morning, it isn't as bad off as I thought. Sure, it might have taken me ten years to write it, but it's actually quite good. In some parts, I forget what's coming and it surprises me. That's pretty good since I wrote it.

Honestly, my eyes can't be the only ones to see this. Leslie is a qualified editor, and I could ask for her help. Of course, I would pay her. Her being my girlfriend doesn't mean she does the work for free. She might be able to help me polish it up, and make it ready to turn into a publisher.

Me: I'm home early. Don't want to talk about it, but working on editing the book. You still on campus?

It's only one, so she might be in between classes right now.

Leslie: At the coffee shop. Next class is in fifteen. I'm sorry you are having such a rough day. TGIF

I've never been so excited for a Friday.

Me: Alright. I'll see you in a couple hours.

I have four hours until she shows up for dinner, and I plan on utilizing that time to get at least five chapters marked up. Leslie plans on getting some work done this weekend, too, and that will push me to work on this even more. She might actually rub off on me and I'll kick my ass into gear and get this done this weekend and talk to her about editing it for me. Or, at least, marking it up where she thinks things can be better.

I set a timer on my phone to count down until four-thirty when I have to change for dinner.

You can do this!

21

LESLIE

*I*t's our first official date outside of the house, and going to Dallas is the best option. The traffic isn't too bad until we get into the city, and then it's a shitshow. Thankfully, he's driving because I don't do well with large amounts of congestion. I'm a small town girl, and people here just don't know how to drive. Whipping in and out of lanes, and it's road rage galore. His hand is on my thigh, sending surges throughout my body.

He gets off of highway 36 and cuts across to the restaurant. I've never been to Landry's before, but he says it has good food, so I'll take his word for it. As long as I'm with him, I could care less.

When we come to a spot in a parking spot, he hurries out and opens my door for me.

"Thank you," I say, standing up and getting my footing. It's been a while since I've worn heels, but it seemed necessary for tonight.

"That dress looks amazing on you. I think red is definitely your color."

As we walk inside, his hand lands on the small of my back, as we approach the hostess stand.

"Reservation for Mills."

The lady checks her tablet and walks us back toward the kitchen in a cozy spot where most of the restaurant can't see us.

"Will this be sufficient?"

He nods, and the hostess leaves us with two menus.

"Nobody is going to see us here. Isn't it nice to get out together?"

He smiles. "You aren't meant to be kept secret. I can't wait until the semester is over."

I take a look at the wine menu, and order a bottle of chardonnay. We are celebrating tonight.

My hand lands on his and our eyes meet. Noah is unlike any man I've ever met, and I can see us being long-term. We are spending so much time together, but I don't want to get ahead of myself.

This career change is going to come with ups and downs and some getting used to, but starting on Monday, I can work on my clients in my free time and see how much I can get done. This will help me figure out how many manuscripts I can handle over the course of the semester. I don't want to overextend myself, but the money needs to continue coming in. The logistics of it will fall into place once I get my schedule down.

Noah picks up the bottle and pours into the two glasses. "Here's to your next adventure. Living the dream, baby."

It's nice to have someone be supportive in my endeavors. My father has always told me I am crazy for wanting to do freelance editing, and honestly, I don't think he ever thought I was going to leave the department. I'm glad I could prove him wrong. He's my dad, and I love him, but following my dream has always been in the back of my head, and I've been working towards it for five years.

Noah just doesn't seem all here tonight. I'm sure there is a lot on his mind because of this whole Adam situation, and the pressure it puts on him and his reputation is bound to cause some issues.

"I know you don't want to talk about it, but it's the elephant in the room. Being together means we need to be able to talk about the hard stuff, too," I say, taking his hand in mine again.

Noah's chest rises and falls and he explains what is going on in detail. I didn't know about the other complaints, and the fact that they are still trying to use them against him is blasphemy. They shouldn't even be in his personnel file, and if I were him, I would get a lawyer, too. He could risk losing his tenure because of something like that.

"Those assholes won't know what hit them when you show up with a lawyer. Listen, you need to take care of that this weekend. That's something you have been working toward, and they can't take it away from you because of their wrongdoing. It's unethical to take money from a donor to cover up a complaint against a teacher. Why should you be held liable?"

The more I hear him talk about the officials at the university, the less I even want to be associated with it. One last semester and then I'm gone for good. Why does he stay there? If they tried to pull this crap with me, I would be out of there.

"Can you just go to a different university? Somewhere where they won't pull shit like this? You deserve better, Noah."

"I can't just up and leave. All the years I've put in for tenure and my reputation, and they are just going to throw it away. None of these fucking complaints are valid, and they have the nerve to threaten me."

He starts to get heated and his knuckles turn white. I've never seen him this upset before.

I get up from my side of the table, and sit in my lap. "Listen, we will take care of this, okay? For now, let's try to have a nice dinner, enjoy some wine, and let the stress go. Can you do that?"

He smiles and kisses me. "Anything for you, Les."

Even with everything going on, for the rest of the night, we don't worry about anything else, but each other's company.

22

NOAH

I must have had too much wine to drink because my eyes open to being back in my bed, not remembering how we arrived back. A celebratory dinner for Leslie, turned into a drinking fest for me. Shit. She must be pissed. Did I ruin her night?

She is passed out next to me, and I get up without waking her. It will take some time to adjust to her new schedule, and now she doesn't have to sleep all day and be up all night.

I go into the kitchen to make a pot of coffee, and while it's going, I go into the den and boot up my computer. With it only being five in the morning, I might as well get some caffeine in my body, and get some editing done. Leslie might want to do something later and getting this out of the way early will clear my calendar for the day.

After grabbing and filling my mug, I sit down in my office chair, and put in some headphones. I like the Read Aloud feature, but don't want to take the chance of waking Leslie up. She needs her sleep.

A couple of hours later, I look over, headphones still on, and see Leslie draped in only sheets.

"I didn't know you were up," I say, taking the headphones out my ears. "Sleep okay?"

She nods, comes and sits on my lap. "When are you going to let me read it? Why so secretive about it?"

I sigh. "I've been writing it for ten years. So, honestly it's probably crap. Am I weird for not wanting anyone else to read it?"

"No, that's pretty normal for a new writer. It's just me," she says, peaking at the screen.

I lean in for a kiss, and to change the subject. "It's about time for me to make lunch. Noon already."

"No, no, no," she says, standing up. "Let me read the first chapter, please?"

How do I plan to get this published without letting someone read it? I bite the bullet and move to let her sit down.

"Okay, just the first chapter and tell me what you think. If you want to continue and help me with edits, then I'll pay you."

"You don't have to do that."

I shake my head. "You aren't doing it for free, Les."

Lunch is calling, and my stomach is growling. I pull out some butter, four slices of bread and two slices of American cheese. Grilled cheeses it is.

What am I going to do if she hates it? Will she even be honest? I mean, I know it's an utter mess right now without going through the whole thing yet. There are probably a million plot holes and the sentence structure could be better.

I flip the sandwiches over, and sneak a peek into the den. Her face is neutral but sitting criss cross in the chair.

The sandwiches come out of the skillet and onto a plate as I approach the den, leaning up against the door and just watching for expressions.

"Noah, did you really write this?" she asks, pointing to the screen. "Because it's actually a great introduction. I sense some dark elements will be coming into play. I would love to work with you on this."

I hand her a grilled cheese and she bites into it. "I can work on it in between clients so I don't have any idea when I could be done with the first round of edits, but if you trust me, I would love to be your editor."

The growling of my stomach changes the subject and I scarf down the sandwich and wait for her to be finished. The only thing covering her naked body right now are my sheets.

"By the way, what happened? I don't even remember leaving the restaurant last night?" I ask, picking her up out of the chair and heading toward the bedroom.

"You got a little tipsy, and had a good time. Don't worry, I took good care of you." She winks.

I lay her on the bed and honestly right now, all I want to do is ripping those fucking sheets off of her, and show her how sorry I am for last night.

It's my turn to make it up to her...

23

LESLIE

*A*fter a quick shower, and stealing one of his t-shirts, I sit down in front of his computer again and start reading. Noah is a good writer, but he shouldn't be so down on himself. Imposter syndrome is a real thing, and once you start heading down that road, it's hard to bring yourself back. First drafts are never shiny. It takes word to get it to where it needs to be, and I can't believe he is trusting me to give him direction.

He brings a cup of tea, and shuts the doors into the den so I can give my full attention to his manuscript. I dive in, and it sucks me in. The first chapter really set the tone for the book and I hope the rest of it matches. If not, I will help him come up with ways to.

About four chapters in, I notice him lingers outside the doors, and it's distracting.

"Go away! I can't concentrate with you staring at me," I laugh.

Noah has to become more confident in his work. I get that it's hard to let someone else read it, but if he is wanting to get this published, then there are going to be thousands of eyes on it, and he has portray that confidence to an agent.

The flow of the work is competent but it's very fast paced, and somehow we need to slow it down and let it sink in with the reader.

We need to find a happy medium. So I continue to make comments throughout the chapters, and what I think might help, or where pacing needs to be slowed down. It's something that is very common in first drafts. So he doesn't have anything to feel bad about.

It's nice to read something for fun again, because in the last few months, all I have had time to read is work for clients. It's not the same. I love it, but this is different. Noah trusting me with reading it means a lot.

By the time four rolls around, I'm almost half way through his manuscript, and for the sake of it, I found myself more focused on reading than editing. So, maybe I should read it through once, and then go back through and start making comments. I don't normally do this with my clients, but I might from now on. He does a great job of pulling me into the story, and if I hadn't noticed the time, I would have sat here and finished it today.

I open up the den doors, and head out into the living where Noah is on the couch reading a Stephen King book.

"If I don't stop now, then I'll never get any client work done today," she says, taking a minute to curl up with him on the couch.

"So, you like it?"

"Noah, it's freaking good. It's a first draft so, of course, there is work to do, but overall it's really good. People are going to love it."

I give him a kiss, and grab my laptop bag so I can begin working on the manuscript for a couple of hours before we go back to bed. My goal is to knock out at least three chapters before bed. I don't want to fall behind because my deadlines are hard, and they can't be moved.

I curl up next to Noah on the couch, and go at it.

24

NOAH

I'm not excited about going to campus today, but after talking to Sulikowski for a little bit on the phone yesterday, he is ready to come in and meet with the director about the complaints. There is legal action to be taken if they don't' agree to remove them from my file, and in turn it won't look go for the university if something like this goes public.

I drop Leslie off at her house on the way to campus, and go straight to the English hall where I find Professor Jones standing at my door.

"What do you want now?" I ask.

"The council wants to speak with you first thing. Let's go."

I follow behind him over to the admin building and into the conference room.

The same set of people are sitting around the table, and one of them has a manilla envelope in front of them.

"So, did you decide to remove the complaints? My lawyer said he will come up here and speak with your legal rep if it's necessary, but I'd really rather not do that."

The director pushes the envelope over to me, and I open it. Fuck!

Inside are three photos of Leslie and me. Someone must have been following us.

"These have been brought to our attention. You know dating a student is unethical, but your assistant is even worse," the director says.

Who would even has a reason to follow me? My fists clench as I look over the photos again.

"Who even gave these to you? She isn't a child. And we met before she was my student."

Most of the room scoffs. "And that changes things? She is still your student. Are you sure you want this to get out? It might not be something we can legally fire you for, but reputation is everything, Professor Mills."

So this is it. They are trying to blackmail me into resigning. I can't be mad at Leslie because she did nothing wrong, but my whole fucking career is about to go in the toilet. All because of stuck up kids.

"With all due respect, unless you are offering me a severance package, I am not going anywhere. My tenure is valid, and like you said, this isn't something you could legally fire me for. Should I call my lawyer?"

This might be a good thing. I can use this as leverage to get a good severance package and then take some time off. The University of Dallas has asked me to come teach up there before accepting this position, and they might need another professor. Sure, I would have to start over, but I don't think the same issues will arise up there.

"I'll talk to HR and see what kind of package we can offer. You should know better than to let your feelings cloud your judgment. What would Janet think?"

I jump out of my chair. "Don't you ever fucking put my wife's name in your mouth. EVER!"

Before I go berserk, I leave the conference room, and go outside to the quad. The whole world is spinning and my career as a teacher might be gone forever.

I go to my office, to wade through my emails from years ago, I archived it in case I ever needed to reach out to them and reply.

. . .

Dear Ellen,

I am looking for an opportunity to teach in Dallas. My current university is looking to downsize, and you have an amazing English program. I would appreciate being taken into consideration for any open positions within the English department.

Thank you,
Professor Noah Mills

I GRAB MY LAPTOP BAG, and go upstairs to lock the lecture hall's doors. Things are going downhill fast, but with a threat like that, they most definitely don't want me to teach today. The director wants me off her campus as soon as possible. I have information that could portray their administration as unethical and that's the last thing they want coming out.

Sulikowski meets me at the coffee shop on campus and I explain to him that the situation has changed, and now they are using my relationship with Leslie as grounds for blackmail. His advice is candid, but he doesn't think I should let them use that information. It's not a fireable offense on its own, but coupled with five complaints on your record, they could use it to get rid of me. So, since they want me out of here so badly, I want one hell of a severance package.

My phone vibrates.

Leslie: Where are you? Office is locked and so is the lecture hall. ??????

With everything going on, I forgot to even tell her.

Me: Come to the coffee shop.

Sulikowski dismisses himself and tells me to call him if I end up needing anything, and I try to drown myself in caffeine.

"What the hell is going on?" she says loudly, and then lowers her voice as students start to stare.

"Well, someone turned in photos of us at Landry's. The board knows and wants me to quit."

Her head flies back. "I'm so sorry. This is all my fault, Noah. We should have just stayed away from each other."

"Don't you dare. Someone was following us, Les. How else would they know where we were? I think the school hired someone. They are worried that I'll tell someone about the donations."

"So, what are you going to do?" she asks, sitting her bag down on the table.

"Get one hell of a severance package and try to see if Dallas University could use another teacher up there. I've got savings put away, but I can't go too long without something."

Here's the thing, if they come after me, then they will be coming after her, too.

"Watch your six. They might try to use you to get me leave. Threatening you with suspension or something stupid."

"Honestly, I can go to college anywhere. There is an online college that will let me finish my degree in two months. It's an accelerated program, but totally manageable now that I don't work at the department. I say fuck him, let's go!"

Right as she takes my hand, my email notification goes off, and I open it from Director Allwood.

Professor Mills,

Attached is the best severance package we can offer after your time at the University. We wish you the best of luck in your endeavors.

Thank you,
Director Allwood

I OPEN up the attachment to see. They are offering me sixty thousand dollars. I can afford to take a year off with that amount of money. I almost jumped for joy.

"It's official. I am no longer employed at this university. Let's get the fuck out of here. That cabin in Arkansas sounds like the perfect escape."

We walk off campus, holding hands, and not giving a fuck who sees.

EPILOGUE
NOAH

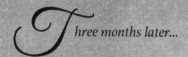

hree months later...

THE STEAM from my coffee is visible as I overlook the woods. There is nothing like waking up to the wilderness and sitting outside. Leslie coming into my life, and showing me I'm able to love someone else again, is exactly what I needed. Teaching has always been my strong suit and passion, but I couldn't let the University treat me that way. After only two days, they announced that I was terminated, and that's when my lawyer reached out to them. See, after examining their faculty handbook, we found nothing in there related to fraternizing with students, and therefore my termination as they called it, was unwarranted. After months of going back and forth, my lawyer got them to settle outside of court, and ended up getting me an additional four-hundred-thousand dollars for wrongful termination. It was a good way to say fuck you to the University, and get what I was owed after all my time there.

"Aren't you cold out here?" Leslie asks, her hands coming around my stomach from behind.

"Not at all."

She wraps the blanket around both of us and snuggles into me. "Isn't this perfect? Why would anyone ever want to go back?"

Her business has grown substantially, taking on six additional clients and making almost three times what she was making as a fire-fighter. She is still doing online classes to finish her degree, but she's almost done.

"Are you sure you want to go back? With the settlement, you don't have to work anymore."

Sure, that sounds nice, but in real life, I would be bored in a matter of days. Being a professor of American Literature is a strong suit of mine, as my knowledge is great and sometimes I enjoy it. The students can be assholes sometimes, but you get used to it over time until it doesn't even phase you anymore.

"Hudson is expecting me next week. And honestly as much as I love it out here, I'm a working man."

She laughs and gives me a kiss, before pulling me back inside to the couch. The last few days have been full of bliss. No cell phones, no computers, just us in this small cozy cabin with a foot of snow which apparently is rare for Arkansas.

A getaway is just what we needed after the stressful few months, but it's back to the reality tomorrow. Leslie finished going through my manuscript and we worked together to polish it up before submitting it to a some agents for representation. Instead of pacing around my living room for a week, she decided it was the perfect time for us to come out here. Get away from it all and just relax.

"Have you checked your emails at all since we've been here?" she asks.

I shake my head.

"Don't you think you should?"

She knows me to well. I'm been chomping at the bit to see if I've gotten any responses, but she asked for no electronics, and wanted to play by her rules.

My laptop bag is pulled onto the coffee table, and turned on. I take a deep breath before opening the browser to my email. Here goes nothing. Three new emails.

Dear Mr. Mills,

I was delighted to find your query letter in my inbox. Your book, At All costs, has piqued my interest and I would love to read more. Could you send me the full manuscript for me to review to make a better decision on whether I would like to bring you on as a client?

Thank you,
Paul Schminke
Literary Agent

MY EYES LIGHT UP, and I look over, realizing Leslie is off in wonderland and not even paying attention. "Babe. Look!"

I get up and start pacing. "What if they hate it? The premise is good, but what about the whole damn thing?"

She takes my hands and wraps them around her waist. "We've discussed this, remember. You won't go anywhere if you hide it in your desk for the rest of your life."

She is so supportive, and has pushed me every step of the process.

I attach the full manuscript to the email.

Dear Paul,

Thank you for your interest in the full manuscript. I have attached it to this email. After you have read it, I would appreciate any feedback you might have, good or bad. Look forward to hearing from you.

Thanks,
Noah Mills

WHEN I PRESS SEND, my heart flutters. Sure, this was the overall goal, but planning it and doing it are two different things. Now that my work is floating out there for people to read and critique is frightening. Some people might not worry, but I spent so many years writing it, and hope to god nobody thinks it's shit.

"I couldn't have done this without you. You know that, right?"

She smiles and leans into me. "You are one lucky man, you know that?"

God, don't I know. One day, Leslie will be my wife, and I'll be the luckiest man in the world.

ABOUT THE AUTHOR

Ashley Zakrzewski is known for her captivating storytelling, sultry plots, and dynamic protagonists. Hailing from Arkansas, her affinity for the written word began early on, and she has been relentlessly chasing after her dreams ever since.

She has opened a TikTok shop that you can get signed paperbacks that come with swag packs. Go follow her on socials.

TikTok: @lovemeashley
    Instagram: @authorashleyz
    Facebook: Author Ashley Zakrzewski

Made in the USA
Columbia, SC
06 November 2024

64c27e79-29e5-4d6c-bf1a-3522097a2624R01